PRAISE FOR FATAL ROUNDS

"Physician-turned-author Rubin knows her way around a hospital and a literary thriller, setting up a bout that unfolds with scalpel-like precision ... A knockout that's just what the doctor ordered for thriller enthusiasts."

— *KIRKUS REVIEWS*

"Heroine Liza is unusual, likable, and unreliable ... A brisk, page-turning read."

— RACHEL HOWZELL HALL, *NEW YORK TIMES*
BESTSELLING AUTHOR

"A bold, intelligent voice is enhanced by sharp wit ... a splendidly peculiar mystery."

— THE BOOKLIFE PRIZE (MYSTERY/THRILLER FINALIST)

PRAISE FOR THE BENJAMIN ORIS SERIES

THE BONE CURSE: "A strong medical thriller—inclusive, skillfully written, and inviting."

— FOREWORD REVIEWS

THE BONE HUNGER: "The reveal is a real shocker, and Rubin's winning lead is well-suited to sustain a series. This is just the ticket for Robin Cook fans."

— PUBLISHERS WEEKLY

THE BONE ELIXIR: "The author's pithy writing keeps the story popping all the way to the rousing final act. A chilling supernatural tale with indelible characters."

— KIRKUS REVIEWS

FATAL ROUNDS

FATAL ROUNDS

CARRIE RUBIN

INDIGO
DOT
PRESS

Copyright © 2022 by Carrie Rubin

Indigo Dot Press
indigodotpress@gmail.com

First edition, 2022

Library of Congress Control Number: 2022910718

FIC031080 FICTION / Thrillers / Psychological
FIC031040 FICTION / Thrillers / Medical
FIC030000 FICTION / Thrillers / Suspense

ISBN 978-1-958160-00-8 (hardcover)
ISBN 978-1-958160-01-5 (trade paperback)
ISBN 978-1-958160-02-2 (ebook)
ISBN 978-1-958160-03-9 (audiobook)

Cover design by Lance Buckley Design

For A and J, my two hearts

1

From a recessed pocket of the waiting room, I watch my stalker enter from the OR suite. In tailored scrubs and a monogrammed surgical cap, he approaches a woman and a teenage boy seated against the opposite wall. Their thighs bounce on chairs the color of honeydew, and their gazes dart back and forth between the OR door and the softly ticking clock hanging above the vacant reception desk. Aside from me, they're the only two people in the room.

When they see the surgeon, they freeze. Even I can tell they're terrified his news will be bad. The mother grips her son's hand, and together they stand. The doctor's failure to notice me, at least for now, gives me a smug satisfaction. *Touché,* I want to say. How does it feel to be watched?

My father's voice interrupts my gloating. *Liza, is this a rational thing to do?*

I push the question away and return to the mother and son. Did her husband survive? Will he ever walk again? Will he make it to his son's graduation? From the woman's tearful phone conversation an hour ago, I gleaned her husband fell three stories off a scaffold onto a pile of metal grating. He's been working extra construction shifts this summer to buy her a new car, one with better traction in our icy Massachusetts winters.

Though my muted emotions might not show it, I empathize with their sorrow and fear. Years of social training with Dr. Lightfoot have taught me how. Still, despite my sympathy, I'm relieved their loved one's trauma brought my stalker to the hospital. As a recent medical school graduate, I know how slow Sundays can be. Though I called the operator this morning to confirm the surgeon was on call, there was no guarantee a trauma would take place.

Dr. Samuel Donovan finally puts the two family members at ease. "Your husband is going to be fine."

"Oh thank God." The woman embraces her son. "We were terrified he might—"

"I won't lie. It was touch and go for a while. He needed a lot of blood, but we managed to pull him through."

Showers of spousal and filial gratitude bathe the surgeon. He shakes his head and deflects their praise, but from my twenty-foot distance, I wonder if his modesty is faker than the plastic leaves on the artificial tree that hides me.

While they ask questions about the surgery itself and the recovery that will follow, I struggle to remain still. Hours in the chair have taken their toll. My tailbone throbs and my calves beg for a stretch. I've been waiting in this quiet room since breakfast, with only a quick run to the cafeteria around noon for a packaged ham and cheese sandwich to carry back with me. But my patience has paid off because there he is, in all his life-saving glory, with his runner's physique, sprinkling of stubble, and aristocratic features.

Maybe I'm being too quick to judge the surgeon. Maybe "stalker" isn't even the right word. After all, I don't yet know his story. Don't yet know why he, a complete stranger, is lurking in not one, not two, but three of my photographs.

I reach up to tuck my hair behind my ears and find nothing but air. *You cut it*, I remind myself. Last week in a salon visit that cost fifty dollars and thirty minutes of exhausting chitchat. But I like my new look. A pixie cut is better suited for the autopsies I'll be doing.

Watching the surgeon interact with the mother and son across the room, I think back to when I first noticed him in my pictures. It was over four months ago, a few days before the residency rank list deadline—the national process that determines where senior medical students match for their residency training. Initially this hospital, Titus McCall Medical Center, was my second choice. Massachusetts General in Boston was my first.

Yet here I am.

On that blustery and snowy February afternoon, I was in my studio apartment putting together a photo book for my mother. With her grasp on reality ever slipping, I wanted something to tether her to this world. The odds of it working were slim, but the album was easy to create with an online photo service, and the hard copy they mailed out would make for a nice memento. With my own software, I was able to play around and embellish the pictures even more. Everything from her childhood years to my dad's funeral went into it.

It was in one of those funeral images that I first spotted the surgeon, though I didn't know he was a surgeon at the time. A graveside shot from four years ago. I wavered on whether to include it in the album. My mother's psychiatrist always stressed the importance of being honest about the loss in her life, but I didn't want to send her into a deeper psychotic state.

In the photograph, my mom was pressed against my father's casket, its silver vault still raised above the cemetery ground and the dirt around its base covered by green cloth. Her fingers caressed the glossy maple wood, and her head hung low. Like everything else in the July heat, her body appeared wilted. Beyond her, off to the right in the wooded background, an unfamiliar man leaned against a tree.

Wondering who it was, I enlarged that corner of the image. With a closer look, I realized I'd seen him in one of the other pictures I'd included in the photo book, the one from my undergrad college graduation a year before.

Baffled, I scrolled through all the uploaded images until I found it. Another outdoor shot, this time of me flanked by my mother and father, both beaming but with my mother gazing up toward the sky. Whether or not she fully grasped my accomplishment, I don't know, but she was ecstatic in the moment, sunlight highlighting her long hair and flower buds coloring the trees. Since my brother, Ned, took the picture, he wasn't in it.

But someone else was.

Off in the background a man stood solo, concealed not by wooded trees like in the funeral picture, but rather by clusters of happy graduates and their families. Upon zooming in, I could tell he was the same man I'd seen before. Dark, neatly trimmed hair, refined features, a fit build beneath his chinos and bland shirt. So understated were his clothes, he hardly seemed notable. But I took note of him then.

A rare tremor of excitement rippled through me, and not the good kind. I leaned closer to my desktop computer and scoured photo after photo, particularly those I'd taken in public venues. My jaw tensed when I spotted him a third time. Or at least I thought it was him, though with the angle of his face I couldn't be sure. It was a photo from 2013, back when my father received an award for his years of legal service to Boston's poor and downtrodden, just a few months after a shooting nearly took his life. Though he survived, it was that injury that prompted him to retire from the law and withdraw his bid to run for city council. Before he left, a high-ranking judge honored him for his service.

The ceremony took place in a hotel conference room, its round tables arranged with linens, candles, and small plates for hors d'oeuvres and desserts. After the service I went around the room, snapping photos of my father's friends and colleagues. Not only would he enjoy the memories, it gave me something to do.

Sure enough, in one of the pictures of a boisterous table of lawyers, a man in a gray suit was standing in the doorway, his face turned sideways. As I zoomed in again, the same dark hair and refined features appeared, at least in profile, and even with the small bit of blurring—the photo possibly taken while he was turning his face—it looked to be him.

After that discovery, I combed through every picture again, even the ones on my camera that I hadn't uploaded to the photo album, but I didn't find him a fourth time. Still, spotting him in three photographs, or at the very least two, seemed far too coincidental.

If only I could have asked my father who the man was, maybe he would have known, but at the time I made up the album, my dad was three and a half years underground. Though I knew asking my mother was a long shot, I tried anyway.

It turned out to be worse than a long shot. It was a disaster. The pictures agitated her, and she descended into her Joan of Arc persona, crying about the king charging the castle and throwing her in the dungeon for being a witch and a heretic. "He'll burn me at the stake, Liza," she yelled. "He'll burn me at the stake."

Though pleased she'd called me by my name, I wasn't pleased to have my trip down memory lane worsen her psychosis. When it came to judging emotional tone, I was a poor navigator, always struggling with how to steer, advance, or retreat. On top of that, I worried the man himself—or at least the picture of him—was responsible for her meltdown, which only heightened my concern about his identity. But her pain hurt my heart, so I tucked the book beneath the sweaters in her fourth drawer, grabbed her guitar, and gently guided her outside to her favorite rock, just inside the mental health facility's iron gate. Once she sat on the stone and started to strum and sing, she was okay, her voice as melodic and soothing as the wood thrushes chirping in the trees above her.

I didn't give up my quest, however. I'm a twenty-seven-year-old living in the information age. It's nothing the internet couldn't give me. But I don't always make the best choices, so I wanted to ask my mother about him first. A simple explanation from her could have kept me from skipping blindly down the wrong track. Since that didn't happen, I returned to my apartment in Morganville, a scenic town in Northeast Massachusetts that's fifteen minutes from my mom's facility and twelve minutes from the hospital I'm sitting in now. At home, I cropped and enlarged the stranger's picture.

Trying Google first, I uploaded the photo and ran a reverse-image search. Several rows of photographs of other men in similar poses with similar backgrounds popped up, but none of them looked like the man in my pictures.

Not to be deterred, I tried another free reverse-image site, but when that one also failed me, I decided to go with a paid website, one that uses facial recognition to search millions of online pages and social media platforms to help determine whether your photo (or someone else's) is being used by catfishers.

After uploading the stranger's picture, the website conducted its search. A few minutes later, ninety-two possibilities spit out—for a fee. After paying ten dollars to get my results, I was rewarded with a winner. The site identified the man as Dr. Samuel Donovan, a trauma surgeon at Titus McCall Medical Center. The web page matched my picture of him to his photograph in the hospital's directory, as well as to other shots in an online professional newsletter.

To say I was perplexed is an understatement. To say I was exceptionally curious is spot on, but although I love a good puzzle— and as someone who's prone to indifference about many things, solving this real-life one is beyond tempting—I've spent enough hours slouched in Dr. Lightfoot's chair to know I needed to tread carefully. *Give it some time*, my shrink whispered in my head as I studied the surgeon's picture. *You have no proof this man is up to anything.*

Even when imaginary, my psychiatrist's counsel is hard to ignore. So as difficult as it was to do, I put my probing on hold for four months and gave the situation time to mellow. I completed med school, attended to my mother, and prepared for my residency.

Still, despite my self-imposed moratorium, I continued to feel something was at play, something wasn't right. Like that time when I was seven and sniffed out the malignant nature of a neighborhood kid well before he locked me inside an old steamer trunk. Or when I suspected my brother's girlfriend would rip him off months before she ran away with his stuff.

So yes, I want to know what Dr. Samuel Donovan is up to, especially if his photo is what set my mother off. While my social circle might be small, I always protect those inside it.

Always.

A voice rouses me, and I remember where I am. Across the waiting room, mother and son take their seats.

"A nurse will come get you once your husband is stable in recovery," Dr. Donovan tells them. He smooths his scrub top and adjusts his fancy cap, which probably cost more than any piece of clothing in my closet.

After another rush of gratitude from the wife, he turns, checks the clock above the reception desk, and strides to the swinging door that leads back to the operating rooms. Before he departs, he glances in my direction and startles. I don't know if this hiccup of hesitation is one of recognition or one of surprise at finding someone tucked away in a room he thought otherwise empty. He exits before I can tell.

It doesn't matter. In three days I'll start my residency training. In three days the two of us will walk the same halls and frequent the same spaces, at least the spaces where the worlds of surgery and pathology collide.

See you in the ring soon, Dr. Sam Donovan.

The bell has rung.

2

According to the American Psychiatric Association, those of us with schizoid personality disorder have little desire to form social relationships. We're also emotionally detached and come off as cold and aloof, having limited interest in the minutiae of other people's lives. Although we can gauge expressions and emotions when they're obvious, we sometimes struggle with more subtle social cues.

In my case, it's yes to all of the above and then some, which I suppose qualifies me for a few other labels as well. Although some have wondered if I'm on the autism spectrum, Dr. Lightfoot says my inconsistent evaluations make that stamp harder to stick.

My father refused to define me by a three-word disorder. "Listen up," he'd say, either out walking with me in the woods or sitting with me in my preteen room, its walls plastered with posters of the human brain. "You are not a list of symptoms, Liza. You are not a diagnosis. You are you, you are special, and you are wicked smart. Most importantly, you have a good heart. Whatever doesn't come naturally, you'll learn to compensate for. You'll learn to play the game."

And so I did, or at least I tried to, having years of weekly therapy sessions as a child and young adult to guide me. Cognitive behavioral therapy, psychotherapy, and—most arduous of all—group therapy. How much the visits with Dr. Lightfoot cost my father beyond what insurance would pay I can only imagine, especially with my mother's schizophrenia.

I still didn't have any friends though, so when I took a neighborhood bullied girl under my wing in third grade, my dad was ecstatic. So much so that I still keep in touch with her today, though why she enjoys my company I have no idea.

If I were more prone to stewing and fretting, I might worry about tumbling down the slippery slide toward schizophrenia like my mother, which, unlike schizoid personality disorder, comes packed with delusions, hallucinations, and disordered thought. Disordered speech and movement too. But the two conditions are separate and distinct. One does not lead to the other. Still, any psychiatrist worth their fifty-minute therapy session will tell you those with the personality disorder may be more at risk for developing schizophrenia, and that schizoids (my label of choice, not my shrink's) often have a family member with schizophrenia.

That's a check in my column.

But my father was probably right. I'm not a list of symptoms. As with any disorder, everyone branded with it is unique. Personalities differ no matter the underlying link between them. For example, some schizoids rarely experience strong emotions like joy or anger. Often we're indifferent. While I don't have much experience with joy, I have plenty with anger. I've learned to control it though. Dr. Lightfoot has taught me that non-violent means can be more effective, and it's been years since I expressed rage with my fists. At least on people. The heavy bag at Brian's Gym is a different story.

I don't parade my diagnosis around for pity or sympathy, not even for likability. To be blunt, I don't care what people think about me. That's the one perk of being a schizoid. I'm only acknowledging it because it shows what I'm up against on this last Wednesday of June as I exit my Dyno Blue Pearl Honda Civic (formerly my father's car) and enter Titus McCall Medical Center where my three-day pathology orientation awaits. Along with a new group of people who won't understand me.

In other words, today my father's guidance, my psychiatrist's cognitive therapy sessions, and my social training will work overtime.

At eight twenty-six a.m., I arrive in a formal conference room within the department of pathology, its walls richly papered and its carpet smelling new. I'm four minutes ahead of schedule and four minutes too early. Now I'll have to talk to people. (Yay me.)

Seated around the center of the oval table, which could easily accommodate sixteen people, are three of my future colleagues. Two men sit on the side farthest from the door, and a woman sits on the side closest. The guys appear to be about my age, but the woman looks to be in her thirties. I grab the leather chair next to her, swivel it back from the table, and sit. My worn satchel falls to the floor.

One of the men rises to greet me. "Boys against girls," he says, grinning. He's sturdy but not overweight, and his hair is jet black. Remarkably, despite a nicked chin that suggests a recent shave, his face already shows a hint of regrowth. He extends his hand. "I'm Waseem Ahmad. Nice to meet you."

His accent is minimal, and his smile is so big that in my attempt to match it, I forget to shake his hand. "I'm Liza. Liza Larkin."

The other man stands briefly. "And I'm John Kim." He brushes a clump of hair out of his eyes and smiles shyly. Though I imagine women being attracted to his handsome features, they do nothing for me.

"And I'm—"

Waseem cuts the woman off. "No, no." He wiggles like an excited child. "Let me say it." His arm wafts through the air toward the woman as if he's unveiling a precious work of art. "And this here is...Jennifer Lopez."

Even my eyebrows lift at this.

She smiles and twirls a threaded bracelet on her wrist, its colorful strands starting to fray. "Yes, yes, have your fun now, but unlike the famous one, I can't carry a tune. And I like to go by Jen, not Jennifer." She notices me eyeing her armband and holds it up. "My daughter makes friendship bracelets for everyone and their pet. Your turn will come."

I don't know how to respond to this, so I simply say, "Pretty."

They banter back and forth about residency hours and night call (which doesn't start for us until next month), and I feel like I can finally breathe. Then a woman rushes in, and my muscles tense all over again.

"Sorry I'm late." She sounds breathless. "Is Dr. Thomas here yet?"

Clearly this is a rhetorical question because it's obvious our program director has not yet arrived.

"Phew." She plops her designer purse on the table, its metal clasp clunking against the wood. "Got stuck in traffic. I thought I'd be able to live with my sister in Boston since it's so close, but after this morning, I might have to rethink that."

Waseem stands and introduces himself, and the whole process repeats.

"I'm Megan Carlson," she announces after we all say our names. She adjusts her sweater set and sinks into the seat next to me. Golden highlights in her tawny hair bring out the flecks in her eyes, and this, combined with her skillfully applied makeup, gives her a more striking appearance than her features would otherwise offer. But like John Kim, her looks do nothing for me. "Where are you from?" she asks me.

"I live here in Morganville. Boston before that."

"Oh really? Did you go to med school at Titus McCall?"

"No. Boston U."

"Cool."

"And you?" I remember to ask.

"Johns Hopkins."

A muscle in my face contracts. According to Google, that's

where Dr. Sam Donovan, my stalker surgeon, did his surgical residency, followed by a fellowship in acute-care surgery in Chicago.

"You have such beautiful skin," Megan says to me. "I'd kill for that complexion."

I put a hand to my cheek. My dad was biracial, and my mom descends from fair-haired Germans on both sides. When her mind cooperates, she even speaks the language. She chose my name, Liza, because it sounds like the German word for quiet: *leise*. Probably because she had so little quiet in her own head.

Based on my colleagues' expressions, my lack of response discomforts them, so I smile—belatedly—and say, "Thank you. Let's hope it doesn't come to that." They all laugh, and balance is once again restored. My behavioral therapy pays off. I have learned to play the game.

Jen has just started asking about research interests when a middle-aged man enters the room. Gray stipples his cropped, ebony hair, and a sportscoat works overtime to contain his broad shoulders.

"Sorry to keep you waiting," he says. "Administrative hassles, you know. They chap my ass." Dr. Darnell Thomas's voice is deep, and the adolescent comment coming from it makes even me laugh. "Welcome to Titus McCall and congratulations on matching here. I enjoyed meeting each of you during your interviews last fall. None of you are academic slouches, that's for sure." He takes a seat at the end of the table. A white board hangs on the wall behind him. "Good thing, too, because you'll be working your butts off, but in a different way than in your clinical months as a med student. No more five patients at once to admit, no more cardiac codes that turn you into sweating pools of adrenaline, no more rectal exams. Well, at least not on living people."

Snickers all around, and I'm relieved to feel this whisper of camaraderie with my fellow first-years.

"You'll be mostly behind the scenes now." The program director looks pointedly at me and then John. "Good for us introverts, right?"

I don't know what my letters of recommendation from med school said, but I imagine my social aversion was mentioned. How could it not be? I had a crummy bedside manner, and I never hung out with the other students. If Dr. Thomas wants to chalk it all up to introversion, so be it. My father's words once again surface in my mind. *You are not a list of symptoms, Liza.*

"Your four years of training will be fairly evenly divided between anatomical pathology and laboratory medicine, and you'll be doing autopsies on a rotational basis to get continuous exposure." Dr. Thomas shifts positions, making his chair squeak. "And as you know, this program is research-heavy. You'll have a required project each year, and we'll discuss that soon enough."

The rest of his talk centers on what our three days of orientation will entail, including general hospital odds and ends like procuring ID badges, Human Resources sensitivity training, and completion of a research ethics course.

"And of course you'll get a hospital tour," he says. "I'll introduce you to as many doctors as I can, so they can put faces to the names they'll read on their reports. Remember, in pathology we're the doctor's doctor. We help them diagnose their patients by reading biopsies, deciphering lab work, and autopsying unexpected patient deaths." He pauses before adding, "And let's just say some doctors are more challenging than their patients."

Everyone nods except me. I wonder if I'm one of those doctors.

After lunch we tour Titus McCall Medical Center with Dr. Thomas. We visit inpatient wards, outpatient clinics, academic offices, and the med school, all of which are housed in interconnected buildings neatly tucked away in a Massachusetts forest.

On the fifth floor, our program director pauses near the hexagonal atrium, which extends five stories below and three stories above. He directs us to one of the many expansive windows that bathe the corridor in sunlight and points off in the distance toward the right.

"You can only see the tail end of them from here, but those are the hospital gardens. They're a great escape when you need a break from organ dissection and microscopes." After a moment of appreciative murmurs from my colleagues, Dr. Thomas claps his hands. "Let's move on. We're not gettin' any younger." Like ducklings, we trail along after him. "I've already introduced you to some of the internists. Now it's time to meet the surgeons. We'll start in their lounge. That's where the action is."

At these words every one of my senses heightens, and as we make our way down three flights of stairs and through two mint-colored corridors, a tingling of anticipation runs through me.

Outside the surgeon's lounge, my reward comes swiftly. Approaching from the other direction is the man I most want to see.

"Samuel," Dr. Thomas booms, clapping the surgeon on the back. The men are of similar height, six feet give or take an inch. "Glad we caught you. I want to introduce you to our new pathology residents."

My fingertips press into my palms.

A smile bathes Dr. Donovan's face. The skin around his eyes crinkles, and when he pulls off his surgical cap, his hair attractively ruffles. Even though I hover behind Waseem, I'm close enough to notice a mole beneath the surgeon's right eye, the only blemish in his otherwise refined face. The blackness of it bleeds into his lower eyelashes, and were he a woman, you might mistake it for a smudge of mascara. I know from my internet search he's forty-two years old. What I don't know is how long he's been a stalker.

Or if he even is one, my father cautions in my mind. I let the comment float away.

"New recruits, huh, Darnell? Did you make them drop and give you fifty?"

"That's next on the tour." Dr. Thomas's voice reverberates down the hallway. Waseem, who I discovered during lunch is fond of celebrity references, has already likened it to that of James Earl Jones's.

Our program director begins introducing us, starting with Megan.

"It's like I already know you," she says to the surgeon. "Everyone at Johns Hopkins still raves about the former resident who helped set up a free clinic. My med school advisor speaks very highly of you."

Dr. Donovan grins, and his eyes sparkle like my brother's do when someone praises his songwriting. "Better than very lowly. Great to have a fellow Baltimore trainee."

Waseem pumps the surgeon's hand and mentions something about having a cousin in Maryland. After Jen and John say a quick hello, it's my turn. When I step out of Waseem's shadow, Dr. Donovan's amicable expression seems to falter. Stalker or no stalker, it appears he didn't expect to see me here.

"Liza Larkin," he says after Dr. Thomas introduces me. "Nice alliteration."

Unimpressed, I say nothing.

"What brings you to Titus McCall? Our cafeteria's famous fish tacos? Trust me, you'll want to stay away from those."

Everyone laughs except me.

"Dr. Donovan is one of the finest trauma surgeons you'll ever meet," Dr. Thomas says.

My program director's comment has saved me from answering the surgeon's question, which I'm not yet prepared to do. After all, it's not like I can say, "*You're* what brought me here." Not in front of all these people. They'll think I'm unbalanced.

Dr. Thomas looks around the hallway and lowers his voice. "A few of the surgeons can be difficult, but Dr. Donovan isn't one of them. He's as patient as a monk. And when he's covering non-trauma surgery, you'll never see anyone cut cleaner tumor margins."

Megan leans toward Dr. Donovan with a lift of her brow. "Well then, I know whose slides I'm moving to the front of the line."

"I'll hold you to it," he says. Though he points a finger Megan's way, his gaze drifts to me. Grin or no grin, twinkle or no twinkle, charm or no charm, I see recognition in his eyes. I see surprise. I see questions.

At least I think I do.

An energetic guy with closely shorn hair hustles toward us, breaking our eye contact. He skids to a halt next to Dr. Donovan, his high-top sneakers squeaking over the tiled floor. His scrubs hug a lean frame, and beads of sweat dot his forehead.

"You get her closed up?" Dr. Donovan asks him.

The newcomer nods. "With stitches so perfect she'll never even know she had surgery."

Dr. Donovan high-fives him. "Guys, this is Trey Washington, fourth-year surgical resident and my right-hand man, at least for another eight weeks."

My colleagues say hi and introduce themselves. When I don't, Megan gives him my name. I manage a nod, but after nearly seven hours with my fellow first-years, my social reserves are tapped. I need a few minutes of solitude before our HR lecture at four.

My indifference must amuse Trey because he smiles and winks at me. I've had enough come-ons from men to know what this means, but not only is his action presumptuous and arrogant, it's wasted on me.

I'm about to excuse myself, make up some pretext and let everyone know I'll meet them at the lecture, when I realize that Trey, as Dr. Donovan's "right-hand man," might be useful to me in the future. So, with effort, I double back, put on my social mask, and give him a proper greeting. This self-serving move is shameful, I know, but the match between Dr. Donovan and me has just begun, and I'll need all the reserve punches I can get. When my group finally strolls away en masse, Trey calls out, "See you around, Larkin."

Megan nudges me in the side. "Looks like a certain surgical resident wants to dabble in pathology."

I turn over my shoulder to him one last time. Dr. Donovan, too, is watching me, but in a different way than Trey.

When we return to the pathology department, I make the acquaintance of one more person—my advisor, Dr. Rina Silverstein, neuropathologist and department chair. She appears to be a youthful sixty, with long hair the color of her surname and a smooth complexion. She seems vaguely familiar, but I can't place from where. Did I meet her during my interview last fall?

"We'll get together for a meeting soon," she says to me, tapping the fitness band on her wrist and marching in her Birkenstock sandals. "A walking meeting so I can get my steps in. No need to invite the sitting disease, am I right?" Before I can answer she adds, "I'm excited to be your advisor, but I hope you'll see me as a mentor too. It's rare to find a resident who knows from the start they want to be a neuropathologist. When I saw that tidbit in your application essay, I quickly claimed you for myself. The brain is a fascinating place with so many unanswered questions. Maybe we'll solve some together."

I nod because it's true. Everyone's liver pretty much works the same. Kidneys too. But brains are different. For some people, they're logical, organized, and trustworthy. For others, like my mother (and yes, sometimes me), they're a prison.

"I look forward to working with you as well," I say and mean it. It's a relief to finally be doing pathology, away from direct patient contact, behind the scenes where I can lose myself in study and research and solve diagnostic puzzles. My colleagues will adapt to my differences. People always do.

"Oh, and put this on your calendar. I'm having my annual get-together for the new path residents in a couple weeks. Dinner at my house, nothing fancy."

To a person like me, her announcement is like knives screeching against stainless steel.

"My husband left for a six-month sabbatical in Rome," she says. "I could use the company. Time apart keeps things fresh, right?" Her smile wavers for a moment but then returns. "It'll be a great way for us all to get to know each other. I'm sure you and your fellow residents will become wonderful friends."

I bite my lip. I don't bother to tell her that's highly unlikely.

3

After three days of being fused to my colleagues, during which I was as polite and interactive as I know how to be, I'm itching to flee the hospital as soon as orientation ends on Friday afternoon. Our residency training officially begins on Monday, July first, just as it does for all residents across the country. I need the weekend to decompress.

I slip out of the conference room, mindful of Megan's lingering gaze on my back. Only a few days in and I've already disappointed her by turning down her invitation to join them for drinks tonight or tomorrow. "It would be nice to get to know each other better," she said as we packed up our things.

Get to know each other better? In three days of meetings, tours, and lunches, I've learned far more about my colleagues than I ever wanted to, including Megan's whispered suspicion to me that despite Waseem's mention of a girlfriend back in the United Arab Emirates, he seems more interested in John. How she managed to surmise such a thing based simply on observation fills me with both awe and respect.

So yes, I've learned enough about them for now. For our entire four years perhaps. The only person I want to learn more about is Dr. Sam Donovan.

Strangely enough, I don't have to go far. Just as I'm exiting the pathology department, he opens one of the double doors to enter it. I wonder why he's here. A simple phone call or computer check could get him any path report he needs.

"Why, Dr. Larkin, hello," he says amiably, holding the door open for me, his nails groomed and his ring finger bare. "Nice to see you again. You settling in okay?"

"Yes."

"Glad to hear it. Let me know if you need anything. Patient histories, surgical notes, whatever might help you with your work."

"Thank you," I say, unsure how to process this generosity.

"You know, it's funny. After I first saw you, it occurred to me who you are."

Does he mean when I spied on him in the waiting room last week? Or does he mean when Dr. Thomas introduced us two days ago?

A med student tries to pass through the doors. Dr. Donovan guides me toward the wall so we no longer block the exit. A framed print of a snowy mountain presses into my shoulder.

"What do you mean?" I finally say.

"Your father was Kevin Larkin, right?"

"Yes," I say slowly. "Why?"

"That was an awful thing when he got shot. I'm glad they caught the nutjob who did it."

"How did you——"

"It was all over the news. A lawyer—an up-and-coming politician no less—gets shot at a political rally. Thank God he survived. You must have been terrified."

Despite my years of social training, I'm not prepared for this. Nor can I read anything in Dr. Donovan's expression. I stare at the mole beneath his right eye, wondering how much I should share. My goal is to learn about him, not the other way around. He has thrown an unexpected jab.

I finally decide on, "I was out of the country when it happened. Mass General discharged him before I got home."

"I heard he died of a heart attack not long after. I'm so sorry for your loss. Was it three years ago now?"

My face heats. "Four." I step closer to him. "How do you know about that? Were you at his—"

An approaching pathologist with cat-eye glasses interrupts us. "Samuel," she says. "What a nice surprise. How was your vacation last month? Did you get back to the old stomping grounds like you planned?" The pathologist, who I met yesterday but whose name I can't remember, turns to me and clarifies. "Dr. Donovan and I grew up in New London, Connecticut. We didn't know each other well, but his dad was the pastor at my church. No giggling allowed during Stern Vern Donovan's sermons, that's for sure."

The two of them laugh, but like I'm back in Sunday School myself, where my mother and father hoped I'd form something akin to human connection, I stand there mutely.

"What brings you to our nerdy neck of the hospital?" the bespectacled doctor asks. "Do you need to see some slides on a patient?"

"I do indeed." Dr. Donovan follows the pathologist into the department. Before he disappears into its carpeted corridors, he turns around and says, "Another time, Dr. Larkin, shall we?"

The double doors whoosh shut behind him. I stand there, my shoulders tense, my head spinning. He's given me no answers, only more questions.

I slow my breathing and exit the hospital.

The first round isn't over.

***

Once inside my Civic, I roll down the window until the air conditioning kicks in and my sweater no longer sticks to my flesh. Whether my sweaty state is due to the summer heat or my encounter with Dr. Donovan, I can't be sure. His talk of my father has me vexed, and I have no way of knowing whether his concern was sincere. I'm convinced he's hiding something, but his words are too cryptic for me to tell.

As I near my apartment, which is south of the hospital and east of downtown Morganville on a tree-lined street with crops of residential apartment buildings, I grab my phone and leave a reminder on my voice-recorder app to Google my father's shooting. See how much of it was in the Morganville news. But first, I need to grab a quick bite from a sub shop and then slip into my workout clothes. From there, I'll go to the gym and box a heavy bag until my muscles hemorrhage.

My place is a five-hundred-square-foot studio with a kitchenette and a bathroom. Aside from the bed, the desk is where I spend most of my time. Two posters decorate the place. One is of the human brain and nervous system. The other is of John Nash, the famous mathematician who had schizophrenia. There is neither dishwasher nor TV. I rarely cook, so the former is unnecessary, and anything I watch can be streamed on my desktop computer or laptop, both of which accommodate any video game I want to play. With my new resident salary, I could afford a bigger apartment, but why? My place has everything I need.

After my mom moved into the mental health facility, I left Boston for Morganville to be closer to her, even though it made my commute to school longer. I tried to keep her at home after my dad died, I really did, but it didn't take a Mensa scholar to see I had nowhere near the caregiver skills of my father. After that failed attempt, I moved her to Home and Hearth Healing.

Three years later I still feel like Judas.

I enter my studio apartment and kick my shoes off. Just as my clothes are about to join them, I hear a rap on my door. With it comes the scent of freshly made baked goods. Though I can't tell whether the mouth-watering aroma is from cookies or brownies, it does tell me who's knocking.

I pull my shirt back on and open the door. April Cummings, my neighbor across the hall for the past ten months, stands beyond the threshold, a tinfoil-covered plate in her hands. Her ten-year-old daughter, Jasmine, must be back in their apartment, which is one room bigger than my own and boasts a complete kitchen. The child's absence suggests a short visit. Good.

"Hey, Liza, I won't keep you long." April's tone is as bright as her yellow tank top. A flowering-vine tattoo runs down the length of one arm. Balloons in flight decorate the other. A pink clip scrunches her over-dyed hair into a spiky bun, and as always when she smiles, her upper lip tries to hide the brown spot on her incisor. "I just wanted to give you these as a thank you for staying with Jasmine last week. I don't know what I would've done without you."

"She was in bed. I didn't have to do anything."

"Maybe so, but spending the night at my place last minute like that was really cool of you. I couldn't pass up a chance at an extra shift, you know?"

I nod because I do know. April works at a twenty-four-hour diner thirty miles from here. It was the only place that would hire her after her prison release two years ago.

"Um, can I leave these on your counter?" She indicates the plate with a tilt of her head.

My social training has failed me. I've left her on the doorstep the whole time. I move back and invite her in. As soon as she sets the plate on my counter, I lift off the tinfoil and stuff a warm and gooey chocolate chip cookie into my mouth.

She laughs. "For someone so fit, you sure have a sweet tooth."

"Don't tell anyone," I say and then remember to add, "Thank you. These are really good, but you didn't have to do that."

"That extra shift helped me pay Sinclair what I still owed him for this month's rent. Hopefully I'll get a few more hours to help with July's."

This apartment complex is too expensive for her, we both know that, but she wants Jasmine in Morganville's school system. It's one of the best.

"Sinclair can be so..." Her face loses its brightness. "So determined."

Mr. Sinclair is our middle-aged landlord. He's brutish, smug, and entitled. The last time I saw him in the hallway, I told him to take it easy on April. He curled his lip and said, "She's lucky I even rent to her. She's a former convict, you know. Spent two years in prison while her kid went to foster care."

"It wasn't her fault," I said. "The drugs were her boyfriend's."

My landlord sucked something out of his teeth. "She transported them willingly."

"He beat her. That doesn't sound willingly to me. She's a good mom."

"Her arms look like a coloring book."

"Tattoos don't determine character," I said. "For example, you don't have any and you're an asshole."

That's when Sinclair, who's about five foot eight like me, got right up in my face and looked me in the eyes. His breath smelled of spearmint gum, and his nose was mapped with the broken capillaries and spider veins of rosacea. I'm not sure what he expected me to do, so I gave a sharp and abrupt jerk of my head, almost headbutting him but not quite. I smiled when he flinched and stepped back. Then he wiped a hand over his mouth and said, "Mind your own business, Larkin, or you can find a new place to live."

I take another cookie and tune back into April who's telling me her daughter won first place in a YMCA art contest. As she tells the story, her maternal pride is so big she forgets about the brown spot on her tooth and smiles widely. I wish she always forgot about it. Anyone who knows April wouldn't worry about brown spots on her teeth or tattoos on her arms. Instead, they would notice how she walks her daughter to the bus during school months and how she takes her to the park behind our building to shoot hoops or jump rope when she gets home from work.

"I better get back to Jasmine," she says. "But thank you again so much." She waves at the cookies. "No rush getting the plate back to me. Whenever you're done is fine."

I nod and escort her out. As she opens her door across the hall, a frizzy-haired girl peeks out. When she sees me, she puffs out her cheeks and crosses her eyes. I wiggle my eyebrows and make fish lips in return. She laughs and disappears.

I close the door, lean back against it, and close my eyes. Brian's Gym is calling.

Sweat drips down my face, my arms, my torso beneath my sports bra. In front of me, a heavy sand-filled bag swings and thuds from my kicks and punches. Similar bags surround me, each suspended by chains that hang from crisscrossing beams on the ceiling.

Other than my runs outside, Brian's Gym is the only place I'll work out. It's small and functional and intended for only the most serious exercisers. Brian knows to leave me alone, and he keeps his place open from five a.m. until midnight. Though he has employees to help run the place and instruct the classes, he seems ever-present.

On this Friday night, four other people take his class. Three men and one woman. All of them are fit; all of them are muscular, and all of them are determined. Like me, they have come for an intense workout. Socializing is not their priority. Same with the handful of other gym-goers on treadmills, cycles, or weight benches.

As always, Brian delivers. My muscles resist and contract as I pound the bag. They release when I pull back. With each punch and kick, I deliver more force until I grunt so loudly, I drown out the *thud* of the bag and the pounding bass of rock music from the wall-mounted speakers.

I kick the bag for my mother's illness. I punch the bag for my father's death. I throttle the bag for all the Sinclairs and bullies and power-hungry brutes out there.

After years of this exercise, my shins are well adjusted to the contact, so bruising is minimal, but were it not for my shock-absorbing gloves, my knuckles would be shredded and my wrists sprained.

Finally, after fifty minutes of pounding and an hour of weightlifting, I head out. By now night has fallen, and only a few cars pepper the lot. I head to my Civic, thinking of my much-needed shower at home. Unzipping a pocket of my gym bag, I reach for my keys.

Before I can grab them, a figure darts out from behind an SUV and jumps me.

4

I stagger from the stranger's impact. He grasps me from behind. My shock has given him the advantage, but it doesn't last long because my instinct kicks in. I throw my head back and strike what might be nose, might be chin. Whatever it is, it's enough for his grip to loosen. I drop low and escape his clutch. He reaches out and grabs the sleeve of my sweatshirt before I get far. I spin around and kick at him, but he jumps back, still clutching my sleeve.

Dropping my gym bag, I try to wiggle out of my sweatshirt. He lunges forward and grabs me in a weird embrace, face to face, my arms pinned down at my side. The glow of the parking lot lights reveals that he's skinny and no more muscular than me, but that doesn't seem to matter, because he's wired and his eyes are crazed. His nose runs, and he sniffles more than he breathes. A tattoo of a pink snake coils up his neck.

I knee him in the groin. He grunts but doesn't release me. Something digs into my back where his fisted hands hold me tightly. For a second we stand there, nose to nose, eye to eye, thumping heart to thumping heart. The dark night is quiet around us, and the only thing I hear is our breathing. His panicky expression suggests assaulting women is not his usual habit, and if I can just free one of my arms, I think I can overpower him.

Something clicks behind me. I imagine a switchblade snapping open. Not wanting to wait and find out I'm right, I grunt, tear my arm free, and poke a finger deep into his eye.

He howls. His grip loosens, and whatever he's holding in his hand stabs me high in the left leg through my gym shorts. My throat emits a cry of surprise, but I don't dwell on the pain. I wrench my other arm free, release the finger from his eye, and punch him in the side of the head. He stumbles back from the blow. I kick his hand, and his weapon goes flying. A punch to his gut comes next, followed by a roundhouse kick that lands on his cheek and splits it open.

By now he's crying. He holds up his hands and pleads for me to stop. I do. Tears have always disarmed me.

He backs away, limping and cradling the hand I injured. Blood leaks down the cheek I kicked. Congested breathing whistles out of the nose I head-bumped. When he seems convinced I won't come at him again, he picks up the fallen knife and hobbles away, disappearing into a copse of trees beyond the parking lot. It isn't until he's fled that I wonder if I should have subdued him. Sat on him or dragged him into the gym or wrapped him up with a bow for the police. I'm not sure what the societal norm is for this.

Checking myself for injury, I rotate my neck, stretch my shoulders, and flex and extend my arms at the elbow. Everything on my top half seems okay, but when I twist at the waist, a pain erupts in my upper thigh near my hip. I reach down to where I got stabbed and find my shorts sticky and damp. Moving closer to the parking lot light, I see blood dripping down my bare leg. At least it's not copious.

I limp back to my gym bag, pull out my towel that's wet with sweat, and hold it over my hip. Then I grab my bag, totter to my car, and get inside.

With my head against the seat, I close my eyes and breathe in and out, all the while pressing the towel over my wound. It doesn't take long for my heart rate and breathing to normalize, and my mind starts to replay the event. Who was the man and what did he want? If he was after money, why didn't he grab my bag and take off? If he wanted to sexually assault me, why not drag me into a van or a secluded area? It seemed he wanted only to hurt me. Stab me and maybe even leave me to die.

I open my eyes and turn on the overhead light. When I bring the towel up from my hip, I see there isn't much active bleeding. Should I go to the hospital anyway? Should I call the police?

Give me a Gram stain and I'll tell you if a bacterial organism is positive or negative. Give me thyroid function tests and I'll tell you if the gland is working overtime or undertime. Give me a tissue slide and a microscope and I'll tell you if the cells look cancerous. But expect me to intuit life's most logical pathways? I'll often pick the wrong one. I just want to go home, eat more of April's cookies, and review my histology textbook before my first day on Monday.

But a part of me knows this is the wrong choice, so as always in questionable circumstances, I conjure my father. What would he, Kevin Larkin, lawyer-and-political-candidate-turned-food-truck owner tell me to do?

"You were attacked, Liza," he'd say. "You were stabbed. You need to call the police and go to the hospital."

I decide to do the first—indirectly, anyway. I wait on the second.

Pulling out my cell phone, I ready myself. Except for my professional duties, I rarely call anyone. I don't even text much.

Releasing my pent-up breath, I open up a contact. Shawna Vasquez-Lane. My one and only childhood friend who, for whatever reason, stays in touch with me. College graduation, med school graduation, even my dad's funeral—she was there for all of them.

Once a bullied, obese girl the other kids called Shamu Shawna, she is no longer either of those things. She's a sought-after hair stylist with the confidence of a bulldog. She lives on Waverly Boulevard in the north outskirts of Morganville, not far from the hospital. She was the one who suggested the town to me when I needed to move closer to my mother's facility.

But it's not Shawna I need right now. It's her wife, Tam Lane, a Morganville police officer.

I sigh and make the call.

Five minutes later, a police officer arrives in a patrol car. The temperature has cooled in the darkened parking lot, but the air remains muggy, and a few mosquitoes buzz and dive. A small crowd convenes outside the gym's entrance, watching the commotion.

Brian has already checked on me and brought out a clean towel for my hip, which has mostly stopped bleeding. The cop starts calling for an ambulance, but I tell him not to. I can take myself to the ER. The wound is superficial, I assure him. A stitch or two should do it, and I don't need the cost of an ambulance.

He asks me to describe the events and I do, leaning against my Civic at first, but then moving away from it to show him how I fought back. He jots everything down and tells me not only is he impressed with my recall, he's surprised I'm so calm. When I shrug and tell him this is my usual state, he studies me with a scrunched-up face as if he finds me peculiar. It's a look I need no social training to decipher.

A Jeep pulls into the lot and takes a vacant spot near my car. Tam gets out, and to my surprise, Shawna does too.

"You okay?" my childhood friend asks as she approaches. She's dressed in yoga pants and a T-shirt with the word *Muse* on it, which I think is a rock band. "Thought I'd come along for a little moral support."

She doesn't hug me—she knows better—but she squeezes my hand, and I don't tense.

"Thank you," I say. I feel relief at her presence, like when my parents picked me up early from a summer camp I never should have been left at in the first place. Despite what I told the cop about being calm, uncomfortable prickles dance up and down my spine like tap shoes. Not so much from the attack itself, but from the spot-light it's put me in. Ben, the cop, is nice though, and Tam tells me I'm in good hands with him.

"I'm sorry you're out here on your night off," I tell Tam.

She waves my words away. "Of course we'd be here. Besides, we dropped Seth off with our neighbor. It's as close to a date night as we've have had for a while." The new parents fist-bump and laugh at this.

Even I can tell they're a good match. Shawna is more feminine, at least in the traditional sense, with long, wavy hair and fashionable clothes. Tam (short for Tammy) is more masculine, with short hair, a rather broad build, and with as much interest in clothes as me, which is to say very little. I described them to my shrink the last time I saw him, almost nine months ago now. (*Too long*, my father whispers in my head.) I asked my doctor if I was stereotyping the couple with my description. It wouldn't be the first time I've said the wrong thing.

"Do they look like you described?" Dr. Lightfoot asked. When I nodded, he said, "Then you're just reporting what you see. There's nothing wrong with that, but as you well know, femininity and masculinity are social constructs that sometimes confine us." He then shifted the conversation to a weird place. "Do either of them appeal to you sexually?" I told him of course not. Then I added, "But neither do you."

He hooted for a long time over that, as if I'd just cracked the funniest joke in the world. It's true though. I have little interest in sex. Many schizoids don't. (*You are not a list of symptoms, Liza.*) But that's not to say I haven't had sex. I have. But only with a couple men in college and one in med school when I drank more than I should have and figured what the heck. "So yes," I told Dr. Lightfoot while he was still chuckling, "men are where my interests lie. If I were to have any."

"Liza? Liza, you okay?"

I blink and realize I've drifted off. The attack has affected me more than I want to admit. I nod, and then, at Tam's request, relay the incident all over again.

"And you're sure you didn't recognize the guy?" she asks.

"I've never seen him before."

"We have a couple units patrolling the area," Officer Ben says, "but no one fitting his description has been found."

"Anyone got a beef with you?" Tam asks.

I think of my landlord, Sinclair, and our last encounter where I pretended to head-butt him, but he's more roar than chomp and too clueless to know someone like my attacker. I also wonder about Dr. Donovan, but it seems extreme. We've barely stepped into the ring together.

"No," I tell her.

She asks me a few more questions, and when Officer Ben has what he needs for his report, he requests I go to the station tomorrow to look at mugshots and meet with a sketch artist.

Tam offers to escort me to the ER in my Civic. "You shouldn't drive right now. Shawna can follow up in our car, and then we'll drop you off at your place when you're all patched up."

I don't want them to do this. I just want to go home and take care of the wound myself, but I don't need my father here to tell me that's a stupid plan. "Thank you," I say.

Before we leave, Shawna says, "You call me if you need anything, okay? Don't be such a stranger." She hesitates. "Look, I know you're still reeling from your dad's death. Doesn't matter if it's been four years or forty, the two of you were so close. Are you still seeing Dr. Lightfoot, to…you know…help with things? It's normal to need someone to—"

"I'm fine. Really. I've moved on." I've said the same thing to Dr. Lightfoot, but he never seems to believe me. Always wants to talk about my dad. So I simply stopped going to my appointments.

Shawna and I say goodbye to each other, and as Tam drives my car with me in the passenger seat, she shifts the conversation to something lighter. "Shawna's planning a big first birthday party for Seth in September. Can't believe he's almost a year old." She smiles and taps the steering wheel at a red light. "She'll want you to come, you know. Me too."

Oh no no no no no, I don't want to. "Okay."

"In fact," Tam's eyebrows lift, "maybe you could help design the invitations. You're so good with all that Photoshop stuff. You could put our heads on a family of cats or dogs or something funny like that."

She laughs as she comes up with more ideas. I tell her sure, but as she talks about birthday cakes and clowns, my mind wanders back to my own birthday party twenty years ago. I was turning seven, and my parents decided we should move beyond the simple family affair of a celebratory meal out or a trip to the kiddie arcade. Too bad, because I enjoyed playing those blinking and clanging games and stuffing my pockets with the strings of prize tickets they spit out.

It was a small party. Four neighborhood girls and me. My mom made a chocolate cake topped with blue icing. My dad set up outdoor activities in the small backyard of our Boston Cape Cod. My brother, Ned, selected party music from his already growing CD collection. The first game on the agenda was musical chairs.

As Ned started the music, a bubbly pop tune I recognized but couldn't name, the five of us girls began circling the four folding chairs centered around our oak tree, its branches providing shade from the midday sun. While the other girls giggled and skipped, I remained stone-faced, determined to get a seat. The moment my brother stopped the music in the first round, a girl in a pink sundress and I scrambled for the nearest chair. Worried she'd get there before me, I shoved her out of the way. The goal was to snag a chair, right?

But my shove was too hard. The girl tripped and fell, and although our plush lawn cushioned her landing, grass stained both her knees and her dress, and she burst out crying. Everyone else fell silent. My dad stared at me, and if a face could sink, his did. My mom, who was well enough at the time to know her daughter was unusual, was similarly dismayed. Ned just shook his head, as if I were already a lost cause.

That was the first time I recognized—really recognized—how different I was from the other kids. There were social rules I was failing to follow. My behavior was un-clanlike. Before then, I guess I saw any discrepancies between us as *their* deficiencies, not mine. I was who I was, and I knew what I wanted. Right then I wanted a chair. I got it.

That probably wasn't the first time I used force, but it's the first time I clearly remember, and at that moment, with everyone gawking at me like I was from another planet, I understood something. If I didn't want to hurt, scare, or anger people, I would need to modify my behavior. I would need to watch the other kids and mimic their responses. See how they connected with each other and then act accordingly. In other words, I would need to learn how to fake it.

Of course, it took me years to hone it, and that wouldn't be the last time I used force (not by a long shot), but fortunately, I had Dr. Lightfoot to help me.

But man, was it ever tiring.

5

Three days into my residency, I sit in my cubicle inside the pathology resident quarters and wait for our chief resident to arrive. He'll be announcing which one of us gets to assist in the first autopsy, a young male found dead in his father's basement early this morning.

To my left beyond the cubicle's wood divider, Waseem chomps gum and plays on his phone. Twenty minutes ago I showed him how to use a video-editing app, and given his fascination with the film world, pathology slides temporarily took a backseat to his new discovery. To my right, John reads quietly from a textbook. It's the same one open on my own desk, next to my microscope and a sleeved cup of Earl Grey tea, which is still too hot to drink. Behind me, Jen asks Megan her opinion on atypical-looking liver cells.

Each of us has a microscope in our cubicle where we'll be doing most of our slide-reading. During downtime, we're encouraged to grab a box of teaching slides from the department library down the hall to sharpen our skills, which is what Jen and Megan are doing now.

Our group of cubicles is positioned in the front right corner of the room near a window. Several more are clustered to our left as well as behind us, one cubicle for every resident, twenty spots in all. One second-year and one third-year resident are in the room with us now. The others are off working in their various rotations.

Restless, I tap my foot. I haven't learned anything more about Dr. Sam Donovan since he mentioned my father, and although I did confirm that my dad's shooting made the Morganville news, I'm still puzzled by how the surgeon made the connection between my father and me so quickly. Since our paths don't cross much, I'll have to get more creative. Patience is important though. Learning the ropes of my new program takes priority. I don't want to blow it.

Until my sutures are out on Monday, five days from now, I can't do much exercise. Luckily, my superficial stab wound from Friday night's attack needed only four stitches, and other than some mild soreness when I put pressure on my hip and a dull ache when I move it, the area's healing well. At least I was able to resume upper body work, and between boxing the heavy bag and lifting weights, I've kept my brain clear.

The cops haven't found my attacker. As requested, I went to the Morganville Police Department the following day. When I couldn't identify my assailant from mugshots, I worked with a sketch artist but to no avail. Despite the beating I gave the guy, there were no reports of a man fitting his description showing up in area emergency rooms, and no similar attacks have been called in. While I am over the incident emotionally, save an extra glance over my shoulder when I leave the gym or the hospital, I still wonder about its randomness.

After listening to Waseem snap his gum for a long fifteen minutes, I'm relieved when our chief resident, Martin Chen, finally enters the room.

"Hello, my loyal first-years," he says, smiling broadly. "Thanks for waiting for me. Who wants dibs on the first autopsy?"

We all stand at once.

The second-year resident behind us groans. "Give it a year. You'll be bribing each other with pizza and beer to take the autopsy du jour off your hands."

"Don't piss on their passion, Smith," Martin admonishes, but his grin remains. "Dr. Carlson here is a budding forensic pathologist. This is her future."

Megan widens her eyes and does a little jump. "Does that mean I can assist then?" Her silk blouse, wedge heels, and wide-leg pants turn my sweater tee, chinos, and penny loafers into an Old Navy ad.

Martin puts one hand on his portly hip and raises a finger in the air with the other. "One, I love your enthusiasm." He lifts a second finger. "Two, there'll be plenty of opportunities to learn autopsy technique." Up goes a third finger. "And three, no."

Megan deflates with a disappointment even a schizoid can read.

"Well, maybe," Martin quickly adds. "It depends on who answers my question correctly, and it's a doozy. Don't worry though. I'll have a softball question follow-up if no one gets it."

The second-year resident sighs behind us. "Ah yes, Martin's famed trivia. You'll soon tire of that too."

Megan's smile has returned. During our teaching rounds thus far, she's answered the most questions correctly. Kate Spade and Gucci are not all she knows.

Scheduled every morning at eight thirty, our teaching rounds take place in a windowless room down the hall from our cubicles. Inside, at a long table supporting a microscope system with ten viewing heads, we take a seat. At the end of the table, behind the master microscope, sits our program director or our chief resident. Any slide they slip onto the stage of the scope can be seen through the lenses of our own viewing heads. Then the questioning begins, often in a quick, shot-fire fashion, which is why the path residents jokingly refer to the room as the Death Chamber.

"Are you ready for the deciding question?" Martin lifts his chin and holds his breath in a dramatic fashion. "The fate of the first autopsy rests in your hands. Or I guess I should say, your brains."

We straighten and nod, and I'm as caught up in this game as the others. My brother and I loved playing *Trivial Pursuit* with our mother, back when her mind still allowed it.

"Okay, here goes. What boxer holds the knockout world record?"

For a moment, there's silence. I blink, unable to believe my good fortune.

Megan puffs air out of her mouth. "That's not a medical question."

"It is if it involves chronic traumatic encephalopathy," Waseem says, making the others laugh, including the second-year resident in the back. "But I think I'm going to need your softball question, chief."

"Me too," Jen says, rolling her eyes. John smiles in agreement.

"Okay, here—"

"Billy Bird," I say, cutting Martin off. He stares at me, as do the others. Their attention makes my cheeks warm in an unpleasant way.

The chief starts clapping. "Well, well, it's always the quiet ones, isn't it? Nice to see we have a boxing fan in the bunch."

Maybe so, I think, but mostly I happened to be in the right place at the right time last month when Brian and some other guys at the gym were discussing this very topic.

I close my textbook, grab my tea, and exit my cubicle to go with Martin. As we head from the second-floor path department to the basement morgue, it dawns on me I should've said something to the others before I left. Something like "good try" or "I just got lucky" or any number of other platitudes to keep me from looking aloof or stuck-up. Over the years, my father and Dr. Lightfoot have counseled me on this many times, but in my eagerness to assist in the autopsy, I forgot to execute the expected response.

Regret slows my pace. Just because I don't care what people think of me doesn't mean I want to snub my colleagues. People often assume my lack of desire to form relationships is selfish and arrogant. Cruel even. But I think it's the opposite. I think it's kind.

I'm less likely to hurt them that way.

———

Dressed in scrubs, protective gowns, masks, face shields, and double gloves, Martin and I stand in front of the stainless-steel table holding the deceased man. A mildly unpleasant scent lingers in the small room, which, with its cabinets, countertops, and autopsy table, is a study in chrome, but mostly I smell the synthetic fibers of my mask.

The corpse is nude and supine, and Martin starts reviewing the body's different types of mortis. During a pathology rotation as a fourth-year med student, I assisted in two autopsies, but it's good to have the reminder.

"You see how he's mostly stiff but not yet at full rigor?" Martin moves a lower limb to show the rigor has not yet set into the legs. "That suggests he's been dead less than twelve hours, which is when peak rigor mortis occurs. And yet see here?" Martin points to the dark-purplish discoloration of the inferior portion of the corpse where blood has pooled in the dependent areas. "The livor mortis *is* set. Push on the discolored part."

I do as he asks. The purple hue remains unchanged.

"See how it doesn't blanch? That means he's been dead at least eight hours. Given the distribution, it also means he either died in this position or someone moved him shortly after death. Of course, it's not always exact, but those two things combined with his body temperature..." Martin glances at me from inside his plastic face shield. "What's that type of mortis called?" he quizzes.

"Algor mortis."

"And how fast does the body cool?"

"About one point four degrees Fahrenheit per hour, but it will depend on what temperature the environment is."

"Good. Just checking to make sure boxing isn't the only thing you know." He winks, and I wish I could be as easy in my skin as he is. Someone who immediately puts people at ease.

Martin cracks his knuckles beneath his gloves and continues. "So those three types of mortis suggest his time of death was between eight and ten hours ago, maybe closer to ten. Since it's one in the afternoon now, that would mean he died between three and five o'clock this morning."

I nod, fascinated as always by the world of science, where facts and logic rule and emotions are shown the door.

Knuckles taken care of, Martin clasps his hands together. "You ready? The forensic pathologist should be here soon. We're very lucky that at Titus McCall we have two medical examiners on staff who handle the local forensic autopsies. Not many pathology training programs have that. Then again, you already knew that since you chose to match here."

Not daring to admit I didn't know that—or at least didn't remember it given I flip-flopped my top residency choice a few days before the deadline—I merely nod. Megan would know it though.

"The guy's young age makes his death suspicious by default, so the forensic pathologist will be our attending on the case. I'm sure her fellow will be here too, so you might not get to do much yourself."

Before Martin can say anything else, the door opens, and Dr. Rina Silverstein, my advisor, enters the room. She wears gloves, but her absence of a gown and face shield suggests she's only checking in. Her hair hangs behind her in a long silver braid.

After greeting us, she visually inspects the cadaver. "I heard you have one for forensics. Dr. Munson's out in the hall."

"That's the forensic pathologist," Martin tells me.

"What've you got?" my advisor asks.

Martin indicates I take over, so I do. "A twenty-seven-year-old man found dead in his father's basement this morning around seven a.m. Time of death is estimated to be between three and five a.m."

"Oh, how sad," she says. "Suspected cause?"

"According to his file," I continue, "his father is worried about a heroin overdose, although he's apparently been clean for a few weeks. He's been living in his dad's basement for the past year."

Dr. Silverstein's gaze tracks to the needle marks on the man's arms, most of which look old. She points to an area high up on an antecubital vein near the elbow. "Is that a fresh one?"

"Might be, but we haven't looked closely yet," Martin says. "We'll let you know what we find. It's a shame though."

"What is?" my advisor asks.

"The guy survived surgery fourteen months ago. Accidentally

shot himself in the gut with his dad's gun. Tried to clean the weapon when he was high."

"That's tragic." Dr. Silverstein sighs and shakes her head.

"Dr. Donovan had his work cut out for him with that one," Martin says.

At the mention of the surgeon's name, my neck tingles.

"He's definitely the best," my advisor replies. "Trauma surgeon or not, he's the one I requested for my gallbladder surgery two years ago. He even paid me a house call afterward." She stares at the corpse a moment longer. "Such a young man. This opiate epidemic is heartbreaking. Assuming an overdose is indeed the cause of death."

Martin snaps his gloves. "We'll find out soon enough."

6

I park my car in the employee lot closest to the pathology department's entrance, which happens to be near the hospital's hexagonal atrium with its coffee and tea kiosk. Only the start of my second week as a resident and already a large cup of tea to sip during morning teaching rounds has become my routine. I'll need it too. Something to buoy me through Megan's inevitable onslaught about why I didn't go out with them for a second weekend in a row.

Even Jen's coming, she texted me Saturday afternoon. And she has kids!

Can't, I typed back.

My phone quickly pinged again. I know you like to keep to yourself but we have to stick together. Four years ahead of us. We're a team.

Not wanting to hurt her feelings but having no idea how to respond, I considered replying with a string of emojis. With my luck though, given my lack of emoji prowess, I'd either end up sexually propositioning her or inviting her to the zoo. So instead I simply typed, Sorry.

Clearing the conversation from my mind, I exit my Civic and head to the atrium. The morning air is clean and fragrant, and my moves are fluid, my stab wound hardly bothering me. A trip to the urgent care center last night got rid of the four stitches. All that remains is a pink scar. Even the attack outside Brian's Gym has become a distant memory.

Must be nice to never be touched by anything, Liza Lou, I hear my brother say in my head. *To have things roll off you so easily like a robot.*

Two years older than me, Ned is a twenty-nine-year-old musician in Providence, Rhode Island. By day he teaches guitar and repairs instruments in a music store. By night he plays bass in an alternative rock band whenever they can get a gig. Not only has he inherited our mother's musical talents, he's inherited her small frame and fine features. Her emotional sensitivity too, and although he doesn't share her psychiatric illness, he struggles with a depression all his own. His "dark fiend" he calls it.

Because my mother's schizophrenia first manifested when she was pregnant with me at the age of twenty-six, my brother wondered if the two might somehow go together. He saw how I turned out and figured two plus twenty made four and that I might be what made our mother mentally ill.

"Maybe it's something in your blood," he once told me when he was depressed. "Just like the dark fiend is in mine."

Although scientifically this is nonsense and he apologized later for saying it, when I see my mother in full-raging psychosis, battling like Joan of Arc or prancing around Home and Hearth Healing's rec room as Meryl Streep, a seedling of doubt plants itself in my brain, no matter how illogical.

Of course, it's easy for Ned to point fingers. He's not the one caring for her. He's not the one who visits her regularly, checks in with her psychiatrist, pays her facility fees through the account set up for that purpose. He's never been able to handle her deterioration, which started to really take flight when I was seventeen and he nineteen.

Unlike many aging schizophrenics, her positive symptoms of delusions and hallucinations haven't improved with age. The opposite, in fact, and my father's death (and her parents before him) only intensified them. Dr. Dhar says she's one of the most challenging cases he's ever had. Says her grief and depression might be what's making her less responsive to medication than she was in the past. Leave it to my mother to be the brittle case.

But I don't take Ned's comment personally. I rarely take anything personally. Ned is who he is—sensitive, trusting, and otherwise kind—and my mother adores him. I will continue to look out for him, just as I did as a child.

Thinking of my mother reminds me of a few things I need to do for her. As I enter the swinging glass doors of the hospital atrium, I grab my phone from my satchel, open the voice recorder app, and start noting these things out loud.

I make it through "download more songs for her playlists" before my voice cuts off. Inside the vestibule, I freeze. Ten feet away near the coffee and tea kiosk, Dr. Donovan pours cream into his cup at the side counter. Dressed in an expensive-looking suit, he's having a heated exchange with a petite blond woman in scrubs. Actually, she's the one who's heated. As far as I can tell, he looks indifferent, but when she keeps arguing, he grabs his coffee and leads her a few feet toward the window behind an abstract metal sculpture that resembles two giant, entwined eels.

The couple is even closer to me now, and before either one spots me, I hurry to one of six chairs that form a U in front of another window. Now, on the opposite side of the statue, with my back to them, I pretend to check something on my phone.

"But I don't understand," the woman says, her words staccato stabs. "I left my husband for you."

"I never asked you to. Besides, your ex is a loser."

"But you promised we'd take things to the next level."

"Sorry, but I think we're better off apart."

Even to me his voice sounds uncaring. Or maybe it's fatigue from repeating himself. Have they had this conversation before? I dare a glance over my shoulder and peer at them through an oval space in the statue where the bodies of the eels have separated.

"Got what you needed from me, is that it? A quick screw. Someone to water your precious plants while you're gone." The woman's cheeks are flushed. "Next!" she calls out to a blonde passing by in shorts. "It's your lucky day. He's on the market again." The stranger startles and quickens her pace.

"Stop it." Dr. Donovan's tone sharpens. "You're making a scene."

"What would your mother think of your assembly line of women if she were alive?"

A muscle in the surgeon's jaw contracts. "You leave her out of this."

The woman snorts. "You've got Mommy issues, you know that? None of us can measure up. News flash, she probably wasn't the saint you think she was."

He grabs the woman's arm and presses against her. Her skin blanches beneath his fingertips. "Stop it," he repeats. "You'll never be the woman she was."

"But—"

"Leave me alone, understand? Stop calling me, stop bugging me, stop chasing after me." His tone hardens to concrete. "Or you'll wish you had."

The woman's head jerks back at his threat.

Whoa. Where'd that Dr. Donovan come from? Is this the same man my advisor and program director have so highly praised? The same surgeon who helped start a free clinic during his already grueling residency? What was it Dr. Thomas said during our orientation? "He's as patient as a monk."

I lick my lips. Something flutters in my chest. *You're not that man at all, are you, Dr. Donovan?*

Finally, the woman steps aside, and Dr. Donovan strides away, smoothing his suit jacket with the hand not carrying his coffee. By the time he reaches the stairwell, he seems once again in control.

I drop my head, hoping he doesn't see me, but when I look up he's staring my way. For a moment, neither of us moves. Then he smiles faintly, shapes his thumb and index finger into an imaginary gun, and aims it at me before he disappears into the stairwell.

The breath I was holding expels. What was *that* supposed to mean? A joke to diffuse the situation? A message? I have no clue. Dr. Lightfoot hasn't prepared me for finger guns.

When I stand and put my phone in my satchel, I realize my voice recorder app is still running. I push stop on the record button. Their entire conversation, at least the part I heard, is now permanent.

My finger hovers above the delete tab, but then I wonder about the recording's usefulness. Instead of deleting it, I label it *SD* for Sam Donovan and close out the app.

A check of my watch tells me I still have fifteen minutes before teaching rounds begin at eight thirty. I march to the kiosk for my tea. Two women whisper behind the counter. It's obvious they're discussing the exchange I just witnessed.

They quiet down when I approach, but after I order my Earl Grey, I summon every ounce of social training I've had and force my lips into a smile. Even to me it feels fake, especially after getting shot by Dr. Donovan's finger, but my need for information exceeds my need to go unnoticed by the world.

I must be convincing because after a bit of back and forth, during which I'm handed a large cup of scalding tea, I learn from the baristas that the woman Dr. Donovan was arguing with is a respiratory therapist. One of them has seen her at the hospital's weekend yoga class. I also learn that Dr. Donovan is "a great guy" who always leaves a big tip and that the woman "must've done something awful to make him angry."

I think I'll have to agree to disagree with that. Unlike the baristas, I didn't only see the fight, I heard it too. How is it that I, a subpar people-reader, am the only one who feels something is off with the man? And why is he in my photos?

I decide the first thing I'll do when I get home tonight is back up that recording onto my computer for safekeeping.

Before I can gloat too much though, a voice cautions me. My father's? Dr. Lightfoot's? My own inner conscience? *Do you really want to go down this road?* it asks. *What if you start something you can't finish?*

I silence it with a burning sip of tea.

7

I nside the residents' room, I help Jen with a PowerPoint issue. When I finish, I select a case of hematology slides from the library to review for the rest of the afternoon. Despite my work, my thoughts wander to Dr. Donovan.

Ever since witnessing his threatening manner toward the woman in the atrium two days ago, not to mention his finger gun, I've taken to calling that version of him "Sam" in my mind. Though others may not see it, his dual nature is as clear to me as the blood cells under my microscope lens.

I place a new slide on the stage. Halfway through my examination of it, Dr. Silverstein enters the room, her hair swirled into a loose bun. A summer dress sways with her movements, and green toenails poke through the ends of her Birkenstock sandals. Though I still can't place where I've seen her beyond Titus McCall Hospital, I'm convinced I have.

"Liza dear, let's have an impromptu meeting." Her hand rests on the wood barrier of my cubicle as she peers over at me. "You're almost two weeks in now, and I want to know how things are going."

I stand, and we exit the residents' room. When I veer toward her office, she laces her arm through mine and pulls me the opposite direction.

"Let's walk while we talk." She feigns marching like a soldier and raises the wrist sporting a fitness band. "We'll stroll around the gardens. The weather's beautiful today, not so hot."

Outside, the sun is bright, and at first my eyes refuse to adjust. I should have grabbed my sunglasses from my satchel. At least the temperature is comfortable, and a refreshing breeze carries the scent of peonies through the air as we near the gardens. Once inside them, tall evergreens hide us from the world. Together, we weave around the maze-like shrubbery and colorful flowerbeds.

Dr. Silverstein rubs her palm over a high hedge and asks me how things are going.

"Fine," I reply.

"Have you learned your way around the hospital yet?"

"Yes."

"Do you have any questions for me?"

"No."

She chuckles. "My son's a lot like you, you know. Quiet, intense, a loner." She bends down to stroke a rose, its petals the same yellow as the embroidered flowers on the hem of her dress. "That's okay, of course, but remember, no one's an island."

This phrase is overly familiar to me. Dr. Lightfoot likes repeating it during our sessions. And yet I am indeed an island. Everyone else is on the mainland.

My advisor stands and resumes walking. "I'm sure it's difficult for you with your mother."

I stutter step on the stone pathway. How does she know about my mother? Was there mention of her in the articles about my dad's shooting? I'm not ashamed of my mom's schizophrenia, not at all, but it unnerves me to have people know about my life when I know nothing of theirs.

When my silence lingers, she says, "I'm not prying. I just want you to know I'm here for you if you need anything."

"Thank you," I manage.

The sound of trickling water reaches us. After we round a

cluster of freshly pruned shrubs, I find the source. Down a flight of concrete steps is a peaceful sitting area with a fountain and four benches, all of them empty.

"Lovely, isn't it?" my advisor asks. "It's a pity people don't take more advantage of it, either this space or the gardens themselves." She cups my elbow as I peer down. "Be careful though. When the leaves are full like this, these stairs are hidden and come out of nowhere. Don't want to take a nasty tumble."

I nod and we resume walking, making our way back to the hospital.

"You're doing great work so far," she says. "You have a knack for slicing the thinnest tissue sections, and your ability to spot atypical cells is impressive for your level of training."

"Thanks."

"Any ideas for your first-year research project?"

I shake my head.

"Well, it's still early. It's clear you're a voracious reader, so I'm sure you'll find some question that needs answering. But remember to give yourself downtime. Go shopping with Megan, see a movie with Waseem, go to lunch with John or Jen."

Won't be happening, I think, although I know Megan would love to get me inside a department store. Twice now, she's declared she's taking me to Nordstrom to buy me a new purse. "Something that doesn't look like it belongs on the side of a horse," she said. Earlier today she flooded our phones with pictures from our orientation, pictures I hadn't even realized she'd taken.

Thought you guys would like to see these, she texted. Excited to get together at Dr. S's this weekend! Let's go out after. First round's on Liza since she was an MIA party pooper last weekend! This was followed by a smiley face emoji and a winky face one.

As if reading my mind, Dr. Silverstein raises an eyebrow. "I'll see you for dinner at my place on Saturday, right?"

I nod reluctantly.

"It'll be good for you. Martin says you're always the last to leave. He's even seen you here on the weekend, and your call duties don't start until next month. Make sure—" My advisor cuts herself off.

"Well, speak of the devil," she says. "We were just talking about you, Martin."

My chief resident fans his hands toward himself. "Nothing but fantastical praise and glowing accolades I hope." He squints at me, the sun bright in his eyes. "Just catching some fresh air, but I'm glad I ran into you. The drug assay results are back on the autopsy you helped us with."

"Did it confirm a heroin overdose?" I ask, relieved to be off the topic of dinner parties and shopping.

"Well, there *was* morphine in his system—which is the measurable byproduct of heroin—but it wasn't very high."

"So he wasn't clean like his father thought," Dr. Silverstein says. "Does Dr. Munson think that's what killed him?"

"Hard to say. You know how it goes with quantitative analysis." He turns to me to explain. "Drug concentrations vary in unpredictable ways postmortem. Makes it hard to know what's truly the lethal concentration."

"So is the medical examiner calling it a heroin overdose?" Dr. Silverstein repeats.

"Given she found nothing else on exam, she probably will. As for manner of death, she's not yet ready to declare whether it's an accident or a suicide. She wants the police to ask the father a few more questions first."

"Sounds like a good one for teaching rounds. It's similar to the case we had last fall, remember?"

"Which one was that?" Martin's hand shields his eyes from the rays.

"Sandy Newmaker, the librarian. The one with all the scars from the dog attack she suffered a few months before she died. Needed surgery and skin grafts to put her back together."

My ears prick up.

"Oh yes, that one." Martin nods in recognition. "She was also an addict. Fentanyl and other opioids if I remember correctly. Given the postmortem distribution of fentanyl, her toxicology results weren't very reliable either."

"So heartbreaking," Dr. Silverstein says. "Two patients survive major trauma surgery only to die a short time later."

Upon hearing those words, I grow as stiff as the antique garden lamp on my left. I'm no statistician, but those odds seem unlikely to me. Opening and closing my hands, I wait impatiently for Dr. Silverstein and Martin to finish talking. I'm eager to get back inside the hospital. I have some research to do.

Just not the kind my advisor had in mind.

When Dr. Silverstein and I return to the path department, the only thing I want to do is surf the internet and learn more about Sandy Newmaker, the deceased librarian, but an unexpected guest in the residents' room keeps me from my search. Seated in my cubicle, messing with my microscope, is Dr. Donovan's "right-hand man," Trey Washington. Gone are his scrubs. In their place, dark jeans and a snug T-shirt.

Though I try to keep the annoyance off my face, I doubt I succeed. Having my space invaded raises my blood pressure. It always has. My brother learned that the hard way when I smacked him in the face after finding him snooping through my closet when I was eleven. Split his lip wide open. Though I don't always feel remorse, I did then. My dad took away my science kit and computer privileges for a month and scheduled bonus sessions for me with Dr. Lightfoot. But that punishment was nothing compared to seeing my dad cry that night when he didn't know I was watching.

"Hey, Billy Bird," Trey says. His use of the boxer's name from Martin's trivia question, along with Waseem's chuckling in the cubicle next to mine, tells me the two men have been discussing me in my absence.

"Don't call me that," I say. "And get out of my chair." At the last minute, I remember to add, "Please."

"Whoa, whoa." Trey stands, his hands raised in self-defense. "Just messing with you."

After switching places with the surgery resident, I reach under my desk for my satchel. Exhaling my irritation, I soften my face. "Sorry. I'm just in a hurry to leave."

"You?" Waseem says. "It's not even five yet. Has the world stopped churning?"

Trey grins. "I think you mean 'turning.'" He leans against the wood divider, his fit, trim body now blocking my colleague from view. A tattoo of an ace of spades on his bicep falls just below his sleeve. "Just so happens I'm done early too. A rarity in surgery. How about we grab a drink at O'Dell's down the road?"

Waseem raises his head above the divider and wiggles his furry eyebrows. His five o'clock shadow is more like a midnight one. I make a face that forces his retreat, and his head disappears. At least none of my other colleagues are around to hear Trey's request. Megan would sigh dramatically and say, "Yes, pleeeease Trey, get this hermit crab out of her crabitat."

"Come on," the surgery resident says. "All work and no play make Liza as dull as her corpses." His casual posture and unwavering eye contact suggest nothing but confidence. Most women would probably jump at the offer. The reason I accept, however, has nothing to do with his chestnut eyes or smooth smile. It's because he's my ticket into Dr. Donovan's world.

At my insistence, we take separate cars to O'Dell's, which is a short drive east on Waverly Boulevard, the opposite direction from my mom's facility and Shawna and Tam's house.

Once inside, we settle into an oak booth that smells of beer and onion rings. Dark accents surround us, and televisions tuned to sports channels flash in the corners, their volume muted in favor of pop tunes bleating from ceiling speakers. Given it's barely past five o'clock on a Wednesday, the crowd is light and we're served quickly.

As we sip our pints—a lager for me, an ale for him—Trey starts with the usual questioning. "So, where're you from?"

"Boston."

"Where'd you go to school?"

"Boston."

"Where's your family?"

"Morganville and Providence."

He smirks and rubs a splash of beer from his chin. "Not much of a talker, are you. Where do you live now?"

When I don't respond, he sighs and proceeds to tell me about himself. I learn about his childhood in Columbus, his obstetrician mother and ICU nurse father, his undergrad and medical training, and his choice of Titus McCall for residency.

It's at this point I feel enough time has passed to finally ask about what interests me most. "What's it like working with Dr. Donovan?"

"Donovan? He's a great surgeon. Learned a lot from him my first three years."

"How long has he been at Titus McCall?"

Trey watches a baseball replay on one of the TVs. "I think seven years now? He went to Harvard for med school and did his residency at Johns Hopkins." His gaze returns to me. "But don't think that makes him a snob. He drives a five-year-old Highlander Hybrid when he could be driving a Porsche, you know?"

"As a trauma surgeon, he must work long hours. Lots of call. Probably doesn't leave much time for anything else."

Trey shakes his head. "Actually, you'd be surprised. They pool with the general surgeons, so they're only on call, like, twice a month. They act as backup in case one of the general surgeons needs them, and they do some clinic time too, but it's a pretty sweet schedule for a surgeon."

"Nice," I say, but my interest lies not in their "sweet schedule" but rather in how much free time Dr. Donovan has on his hands. Free time to lurk in strangers' photographs. "No tantrums then? No instrument-throwing? Some surgeons are famous for that."

"Nah. Again, he's pretty low-key." A hesitation. "Well, he doesn't like to be challenged—what surgeon does?—and he definitely likes things a certain way. You know, high standards, wants others to meet them, that sort of thing. I suppose that's what makes him such a good surgeon. Patients love him."

"How so?"

Trey sips his beer before answering. "He takes a real interest in them. And not just pre- and post-op. He stays in touch with some of them. Likes to see how they're doing down the road, especially those who survived against all odds. They love that."

"How do you know he stays in touch with them?"

"They stop by to say hi, drop cookies off when he's seeing follow-ups in clinic." Trey grins. "Sometimes they even try to set him up with their daughters."

"So he's not married?"

"No." Trey's smile fades. "Oh shit, you're into him, aren't you? That's what this is all about."

I puff out my cheeks. "Hardly."

Dang it. I pushed too hard. I've made my inside man suspicious. Maybe it's best to be honest about Dr. Donovan. Well, at least about one thing. I plan on keeping his creepy photo-stalking to myself for a while.

"I saw him in the atrium the other day with a woman," I say. "He was rough on her. The opposite of what everyone says about him. So I was curious, that's all."

Trey exhales and relaxes back against the padded booth. "I don't know about that, but I do know the guy's got a lot of female fans. I'm sure he's had his moments." He starts flipping his soggy bar coaster between his fingers. "But look, he...well, he did me a solid in my second year. I effed up big time, and he... Let's just say I could've been kicked out of the program if it wasn't for him. I've got nothing bad to say about the guy."

I nod and throw in a smile for good measure, but on the inside I worry Trey won't be much help to me after all. I stare at the tattoo on his right bicep. "What's with the ace?"

He lifts his sleeve, and three other aces pop into view, one in every suit and each in a free-falling fashion that starts high on his deltoid. "Just a reminder to always have an ace up my sleeve."

I'm not sure what he means by this, but I can't fault his logic. We should always have an ace or two up our sleeve.

"I've shown you mine, now you show me yours," he says.

"Show you my what?"

"Your tattoos."

"I don't have any."

He seems surprised by this. "Really? An off-the-beaten-path woman like you?" He looks at my ears. "No piercings either?"

"No."

"Why not?"

"What's the point?"

He snickers, and when my silence persists, he fills it. "So, miss pathologist, can you tell me something else about yourself besides your indifference to body art and your inconceivable preference of lagers over ales? What do you like to do in your spare time?"

"Read, exercise, video games, graphic design."

"You like movies?"

"Not really."

"Skiing?"

"No."

"Dancing?"

"No."

"Shopping?"

"No."

Laughing, Trey rubs a hand over his closely shorn hair. When I raise my beer to drink, he clicks it with his own. "At least there's one thing I know about you, Dr. Larkin. You're definitely not like any other woman I've met."

No, I think. *I'm probably not.*

8

Early Saturday morning I go for a run, enjoying the stillness of the hour when the birds are awake but the rest of the neighborhood sleeps. A sparkling veil of dew blankets the grass, and the brilliant oranges and pinks of the sunrise make their final appearance before the day officially begins. I don't listen to music. Nature and my thoughts are enough.

Normally, I run the trail of a nearby park. Six times around nets me almost five miles. Or sometimes I use the track at the high school. But today I wind my way around the residential neighborhoods. Some blocks have sidewalks. Others require using the road. The scar over my stab wound throbs in discomfort, but it's not too bad. According to Tam, they still haven't caught the guy who attacked me. Probably never will.

In my quest to learn more about Dr. Donovan, I've queried as many people as I can, mostly my senior residents, but the answer is always the same: "He's a good guy and a great surgeon."

After Martin got curious, wondering why I wanted to know so much about the man, I backed down. I'm not ready to tell anyone my suspicions. That would be premature. So for now this match is between Sam and me. Hopefully, by later this morning, I'll have some answers. I plan to visit the library where Sandy Newmaker worked. She was one of the two patients who died of unclear causes not long after having trauma surgery.

Back at my apartment, I shower and eat two bowls of Cheerios, followed by a doughnut. The library doesn't open until nine, so to make the clock tick faster, I mess around with the orientation pictures Megan sent me. In one, I Photoshop Jen's head onto Waseem's body and vice versa. In another, I do the same with John and Megan, and then again with Dr. Thomas and me. I send the doctored photos to my phone to share with my fellow first-years later. Maybe they'll enjoy them. Maybe the gesture will check off a box in the "effort" column and get Megan off my back. God knows I'll need the goodwill to survive Dr. Silverstein's get-together this evening.

I make myself another cup of tea, sink back on my desk chair, and review in my mind what I learned about Sandy Newmaker three nights ago, after my drink at O'Dell's with Trey. From Dr. Silverstein and Martin's conversation in the hospital gardens, I already knew the woman was a librarian addicted to opioids and that she required surgery after a vicious dog attack. Though I wanted more information about her hospitalization—for example, who her surgeon was—I didn't dare access her medical records. Without a professional reason to do so, I might get in trouble. HIPAA laws are not to be taken lightly. When I was a med student, a nurse lost his job after two violations.

So instead, I relied on Google, and as usual it didn't disappoint. A search of "Sandy Newmaker" plus "librarian" took me to the website of the local library in Perry, Massachusetts, a town about a half hour west of Morganville. Sandy Newmaker wrote book reviews for their weekly "What We're Reading" column, which is why her name appeared. The other morsel I learned was that she was a runner, and an impressive one at that. Her name popped up with the Boston Marathon and other races around the northeastern states. None after 2016 though.

I found no social media accounts, at least not in her name. The only other piece of information I discovered from my internet search was her obituary from October, almost nine months ago. She died unexpectedly at the age of thirty-one (no cause of death listed) and was survived by her parents and two brothers. It didn't appear she was married or had children.

Armed with that good start, I plan to scrounge up every social skill I've harvested over the years and visit Perry Public Library today. Maybe someone working there will share more specifics. I've saved Dr. Donovan's picture from the hospital's staff directory to my phone and intend to show it around.

Finally, eight thirty arrives. Dressed in shorts, a cap-sleeved shirt, and sandals, I exit my apartment and lock the door behind me. When I head down the hall, I stop dead at what I see. Like a grenade, anger explodes in my belly.

Near the building's exit, April cowers in her waitressing uniform, probably on her way out. Rubbing up against her is our landlord, Mr. Sinclair, his hand slithering up her skirt like a snake. From the trapped-rabbit expression on her face, she's not enjoying his affection.

I clamor down the hall, clearing my throat as if my cereal still clogs it. Mr. Sinclair startles and steps back. When he sees me, his face tightens and his hands form fists, but when I keep charging forward he presses back against the wall. I stop barely a foot away from him.

"Hi, April," I say, glaring at Sinclair. "Have a good day at work."

She swallows and nods and then hurries out the door. Once she's outside, she peers back through the small window and mouths a wide-eyed *thank you*.

Sinclair starts to leave too, but before he can, I press him back against the wall and grab his polo shirt at the waist. The soft flesh of a middle-aged stomach peeks out at me.

"How dare you touch me," he stammers. He tries to yank free, but I hold on.

I rub his soft belly, mindful not to take my anger too far. "Like you touched April without her permission? Hoping she might make her rent payment some other way?"

He goes to swat my arm away, but I've already released him and stepped back.

"You're lucky I don't evict you." Even though he's free of my hold, he jerks his arm away like a defiant child.

I bark a laugh. "Yeah, right. Go ahead and try. I'll pass on how you're willing to take sexual favors in place of rent."

His face remains pink. "Do you hate men, is that it, Larkin? You one of those pissed-off feminazis?"

"I don't hate men. I don't hate women. I just hate assholes." I pull out my phone. "How much does April still owe you for July's rent?"

He straightens his hair, trying to regain his cool. "Four hundred dollars."

"Fine." I unlock my phone, open my PayPal app, and spend a minute scrolling and tapping. "There. I've just sent that plus her August rent to your business account. Now leave her the fuck alone."

I burst out the door toward my car. Once inside it, the seat hot on my bare thighs from the sun, it takes a little time for my calm to return. Most everything easily rolls off me, but sometimes anger likes to stick around. Once it dissipates, I put my car in reverse, eager to get to the Perry public library and confirm what I suspect I already know.

A call on my cellphone tells me it's not going to happen quite yet. It's Home and Hearth Healing, my mother's mental health facility. I put my car back into park and answer. Luis Vargas, my mom's favorite nurse, is on the line. He asks if I can come to the center.

"Emily's catatonic," he says.

Inside the rec room at Home and Hearth Healing, my mother is anything but catatonic. She's standing on the couch near the fireplace, bare feet shuffling back and forth over the cushions, hair tangled, fingers tapping each other, speech rambling in a disorganized and unintelligible fashion. Still, the name *Hitler* is clearly heard.

Luis speaks calmly to her, trying to coax her down. A few residents titter nervously nearby and watch the spectacle, but most have been escorted out. From what I can see, the Saturday visitors have been too, and I'm grateful for the center's discretion.

Not only am I disturbed to see my mom is deep in psychosis, I'm disturbed to find it's her concentration camp delusion. My mom is of German descent, but she's not Jewish, and it seems wrong for her to believe she's been persecuted as such. But a schizophrenic brain in full-blown psychosis is not one to be reasoned with.

On the best days (which are few), she's herself, talking to me like a mother talks to a daughter, which is to say with love, praise, and advice. On the good days, she's still Emily, but she's a withdrawn and quieter version of herself, playing guitar outside or sketching in the rec room. On fair days, she's Meryl Streep, seeing the world through the eyes of an actress and sharing stories of her days on set, often in a disorganized manner. On bad days, she's Joan of Arc, persecuted by the king and trying to avoid being burned at the stake, although she's still in strong, I-am-woman-hear-me-roar form. On the worst—and thankfully rarest—days, she's Anna, a concentration camp prisoner, destined for the gas chamber. In this delusion, she's lost most of her fight.

I go to Luis's side. Like all the nurses who work there, he's dressed in tan chinos and a white shirt. When I see the dark circles under my mother's eyes and the terror that resides within them, my chest cinches. Already petite, her frame seems thinner than when I was here just a few days ago.

"What happened?" I ask Luis. "You said she was catatonic."

"She was at first. She was outside on her favorite rock, playing guitar and singing, and then she suddenly went still." His usual calm sounds frayed. "Her guitar fell, but she still didn't react. Maisy here saw it, didn't you, Maisy?"

A tall, angular woman with curly hair nods. Her arms are wrapped around each other in an awkward fashion. Though she hasn't been at the center long, I recognize her from past visits, as she's frequently by my mother's side. She keeps nodding long after what's necessary and in a sing-songy voice says, "She just frooooze up completely." Still nodding. "Wooooouldn't move at all."

Luis sighs and runs a hand through his thick hair. The movement shifts his glasses, and he rights them in place. "Five minutes after I called you, she started moving, and we were able to get her inside. I thought she'd be okay, but when she finally started to talk, she claimed Hitler was watching her, tracking her every move, and…" the nurse clears his throat, "she said he'd already killed her family and that she was next. That's when the agitation started."

"Does she need haloperidol?"

"Dr. Dhar gave us a treatment plan, yes, but I wanted to try this first. I only called you because you said you want to be informed of things right away."

"I do, thank you."

To my right, Maisy finally stops nodding and leaves the rec room, her arms still wrapped in their weird embrace.

"Dr. Dhar's away at a conference today," Luis says. "We talked by phone. He wants to meet with you on Thursday afternoon. Talk about some med adjustments for Emily. She's been more paranoid of late. Thinks someone's spying on her."

I nod, and I'm about to reach for my mother and try to sit her down on the sofa, knowing full well Luis will be more effective than me, when he breaks into song. He sings beautifully, and the melody he chooses is soft and soothing.

After two minutes of his angelic voice, my mother stops shuffling back and forth on the couch cushions. She stops rambling, and her fingers stop tapping. As Luis keeps singing, he reaches out for her hand. She grasps it. Slowly she steps off the couch. Her eyes catch mine for a moment, but there's no recognition. Though I'm used to that, it still hits like a brick.

Luis nods at me and escorts my mother to her room. I don't follow right away, giving him time to settle her in. Like with my chief resident, I think of how wonderful it must be to be a Luis. Someone who can calm someone through song instead of antipsychotics. I know this isn't always the case, and he'll be the first to tell me he got lucky, but still, I marvel at people like him and Martin. People so in tune with others. I'll always be a solitary island around them.

When I finally leave the rec room and stroll down the sage-tiled hallway that leads to my mother's room, I see Maisy inside her own, along with an orderly I don't recognize. The sing-songy woman is sitting on the end of her bed, trying to wrap her afghan around her, but the orderly, dressed in white pants and a white polo shirt, holds a corner of it in a teasing fashion and won't release it. He looks to be in his thirties, medium build, dark hair. Striped socks peek beneath his pants and provide the only splash of color.

I pause to watch them. At first, I wonder if this is a game they play, but when I scrutinize Maisy's face and try to read her expression, it doesn't seem to be one of amusement. The man, not realizing I'm standing in the doorway, tugs harder on the blanket.

When Maisy starts whimpering, I speak up. "Maisy, do you need help?"

The orderly releases the blanket as if it were on fire and looks up at me. "Oh, hi," he says.

A smile lights up his oblong features. I can't tell if it's genuine or not, but I don't like the teasing I just witnessed.

"I'm Pete Parsons, a new orderly here." He extends a hand, but I don't take it.

"Then I guess you've yet to learn that teasing is only fun when both people are into it," I say.

His smile fades, and if he's about to say something else, I don't wait for it. Instead, I head to my mother's room.

I don't like this new orderly. What I observed doesn't sit well with me. Could he be the source of my mother's new paranoia? Paranoid delusions are certainly nothing new for her. She was once convinced my father was trying to poison her with her medicines. Another time she thought I was conspiring with the king to throw her in the dungeon and leave her there to rot. So hearing that she thinks someone's spying on her is not a bombshell revelation.

But what if it were true? She never leaves the facility, so it would have to be someone inside, either another resident or an employee.

Maybe even a visitor. It may be nothing, but having just viewed a bit of sadism by the new orderly, I can't blow my mother's paranoia off. I usually visit three times a week. I'll bump it up to four if I can and talk to Dr. Dhar next week.

Inside her room, which is a comfortable space in shades of lavender and butter cream, she's lying calmly on the bed with Luis seated next to her. Together they sing "Sunshine on My Shoulders." My breath catches at the sound. It's the song she sang to me when I was a little girl, back before her disease blossomed into what it is now. My eyes sting, and I find I have to blink rapidly. Not since my dad's funeral has my chest squeezed so tightly.

Not wanting to disturb them, I tiptoe to Luis and do the only thing I can to show my gratitude. I place a hand on his shoulder and make eye contact. Coming from me, this is a huge gesture. Then I slip quietly out of the room.

As I pass Maisy on my way out, I look for the new orderly and make sure he's not bothering her. He's no longer in her room, but someone else is, and the shock of seeing her sitting with Maisy pinches off the sorrow in my chest. My eyes open and close a few times to make sure it's really her I'm seeing.

So *this* is where I've encountered Dr. Silverstein before. I must have noticed her briefly in the center when she was visiting Maisy, sometime before I started residency.

My advisor looks up at me. Her expression is not of surprise at all. It seems to be one of understanding, suggesting that, unlike me, she remembers our paths crossing here. That explains how she knows about my mother. Maybe she wanted me to take the lead on discussing it. I feel a bit sick. What if she just witnessed my mother's meltdown?

Having my two worlds collide likes this throws me off balance. I reach out and put a hand on Maisy's doorframe to steady myself. Lowering my head, I channel Dr. Lightfoot's breathing technique and seize on it now.

When I finally look up again, my advisor merely smiles and nods. Then she lowers her head and lets me leave without saying a word.

It's eleven thirty by the time I reach the Perry public library to ask about Sandy Newmaker. Not even noon yet, and I feel like I've lived through a whole day. My itch to go pound the bag at Brian's Gym is intense, especially after spotting Dr. Silverstein at Home and Hearth Healing, but my desire to learn something new about Dr. Donovan is greater.

Housed in a small historic building, the library's interior is rife with shadowy corners and exudes a musty smell. I wouldn't care if it smelled like fresh mulch. Surrounding myself with its books would be a pleasant way to spend the day.

Running my fingers over the spines of the new releases in nonfiction (my preferred genre, especially the ones on mental health), I make note of the titles. My father's personal library held a decent collection, but I read through its contents long before I had to sell the house. After his fatal heart attack and my mom's institutionalization, I recruited Ned to help sort through their belongings and get the place ready to put on the market.

At first my brother was there more in body than in mind, his dark fiend at play as he struggled to grasp the new reality facing us as brother and sister. Eventually, however, he rose to the task, as he's been known to do once I lay things out for him, and together we made a decent team.

I let the memories go and redirect my focus to the checkout counter, behind which a hunched, older woman stands. Her reading glasses dangle from a chain around her neck as she shelves books in an area marked *Reserved*. Her hearing must be stronger than her bones because when I approach, she turns around before I say a word.

"Hello, dear. What can I help you with?" Her voice carries a faint tremor.

I inhale. Here goes. "I was wondering if Sandy was working today? Sandy Newmaker?"

The elderly woman's face loses its light. Guilt washes over me. Deceiving nice people is not how I enjoy spending my time.

"I'm sorry to be the one to tell you," she says, "but Sandy passed away last October."

I try to look shocked. "That's terrible."

"Were you a friend of hers?"

"More of an acquaintance. We met running marathons. I was passing through Perry and remembered her saying she worked here, so I thought I'd stop by and say hi." I strive for pensive. "Guess that explains why I haven't seen her at any marathons for a while."

"She had a terrible go of things, the poor woman. She injured her knee running a couple years back. Tore some ligaments, I guess. Despite having surgery on it, her life traveled south after that."

"I'm very sorry to hear it." My fingers jiggle the keys in my shorts pocket, and I force them still.

The librarian reaches for the chair behind her computer and eases herself down, smoothing her cardigan along the way. Given how empty the place is, maybe she's happy for the company. "Sandy got so depressed after that knee injury. She couldn't run anymore, and with all the pain she was having, she couldn't get off the…" She hesitates and bites her lower lip.

I want her to keep talking, but I don't want to make her suspicious. Treading carefully, I wrinkle my brow in what I hope looks like concern. "She couldn't get off the pain meds? Is that what you were going to say?" I remove my hands from my pockets and place my palms over my heart. "I'm a doctor. I've seen that happen all too often."

"Oh dear, I imagine you have. Poor Sandy got so addicted to those things after her knee surgery. Then that awful dog attack happened and made things even worse. I'm amazed she survived that second surgery. It was far more extensive than the knee one. Had to stitch up her limbs and her neck, close a gash in her belly, reattach a finger. The dog nearly killed her. After all that, the poor woman completely fell apart. My boss eventually had to fire her. Broke his heart to do so, but it had to be done. She couldn't function." The librarian leans so far forward on her chair I worry she'll topple over. Her voice drops to a whisper. "I heard after that, she even took to heroin. Couldn't get her hands on enough pills anymore. No job. No money."

It always surprises me how much people open up once they learn you're a doctor. As if the medical degree grants an automatic pass to the next level of intimacy. Makes me think of something a family practice attending told me back in med school. "Normally I don't mind," he said. "It's an honor. But sometimes I just want to get my groceries."

The librarian flaps her hand. "So heartbreaking to see such a good woman go down like that. We were all sad when she died. We hoped after her surgery for the dog attack she'd get clean. She got a second chance at life with that." The woman dabs at her eyes. "But she didn't take it."

"Was it a drug overdose?"

She nods, and I murmur how sad that is. What I don't mention is that according to my chief resident, the medical examiner couldn't conclusively say there were enough drugs in Sandy's system to kill her.

I ready myself for my next words. I practiced them earlier. "You know, we had another friend who sometimes ran with us. I wonder if he knows she died." I tap my chin and stare at the books on the cart next to her, as if I'm considering something. "Oh, wait." I grab my phone from my satchel and pull up Dr. Donovan's picture. "Maybe you can tell me if he comes in here. I don't think he lives too far from Perry."

"Sure, dear." She lifts her reading glasses and puts them on, the chain swinging back and forth in front of her crepey neck. After a beat, she says, "Yes, he's been in here."

My fingers tighten around the phone. I don't dare speak out of fear it'll reveal my excitement.

She removes her glasses and drops them to her chest. "But I don't think I've seen him around since Sandy died. 'Course, maybe my boss or one of my coworkers has. I wasn't aware they knew each other."

"Hmm, well, maybe I'll give him a call." I measure my words

carefully, struggling to stay in the moment, but my brain is already in overdrive trying to make sense of what I've just learned.

I thank her for her time, express my condolences again, and listen with a plastic smile as she talks about the library's upcoming changes. When I get back to my car, the front window of which has been gifted a big streak of bird poop in my absence, the thoughts rush at me.

What was Dr. Donovan's interest in Sandy Newmaker? Was he the one who performed surgery on her after the nearly fatal dog attack? If so, why was he spying on her? Then again, *was* he spying on her? Or was he simply visiting the library? Maybe he lives here in Perry and not in Morganville like I assumed. I tried Googling his address, but his only connection to real estate was a condo in Baltimore, presumably purchased for his residency training and since sold.

As always, the best way for me to process things is through exercise. I already jogged this morning, so I'll head to Brian's Gym for some boxing and core work. Afterward, I'll jot down my thoughts about what this all means.

Then I remember Dr. Silverstein's get-together tonight. With a groan, I smack the steering wheel. I have no choice but to go. She's my advisor.

Yay me.

Before I drive away, I pull up my email and find the invitation with her address. I enter it into my GPS now in case I'm pressed for time after my trip to the gym.

In the meantime, I'll think about Sam, the man who performs surgery on a woman like a Dr. Donovan and then spies on her in the library like a Sam. The same Sam who's in my pictures, a Sam no one in my family knows. At least I don't think they do.

Is he merely a stalker or is there something more sinister at play? An awful thought wiggles its way into my head, but I shove it back down. Not wanting to jump to conclusions—Dr. Lightfoot says nothing good comes from that—I realize I'm going to have to dig further, but it'll probably come with some risk.

That's okay. I think I'm up to the match.

9

Four days have passed since my visit to the Perry library. I wait inside the pathology conference room for surgical path rounds to begin, hoping Dr. Donovan will show. It's my third attendance at one, but I've yet to see him here.

Designed for residents, pathologists, and surgeons who wish to attend (though mandatory for first-years unless we're busy elsewhere), the rounds benefit both specialties. Not only do the surgeons get a front-row seat to the microscopic results of their biopsies and tumor resections, the pathologists get to learn more about the patients. A chance to see them as an entire person, not just stained cells on a slide.

One chair over, head lowered toward his iPad, John Kim reads a journal article I sent him about bone tumor classification. I found it in one of my online journals this morning and thought it might help with his research project.

On the other side of the table, Jen and Waseem discuss how much meat they'll need for Sunday's barbecue. The mother of three has invited each of us and a plus-one to the social event. Though I feel less obligated to attend than I did Dr. Silverstein's dinner party (not to mention I've never brought a plus-one to anything in my life), I'm thinking of inviting Trey. Jen's barbecue makes for a good opportunity to get closer to him should I need his behind-the-scenes access to Dr. Donovan.

My two colleagues leave me out of their poultry and beef discussion. They've learned not to engage me in small talk. If only Megan would do the same. She's not here yet, but we've reserved a spot for her near us at the end of the table, farthest from the screen.

I look at my watch for the hundredth time. Three minutes to go before the conference starts. A few path attendings and surgeons have arrived, some with coffee cups for a three p.m. pick-me-up, some with lunch not yet eaten. A few senior residents pop in too, including our chief, Martin Chen, but still no Dr. Donovan.

I think back to Dr. Silverstein's dinner party on Saturday, which I managed to survive thanks in part to my doctored photos of Megan's orientation pictures. The head transpositions and thought bubbles I subsequently added kept my colleagues in stitches, which in turn deflected their questions away from my personal life. In one photo, I even added the actual celebrity Jennifer Lopez, making it look like she was standing right next to our own Jennifer Lopez. Jen seemed to enjoy that and joked about having the "real" one take her kids for the day so she and her husband could finally have a break.

To my relief, Dr. Silverstein said very little about my mother's debacle at Home and Hearth Healing earlier that day. She did, however, thank me for bringing cookies (store-bought), slip me an extra beer, and say, "I think you could use this." Then she reminded me she was always there to talk to if I needed. "You see, Liza, I know what it's like to have a loved one change." I thought she meant Maisy, but she blinked a few times and said, "My husband's mind is slipping. Just a bit, at least for now, but enough that he wanted to get his Rome sabbatical in before it's...well, before it's too late." I felt sorry for her and offered a learned platitude I hoped was adequate.

A familiar voice outside the room jars me back to my surroundings. Moments later, Megan enters the conference room. Her new designer purse doesn't surprise me. Her lighthearted banter with Dr. Donovan does.

Dressed in a tailored suit with an elegant sheen, far fancier than the dull clothes he wore in my photographs, Dr. Donovan laughs at something Megan says. His dark hair is neatly groomed, and I swear I can smell his sandalwood cologne all the way down here at the end of the table. Trey isn't with him.

Waseem pats the empty seat for Megan. She leaves Dr. Donovan's side and joins us. She greets me, but I'm not sure I respond because I've just locked eyes with the surgeon, and my focus is glued to him. The gaiety he had with Megan vanishes. A hardness sets in his eyes and jaw and is directed at me. Maybe he's found out I've been asking about him. Maybe he knows I visited the Perry library.

When Dr. Silverstein enters the room, he watches her approach me. Does he know she's my advisor? She leans over and tells me what a nice job I did on the cytology specimens from this morning. I thank her, and she takes her seat. When I look back at the surgeon, his attention is no longer on me. Instead, he's congratulating a colleague on an aneurysm repair she pulled off. It appears Dr. Donovan the surgeon is back in place.

As the lighting in the room dims, I try not to stare at him, even though he's in my line of sight when I look at the screen. Dr. Thomas puts up the first microscopic slide, a section of kidney from a woman with lupus. Sections of pancreas, ovary, and intestines from other patients follow. The surgeons and their residents ask questions. Our attending pathologists respond.

My nemesis appears genuinely interested in the pathological findings from the biopsies taken from his patients and those of his colleagues. He jots down a note here or there. It seems he's forgotten about me for the time being, which is fine because I too am enjoying the presentations.

Soon, I'm fully relaxed, so much so that when I unexpectedly hear my name, I jump in my chair. Dr. Donovan is asking me a question about a case. First-years are supposed to be silent sponges in this conference, nothing but quiet observers. Though it's difficult to tell in the darkened room, I imagine everyone around the table is as surprised as me by this breach in protocol.

Too caught off guard to be angry, I say, "What was that again?"

"I asked how common a liver angiosarcoma like this is?" Dr.

Donovan points to the screen, where a tissue slide displays a vacuous labyrinth of pink, purple, and blue.

"Not very common." My voice sounds small in the large room. "Maybe about one percent of all liver cancers."

"And what's the tissue of origin?"

"Blood vessels." Why is he doing this? What's his angle?

"At what stage are most diagnosed?"

"A late one."

"How do we treat it?"

I hesitate. "I'm not sure."

"Oh come on, you can do better than that."

Every head in the room is turned my way. Though the attention makes my underarms dampen and my mouth go dry, it's anger that tenses my muscles.

"What about—"

"Whoa, whoa," Dr. Thomas says, cutting the surgeon off. He laughs and adds, "I'm all for resident education, but maybe we better move on."

Dr. Donovan chuckles too. "Sorry, Darnell. Got carried away. Dr. Larkin was doing so well it seemed a shame to stop. She's curious about so many things." He peers down the table at me.

I return his gaze. Despite my anger, I feel a tiny rumble of pleasure to know I've gotten under his skin.

Martin's pager goes off, breaking the silence that's consumed the table. My chief resident stands up. "Come on, Liza, we have an autopsy to do."

Confusion deflates my fervor. It's not my turn for another autopsy. It's Megan's, and then after her, Waseem's. A glance at Megan suggests she's fully aware of this too, her lips a tight line, but she says nothing. Martin's uncharacteristically brusque tone has left no room for questions.

When he and I clear the conference, he hustles me down the hall. As we descend the stairs toward the morgue, he asks, "What in the world was that about? Sheesh, no wonder you were asking me about the guy. Did something happen between you two? Did you do something to piss him off?"

What should I say? Though I have my suspicions about the surgeon, I have no proof he's tied to two patient deaths. Martin will think I'm nuts. I rummage for a lie. "We were discussing a patient the other day. He was really busy, and maybe I asked him too many questions. Disagreed with him about a couple things too."

Martin holds the basement door open and studies me. "That doesn't sound like you. Doesn't sound like him either." But he must buy my excuse because after I step into the hallway, he says, "Talk about a passive-aggressive payback."

As we prep for the autopsy room, donning full body coverage, double gloves, face guards, and masks, I ask why I'm here instead of Megan.

"Are you kidding? You needed rescue from that weird drama. Megan can do the next two."

Fair enough, I think. Hopefully she'll think so too.

By the time we enter the chilly autopsy room and cross the tiles to the stainless-steel table and the body that lies there, I'm back to my academic disposition. The pathologists' assistant is in the back of the room rinsing something in an industrial-sized sink. He greets us over his shoulder and says Dr. Munson will be here shortly.

My second corpse is yet another man not much older than thirty, but this one's in a much worse state than the first. More noxious smelling too. His decaying, chewed-up body looks like it served as the main course for an animal or two.

"He was found in the wooded area of Roster Park earlier today," Martin says, readying the equipment. His eyes are watering, and by the way he gags a few times, it appears the smell of the body affects him more than it does me. "Forensics has already examined his clothing and taken the collections they need. As always with this type of death, the ME and her fellow are in charge, but they said we can observe."

He points to the mauled body. "Looks like he's been there a while. No obvious cause of death yet, but the wildlife damage could be masking an injury. His head and neck are mostly intact though. The crime scene tech said it was partially buried in a crevice where not much air got in. Less decomposition that way. From the hole in his nasal septum and the saddlebag nose, you wonder about cocaine abuse. Maybe he got lost and…"

Martin's voice fades into the background. The smell fades into the background. The sound of the sink's running water fades into the background. Even the mottled, torn, and shredded tissue fades into the background. Only one thing on the body holds my attention. Something the animals haven't destroyed.

I grab hold of the stainless-steel table and stare at the deceased man's neck. With my eyes, I trace what's left of the pink snake that coils from collarbone to chin. I've seen that tattoo before. In the parking lot of Brian's Gym.

This decaying, chewed-up corpse splayed on the autopsy table is my attacker.

Or at least he was.

10

The next twenty-four hours feel like a dream. Discombobulation is a rare state for me, and it takes a lot of running, boxing, and core work to orient myself again. It appears my attack in the parking lot nearly three weeks ago affected me more than I realized. Autopsying the man who jumped me was as surreal as an acid trip. I can't help but wonder if there's a connection between his death and my attack itself.

At four o'clock on Thursday, I leave work and drive to Home and Hearth Healing for my appointment with Dr. Dhar, my mother's psychiatrist. Thanks to a downed power line that's reduced a stretch of Waverly Boulevard to single lane traffic, the trip takes longer than usual. I crank the air conditioning and think about my attacker's postmortem exam.

Though Dr. Munson found nothing to point to homicide—no bullet holes, no stab wounds, no evidence of strangulation—she did find signs of chronic stimulant abuse, including cardiovascular changes. Thinking back, I remember how wired he was, how crazed he looked, how he kept sniffing like his nose was running. All are consistent with cocaine use. Maybe, like Martin suggested, the junkie simply wandered into the park and died. Had a heart attack, got turned around in the woods, fell and got his head stuck in that crevice, whatever. But it seems an odd coincidence.

Not far beyond Shawna and Tam's place, I pass the crew of electricians working on the downed power line, and traffic once again flows on both sides of the road. As the spacing between cars grows and vehicles turn off behind me, I notice a beige sedan two cars back. It looks like the same vehicle that pulled out behind me when I exited the hospital. Maybe an old Taurus, but it's too far away to get a glimpse of the driver in the rearview mirror.

It's just a fluke, I tell myself. Waverly Boulevard is a major artery for the northern half of Morganville. Lots of cars drive the winding road in its entirety. No need to become paranoid like my mom. *Maybe it's something in your blood*, my brother whispers in my mind.

I turn right onto Sherlock Road. Home and Hearth Healing is less than a mile down. Before I head there, I pull into a strip mall on the left and park outside one of Morganville's many doughnut shops. Trees and doughnuts. New England has a surplus of both.

A few minutes later, armed with a box of pastries, I drive the remaining distance to the facility. In the heavier traffic, the beige Taurus is no longer following me. If it ever even was.

The interior of Home and Hearth Healing is homey and warm and smells like spiced apples. Gingham furniture, light-wood accents, and colorful flowering plants make the country-home appearance complete. At a desk against the far wall, I greet the young receptionist, Tiana, who was the one who buzzed me in. When I hand her the box of doughnuts, her lips purse together. "Ooh, you're so good to us, Liza. Thank you."

She takes her usual cinnamon twist and tells me Dr. Dhar is waiting for me in his office. As I make my way down the hallway, the inevitable odors of institutional life replace the spiced apples, but it isn't unpleasant. With the amount of money that goes into this private facility, the atmosphere is as far from a state hospital as you can get. As always, I'm grateful my mother has the means to be in such a nice place, and I try never to take it for granted.

When I peek inside the rec room, I do a double-take. One of the residents, a stubby man with dysmorphic features, has just fallen.

Next to him stands Pete, the new orderly, and I swear in my blink of a glance I saw him purposely trip the poor man. I can't be sure, and when I backtrack for a second look, Pete is helping him up. "You okay, buddy?" he asks.

The orderly gazes toward the door and spots me. After a long moment, he smiles and waves before escorting the man to a chair. Continuing down the hallway to Dr. Dhar's office, I wonder what I just saw.

The psychiatrist greets me as soon as I knock. He's a thin man with even thinner hair, and his small space is as neat and as organized as my own. Above his desk hangs my favorite photograph in the facility, maybe my favorite photograph anywhere. In it, a little girl in the foreground of a chaotic New Delhi street stares at the photographer with the grayest eyes I've ever seen. Her expression seems somewhere between a smirk and sadness. Dr. Dhar says the girl reminds him of me, but I'm not sure what that means.

After the requisite small talk (yay me), Dr. Dhar straightens to full posture and his face grows serious. "I was very sorry to hear about your mother's incident last weekend. I feel bad I wasn't in town."

"That's okay. Luis managed to calm her down without extra medication."

"He's a lifesaver, for sure. Of course, had he felt incapable of diffusing the situation, he would have asked the doctor on call to come in. You know that."

"I do. Your staff does a wonderful job." My thoughts drift to the new orderly, and I wonder if I should mention him to Dr. Dhar.

"I adjusted the dosage of some of your mother's medicines." The psychiatrist hands me a printout of my mom's drug list. "Is this agreeable to you?"

As a doctor who's rotated through psychiatry and as a daughter of a schizophrenic mother, I'm well versed in the world of psychotropic medications. "Looks good," I say.

"Of course, it will take a few weeks to see results, but she hasn't worsened since Saturday so I think we're on the right track."

"Why do you think her paranoia's worse? It's part of the illness, of course, but it seems more than usual. Luis says she's convinced someone's spying on her."

Dr. Dhar picks up a fat pen and rolls it between his fingers. "It's not just paranoia, her psychosis is worse too. She's spending more time as Joan of Arc or Anna." The latter is the Holocaust victim, the despondent persona that distresses both the staff and the other residents. "She's spending less time outside as well, which is a shame because playing music out there is her greatest joy. It's good for the other residents too. We all love listening to her." He smiles, and I appreciate his respect for my mother. "But she tells me they're watching her through the bushes."

"They, as in plural?"

He shrugs. "Sometimes it's *they*—the king and his men, you know. Other times it's just a *he*." The psychiatrist drops the pen and steeples his fingers. "Hopefully, the medication adjustment will get her back to baseline, which," he looks at me and frowns, "isn't the mother you knew, but it's at least a mother who recognizes you and interacts with us, no matter how languidly."

I nod and swallow. It's been a while since I've seen that Emily. Except for brief periods, most of her seemed to die with my father. "Anything else?" I ask him.

"Not unless you have any questions."

Pete again comes to mind. I hate to get a staff member in trouble unnecessarily. What if I'm wrong? Making social assumptions hasn't always gone well for me. Still, something about the guy seems off. It's better to err on the side of caution, isn't it?

"How long has the new orderly been working here?" I ask.

"Pete? Two, three weeks maybe. Why?" When I don't answer right away, Dr. Dhar angles his head. "Is there a problem?"

I pick at a fingernail. "I'm not sure. It's just that the last time I was here he was teasing Maisy. It didn't seem like she was enjoying it. And then today…well, I'm not sure what I saw. Maybe just keep an eye on him?"

He peers at me through dark lashes. "Yes, of course I will. I do so with all my staff. Let me know if you have any other concerns."

We shake hands, and I exit his office. Before I go, I cross over to the other hallway and peek into my mother's room. She's sleeping peacefully, her blond hair fanning her face and her hands clutching the alpaca blanket I bought her last Christmas. She loves its softness. Worries every time we wash it, as if she'll never see it again.

Something on her dresser catches my eye. It's the photo book I made for her and then buried under her sweaters when it seemed to set her off. Knowing she dug it out to look at it gives me hope. Maybe the med changes will bring my mom back. At least for a little while.

On my way out, I stop once again at the receptionist's desk to show Tiana a photograph of Dr. Donovan. In case my mother really is being spied on, I need to confirm Sam is not a visitor.

Tiana studies the picture on my phone. "No, I don't recognize him. Why?"

"Will you call me if he comes in?" I ask. Tiana works the three to eleven shift, so there's a good chance she'd spot him if he stopped by.

"Sure, but…should I be worried?"

I force a smile. "No no, nothing like that. Just an old…family acquaintance." Which I suppose is technically a version of the truth.

She assures me she will, and we say our goodbyes.

Outside, the parking lot remains as quiet as it was when I entered, most of the cars probably belonging to staff members since few visitors were inside, but as I back out my Civic and drive toward the exit, a vehicle catches my eye and makes my skin prickle.

Parked in the very last spot is a beige Taurus.

I ease my car behind it. Up close, a number of paint scratches and nicks stand out, including a dented back door on the driver's side.

Something's not right. It's more than paranoia, I'm sure of it.

After putting my car in park, I grab my phone and snap a picture of the Massachusetts license plate, which is rusted and bent and in worse shape than the Taurus itself. I look around. Seeing no one, I get out and take more pictures of the car, all from different angles. Just in case I might need them.

After I leave Home and Hearth Healing, I head back to the hospital to finish a presentation on small cell cancer of the lung. I'm scheduled to give the talk to my fellow first-years tomorrow. Most of it's prepared, but I need to review a few more slides and find a couple more cases from our study files. It should take no more than an hour. Even with another half hour to review it, I can easily make Brian's eight o'clock heavy-bag class.

Inside my cubicle, my colleagues gone for the day, I devour a slice of pizza from the cafeteria. My side of broccoli smells like wet dog, but I eat it anyway, and my piece of chocolate cream pie, although decent, is no match for my neighbor's desserts.

I lick my fork clean and consider doing the same to the plate when my cell phone buzzes. Having no social life, I get few calls. It's usually the center about my mother, or Shawna or my brother, Ned. Sometimes it's a telemarketer or a scammer, but those numbers are quick to get blocked.

This time the call is from Shawna. We spent enough time together as kids that I don't bristle like the Grinch at the thought of answering.

"Just checking in to see how you're doing," she says after I greet her.

"Fine." Remembering from Dr. Lightfoot that this is not particularly helpful dialogue, I add, "Other than a faded bruise and a scar, my stab wound is pretty much healed. Thanks again to you and Tam for coming out that night. It helped having a cop I know there."

"Of course. We were happy to. Are you sleeping okay?"

"Yes."

"Having any flashbacks of the assault?"

"No." Technically, this is true, but I don't mention my shock of seeing my attacker on the autopsy table yesterday or my paranoia of being followed today.

"Wow, what I wouldn't give for your ability to shut things off."

"You sound like my brother."

"Just don't be surprised if things catch up with you. They often do."

"Okay. Thanks." I change the subject. "Tam asked me to fiddle around with some funny invitations for Seth's birthday party. I'll email them to you."

"That's awesome. Thank you for doing that. I want his first birthday to be special."

We chat a bit more, and though I try hard to hold up my end of the conversation, I'm not sure I succeed. As she's telling me about one of her demanding clients at the salon, something rustles outside the residents' room.

I push my chair back and stand. With my phone against my ear, I check the hallway. Darkness from all the rooms, including Dr. Thomas's office on the left and the Death Chamber on the right, where we have morning teaching rounds.

I return to my seat. Shawna is wrapping up the call. I don't want to say anything about yesterday's autopsy surprise, but my father's voice is insisting I do. At least to Tam. She'll want to know my attacker is currently in the morgue. I just hate reopening that box.

I sigh. "Before you go, could you put Tam on the phone?"

"Sure. Why?"

"It's just…I have an update on my attacker. As a cop, she should probably know."

"What? We've been talking for ten minutes and you just mention this now?" Shawna pauses, probably in frustration. "Hold on, I'll get her."

A few seconds later, Tam's laid-back voice says, "What's up?"

Suspecting Shawna has put me on speakerphone, I relay the autopsy from yesterday and how I think it was the same man who attacked me. "I recognized his neck tattoo," I say.

"Did you tell the medical examiner? The police?"

"No."

When Tam doesn't respond, I imagine her and Shawna exchanging glances and shaking their heads in exasperation. This is why I don't like getting close to people. I always disappoint them.

I go on. "Cause of death isn't clear yet—we're waiting on toxicology results—but Dr. Munson is thinking cardiac arrest from cocaine intoxication. The guy's heart muscle is big, and he's got coronary artery disease atypical for a man his age. Other findings of cocaine use too. That fits how he seemed the night he jumped me."

"Yeah, I heard about the body in the park. They got an ID on him a little while ago. You didn't know?"

"No, but I haven't seen Dr. Munson yet today."

"Sheesh, I didn't know the guy was *your* guy." Tam exhales into the phone. "Listen, Liza, I'm not a detective. It's not my investigation. I know you want to put this behind you, but Vance—that's the detective on the case—is gonna wanna follow-up with you. I've got to pass this on to him. I'll help you, but you're gonna have to talk to him."

"I figured as much." I'm already regretting speaking up. I just want to be left alone.

"Is there anything else you want to tell me?"

I think of Dr. Donovan and my suspicion that he's a stalker. Or worse. Maybe now is the time to come forward. But what would I say? That I switched my top residency choice to spy on him? That I'm cozying up to his right-hand resident for purely selfish reasons? That I'm playing detective in public libraries and spinning stories to sweet old librarians? Even to me those sound like the actions of a lunatic. No, until I have more ammunition against him, I can't pass any of this on to Tam.

"No, that's it," I say. "Thank you."

After a few final pleasantries in which Tam humorously grumbles about Seth cracking her phone screen during his new throwing phase and an upcoming trip to visit Shawna's family in Maine, we disconnect.

Five minutes later, I'm engrossed once again in small cell lung cancer. Peering into my microscope at purplish-blue cells, I move the stage until I find the shot I want. Then I secure a plastic holder to my microscope eyepiece, slide my phone into it, and tighten the phone in place. This allows me to snap a picture of the cells. After checking to make sure the placement's still good, I take the picture and hunt around the slide for other good shots. I only need a few more, and then I'll upload the photos to my Power-Point presentation. How the world functioned before technology is beyond me.

Footsteps enter the room, and I jump in surprise. When I look out from my cubicle, Dr. Donovan is ambling toward me.

I grab the arm of my microscope. I'll bash him in the head with its base if I have to.

"Working late, I see." He smiles and sits on top of Waseem's desk one cubicle over. His neatly styled hair and button-down patterned shirt don't suggest recent surgery. An afternoon in clinic maybe? But the clothing doesn't seem fancy enough for that either, not by his usual standards. No expensive suit. No silk tie.

"Presentation tomorrow," I offer warily. My hand eases up on the microscope but doesn't let go completely. Yesterday during surgical path rounds he came at me in a room full of people. Tonight it's just the two of us.

From his higher elevation on Waseem's desk, he looks down at me over the wooden divider. "Your advisor tells me you're a smart one."

I say nothing.

"Forgive me for throwing you off at rounds yesterday." He studies the cuticles of his right hand, which are better groomed than my own. "But this *is* a teaching hospital, after all."

"You didn't throw me off."

He moves on to examining his left hand. "Heard you had an interesting autopsy yesterday."

How does he know that? From Martin? From Megan? After all, the two of them were quite friendly before surgical path rounds. Or did he overhear me talking to Tam a few minutes ago?

I lock eyes with him. "Funny, you seem to know a lot about me. Am I that fascinating?"

He laughs, and it reaches all the way up to his hazel eyes. This close to him, under the fluorescent lighting, I notice their coloring is mismatched. The right eye has less green in it than the left, as if the mole beneath it has leached the pigment. Considering his dual personality, it seems fitting.

Soon his smile fades to lips only. "It seems *you're* the one who's fascinated with me, Dr. Larkin."

I pause for a moment, wondering how much of my snooping around he's discovered. "Maybe so," I finally say. "But I'm not the one who crashes college graduations and family funerals."

"I have no idea what you mean."

"You know exactly what I mean."

He tilts his head. "You seem to be a confused young lady. Nonetheless, public events are public for a reason, aren't they?"

"By the way…" I release the microscope, my confidence growing. Elegant or not, he's just another bully, and like the others before him, I'll bring him down. "You wouldn't happen to own a beat-up beige Taurus, would you?"

If my question surprises him, he doesn't show it. At least I don't see it. He bites his lower lip and then slips off the desk and plops down onto Waseem's chair, wheeling it toward me. When I sit up quickly, he leans forward until our foreheads are only a foot apart.

"What a shame to have another overdose on your table. This drug epidemic is really tearing New England apart." He shifts an inch closer. "It's amazing what an addict will do for one more hit, isn't it?" After a beat of silence, while I scour my brain for the meaning behind his statement, he slaps his thighs and stands. "I've taken up enough of your time."

I want to throw the final punch, get the last word, say something clever that'll make Round 2 a draw. After all, Round 1 in the conference room yesterday went to him. Yet nothing comes to mind.

I grind my teeth, a habit I thought I'd long since abandoned. When I loosen my jaw enough to speak, I say, "If something were to happen to me, my cop friend would be very interested to discover what I've left behind with someone for safekeeping." This is a complete bluff, but his oblique reference to my welfare suggests a security blanket is in order. Maybe there's cause for some fear after all.

He pauses in the doorway, his back to me, his hands clutching the solid frame on either side. Turning his head slightly, he speaks to the empty cubicles on his left. "I don't know what you're talking about, but here's a piece of advice. I suggest you focus on your residency, not on me. It would be terrible if you lost your position."

He exits, putting Round 2 in the bag.

Sam: 2

Liza: 0

11

Inside the hospital's fitness room, I roll out my yoga mat, its vinyl reeking of synthetic polymers. Not surprising, considering I bought it at Target less than an hour ago. As I uncurl the bottom edge and flatten it onto the wood floor, I marvel at the things we endure in the name of information.

Next to me is the woman Dr. Donovan argued with in the atrium almost two weeks ago. Her trim frame is dressed in yoga pants and a sports bra, and her blond hair is pulled back in a pony-tail. Up close, I see freckles on her nose and a small port wine stain shaped like a turtle just above her elbow. Although she doesn't know it, I purposely waited back by the free weights for her to arrive. As soon as she staked out her territory in the middle of the room with her mat and water bottle, I claimed the spot next to her.

Not counting Brian's heavy-bag class at the gym, you couldn't get me to do a group fitness class if you bribed me with a thousand dollars, but my desire to learn more about the woman who slept with Dr. Donovan exceeds my aversion to the twenty-plus bodies who'll be downward-dogging and triangle-posing around me. I say a silent thank you to the gossipy kiosk baristas who mentioned they'd seen the woman here on weekends.

An online search of the hospital's wellness program revealed the four o'clock start time for yoga on Saturday and Sunday. I figured I'd start with Saturday's class and hope she came. The Sweat Lodge —which is what I heard one of the other attendees call the room while I was waiting in the corner—is actually an impressive offering for employees to take advantage of: weights, five treadmills, three elliptical machines, and one stairclimber, not to mention aerobic and yoga classes offered throughout the week, all taking place on this springy wood flooring where I stretch my muscles now.

Two days after my tête-à-tête with Dr. Donovan in the path department, I'm more determined than ever to uncover his secret. If he thought his veiled threat would stop me, he thought wrong. I'm not ready to call him a killer yet, but I *am* ready to advance to the next round. Since Google refused to tell me where he lives, I'm hoping this scorned woman will.

It's going to take all my willpower to pull this off though. Not only will I have to engage the woman after class, I'll have to get her to open up to me. Asking Trey for Dr. Donovan's address is an option, of course. He's coming to Jen's barbecue with me tomorrow. (Yay me. A social event *and* a date.) But this woman can offer me more intimate details than Trey. Plus, it's best not to overuse the right-hand man and make him suspicious. Not yet, anyway.

A thirty-something-year-old man in gym shorts and a T-shirt heads to the front of the room. Our instructor, probably. I realize I better say something quickly to the woman next to me before we begin. I catch her eye with a smile. She returns the gesture.

"This is my first time in the class," I say. "Is it difficult?"

She shakes her head and stands in mountain pose, ready to begin. "It's for all levels. Just do what you can."

I thank her and add, "I'm Liza Larkin, by the way."

The instructor welcomes us and introduces himself as Mark. Even from a few rows back, I see the pinkness of a nose that's been out in the sun too long, especially for someone with his red hair and fair coloring.

"And I'm Shelly," the woman manages to slip in. "Shelly Parsons."

Parsons. The name sounds familiar, but I can't place it. Mark starts giving us a list of instructions, and I shift my attention to him. Since Brian often incorporates yoga poses into our stretch routines, I'm familiar with most of the positions.

For the next fifty minutes, we twist, fold, and elongate. In all four directions, legs, arms, and buttocks crowd my visual field. Mark weaves around us, adjusting a right-angle pose here, a spinal twist there. I pray he doesn't touch me, but my prayer goes unanswered. During reverse triangle, he presses his hand on my back to further my stretch. It takes more muscle strength not to untwist and bite his fingers than it does to hold the pose, but I manage to breathe through it, and soon he moves on.

I pass the time by thinking about the positive feedback I received on my presentation of small cell lung cancer and the uncomfortable, but fortunately brief, discussion I had with Vance the detective about my attacker showing up on the autopsy table. It helped to have Tam with me—I met her at the Morganville police station during lunch yesterday—and although the investigation is not closed until the toxicology report comes back, my part in it is done. What I left out of the discussion was Dr. Donovan's subtle insinuation he was the one who put the man up to it. I need more proof before I make those kinds of accusations.

As I fold into a forward stretch, my thoughts shift to Dr. Lightfoot. I didn't respond to his email yesterday, asking when I might schedule another appointment. "It's been months since we've seen each other," he wrote. "It's risky to go so long between visits, especially with your dad no longer by your side."

A part of me knows my shrink is right. He usually is. But he's not my focus right now. Sam is. Dr. Lightfoot will only distract me from our sparring. Worse, he'll question my choices.

When the yoga class ends, Shelly and I drink our water, wipe off our sweat, and roll up our mats. A few people head to one of the cardio machines or the weights, but most call it a day. Mark's touch on my back was the least of my worries. Now comes the hard part.

I find my smile. "Well, that wasn't so bad," I say to Shelly as she stretches out her neck.

"Mark's really good. The woman who teaches Sunday's class moves through the poses too quickly."

"Do you attend both?"

"When I can. I usually have to work one of the weekend days though."

"What do you do here?"

She hangs her towel around her neck. "I'm a respiratory thera-pist. You?"

"One of the first-year pathology residents."

"A newbie, huh? Fresh blood for the hospital." She retrieves her gym bag from a cubby at the back, and I follow her. She smiles at me, but I sense a sadness about her. Then again, I'm the last person who should be deciphering emotional cues.

"At least pathology is less grueling than the other residencies," I say. "Probably more new stuff to learn though. It's kind of like another round of med school."

"I imagine so. Gets you back to your anatomy roots."

"Exactly." This is it. Time to take it to the next level. By the way she's dawdling, she doesn't seem to be in a hurry to go anywhere, so I may have a shot. "I don't quite know my way around the hospital yet or understand the computer system too well." This is a lie. I figured it out quickly. "I don't suppose you have time for a coffee in the cafeteria, do you? Maybe you could help familiarize me with things."

Luckily, she bites. She even seems relieved. "That sounds great. In fact, if you don't have any plans, why don't we head out for a drink instead? I could really use one. It's Saturday night. No sense spending it alone if we don't have to."

"That'd be great," I lie again, wanting nothing more than to spend the evening alone. But the charade is necessary. I'm stuck in limbo with Sam. As my dad used to say, it's time to crap or get off the porcelain.

"Do you know O'Dell's?" she asks.

I nod. It's where I went with Trey.

Twenty minutes later, we're seated there. Different booth, same smell of onion rings, same draft lager for me. Shelly orders a whiskey sour and a shot of tequila. Guess she wasn't kidding she needed a drink.

Somehow, between leaving the hospital and driving over here, she has managed to comb out her hair and apply makeup. I even smell perfume. She's pretty and petite, and I imagine she's exactly Dr. Donovan's type.

Although not one to worry about my appearance, I don't want to look like a troll, so I run fingers through my blunt hair and make sure nothing's too out of place. Beyond shaving the necessary parts and basic hygiene, the only grooming I regularly do is shaping my eyebrows. My mother showed me how when I was a young teenager. "Eyebrows can make or break you," she advised. "With your perfect coloring, you don't need makeup. Well-shaped brows will do the trick." She must've been right because so far they've gotten me by.

We spend a few minutes talking about hospital life at Titus McCall. I ask questions I already know the answers to, and she responds helpfully.

When the drinks arrive, she downs the shot and starts on the whiskey sour. "So, tell me about yourself."

I keep it brief with the basics—where I went to school, where I live, jobs I've worked, including data entry in college and cleaning an ice cream parlor at night during med school.

"Wasn't that boring?"

"It wasn't so bad. Both jobs let me work alone, which I liked."

"That would drive me crazy. I need people around."

Perfect segue, I think. *Here goes.* "So you're not married?"

She swallows a mouthful of whiskey sour. "Not anymore." Her tone is more bitter than her drink. "The divorce isn't final yet, but I kicked his ass to the curb." Gone is the tranquil yoga practitioner.

"Boyfriend?"

"Ha. I *thought* I had one." She finishes her drink and raises the glass to signal the waitress for another. I've barely dented my beer. "Sorry," she says. "I don't mean to be all pissy. You don't want to hear about my problems."

Oh yes, Shelly, that's exactly what I want to hear. "I don't mind. Really. You've been a big help to me with the hospital stuff."

She looks at me and smiles, her eyes already glazing from the alcohol. Her second drink arrives more quickly than the first, and she takes a swallow. "Let's just say I left a man who tormented me, only to leap into the arms of a man who ignores me."

Having no interest in the former, I inquire about the latter. "Are you still together? With the ignorer, I mean?"

It's like I've turned on a spigot. Between her gulps of whiskey sours, I learn that her boyfriend was all charm and affection at first. "Took me to fancy restaurants and bought me little gifts. Truth be told, I didn't care about either of those things. It was all kind of superficial. I just liked spending time with him, you know?"

I nod as if I do. My beer is halfway gone. Her second drink has one or two swallows left.

"But time was the one thing he stopped giving me. He's busy, I get it. He's a surg—" She covers her mouth. "Well, let's leave occupations and names out of this." Her words start to slur, and I understand I'll be driving her home. "We'd make a date and he'd cancel it. Sometimes at the last minute. He'd claim he got called in to work, but a couple times I checked and it wasn't the case."

I lean forward. "What do you think he was doing?"

Her eyes roll and her lips make a sloppy *pfft* sound. "Hell if I know. He's a big hiker. Says he likes time alone to think. Whenever I wanted to go with him, he'd say no, but ohhhh, who's the first person he asked to fetch his mail and water his stupid, precious plants when he left town? Me." She *pffts* again. "And now he's completely ghosted me. What an ass."

When she summons the waitress for another drink, the young woman fails to hide her surprise. I assure the waitress I'm driving. Another whiskey sour soon arrives.

"You know what I think it is?" Shelly swallows more alcohol. "I think he's stunted emotionally. Can't get too close to anyone, maybe because he's still grieving over his mother. Guess she was a talented gardener. Designed flower beds that got featured in home and garden magazines. She died six years ago, but he doesn't seem to be over it. Or maybe it's simpler. Maybe he's met someone else, or maybe I just didn't live up to his expectations." She sighs and gazes off somewhere above my head.

"What about his father?"

"Doesn't think as highly of him. Sounds like the guy was a strict disciplinarian and a boozer, despite being a pastor, but that's about all my boyfriend—sorry," she holds up a finger and slurs, "*ex-*boyfriend—would say. But I get the impression he wishes his father was the dead one."

"Does he live in Morganville?" I ask.

"Who, his father?"

"No. Your ex-boyfriend."

Shelly stares at me a moment, and I wonder if she's suspicious or just trying to focus her vision. "He does. In a gorgeous house with a gorgeous view." She scoops up her drink, some of it splashing over the side. "Oh man, I'm drinking too much. Sorry." She takes just a sip now.

"Don't be. Sounds like you need it. I'll drive you home. You can get your car tomorrow."

She seems grateful. Unfortunately, she also seems to have forgotten what we were talking about.

"What's his view?"

"I'm sorry?" she asks.

"You said he has a great view."

She nods like a bobblehead. "Oh yes. It's down in Cheshire Hill Estates. He bought a house there not long ago. Had it renovated. You know the area?"

"I do." The recent home purchase might explain why I couldn't find his address on Google. Maybe he rented before then.

"Yeah, well, he's got that house at the top of the hill, the stucco one with the medieval-looking stone and giant windows." She makes clumsy wide arcs with her arms. "You know which one I'm talking about?"

My fingers tighten around my beer glass. I do indeed. Shawna loves to drive around that area and look at the fancy homes. The one Shelly's describing is Shawna's favorite.

"It's a beautiful house," I say. "Must be really expensive."

"Ridiculously expensive, I'm sure, especially for one person. The guy's kind of a show-off. Most of the time, anyway."

When she doesn't continue, I press for more. "What do you mean?"

"Well, he's rich. Nice suits, custom-made scrubs, and a watch that must've cost a buttload." I wonder if she realizes she's just hinted at his occupation. Not that I don't already know it. "But his SUV isn't all that fancy, and before we were dating, I saw him downtown once dressed in clothes that made him look like Walter the accountant." She bursts out laughing, and I pretend to laugh too. "Pleated tan pants, gray shirt, knock-off shoes. If I hadn't known better, I'd have thought he was dressing up for Halloween. I'm not sure what was up with that outfit."

While she laughs again, I consider the significance of what she's just told me. In my pictures he was rather bland too. Like someone who wants to blend in.

Shelly spends the next forty minutes talking about things that don't help me, including her soon-to-be ex-husband "if the damn divorce ever goes through." But I listen patiently anyway. She has helped me a great deal. It's the least I can do.

"He hit me once, you know," she says, referring to her ex-husband. "When I threatened to leave him over it, he never did it again, and I never did report it. Probably should have. But oh, was he jealous. Always thought I was carrying on with someone else. Eventually I did." She wipes her eyes, and I worry she'll cry. Thankfully, she doesn't. "He had such a mean streak to him. Sadistic, really. Would do things just to set you off. Like a bully, you know?"

"Do I ever," I say. "I've encountered plenty of them over the years." Not as my own tormentors usually, but as other people's. Poor Shawna paid her dues. Even with my protection, kids called her names, ridiculed her, excluded her. The girls were especially mean. She tells me that at least with me around, she could finally breathe. I'm happy if that's the case.

"Plus, my ex could barely keep a job," Shelly is saying. "Guess he got a new one recently. Hopefully they won't fire him. I don't want him sniffing around my salary." She shakes her head. "Wow, I really can pick 'em."

Finally, the respiratory therapist tapers off. She yawns and says maybe she better get home, apologizing again for monopolizing the conversation. I tell her not at all. I'm happy to listen, happy to have someone to pass the time with.

That last part's a lie, of course, but thanks to this nice woman who can't hold her liquor, I now know: One, where Sam lives. Two, that he's often off doing things unaccounted for (like stalking people?). And three, that sometimes when he's out and about, he tries to blend in, something the normally charming and wealthy Dr. Donovan would never do.

Oh yes, I've learned a fair amount about Sam. I click Shelly's empty glass.

Round 3 goes to Liza.

12

From the driver's seat of my parked car, I sip black tea from an aluminum travel mug and watch Dr. Donovan's house in the south part of Morganville. It's Sunday morning, exactly one month from when I first spied on him in the surgical waiting room.

I'm a short distance back on the street. Two other vehicles, one a small moving van, the other a BMW, are parked in front of me for cover, but my view of his front door is perfect. Though always grateful for my dad's Honda Civic—it's far more reliable than the old Plymouth I used to clunk around in—I could do without its vibrant blue coloring. Doesn't blend in as well as…let's say…a beige Taurus.

It's a majestic home, no doubt about that. Sitting at a higher elevation than the rest of the houses in Cheshire Hill Estates, it shouts, "Look how special I am." Not excessively large—though still too large for one person—it's unique with medieval-looking stone accents, Mediterranean-style stucco, and a rounded turret on the left. Expansive windows line the main floor, and a small wrought-iron balcony extends from an upstairs room. Exotic flowering plants with large red blooms flank either side of the carved front door, and despite the July heat, the rest of the landscaping is equally lush and ripe.

My binoculars rest on my bare thighs, the inseam of my shorts not long enough to cover my quadriceps, which are sore from last night's weight session. With Jen's barbecue later today (yay me), I wasn't sure I could fit my workout in, so after driving Shelly home from the bar last night, I stopped at the gym to lift weights and process what she'd told me. Hopefully she's not too hungover this morning to rescue her car from O'Dell's. I could've offered to drive her to the bar to retrieve it, but something else is on my agenda. Now that something else just needs to exit his house.

Another thirty minutes pass. My bladder begins to regret the large mug of tea I'm plying it with. Occasionally, I raise my binoculars. No movement yet inside those massive windows. Hopefully the surgeon hasn't left yet. He's not on call—I checked—but that doesn't mean he doesn't have other things to do. It's those other things I hope to learn about.

Just as I reach for my bag of cashews and tear open the corner, Dr. Donovan's front door opens. I shoot up in my seat and bang my hand on the steering wheel. The cashews go flying over the passenger seat and floor mat. I ignore the mess and focus on the surgeon.

Dressed in Nikes and running shorts with a belt for his water bottle, he exits his palace, locks the door, and starts jogging in the opposite direction from where I'm parked. The fact he's shirtless confirms he's vain Dr. Donovan and not blend-in Sam. What a douche.

When he's out of sight, I clean up the cashews, grab my pathology journal from the backseat, and start reading an article on immunologic markers. Hopefully his run will be short. For a second, I consider following him, but whether by car or by foot, the tail would be too obvious. Instead, I finish the article and two more on top of that. Halfway into the fourth one, Dr. Donovan comes preening down the street. He slows to a walk and then stretches by his mailbox, allowing the whole neighborhood to feast on his glistening torso and limber joints. Unable to resist, I zoom in with my phone camera and take a picture.

When he unlocks his front door, I raise the binoculars in time to catch him enter a four-digit security code into a blinking panel to his right: 9536. Once the system is disarmed, he closes the door and disappears from my view.

Well. What do you know. Sometimes the world gives us a gift. Even to someone like me.

With a smile, I open my notebook app and type the numbers into my phone. I can picture my father pinching the bridge of his nose and shaking his head. "Why are you doing that?" he'd say. "Breaking into a man's home is an irrational and reckless choice." Of course it is. I'd have to be desperate to do such a thing. Regardless, contingency plans are always wise.

Twenty minutes later, I'm rewarded again. The double garage door opens, and Dr. Donovan's Highlander backs out of the driveway. There are no other vehicles inside. No beat-up beige Taurus with a rusted license plate. Maybe I wasn't being followed last Thursday after all, which would mean he wasn't at Home and Hearth Healing either. That's a relief.

When the Highlander pulls out on the street, I snap a picture of the license plate number. Now I'll know which vehicle in the hospital parking lot belongs to him. I pull out and follow.

Stop one disappoints me. It's the hospital. Is he working a shift? Has he come to do charting? Neither extravagant nor dull, his jeans and button-down shirt hold no answer.

In a parking spot several cars away, I decide to give it a half hour. I don't dare use the bathroom. Maybe he's just running a quick errand. But as the minutes tick by, my irritation rises. Today could be a bust. Mindful of the gas my idling car is using, the day too warm to turn off the air conditioning, I give it five more minutes. Then I shift the gear into drive. As I'm about to pull out, Dr. Donovan comes trotting toward his car. When the Highlander nears the lot's exit, I take off and follow it. Maybe something useful will still happen.

Stop two isn't much better. A local restaurant that promises

Sunday brunch until two. He disappears inside the restaurant's side door only to reappear a few minutes later on the front terrace, where he's seated beneath the shade of an umbrella. The rest of the tables are full. From across the street, I remain in my car and pick up my binoculars. For twenty minutes, I watch as he snarfs down an omelet, melon pieces, and orange juice.

Enjoying yourself, tiger? I hear my father say. *Feeling foolish yet?*

And yet, the more I watch the surgeon the more I notice how *he's* watching the waitress, not only during their banter but while she serves other tables as well. Tall and thickset, she appears to be in her mid-forties. A limp slows her pace but doesn't seem to hinder her work.

Dr. Donovan would not be physically drawn to such a woman. She has none of Shelly's attractiveness or womanly appeal. So why the interest? Is she simply a friend? Is she one of his former patients? One of those he likes to stay in touch with, as Trey told me at O'Dell's?

With renewed vigor in my voyeurism, I crunch what remains of my cashews. Soon we are on our way again, my Civic always a few cars back from his Highlander. My bladder is in all-out protest mode now, but it'll have to wait a while longer.

A small auto-body shop not far from downtown is stop number three. With its modest-sized lot and two-garage limit, I assume it's a small-time operation, probably just a single owner. That would explain the mechanic tinkering with the undercarriage of a jacked-up Camry on a Sunday.

Sam pulls up to the curb on the opposite side of the street and parks his SUV. Not wanting to be seen, I choose the McDonald's a block down. He's quite a distance away from me now, but my binoculars don't care. While he stares at the man working underneath the car, I stare at him. "What are you looking at?" I muse out loud.

I have no idea what he's doing. I only know it's not normal behavior. And this is coming from someone like me.

Nonetheless, a moment of uncertainty grips me. Have I gotten it wrong? Have I created something from nothing?

Two years ago as a third-year med student, I thought a group of fourth-years was planning something against me. They stopped talking when I came near, whispered when I left the room, that sort of thing. Normally, such shunning wouldn't bother me—I don't care whether people outside my circle like me or not—but I didn't want to be the recipient of a prank.

Turns out it was nothing of the sort. They were discussing nominating me for the best junior research project. I won too. When I later told the story to Dr. Lightfoot, he reminded me that it would be easier to go through life assuming people have the best of intentions, not the worst.

Is that what I'm doing here?

I shake my head. I'm onto something, I know it. Two former trauma patients have died of drug overdoses that may not have been drug overdoses. He spied on at least one of them, the librarian, and today he spied on a waitress and a mechanic. And let's not forget that shortly after he spotted me lurking in the surgical waiting room last month, I was attacked in the gym parking lot and that attacker is now dead.

No. I'm not wrong. Sam is up to something, and it needs to be stopped. I just don't know what *it* is yet. I have my suspicions, but I'll need access to medical records to prove it.

After five more minutes of watching the mechanic, he's on his way and so am I.

How much longer I can go without using a bathroom is a game I no longer want to play. I tell myself I'll find one during the next stop. We head north, passing several posted signs for Morganville's summer festival with its art fair and musical groups. My brother's band performed at it once. I remember it starts today and runs for the week. I have no intention of going.

We continue north toward Waverly Boulevard. Wait…is Sam driving back to the hospital? Why would he do that? But at Waverly Boulevard, he turns left, not right, so he's clearly headed elsewhere. After a mile of winding road, me still three cars behind him, we pass Shawna and Tam's house. Set back from the street and not nearly as elegant as Dr. Donovan's place down in Cheshire Hill Estates, it's a nice ranch home, one they've put a great deal of work into. It's silly, but I breathe a sigh of relief when we pass it.

But where is he going?

A half mile later, he makes an unexpected, quick right turn onto Sherlock Road.

My fingers tighten around the steering wheel. My mother's mental health facility is on Sherlock Road.

I'm determined to follow him, but I'm still three cars behind and the vehicle in front of me shifts to the right turning lane before I can. Instead of immediately turning, the driver idles there, as if not sure where to go. Two people in the front seat appear to be arguing.

As I wait for the driver to make up his damn mind, I sweep my brain for the destinations on Sherlock Road, someplace else Sam might be going other than my mother's facility. There's the small strip mall on the left where I get my doughnuts for the staff. Next is Home and Hearth Healing on the right, and a mile beyond that lies Redwood Lodge, a hotel and conference center. Beyond that I'm not sure, since Sherlock Road ends in a T-intersection.

Blasting my horn, I tell myself Sam is headed to either the strip mall or the lodge. The other option is too grim.

Finally, the car in front of me turns right. I follow behind, trying not to tailgate, but I've lost precious time. The Highlander is no longer visible on the road.

The vehicle that slowed me down turns left into the strip mall and makes a U-turn. As I pass, I scan the lot but see no black Highlander.

I speed up toward my mother's center and try to keep breathing.

When I reach Home and Hearth Healing, I drive twice through its parking lot, which, although not huge, is divided into two parts by a strip of landscaping that's dense with shrubs and flower beds.

Sunday is a big visiting day, and the lot is packed. No black Highlanders though. This should comfort me, but it doesn't. I find an empty space and pull into it, leaving the car idling. I need to think for a moment.

Do I drive down to Redwood Lodge to see if he's there? Could his car be somewhere in between? Just because it's not here or back at the strip mall doesn't mean it isn't parked on one of the wooded side streets surrounding the center. What if he left it somewhere else and walked to the building?

I turn my car off. It's better to check on my mother, even if it means missing out on wherever Sam is headed now. Plus, I can use the bathroom before my bladder bursts.

Hurrying toward the two-story building, I jog to the front entrance. The rest of the facility is surrounded by tall iron fencing. Though the wrought iron is ornate and pretty, it's inescapable. On the other side of the fence, I see and hear visitors and residents enjoying the summer day.

After I'm buzzed in, I greet Tiana and head straight to my mother's room. My rushed hello to the receptionist probably seems rude, but I'll have to make up for it another time.

My mother isn't there. After using her bathroom, I discover she's not in the rec room either, nor the cafeteria. I'm about to head outside when I see Brenda Morrison, one of the nurses. She smiles and says my mother's having a great day today. Rather breathless, I ask where she is. I'm told she's outside on her rock with her guitar.

I stride to the exit nearest my mother's favorite spot. As soon as I see her on the rock under the giant oak tree, I relax and slow my pace. Surely her being out here is a good sign.

All around the yard, residents and visitors lounge on Adirondack chairs or snack at picnic tables, but the closer I get to my mother, I realize how odd it is that she's neither playing her guitar nor singing. Other than her honey hair that lifts in the gentle breeze, she's sitting there, frozen, her guitar clenched in her hands.

"Mom?"

She blinks but says nothing.

When I step closer, she blinks faster. Her behavior confuses me, not because she hasn't reacted this way before—she has—but because only moments ago, Brenda told me my mom was having a great day. This does not look like a great day.

"Mom, do you want me to take you to your room?"

"Shh, Liza, quiet. He'll see us."

"Who?"

"The man in the bushes."

My mouth opens, then closes. The juxtaposition of her words would mean nothing to anyone else, but to me they mean everything. They mean she's clear enough to use my name, yet her words are those of paranoia.

A tree behind her on the right rustles. I whip my head in its direction. Probably just the wind, but…

Not wanting to feed my mother's delusion but knowing Sam was in the vicinity a short while ago, I step forward into the dirt and peer around the giant oak tree, its branches scratching my arms. A dense cluster of evergreens fills the space behind it, and although they block out most of the iron fence that locks us in, a small stretch of road beyond them is visible. No one's there.

I return to my mother and release a few strands of hair the wind has trapped in her eyelashes, which are so fair they're difficult to see in the sunlight. "There's no one here, Mom. I don't see any—"

My sentence cuts off. Pete, the orderly, approaches us. Where he came from I have no idea. He locks his dark-shadowed eyes on mine and holds me in them for a long beat. I can't tell whether he's angry or merely deep in thought, but three days ago I raised concerns about him to Dr. Dhar. Though the psychiatrist would never use my name, it wouldn't be a big leap for Pete to figure out who the whistle blower was.

When the orderly passes, I lightly touch my mom's shoulder. She continues her stillness. "Is that the man you saw?"

Her silence lasts so long I assume she won't answer, but then, in a voice that sounds pinched, she whispers, "Didn't see. Heard."

"What do you mean?"

In lieu of response, her body goes lax and her guitar starts to tumble. I snatch it before it hits the ground.

"Sweetie, can you take me to my room? Very tired."

I oblige, but on the way toward the side entrance, tiny bolts of electricity spark inside my body. My mother is with it today. She's using my name. Not only that, her term of endearment means she knows I'm her daughter, and she's speaking organized sentences. I glance over my shoulder at Pete. He's helping an elderly woman into a wheelchair.

When it comes to my mother's safety, am I focusing on the wrong man?

13

Jen told me her barbecue party was casual dress. As my car approaches her home, I hope that means shorts and a V-neck tee because that's what I'm wearing.

After today's adrenaline rush of tailing Sam and worrying about my mother at Home and Hearth Healing (I showed Dr. Donovan's picture around to every staff member there, all of whom confirmed they've never seen him at the center), I at least spruced up with a shampoo and shower. I even added a necklace my mother used to wear, a black onyx stone in the shape of a treble clef. One of her music students bought it for her back when she was still teaching.

Jen's two-story house isn't very big, but judging by the bikes, soccer nets, and hula hoops scattered in the yard, it gets a lot of kid traffic. Similar kid-friendly homes line the street. At the sight of the toys, med school pediatrics pops into my mind. Talk about a horror movie for Waseem's must-see list. Definitely not my strongest rotation. For two months I lived in fear of dropping a baby.

Psyching myself up for yet another social event I don't want to attend, I open the driver's door and exit my Civic. A box of truffles from Sally's Chocolaterie down on Main Street rests in my hand.

Even from the curb, I smell the mouthwatering scent of grilled meat.

Trey pulls up shortly after. Like me, he's dressed in shorts and sandals. His T-shirt bears the logo of a local brewery. Just because I'm not interested in sex doesn't mean I can't appreciate an attractive package, and Trey Washington is one.

"We could've driven together," he says, raising an eyebrow. "It's not like I'm going to tie you up and stash you in my trunk, you know."

"I'd like to see you try." My lip must snarl because he pulls his head back and holds up his hands.

"Whoa, take it easy. It was a joke." He grins. "Besides, trunk-stashing doesn't happen till the third date."

He's wrong to think this is a date, but I allow him the illusion. Together we head to Jen's front door. It flies open before I even knock.

"Liza, Trey, so glad you're here," Jen says with a big smile. In a summer dress, with her chestnut hair loose and her arms extended, she looks like she's about to hug me. At the last second, she remembers not to. When I hand her the chocolates, she coos, "Oh, these are my favorite. You shouldn't have."

We step into a foyer that separates living room from dining room. Signs of children are everywhere. A moment later, Megan bursts through an arched door from the kitchen. "Oh my God, Liza, you came!"

Beyond the kitchen, a sliding door leads to a patio where a group of people are congregating. The evening sun ducks behind a cloud, shadowing the partygoers. Festive music flows throughout the house. I steel myself for what's to come.

Unlike Jen, Megan embraces me. (Yay me.) The wine glass in her hand sloshes its contents. As always, she looks ready for the runway, dressed in Capri pants and a blouse with a scooped neckline. Her tawny hair is twisted in an elegant but practical braid. "So good to see you." She turns over her shoulder and yells toward the patio. "Hey, Waseem, John, you guys won the bet. Liza's here!"

Waseem and his five o'clock shadow slide open the screen door and bulldoze in. John follows behind, and the two clink beer bottles. Waseem's appears to be non-alcoholic.

To Megan, John says, "Fork over the dough."

"Et tu, Brute?" I ask my studious counterpart.

He laughs and raises his beer.

Jen calls in her husband and kids from outside, and introductions begin all around. After I nod to them, wondering if I'm supposed to shake their hands, the children—two boys and a girl—quickly lose interest and blast back outside. Jen's husband thanks us for coming and then kisses his wife on the cheek and tells her the burgers and chicken are almost ready. He heads back outside as well, and Jen shoos us along with him, handing me a bottle of beer before I step out. "Hope you like this kind," she says.

"It's fine." I take a sip, and it is.

Maybe I'll survive this gathering after all. Dr. Silverstein's dinner was a good practice run. Come Megan's Christmas party, which she's been threatening to throw, I'll be a regular party animal.

When I step onto the patio, I almost drop my beer. The last person I expected to see here is standing next to Jen's husband, accepting a grilled burger onto a bun.

Dr. Donovan.

My mouth drops open. Megan must see it because she says, "Cool, isn't it? Samuel is my plus-one."

Hearing her say that name spins me into a deeper muddle. It's either Dr. Donovan or Sam. The surgeon or the stalker. There is no in-between Samuel. There is no plus-one. There is no barbecue-attending boyfriend.

My hands fist at my side. He doesn't belong here.

The misplaced surgeon catches my eye, a plate of hamburger, potato salad, chips, and salsa pressed against his waist. His designer polo shirt and preppy shorts scream Dr. Donovan, but with the way the air snaps and hisses between us, I know he's not here for Megan.

He's here for me.

After three corn chips, two bites of potato salad, and half a chicken breast glazed with a barbecue sauce so succulent my father would have begged for the recipe for his food truck, I can't eat another bite. My stomach is too riled with a simmering anger.

Woozy from too much beer and not enough food, I sit in my kiddie chair at the edge of the patio, its sides digging into my hips. I want to confront Sam. I want to ask if he spied on my mother today while she was playing guitar on the rock beneath the trees, the one place in the world that brings her peace but is now tainted with fear. I want to tell him he better not have because if he takes one more step into my world, he'll regret it.

Unfortunately, I've been unable to do any of this. Dr. Donovan has stayed in his Megan cocoon, the two of them laughing in their lawn chairs—they got the good ones—while he scoops up a dollop of spilled salad from her capri pants and refreshes her wine glass whenever it's the slightest bit empty. At one point he stands, raises his own glass of Chardonnay, and against the red-orange of the setting sun gives three cheers to Jen and her husband. "To the Lopezes for this wonderful party. To the Lopezes for freeing us from the hospital. To the Lopezes for their hospitality."

Everyone claps. Everyone loves him. After his toast, the last person he looks at is me. In his beaming expression, I read his thoughts. *You see, Liza? You're no match for me. Who would ever believe you? I'm popular and fun. You're a weird social outcast with crazy in your blood.*

As if he's actually spoken the words, my entire body tenses, and my plate starts to slide off my lap. Despite my shaded spot under the awning, heat rushes to my neck and face.

"You okay?" A hand reaches out to steady my plate.

I blink, and Trey comes into focus next to me. I forgot he was even there. Polishing off my third bottle of beer, I nod. Then, as an afterthought, I shake my head. "I don't feel too well. Just give me a minute."

This isn't true. I feel fine. Well, a little drunk, but still fine. I just need a moment to think. I hand him my plate and hustle into the house. After wandering a few feet down a hallway whose wallpaper is hidden by an onslaught of family photographs, I find the bathroom. I stumble into it and close the door. Leaning against the vanity, my back to the mirror, I begin my deep breathing exercise. "It'll help you diffuse your anger," Dr. Lightfoot has told me. "You have the affect of a turnip until something sets you off. Then you're all fire and flame. You need a way to control it so it doesn't control you."

Slowly, my ire dissolves. Regardless, the things I heard Sam say in my head are true. Who would believe a word I said against him? That's probably why he's gotten so cozy with Megan. He wants everyone in my world on his side. If I want them to believe me, I need to connect him to something. I need to find something that proves he's not the benevolent surgeon they all think he is.

After a few more minutes of deep breathing, an idea surfaces. My eyes snap open. To prove Dr. Donovan is a stalker and somehow connected to the deaths of his former patients—people like the heroin addict and the librarian in Perry, whom I'm still not sure he operated on—I need access to medical records. Up until now I assumed this was an obstacle I couldn't get around. As a pathology resident, digging through electronic charts of former surgical patients would land me in deep muck.

But what if I can convince Dr. Silverstein and Dr. Thomas it's all in the name of research?

I pace the small bathroom, trying to avoid the bath toys on the floor. Dr. Silverstein already knows my mother is in a mental health facility, and by now maybe Dr. Thomas does too. They know of my interest in neuropathology, and, by default, my interest in psychiatry. What if I told them I wanted to do my research project on people who survived serious trauma only to die a short time later from another cause?

It might be interesting to detail those causes of death, I'll tell them. Was it suicide from depression? Was it an overdose from pain meds the patient couldn't quit? Was it a freak accident completely unrelated to their trauma or trauma surgery? Not a particularly useful study for pathology, but since I'm only a first-year resident, maybe they'll allow the deviation.

When I turn around to face the mirror, my expression is back to neutral, my breathing practice successful. I nod. Yes, this idea could work.

Opening the bathroom door, I start back to Trey. He's probably wondering—

I stop short. Coming down the hallway is Dr. Donovan.

"You're missing the party," he says, swaying his hips to the musical beat in the background, his body blocking my exit. Generations of happy Lopezes surround us.

I say nothing.

"We haven't had much chance to talk tonight." His dancing stops, but he flashes that perfect smile. "I'd like to get to know you better."

"In the hallway?"

He runs a finger along a gold picture frame, Jen's three children inside it. "For example, was Titus McCall your first choice for residency?"

"Nope. Mass General. Guess you could say I had a change of heart."

"Their loss, our gain." He shifts over a foot and studies another photograph. "Such a nice family, aren't they? Cute kids." His gaze returns to me. "Family's important, don't you think?"

"You certainly have a strange fixation on mine."

"You must miss your father terribly."

Heat rumbles in my belly. "Have you stopped by the Perry public library lately? Lots of changes going on there, I hear. That sweet old librarian filled me in on so many things."

"It's a beautiful historic building. Nice place to visit."

"You don't fool me, you know. I see who you are. You made a big mistake entering my world."

His *tsks* his tongue and knits his brow. "Are you sure you're stable, Liza? Do I need to warn Trey about you?"

I try to gauge if he's bluffing. Would he turn Trey against me? That could backfire. It could make Trey curious as to what prompted the badmouthing and put a spotlight on Dr. Donovan that the surgeon surely doesn't want.

"I don't know," I say. "Do I need to warn Megan about you?"

He laughs and pokes my forehead, making me jerk back. "You're fun, Dr. Larkin. I like you."

At that moment, one of Jen's sons comes barreling down the hallway. "Excuse me," the boy says, darting past us to the bathroom.

Dr. Donovan puts his hands in the pockets of his preppy shorts. "I better get back out there. Nice chatting with you." He starts to leave but then turns around one last time and says, "I bet you get your great sense of humor from your mom." He simultaneously winks and clicks his tongue. "I sure would like to meet her sometime."

———

Five minutes after I get home from Jen's barbecue, I'm already at my desk on my laptop, putting together a research proposal to present to Dr. Thomas and Dr. Silverstein. I need to frame it carefully, need to convince them the project has relevance to pathology somehow. Though still present, my anger over Sam's verbal left hooks has dissipated to a low boil, even if he has won Round 4.

While I'm weighing various research approaches, someone knocks on my door.

My immediate thought is Sam, but just as quickly I dismiss it. Even if he's followed me and knows where I live, he won't come after me. At least I don't think so, not when I bluffed last week that incriminating information will make its way to my cop friend should something unexpected happen to me.

The knocking repeats, and I assume it's April. I have to answer. One glance in the parking lot will show her whether I'm home or not.

A moment later, I find both April and Jasmine on my doorstep. Jasmine is dressed in Hello Kitty pajamas, and April is wearing shorts and a tank top covered by an apron, which in turn is covered by old baking stains. A large plate topped with a sponge cake is in her hands. Jasmine holds a bowl of cut strawberries.

April raises her offering. "We come bearing treats."

I've got to hand it to the woman. She knows my weakness.

I usher them into my small space, and April sets the cake on my kitchenette counter. She's quiet for a few seconds, her eyes lowered, her fingernails scratching at the vine tattoo coursing down her arm. "I found out you paid my rent," she says, "both for what I still owed this month and for August." Her lower lip trembles, and I'm worried she's going to cry. "I don't know how to thank you."

"It's no big deal."

She looks at me. "No big deal? Hardly. You have no idea what a godsend that was. Sinclair would've kicked me out. Or worse he would've…" Her comment trails off, probably for Jasmine's benefit.

"Sinclair's an asshole."

Jasmine giggles, and I realize what I've just said.

"Um, sorry. I mean, Sinclair's a jerk."

April laughs. "No, you were right the first time. It's nothing Jasmine hasn't heard me say a million times." She grows serious again. "I'll pay you back, I promise."

"Don't worry about it." I grab a few mismatched plates from one of the three cupboards in my kitchenette.

"On no, I have to pay you back," she says urgently. "I wouldn't feel right otherwise. It might take a few months though."

"Take a year if you need." I pluck out three forks plus a knife that looks like it'll work for cutting the cake.

I must be licking my lips because Jasmine whispers, "Told you she'd like the cake." Then she giggles again.

April starts cutting it. After removing two big slices, she thumps her forehead. "I forgot the whipped cream. What a dummy." She smiles, and the brown spot on her tooth pops into view, which tells me she's genuinely happy. If only all people had brown spots to help me gauge their emotions, my life would be easier. "I'll just run and whip some up. Be right back," she sings and hurries out the door, leaving it ajar.

I stare at Jasmine. Jasmine stares at me. She giggles for the third time. This is the longest we've been alone together. That time I slept at April's so she could work a last-minute night shift, Jasmine was already in bed. I don't know what to do with ten-year-old kids.

Luckily, she speaks before I have to. "Your posters are weird."

I study the one with a brain and nervous system on a black background. "I suppose they are."

"Who's that?" She points to the other poster with the gray-haired man on it.

"That's John Nash. He was a mathematician."

She makes a face. "Why would you have a poster of him?"

I shrug. "He was really smart. And he had schizophrenia."

"Schizo what?" Before I need to respond she loses interest in the poster. "Why don't you have a TV?" She wanders a few feet into my apartment which brings her almost to my bed.

I point to my desk. "My computers have everything I need."

From across the hall, April's mixer whirs to life, and I can almost taste the cream and sugar whipping into a white fluff. Jasmine does a three-sixty turn in my small space. "You don't have much stuff. What do you *do* all day?"

I shrug. "I work. I read. I play video games."

"Do you have any other games? Do you have *Sorry*? I love *Sorry*. I love *Operation* too."

I shake my head. "My brother had those games when we were little, but I don't have any of them here."

"Oh." Her shoulders slump.

Wanting to make her happy but having no idea why, I say, "I have a Rubik's Cube."

"You do? Can you solve it? Can I see?"

I cross over to my closet, its clunky door resistant to sliding ever since I kicked it in anger after Ned canceled a visit to my mother. I reach up on the top shelf and retrieve the six-sided cube with its colorful plastic squares. "Here. Mix it all up for me."

Jasmine does, and when she finishes she hands the cube back. I eye the second hand on my watch. The kitchen appliance across the hall grows silent, and in the time it takes April to return with a bowl of whipped cream, I have the cube halfway solved.

"Mom, you have to see this." Jasmine jumps up and down. "Look how fast she's solving it."

I click and turn, twist and flip. Thirty seconds later, the colors are all lined up. I hand it back to Jasmine. By the look on her face, you'd think I just pulled off time travel.

"Still took me almost a minute," I grumble. "I've done better."

I return to my counter and dig into the giant piece of strawberry shortcake April has just served me. Then I close my eyes and enjoy a momentary slice of heaven.

14

One week ago, the day after Jen's barbecue, Dr. Thomas and Dr. Silverstein agreed to sign off on my research project. It was after teaching rounds in the Death Chamber, during which Megan once again smoked us all by knowing the most answers. I waited until my colleagues cleared the room and then asked the program director if we could talk in his office. Once there, we were joined by my advisor.

At first their response to my request to research cause of death in people who previously survived life-threatening trauma came in the form of skeptical brows and lip chewing, gestures easy for me to decipher. Then Dr. Silverstein smoothed her silver braid and said, "I like the philosophical bent it has."

"Me too," Dr. Thomas said. "But it doesn't really advance the field of pathology per se."

"True, true." My advisor nodded her agreement. "But it's only a first-year project. It's not really meant for publication yet. It's mostly to go through the motions of setting up a project on her own, working through IRB, learning to data mine, basic statistics, that sort of thing."

I didn't mention I was already pretty good at those last two, thanks to my part-time job of data entry and analysis in college. As for getting IRB approval—the Institutional Review Board process that helps ensure ethics in research—I figured the project would snare a quick green light. It might even be exempt, given that all I'd be doing is a retrospective chart review. I'd also omit patient identifiers in my analysis.

"Yes, good point," my program director said to my advisor. "Plus, it should make for an interesting presentation at Resident Research Day this spring. Not the same old, same old. There's only so many times we can hear a case study of pheochromocytoma or mature teratoma." His normally baritone pitch rose in what I assumed was mock excitement. "Oh look, that tumor has teeth and hair in it!"

They both laughed, and I pretended to laugh with them. Ovarian tumors with everything from teeth to bone to hair were pretty cool in my opinion, but I suppose when you've been in the field as long as my attendings have, those types of things lose their appeal.

So it was settled. My research project was approved by my program director and my advisor. This morning an email confirmed it was also approved by the Institutional Review Board.

After a quick dinner of lasagna and salad in the hospital cafeteria, I can finally get started. I head to Titus McCall's medical library. "Let's see what you're up to, Sam," I whisper to myself in the stairwell.

Since the barbecue, we've only encountered each other once this past week, at surgical path rounds on Wednesday. He said nothing to me. Didn't even look my way. The same couldn't be said for him and Megan. Lots of glances exchanged there. What's going on between them I hate to think, but it seems unlikely he'll hurt her. At least not physically. Emotionally is a different story, one Shelly Parsons could tell all too well.

I attended another yoga session with the respiratory therapist last Saturday. Though I had to grit my teeth to endure the group class, not to mention more of Mark's touching while I folded into a pretzel, I thought I might hurt Shelly's feelings if I didn't show. She might think I vanished because of her drunken display the week before. My social training in action. Dr. Lightfoot and my father would be proud.

But neither Shelly nor Megan are my focus right now. Dr. Donovan is. He probably thinks his veiled threat against my mother will make me stop snooping into his affairs. If only he knew I'm just getting started.

Inside the hospital library, which is an intimate room on the fifth floor, I take a seat behind a computer terminal that has access to HealthEMR, the electronic medical record system used by Titus McCall and its affiliated clinics. Much smaller than the med school's library, Titus's holds textbooks and professional journals from the various medical specialties. Newspapers, too, though I suspect it's only the older doctors who read those.

The pathology department has computer monitors with access to HealthEMR as well, but I prefer to escape the area tonight. Now that it's after six, most of the residents and faculty have departed for the day, but I don't want to risk another run in with Dr. Donovan. Not yet anyway.

I do, however, need to search the medical records of patients whose deaths he might be responsible for. It's the only theory running through my mind. I find it hard to believe he's simply stalking people. That's obviously part of it, but a stalker focuses on one person. Sam focuses on many.

Another thing keeps running through my mind as well, a niggling that's filled me with a low-grade nausea all week. If I'm being honest, it's been there ever since I first suspected Dr. Donovan of deadly deeds. I can't bring myself to articulate it though, either mentally or verbally. It's too awful to consider. Besides, it's impossible. Logistics-wise, it's impossible.

And yet the man is in my photos…

Once I log in my credentials, I enter HealthEMR. Unlike the residents in other specialties who directly care for patients, I haven't spent much time in the system, only a few times to check histories on patients whose slides I've read or whose gross tissue I've dissected and prepared for examination. But the software doesn't take a tech genius to figure out, and soon I begin my chart search, using the additional access I've been granted through IRB approval that enables me to search via key words.

Navigating the system might be easy, but knowing how to find the data I need isn't. I still have eight months to work on my project, and the details I proposed to my program director and advisor may very well take that amount of time to complete. It's a lot of information to sort through. The hospital does almost two hundred autopsies a year, and I've proposed going back ten years.

The goal for my legitimate research project is to find the cause of death for patients who survived trauma surgery only to die less than five years later. Of course, not every deceased patient who had trauma surgery at Titus McCall will have had an autopsy here. Maybe even no autopsy at all. But I have to define my limits somehow.

The strategy can be dealt with later. For now, I'm only interested in patients with uncertain causes of death who are linked to Dr. Donovan, and since physicians aren't system administrators, he won't know I'm snooping.

Because we're almost into August, I start with the first seven months of this year, 2019, and enter the search terms *autopsy* + *Donovan*. A string of charts pop up, labeled by name and birth date. To narrow my search, I decide to add the words *trauma* and *surgery*. After all, Dr. Donovan doesn't just perform trauma surgery. Trey told me he does some general as well, and Dr. Silverstein's missing gallbladder is proof of that.

With the additional search terms, the list on the screen drops to two charts. Much more doable. The first is a forty-nine-year-old man who died last month. According to his autopsy report, he suffered a massive heart attack. On the postmortem exam, which I assume was done because of his relatively young age, several of his coronary arteries were found to be blocked. His trauma surgery was performed in 2012 after he sustained multiple injuries in a car accident. That's the same year Dr. Donovan started at Titus McCall. Since his death occurred more than five years after his surgery, I won't include it in my official research project. More importantly, since the cause of his death is clear, I won't include it in my case against Sam.

The second chart from 2019 on my screen belongs to the heroin addict whose autopsy I observed earlier this month. Because of the small amount of morphine found in his system, his death was attributed to an accidental heroin overdose. Even though postmortem toxicology can be unreliable, the death still seems suspicious to me, especially since his father thought he'd been clean. The young man's trauma surgery was in 2018, after accidentally discharging his father's gun into his gut. As I already know, his surgeon was Dr. Donovan, but it's nice to have the chart confirm it.

I crack my knuckles.

Case number one for my private study.

The same search terms for 2018 yield two more charts. Sandy Newmaker, the librarian once employed by Perry Public Library, is one of them. She, too, died of an assumed drug overdose, though as with the previous patient the toxicology testing was inconclusive. Also like the previous man, she underwent trauma surgery, but hers was nine months before she died and was due to a vicious dog attack.

The surgeon on record? Dr. Donovan.

Bingo. Case number two.

The library door creaks open. Startled, I look up from my terminal. A balding physician in a white coat munches the remains of an apple while rustling through the newspaper selections stacked in a metal rack by the door. He chooses *The Wall Street Journal*, nods my way, and takes a seat in one of four upholstered chairs surrounding an oval coffee table. By the noisy way he chomps his apple, I'm glad it's almost gone.

The interruption affords me a stretch. My neck cracks, and my eyes blur a bit when I blink them. After some spine twisting and shoulder rolling, I return to the second chart from 2018. It belongs to a fifty-nine-year-old woman, a physician who died in April of that year.

Reading her autopsy report, which is incomplete because the postmortem was halted shortly after it was started, I learn that the cause of death was suspected to be a ruptured cerebral aneurysm or heart attack. The reason the autopsy was stopped was because while sifting through her will and other paperwork, her family found a contract with an anatomical gift program at a nearby medical school. As such, an autopsy was not allowed at Titus McCall. Any further examination of the body would have been done at the receiving med school, the records of which Titus McCall doesn't have. From the pathologist's truncated autopsy report, however, it was felt that since she died at home alone and had no other signs of foul play, a brain bleed or heart attack was the cause.

Combing through more of her records, I discover she survived trauma surgery after a car accident in February 2017. A psychiatry note says the accident took an emotional toll on her, and she retired from medicine shortly after to focus on painting, something the artist in her always wanted to do, especially since primary care medicine had burned her out. Her surgeon?

Dr. Donovan.

Possibly case number three in my private study.

With this find, my heart starts beating faster. That's three people who've died of uncertain causes not long after having trauma surgery performed by Dr. Donovan. That can't be a coincidence. Of course, I haven't looked at the other surgeons yet. Maybe the same occurs for them. Maybe my skewed data mining is creating connections where none actually exist. Still, three cases in two years seems unusual.

The library door closes. I look up and see the doctor reading the paper has left. In my engrossed state, I forgot he was even there. The clock on the screen tells me I've been at this for over an hour, but I can't stop now.

I move onto 2017, and after several minutes of opening electronic documents, most of which reveal nothing, I discover one that fits my criteria: a forty-three-year-old man who had trauma surgery in May 2016 after a farming accident. He died in August 2017 from a suspected heart arrhythmia. Although he had no documented history of this and the medical examiner couldn't determine it on exam, he passed away at home with no evidence of foul play and had a negative toxicology screen so it seemed a reasonable possibility. Like the physician I found earlier, he was alone at the time, his wife out of town with the kids.

His trauma surgeon was Dr. Donovan.

My hands start to shake. I move on to 2016. Another patient matches my search terms: a thirty-seven-year-old woman who died in December of that year from suspected complications of obesity. Like the others, she was home alone at the time of death. Also like the others, she had a history of surgery done by Dr. Donovan, this time for an invasive skin infection in October 2015, acquired from a leg wound.

Case numbers four and five, and I'm not even into 2015. It's possible others have been missed, my search terms not picking them up. Since Dr. Donovan started at Titus McCall back in 2012, I have four more years to check.

My God, could he really have killed these people? Though my evidence might be flimsy, the odds seem too small for there not to be a link. But why? Why would he save them only to kill them later? And how does he do it? There's no sign of struggle on their autopsies, no marks of strangulation, no bullet holes or stab wounds, no toxins. As a surgeon, Dr. Donovan would have access to many drugs, any number of which would be deadly in an overdose. Most would show up on autopsy, but not all.

My body feels like a mixer has twisted all my muscles, but even though it's getting late and I've missed Brian's heavy-bag class, I forge ahead. I can't stop now.

I enter my search criteria for 2015, the pads of my fingertips pulsing on the keyboard. HealthEMR hunts for my information. After a pause, a name pops up.

When I see it, I cry out in alarm, something I haven't done since I tripped barefoot and tore off a toenail five years ago. I can't help it. My shock is too great. Whether or not the unarticulated thought has been niggling in the depths of my mind, the shock of seeing it confirmed is just too great.

No. Not possible. No way. His surgery wasn't even done here. It was done in Boston.

I blink. I can't be seeing what I'm seeing.

And yet it appears I am.

The name of the patient on the screen belongs to my father.

15

I stare at the name on the computer monitor, my breaths choppier than the waves off Cape Cod. My brain tries to process its meaning.

Larkin, Kevin N

It makes no sense. My father had surgery in Boston. It must be someone with the same name. But the same birthdate too?

With an unsteady hand, I guide the cursor over my dad's name and click the chart open. The medical entries are few. Instead of making me feel better, this only helps confirm it's my father's chart. He was always a patient of Massachusetts General and its affiliated clinics. Any Titus McCall records would be limited. Up until now, I assumed they'd be nonexistent, but the date of the lone hospital admission on file—March 16, 2013—confirms it's my father. That's the date he got shot. It's also the date I arrived in Greece for my field study.

My tongue is a lead sinker in my mouth. I click open the discharge summary and read what I can't believe I'm reading. *After a gunshot wound to the lower abdomen, Kevin Larkin, a fifty-four-year-old male, was brought to Titus McCall Medical Center by ambulance for emergent surgery.*

Scrolling quickly through the summary, I look for what I now know will be there, even though the thought of finding it makes me want to puke.

There it is. The name of the trauma surgeon who operated on my father.

Dr. Samuel Donovan.

I collapse in my chair. Gripping the armrests, I stare stupidly at the blurring words on the screen. A fireball whirls in my gut and works its way up to my chest, my arms, my neck, my face.

I want to scream. I want to charge through the hospital corridors and throw crash carts through its pretentious floor-to-ceiling windows. I want to take a giant machete and slash its grandiose gardens. I want to smash its wellness center's dumbbells into its wellness center's shock-absorbing floor. Mostly I want to break down Sam's door in his fancy-pants Cheshire Hill Estates and beat his aristocratic face to a pulp.

Dr. Lightfoot forces his way into my head. I try to shove him back out, but his will to be heard is too strong. *Don't let rage control you, Liza. Not when your response has been violence in the past. Just because you were defending other people doesn't excuse it.*

My psychiatrist's words repeat over and over in my mind, each sentence syncing with my breathing. I know he's right, and until I calm down, I won't allow myself to look back at my father's chart.

Dr. Lightfoot's warning dates back to when I broke a girl's arms. I was fourteen, she was fifteen, and she was relentlessly tormenting Shawna. Not just with *Shamu Shawna* taunts—that was child's play by then—but with awful, horrible things. Things like putting dog shit in Shawna's backpack. Things like spitting in her lunch. Things like hanging used condoms on her locker. So I made the girl stop. I broke her arms with a bat. Well, one arm. The other was just contused. Not easy to do cruel things when one arm is in a cast and the other is in a sling. Simple as that.

But I paid the price. Dearly. Suspension from school, juvenile court, time away from my family. Thank God my dad was a great lawyer. Thank God my grades were topnotch. Thank God the girl had her own delinquency troubles. Thank God my grandparents had money to pay off her family and avoid future lawsuits. Otherwise I might not be a doctor today.

I close my eyes and focus on my breathing. Violence won't help me, I know this. It'll only make Sam win. There are better ways to topple him, and years of learning how to channel my anger into more creative schemes will allow me to do it.

I will my muscles to relax. When they finally do, at least to the point where my hands unclench, I open my eyes and think more clearly.

My father was shot in the lower abdomen at a political rally over six years ago. The event was held inside the River Road Convention Center, which is about halfway between Morganville and Boston. The rally included information booths, as well as food stands, kids' games, and a stage for musical performances. Given my father's plan to run for city council, he was enthusiastic about the event.

It took place in my junior year of college, on the same Saturday I flew to Athens for a ten-day forensic anthropology field study. The school-sponsored, spring-break trip was a Christmas gift from my parents. Even though neuropathology was my future, it was a great opportunity. I studied skeletal remains, decomposition patterns, and other details of crime scene analysis. As an aspiring forensic pathologist, Megan would have loved it, and she would have been a far better socializer than I was.

While in Greece, I knew nothing of my father's shooting. He insisted to my family that I not be called back to the States. Maybe he was worried how I'd react. Maybe he just wanted me to enjoy my trip. Regardless, he pulled through without a problem, recovered well, and saw no reason for me to come home early. In our few email communications—I didn't use my cell phone to avoid the international costs—he mentioned nothing of it.

It wasn't until I got back home that I learned a political zealot had decided to vote with bullets instead of a ballot and pen. How he managed to get a gun into the center I don't know, but he fired three shots before bystanders took him down. My father took one bullet, and a woman took two, but both of them survived.

I was angry at the time. Told my father he should've called me.

But he said he was healing well and ready to move on. "You know me, tiger, I don't like to dwell on things, and I don't want to talk about it. Might be making some life changes though."

He stuck to his word. Not long after, he retired from the law, gave up any pursuit of political office, and bought a food truck, which had always been his dream once he retired. He simply decided to do it earlier than planned. He called it Emily's Ribs and set it up at Dewey Square in Boston and sometimes at sporting games.

The truck quickly made a name for itself. Customers flocked to my dad's barbecued meats and hearty sides, and even though he netted a fraction of his former salary, he was finally at peace, at least employment-wise. My mother's deterioration took its toll family-wise. She loved having a truck named after her though, and in her increasingly limited periods of lucidity, she joked that at least her name would live on even if her mind didn't. None of us laughed.

Thanks to the smart investments my dad made as a lawyer, along with his pension and my mother's inheritance from her parents, who died in a car accident when I was twenty-one, they still lived comfortably. He continued to contribute to my college and med school education, a gift I'll never be able to repay him for. A month before my second year of med school started and not even two years into living his dream, he died. Suffered a heart attack in his food truck while closing up.

Had his employee, Toby Gilbert, been there, he would've been able to call an ambulance and give CPR, but that Saturday was a slow one, and my father let Toby leave early. My dad died alone. His body wasn't found until that night when someone wandered by and wondered why the truck's window was open but no one was manning it. The bystander peeked inside and got the shock of his life. He called 911, but it was too late.

After the funeral, my mother crumbled quickly. Without the daily attention of my father, she spent too much time alone. Ned was off in Rhode Island, curbing his grief and depression with music. Maybe some drugs too, but for once I understood his pain.

I moved back home to live with our mom, but her care needs

were too great. When I returned to school, I fell behind in my classes. With permission from the dean, I dropped out for the year to see if I could help her get better.

That was a fool's errand. Despite frequent psychiatric therapy (including several hospitalizations), good drug combinations, and my constant attention, she continued to spend more time in psychosis than out.

Finally, after discussing it with Ned, who bucked up enough to agree it was for the best, I admitted her to Home and Hearth Healing. Her psychiatrist recommended it. My paternal grandparents recommended it. My mother's friends recommended it. Even my dad and my mom's parents had discussed it when they were still alive. My father had drawn up papers for the inevitable day he knew would come. Still, my guilt was immense. And this is coming from a schizoid.

After my mother was institutionalized, I enrolled back in med school in the fall of 2016, sold my parents' house, and got my apartment in Morganville. Between the college money my father left me and my part-time job, I was able to afford the small studio. Far cheaper than living in Boston, and it was closer to my mother too. Whether or not Ned is still living on his small inheritance, I don't know. Maybe he spent it on his music and recordings. But most of the money my father left the three of us goes to my mother's care. On that I insisted.

But now, as I sit like petrified wood in the deserted hospital library, the computer screen in front of me long since gone dark, I realize all this time I've been wrong. Tragically wrong.

When my father was shot, I assumed his trauma surgery was done at Massachusetts General. Why wouldn't it be? That's where he always went for care. My mother too. Even his surgical follow-up four weeks later was there. I know this because I was going to skip class to accompany him, but he insisted I didn't. He said my mother was having a good day and was going with him to Mass General. He even mentioned the surgeon's name—Dr. Jill Peters. Although I forget a lot of extraneous details, I clearly remember that.

What I now realize, however, is that he must've switched his follow-up appointment to Dr. Peters in Boston, which was closer to home. It was only because he'd been at the convention center when he was shot that the ambulance took him to Titus McCall. Same distance but quicker to get to because of less traffic.

Something clicks in my brain. I put my hand on the mouse and wake the screen up. My dad's autopsy was done in Boston, that much I know. I remember reading the report. Cause of death was listed as sudden cardiac arrest. Though he had no history of heart disease, one of his coronary arteries was partially blocked, so it seemed a likely diagnosis. Yet if the postmortem was done in Boston but my search terms picked it up in Titus McCall's records, that must mean there's a copy of it here too.

I check under *Scanned Documents*. A cover letter shows it was indeed faxed over from Massachusetts General. What it doesn't say is who requested it.

But I know who it was, and I know why he requested it. He was worried what the autopsy would show.

My earlier heat returns. My jaw hardens, and a sharp mass forms deep in my chest.

All this time I thought a trauma surgeon in Boston had operated on my father, but that wasn't the case. It was a Titus McCall surgeon. It was Dr. Samuel Donovan. It was Sam.

And two years later my father was dead.

That's why Sam is in my pictures. The surgeon wasn't there for me. He wasn't there for my mom. He was there for my dad, spying on him, just like he spied on the librarian and just like he's spying on the waitress and mechanic now. I can only assume they're his former patients too.

I no longer care that it's after ten p.m., or that Martin gave us three papers to read before tomorrow's teaching rounds, or that my butt is sore from sitting. For the next ninety minutes, I search through 2014, 2013, and 2012 for charts that fit my criteria.

Only one more patient surfaces—Ted Overton, a fifty-year-old alcoholic who died in November 2014 from suspected liver failure. Once again the cause of death wasn't certain because his liver disease, while advanced, was not severe enough to expect death.

Like the other patients I found, he had previous trauma surgery. His was in December 2013 after surviving—barely, it seems—an impalement.

So that makes case number seven, my father being six. Seven cases where a patient Dr. Donovan operated on died within a few years of surgery, each with an inconclusive cause of death, at least in my opinion. Seven cases in the seven years Dr. Donovan has been at Titus McCall.

As for what it all means, I don't know. He saves them. He stalks them. He kills them. Why? What's his motive? How does he choose his victims?

Perhaps most importantly, will he do it again, and if so, how soon?

These are questions I have no answers for. I only know that I have to use all my cognitive strength to resist picking up the computer and hurling it across the room. I can't allow this psychopath to get away with killing my father. I won't allow it, and I refuse to let him kill anyone else.

But Dr. Lightfoot is right. Violence is rarely the best course of action. I'll have to find another way.

16

During teaching rounds the next morning, Martin asks me a question. I barely make sense of his words. Instead, I stare into the lens of the viewing head, blue cells from a bronchial washing swimming in front of my eyes. The purple nuclei seem to mock me. *Sam killed your father, Sam killed your father, Sam killed your father.*

The surgeon is all I can focus on. That and making sure he doesn't kill anyone else. Since violence is off the table, and since even I know I need more proof before taking this to Tam, tonight I'll contact the families of some of his victims. See if he was stalking them too.

"Liza?"

Martin is still talking to me.

"Um, I'm sorry, what was the question again?" Given my inability to concentrate, the Death Chamber is living up to its nickname this morning. Worse, Dr. Silverstein is sitting in. Sometimes attendings like to join us to offer their insights. Normally I welcome it. Today I don't.

"What's the cell pattern suggesting?" my chief repeats.

I glance up. His normally cheery demeanor is replaced by something else. Concern? Anger? Confusion? I'm too jumbled to tell. My gaze returns to my viewing head. "Hmm, they seem…they suggest…" Even though cytology has been my forte at teaching rounds, the cells might as well be Arabic letters. Though my ineptitude doesn't embarrass me, I worry how unhinged I must look to my advisor.

"Liza, are you okay?" she asks.

I sit back and rub my forehead. "I'm not feeling too well."

"Heavens, your face is flushed. Do you have a fever? Enterovirus is going around, you know."

"Maybe." But my fever is not from illness. It's from something far more sinister than a summer virus.

"You better go home for the day," my advisor says. "Get some rest and drink lots of tea."

Her tone is soothing, just like my mother's used to be. I travel back to the second grade when a case of strep throat plagued me. My mom, still a music teacher at the time, stayed at my bedside. A miserable day became one I never wanted to end. *The Price Is Right, Family Feud, Press Your Luck,* we watched them all. Game shows, which were like puzzles in motion to me, were the only TV I was interested in.

I push back from the table and slowly stand.

"Summer viruses are the worst," Megan says. "I hope you feel better soon."

Murmurs all around from my colleagues. Despite not being sick, I find comfort in their well-meaning platitudes, and if that's the case, I really must be on loose tethers.

Fortunately, Waseem breaks the lovefest. "And someone please wipe down her viewing head. The last thing I need is a case of diarrhea." They all laugh, and before I leave, he adds, "Hope you nip this thing in the butt soon, Liza." His word error, likely intentional, invites another round of mirth.

I wobble to my cubicle to grab my satchel.

Oh yes, Waseem, I intend to. If it's the last thing I do, I intend to.

I leave the path department and stroll down the corridor, staring blankly out the windows. The midmorning sun tucks itself behind a cloud and then pops back out, blinding me for a moment. Behind a white pillar, a guy in scrubs is leaning against the glass. When I realize it's Trey, I slink past, hoping he doesn't see me. There's too much on my mind to talk to him now.

"Oh, hi, Liza."

The greeting comes without his usual swagger and charm. Though I want to keep walking, my social training forces me to stop. "You okay?" I ask.

He pushes away from the window. His shoulders remained hunched. "Sure, everything's good. Just post-call and tired." He fidgets with the pager attached to his scrubs.

When he offers nothing else, I say, "Well, I have to go. Talk to you later." I imagine Dr. Lightfoot shaking his head at my insensitivity, but Trey can't be my focus now.

"Oh yeah," he says. "Sure."

I leave before he has the chance to change his mind and tell me what's wrong.

Inside my car, I slip off my sweater hoodie and blast the air. Not even nine thirty yet and it's already too warm for anything beyond my short-sleeved blouse. I consider going home to change into shorts, but my gray slacks will look more professional should I need to knock on any doors.

If Sam stalked my father and the librarian, I have to assume he stalked the other deceased patients too. That's what I need proof of today. What about the waitress and mechanic? They're still alive. Shouldn't I warn them about Sam?

After pondering this for a moment, I decide no, not yet. They'd have no reason to believe me, and they might even report me. My best move is to gather more proof and give it to Tam. She can take it from there.

In the parking lot with my car idling, I make a game plan. Before I left the hospital library last night, I jotted down addresses and phone numbers for the six victims other than my father. I pull the list and a pen from my satchel. After swinging the visor over to block the sun from the driver's side window, I review the names.

The first one I check off is the librarian. I've already spoken with her elderly colleague and confirmed that Dr. Donovan was seen in the Perry library.

I also check off the most recent death, the heroin addict whose autopsy I witnessed. His father will be too raw from his son's passing, and I'm not skilled enough to make sympathetic inquiries. "Hey, was your son being stalked by his surgeon? I think he killed him." That wouldn't go over too well.

Lastly, I cross off the other 2018 death, the fifty-nine-year-old physician who died of a suspected ruptured brain aneurysm. Her chart indicated she was a widow, and her only daughter, whose number I don't have, lives in North Carolina. Poking around the doctor's former clinic to interview her colleagues would be too risky and raise too many suspicions.

My body temperature cools. After adjusting the air conditioning, I review the 2017 death, a forty-three-year-old man who died from a suspected arrhythmia. I give myself a pep talk, take a few deep breaths, and then call the home number that was listed in his chart. Within seconds I learn the number has been disconnected. If that's the case, it's likely his family moved. I dig my iPad out of my satchel, open up an online realty site, and enter the home address listed in the man's chart. The house was sold to a new buyer in 2017. I check him off too.

That leaves the 2016 and 2014 deaths. The first is the thirty-seven-year-old woman who died of complications of obesity. Steeling myself again, I call her home number, hoping but not really expecting to find someone there on a Tuesday morning, assuming it's still even her number. Fortunately, a man answers. I begin the spiel I've practiced.

"Hi, I'm Dr. Patton, a resident at Titus McCall Medical Center. I'm doing a research project on long-term post-operative outcomes." Technically this is the truth, minus my name change. "Is this Mr. Temple, Carol's husband?"

A tentative *yes* comes through the phone line.

"Great. I'm calling to check on Mrs. Temple. I understand she had surgery for a serious skin infection in 2015."

The long pause that follows makes me wonder if this is yet

another example of me not thinking things through like a normal person. I'm about to hang up when the man says, "Your information is only half correct. She did have surgery, but she died two and a half years ago."

"Oh, I'm so sorry." I hope my tone matches my words. "I should have spotted that in her chart."

"It's okay."

With his quickness to forgive me, I relax a little against my car's seat back.

"Carol was a wonderful woman," he says. "That infection was awful. Just awful. They almost had to cut her leg off, but that doctor saved her."

"Dr. Donovan, you mean?"

"Yep. That's the one. He was incredible. Great man too."

"How so?"

"Carol wasn't just a patient to him, she was a person. He even made house calls."

My fingers squeeze around the pen. "He did?"

"Yep. A few times. Even well after the surgery. Stopped by her thirty-seventh birthday bash too. Not many docs would do that, you know."

I scribble this unusual piece of information down.

His voice hitches. "But she died a short time later. They said it was because of her weight, but I don't know. Aside from that skin infection, she was real healthy."

He sniffs as if he might be crying, and I don't enjoy being the one to cause him pain. I wrap things up. "She sounds like she was a great woman. Again, please forgive my phone call. I'm embarrassed I wasn't better prepared. I'll let you go now."

"It's all right. Feels good to talk about my Carol. Say, what was your name aga—"

I disconnect. I now have proof Sam was watching Mrs. Temple too. That's three patients he's stalked and three patients who are dead. Why did he choose them? Was it random? Or is there a connection I'm failing to see?

My stomach growls. I haven't eaten a thing since learning last night that my father was Dr. Donovan's patient. Didn't even stop at the kiosk in the atrium for my morning tea.

My needs can wait. There's only one name left on my list. Ted Overton, the 2014 death, a fifty-year-old alcoholic who died of suspected liver disease. He's the earliest one I found. Does that mean he was Dr. Donovan's first victim? Were there others I missed? Or did he kill even before he started at Titus McCall in 2012? Seems unlikely he could've gotten away with it for so long. Then again, I remember reading about a nurse who killed hundreds of people over his sixteen-year career.

Shit.

I dial the home number for Ted Overton. No answer. Maybe I won't get as lucky with this one. I try again but after letting it ring and ring, I give up. The fact it doesn't go to voicemail isn't a good sign. His address is local. Though there's no guarantee his family still lives there, I'll drive by it just in case. Given its proximity to a doughnut shop, I can solve two problems at once.

When I get there, my hope of finding a fourth source of proof is squashed. The address that was listed in Overton's chart back in 2014 is no longer residential. The mid-century home has been converted to a dentist's office, complete with a tooth-shaped sign in the corner of the yard and a small parking lot holding three cars.

I pull into the doughnut shop and order a breakfast sandwich, a vanilla-cream pastry, and hot tea at the drive-through. Despite the setback with Overton, I try not to be discouraged. At least I have three cases, including my father, to present to Tam. Will that be enough?

My mind drifts to Dr. Donovan's house, the security code still in my phone. What might I find inside his place? I shake my head. Dead or not, my father would never forgive me. And how would I get in the door? It's not like I can smash open a window in that neighborhood. Having the code is one thing. Having a key is another.

While I'm eating my doughnut in the car, another thought comes to me. I thump the steering wheel. Powdered sugar from my fingers sprinkles everywhere. Why didn't I think of it sooner? Maybe Sam frequented my dad's food truck.

I shove the rest of the doughnut into my mouth and grab my phone. A glimpse of my face in the rearview mirror tells me I look like a crack addict. White powder cakes my lips and blots my fingertips. I don't care. I pull up my contacts. Relieved to find his number still there, I fire off a text to Toby Gilbert, my dad's food-truck assistant. Since I haven't spoken to him since the funeral, I identify myself.

This is Liza Larkin. Need to talk to you. Call me ASAP.

Finally, I wipe my hands, pull out of the doughnut shop parking lot, and drive back to my apartment. A positive ID of Dr. Donovan from Toby Gilbert might be my most important proof of all.

17

The next three days move like thick New England syrup. After collecting and organizing my evidence against Dr. Donovan on Tuesday, which arguably is pretty thin but should still cast suspicion his way, my plan was to rush over to Shawna and Tam's house and pass the information on to Tam.

Need to talk to you about something important, I texted her on Tuesday.

In Maine at Shawna's parents, she responded. Remember I mentioned our trip last time we talked? Back Friday night. If can't wait till Saturday give me a call.

Damn. I didn't remember their trip. I should've put it in my voice recorder. Knowing it was best to relay my findings to her in person, I texted that I'd come by on Saturday.

So I pass the days working, exercising, and running errands. I get my hair cut, keeping it short and fuss-free. I stock up on as many groceries as my tiny apartment can hold. I slice excised tumors and organs into tissues sections. I help Megan diagnose her malfunctioning-laptop problem. I read slides and pass my findings onto an attending. Sometimes my conclusions are correct, and the path reports get added to the patients' charts right away. Sometimes my conclusions are wrong, and corrections are made first. I work on my research project—my real research project—finding other cases to include in my paper, cases where surgeons don't murder their patients. I respond to questions during teaching rounds, my colleagues happy my "illness" was short-lived.

Though I'm antsy to pass my findings on to Tam, now that everything is in place, my baseline calm has returned. Mostly. Just to be safe though, I don't allow my mind to linger on the fact that Sam murdered my father. If I do, the fury inside me grows so hot that even the most grueling workout can't cool it.

But I have no doubt he *did* kill my father. Toby Gilbert, my dad's food-truck assistant, called me Tuesday night. After a few beats of small talk (yay me), I texted him Dr. Donovan's picture.

"Hold on," he said. "Let me look at it." His voice was back in seconds. "Yeah, I think I recognize the dude. That mole under his eye, you know? He didn't order anything but asked me about your father."

My stomach tightened. "What do you mean?"

"I was working the truck alone while your dad took your mom to her…er…an appointment."

"And?" I asked with impatience, wondering why people felt the need for a euphemism when referring to psychiatrists.

"And he asked when your dad would be back."

"What did you say?"

"I told him tomorrow. Why?"

"Was that…" I cleared my throat and tried again. "Do you know what day that was? Was it the day before my dad died?"

"Jeez, Liza, why're you asking that?"

"Was it?"

A pause, during which I hoped Toby was searching his brain and not wondering whether I'd just gone over the crazy cliff. Finally, he said, "I dunno, maybe. I left early that day though, you know, the day your father…" His voice faltered, and it hit me that the conversation might be difficult for him. I should have eased into it, just as Dr. Lightfoot has trained me to do. My dad's death wasn't Toby's fault, but it made sense he would harbor guilt over not being there when he died.

Still, that's all I needed to hear. From that moment on, what little doubt was in my mind that Sam killed my father was squelched. Now I just need to get the police to prove it.

When five o'clock Friday finally arrives, I don't linger like I normally do. I leave the path department to go visit my mom before Brian's heavy-bag class. I worry Trey might ask to meet up, but I haven't heard from him since our passing in the hallway a few days ago. He seemed off at the time. As I exit the hospital atrium, I open up my voice app and make a reminder to text him later. It's smart to keep him on my side.

Inside Home and Hearth Healing, I greet Tiana behind the receptionist desk. She's rubbing at something pink in her raven hair. "Got a little too close to Maisy and her yogurt earlier." She laughs as she cleans out the dried goop. "Looks like I missed a spot."

At the mention of food, I realize I've forgotten to bring dough-nuts. When I apologize, she waves it away.

"Doughnuts or no doughnuts, we're always happy to see you. I wish other family members visited as often as you do. It makes the residents so happy. Besides, after reading about this, I'm not hungry." She holds up a magazine article. My face must register disgust because she says, "Right? Making crafts from your placenta? Everything from art to jewelry to plates. Ew."

"Did you know some women eat them?" I say.

Tiana blinks at me. Her eyelashes seem too long to be anything but synthetic. Regardless, they suit her. "Well, I didn't think anything could convince me to start my diet, but you just did. Congratulations," she says, laughing.

"You don't need to diet," I say.

"I know, but I don't need to eat doughnuts either."

"None of us do, but then what would Morganville do with all those empty buildings?"

This gets another chuckle from the receptionist, which is good because I've exhausted my social stores on this exchange.

"Your mom is in the rec room, by the way."

"How's she been today, do you know?" When Tiana's face shadows, I prepare myself for the worst. "What happened?"

"Nothing bad, sorry to worry you. It's just…um…she and the orderly had a little run-in." She quickly adds, "But it was just a misunderstanding."

My radar is on high alert. "Pete?"

"Yes, Pete Parsons. Emily's blanket went missing—you know, that super-soft one you bought her?—and she thought Pete stole it, but really, he just thought it was someone else's. He hasn't been here that long and—"

The remainder of her words are lost on me because a connection I failed to make two weeks ago now snaps into place. "Did you say 'Parsons'?"

"Yes, Pete Parsons, why?"

Surprise mutes my tongue. Shelly, the woman Dr. Donovan dumped, the woman I've suffered two yoga classes for, shares the same last name. It can't be a coincidence.

I recall our conversation in the pub. How she mentioned Pete the husband had a sadistic streak. That definitely matches Pete the orderly. Twice I've questioned his behavior, once when he seemed to be teasing Maisy and the other when I worried he purposely tripped a resident. I'll need to inform Dr. Dhar of this new information.

"Liza? Earth to Liza."

I refocus on Tiana. "Has Dr. Dhar left for the day?"

"Actually, no. He had to visit a resident in the hospital today, so he came back to finish some work."

Halfway down the hallway I remember to turn around and thank her.

"Of course. Always." She licks her lips and rubs her hands together like a madwoman. "Next week we'll share some placenta pie."

I find Dr. Dhar not in his office but in the rec room, flipping through books on a shelf as if looking for something. My mother is seated on a wide sofa on the other side of the room, teaching Maisy how to play the guitar. This blossoming friendship comforts me. My mom seems peaceful with her.

Dr. Dhar smiles when he sees me. He points to the books. "Rumor has it one of our younger men is drawing penises in some of the books." He plucks out a tattered paperback of *A Tale of Two Cities* and shuffles through its pages. "Aw, here's one." He holds the book open to me.

"At least you can't fault his skills."

A few feet away, a woman with blue hair looks up from her easel and snorts. The psychiatrist laughs too. "Yes, he does have a knack for anatomical detail." He tosses the book in a pile on a nearby table, where it joins five others.

"Can I talk to you?" I ask.

"Of course."

I lead him to a closet full of art supplies. Once out of ear range of the scattered residents and staff members, I relay what I heard about Pete from Shelly. "She called him sadistic. Used that very word."

His face grows serious, and he admits some of the other residents have seemed put off by the orderly.

"What if he's the one spying on my mother?" I add. "She claims someone's watching her from the bushes. What if he's—"

Dr. Dhar holds up a hand. "We have no evidence of that. Let's not create something out of nothing."

I worry this is somehow a dig at me. As if I'm imagining the whole thing.

"But I'll talk to him," the psychiatrist says. My expression must suggest this isn't good enough because he adds, "I can't fire him without proof of actual misconduct. I'll have the other staff members keep an eye on him."

Realizing this is the best I can do for now, I thank him and go join my mother and Maisy. Though my mom doesn't use my name when I sit down next to her, her speech is organized and her demeanor relaxed.

While I sit and listen, she and her groupie strum a few songs. Maisy's long fingers are as gangly as the rest of her body, but the two women seem content, and it feels good to just sit there and watch them, even if Maisy can't pluck the right notes.

Now that I know it was my father Sam was after, the only reason he'd have to go after my mother is to get back at me. Fortunately, after I talk to Tam tomorrow morning, the police will make sure he never hurts anyone again.

18

Located on Waverly Boulevard, Shawna and Tam's house is set far back from the road, well-hidden by the densely forested grounds. As with most of the homes on the winding street, you have to look twice to notice it's there.

Because of the road's scenic offerings, it makes for an attractive jogging path, but the lack of sidewalks and abundance of curves make for a potentially dangerous one. Despite Tam's disapproval, Shawna often jogs the route. She says it frees her mind. "When the traffic is light, I feel like the only person in the world," she once told me. "Just me and Mother Nature, two moms getting their sanity back."

After a lot of bickering, Shawna and Tam came to an agreement. Shawna can jog it but only if she runs against traffic, wears reflective clothing, and doesn't take Seth. If he tags along in the jogging stroller, she needs to take a different route. "I wouldn't have it any other way," she told me.

When I spot their graveled driveway marked by a gray mailbox, I pull my Civic up to their home and park in front of the two-car garage.

At twenty-two hundred square feet, the ranch home with

maroon siding, white shutters, and a wrap-around porch is good-sized for a family of three. The lot is spacious too, with part of the backyard fenced in for their border collie, Betts.

Though I could count on two hands the number of homes I've visited in my lifetime, I've been to Shawna and Tam's place the most, at least in my adult life. They've lived here for three years, moving in shortly after their wedding. Instead of a honeymoon spent surfing or snorkeling, they used the two weeks to settle into their new house. They've invested a lot of time, money, and hard work into it, and it's their respite from the world. If a home and family were what I desired, theirs is the path I would emulate. Tucked away from humanity and yet still part of it when need be.

I exit my car, crunch my way to the stone pathway, and climb the porch steps. My satchel bounces against my side. Tam opens the door before I even knock.

"Sorry about the gravel," she says as I pick a stone out of my sandals. "I'd pave the driveway if it wasn't longer than a drug dealer's rap sheet." Dressed in jeans, a plain tee, and an unbuttoned cotton shirt, she holds the door open for me. "Good to see you." She ruffles her short hair and points to a pile of suitcases and infant travel paraphernalia in the corner of the living room. "Ignore the mess. We drove back last night. Haven't had a chance to unpack yet. Traffic on 95 was a nightmare. Typical August in Maine, I guess."

Inside the air-conditioned home, she leads me to the coffee-colored sofa, where I smell the beverage itself wafting from the kitchen. After I sit down and drop my satchel on the speckled carpet, I remember to say, "Sorry to bug you so soon after you're back. I appreciate you letting me come by."

"You're always welcome, you know that." She stuffs her hands in her pockets. "Shawna thinks the world of you. We both do."

Shawna's ongoing warmth for me (and by default, Tam's), despite my abysmal reciprocation, remains one of life's greatest mysteries.

The back door slams. Seconds later, Betts darts into the living room. She jumps into my lap and licks my face. I nuzzle against her black-and-white coat, which feels like it's recently been brushed.

Once our greeting is consummated, the border collie circles around on the couch a few times and then plants herself right next to me. While I pet her, Shawna comes in, a pink-cheeked Seth on her hip. Even clad in jean shorts and a zip hoodie, she's more put together than me.

After yanking a clump of her wavy hair from Seth's grip, she says, "So glad you could stop by. Coffee or tea?"

"No thanks."

"I've been wondering how you've been since that awful attack."

I shrug. "It wasn't so bad, and my hip is all healed up."

She shifts Seth to the other side. "Well, thank God it wasn't worse. Not that I want anyone dead, but at least the guy won't be coming after you again."

Not that one, at least. "Oh, I almost forgot." I reach into my satchel.

While I fish around inside it, trying to remember which pocket I put the envelope in, Shawna says, "You really need to let me buy you a purse for Christmas. That bag looks Army-issued."

"You sound like Megan, one of the other first-year residents." I find the envelope and reach inside it. "Here. To thank you for hearing me out this morning." I hand the Crate & Barrel gift card to Shawna. The home store is her weak spot but one she rarely indulges in. To Tam, I hand over an L.L.Bean card. "Sorry. Maybe I should have wrapped them."

"Oh sweetie, that's so thoughtful." The look in Shawna's eyes is not unlike the one Betts is giving me now. She hands Seth to Tam and sits down on the couch, the dog between us. "This is very kind of you, but please, you know you don't have to give us gifts when you come here."

"My mom always taught me not to come empty-handed." I worry I should have brought something else. Knowing not to come empty-handed and knowing what gifts to bring are two different things.

Shawna reaches out and squeezes my arm. Neither of the women speak, but the weight of their stares makes me squirm. Even Seth and Betts look at me. Just when I wonder if I'm supposed to keep talking, Shawna says, "Well, thank you again. You have such a good heart."

As always, I struggle to reconcile Shawna's version of me with my own, but I'm relieved we can finally move on.

Tam lowers Seth into a play fort, a sturdy plastic structure with more knobs and gadgets than a pilot's control panel. The ten-month-old quickly goes to work swatting, rattling, and mouthing. Tam takes a seat on the floor next to him. "So what's up? You mentioned you had important information for me. I assume it's okay for Shawna to hear too?"

I nod, and from my bag I pull the files I've prepared on Dr. Donovan. My fingers are so fidgety I almost drop the papers on Betts's head, which is now resting on my thigh.

After a couple deep breaths, I relay what I've learned about Dr. Donovan, from when I first noticed him in the background of my photographs to discovering he killed my father. For twenty minutes, I spew findings and facts, observations and conversations. Other than a school presentation, I can't remember when I've ever talked so long or so animatedly. Several times I try to slow my voice but am not sure I succeed. Where has my even temperament gone?

Finally, I finish. When I do, neither Tam nor Shawna say anything. Shawna rises and returns a few moments later with a glass of water. She hands it to me. While I drink it, I notice the two of them stare at each other. Their shock over what Dr. Donovan has done must have rendered them speechless.

As their silence continues, I start to worry. Have I left something out? I hand my papers to Tam. "It's all here. I didn't include the patient names though. Not yet, anyway. That would violate HIPAA and my research approval."

Tam flips through the sheets I've prepared. In my opinion, she doesn't give them ample time. Seth breaks his parents' silence with a loud squeal. Betts raises her head from my lap, but when I resume petting her she lowers it once again.

With a slow exhale, Tam sits up straighter on the floor and raises her eyes to me. "Wow, this is some interesting stuff you've given me." She rubs her chin, her lips parted. I don't understand her hesitancy. "But you see, it's kind of circumstantial, don't you think? And, well, from what you just told us, he's a pretty popular surgeon in the area."

"It's obvious it's an act."

When I say this, Tam glances at Shawna, but instead of weighing in, Shawna stands and mumbles something about getting Seth's bottle. I look at the happy baby. He doesn't seem hungry to me.

"What's wrong?" I say, digging my nails into my palms.

Tam leans forward. "Oh, nothing, nothing." She sounds as if she's speaking to Seth. "It's just...well...there's not a lot of real proof."

"No proof? What about my photos?" I point to the pictures I gave her. "He's in all three."

She flips through them. "Two, maybe, but I'm not sure this is him at the award ceremony."

"What's it matter? He's clearly in two." My voice once again is not my own. That familiar flush of anger rumbles in my belly. "How do you explain that?"

"You're right, it's weird," she says quickly. "But you could argue it's a coincidence. They're public events. Maybe someone he knew was graduating and that's why he's in this one."

She holds up the picture of my college graduation, where I'm flanked by my parents and Sam is in the background between some other families.

"Look at all those people around," she says. "Even your father must not have seen him in the crowd, or he would've said something to you." She raises the funeral photo. "As for this shot, you just told me he checks in on his patients after surgery, wants to make sure they're doing well. He visited your dad's food truck. He visited the librarian at the library. Maybe he felt really bad about Kevin's death. Wanted to pay his respects at the funeral without intruding on you and your family. He wouldn't be the first doctor to attend a patient's funeral."

"No." I scoot to the edge of the couch, disrupting Betts's slumber. "I said that's what people who *know* him say, but he's got them fooled. His wanting to make sure the patients are okay is just the excuse he uses."

"Yeah, but you see, there's no proof of that." Tam's voice continues in the same soft tone, which I don't like one bit.

My mouth opens. Nothing but a sputter comes out. Seth starts to whine in his plastic fort. I try again. "Yeah, but what about the waitress and the mechanic he's spying on now?"

Shawna returns with Seth's bottle. From the consistency and color of the contents, which I recognize from my med school obstetrics rotation, it's breast milk. Shawna told me Seth weaned himself a month ago, but she still pumps to "give him the extra IQ points." She scoops him up and retakes her seat on the couch. He readily takes the bottle, which shows how much I know about babies.

I return my attention to Tam, waiting for her response. In that same calm voice, she asks, "Is it possible Dr. Donovan was simply eating at the restaurant and not actually spying on the waitress?" When I don't refute it right away, she continues. "And maybe he was just deciding whether or not to use that auto-body shop. Do you know if the waitress and the mechanic were actually his patients?"

"No, but..." My brain scrambles for something to further my case. "You could search his house, right? I'm sure you'll find something. A weapon, drugs to subdue his victims, souvenirs from his kills."

Shawna shifts on the couch. Tam blinks at me and rubs her neck. "Look," she says. "The police can't search someone's property without cause." She raises the stack of papers I gave her. "I can see how odd it seems that all seven of his patients died within a few years of surgery, I'll give you that, but all of them have legitimate causes of death."

"Not necessarily," I say, but I can now see I'm losing the fight. My earlier hope of getting Tam's help to stop Dr. Donovan is disappearing faster than the milk in Seth's bottle. "In some of the cases, the medical examiner assumed the cause of death but couldn't really prove it."

"Still..."

My cheeks grow hot. "Seven people is a lot, Tam!" Betts startles against my thigh. I don't blame her. I startled even myself. I remember my mother ranting on the couch at Home and Hearth Healing a few weeks ago and lower my voice. "One of them was my father."

"Oh sweetie, we know." Shawna reaches out to me, gripping Seth in the crook of her other arm. He holds his bottle and sucks down what's left of the milk. "It's awful about your dad, and I can absolutely see why you'd make this connection. I'm sure you're still trying to process it all. Grief is a funny thing that way."

"Do you remember seeing him at my dad's funeral?" I ask her. "You were there."

She hesitates. "I wish I could say yes, but I don't remember. Like Tam said, a lot of doctors go to their patients' funerals, so it's possible, for sure."

I may be socially inept, but I'm not stupid. I can hear the patronizing tone in her voice. Though I'm sure it stems from kindness, it frustrates me nonetheless. Why can't I make them understand?

"Tell you what." Tam stands from the floor. She drags over the ottoman from a corner chair and sits on it in front of me. "How about you finish your research. Look through the other surgeons. See if you find cases of their patients dying not long after surgery. If you do, it might make you feel better. Might show the randomness of it."

"It's not about making me feel better." The fire in my voice is back. "It's about uncovering what he's up to. That's the whole reason I ranked Titus McCall first. What if he does this again? We have to save—"

Tam holds up a finger to stop me. "What was that again?"

"I said it's about making sure he doesn't hurt anyone else."

"Not that part. The part about you ranking Titus McCall first."

Shawna puts the bottle down and repositions a sleepy Seth in her arms. She looks pointedly at me. "Liza, are you telling us the reason you moved Mass General down to second place and Titus McCall to first is so that you could follow this man?"

I frown. "So what if I did? It's near my apartment. They're both great training hospitals."

Tam pinches her nose. In that moment, she reminds me of my father, who's probably pinching his own nose beside her. "But do you know how cra—" She stops short, but I know what she was about to say. She starts over. "Do you know how odd that sounds? By watching him, dare I say *stalking* him, how is what you're doing any different than what you're accusing him of doing?"

"Because I'm not a killer. Jesus, do I need to spell it out?" I stare back and forth between them. I can't believe it. The look Shawna's giving me is not unlike the looks people give my mother.

"Liza," she says calmly. "When's the last time you saw Dr. Lightfoot? You know he helps you make sense of things. Helps you maneuver life's—"

"Oh my God, how is that the point here?" I feel like pulling my hair out. Instead, I take a deep breath and try again. "Don't you see? Sam's been threatening me, even hinted he sent that junkie to attack me, and now that guy's dead. His threats are subtle, it's true, but they're there. I think he's following me too, and he might even be watching my mother. She says someone's been spying on her behind the bushes near…" I don't finish my sentence. What's the point? Even I can hear the lunacy of my words. But my inability to adequately express myself doesn't make Sam's actions any less real.

I sigh. Looking at my friends, I see that I'm on my own. The proof I thought I had is not proof at all. Even as Tam is assuring me she'll hold onto my files and find out if Dr. Donovan has any complaints in his background, even as Shawna tells me she's here for me and that she'll be sure to check in on me more, even as Seth winks his sleepy eyes at me and Betts rubs her nose in my hand, I know that I'm on my own.

The only person who can stop Sam now is me.

19

Tam's inability to help me this morning leaves me frustrated and angry, but I try not to stew for long. An hour of heavy-bag punching and kicking at Brian's Gym and another twenty minutes of core work dull the heat in my belly.

I *will* bring Sam down. One way or another, I'll bring him down.

Back in my studio apartment, I shower and throw on a clean pair of gym shorts and a racerback tank. If I hurry, I can make the four o'clock hospital yoga class. Though I could do without Mark and his hands-on approach, not to mention his verbal mantras, fifty minutes of stretching is a small price to pay for more dirt on Dr. Donovan, providing Shelly Parsons is there. Now that I'm on my own, I'm going to have to push harder for usable information.

Inside the Sweat Lodge, five yoga mats cover the floor. Shelly is on one of them. Only one treadmill is in use, and the free weights collect dust in the corner. Mark isn't here yet.

I unroll my mat next to the respiratory therapist. She doesn't seem to notice me at first.

"It's dead in here," I say, smiling her way.

Her eyes blink in recognition. "Oh, hi. Yeah. First weekend of August. A lot of people are probably on vacation."

While she folds down into child's pose, I stretch out my hamstrings. "Guess what I learned?"

She doesn't move, just remains face down in her pose. I hear her say a muffled, "What?"

I wonder what's wrong. During the last two classes she was more upbeat, even after Dr. Donovan dumped her. And she certainly didn't hold back at O'Dell's, where whiskey sours loosened her tongue like an oil can. Maybe I'm reading her vibes wrong. Maybe she just wants me to leave her alone.

"I think your ex-husband is working at my moth—" I catch myself. No need to make this more personal than it has to be. "At my friend's mental health facility."

Shelly bolts up from her child's pose so quickly I worry she'll slip a disc. "You're shitting me."

"Pete Parsons? Dark hair, bags under his eyes, colorful socks."

"Oh my God, that's him." She unfolds her legs, sits on her butt, and pulls her knees to her chest. "Of all the wrong places for him to work. Such a sadistic bastard." She stares hard at me, and just as our instructor shuffles in with his royal blue mat, she says, "You better warn whoever's in charge there about him. I wouldn't trust him alone with a patient." She taps her temple. "He'll mess with their heads."

Mark directs us into downward dog, so I say nothing else, but Shelly has confirmed my suspicions. While Pete is not my main focus, I can't lose sight of him.

Thanks to the small class size, I get extra helpings of Mark's touches and dippy words of encouragement, so much so that I'm ready to yank the red hair right out of his scalp. I control myself, and when the session is over, I capitulate to the relaxed state of my body, once again recognizing how good it feels after the class. Maybe this yoga stuff deserves more of my attention. God knows Dr. Lightfoot was always pushing it on me. (*You really need to answer his email, Liza.*) But I'll only practice it in the privacy of my apartment, where Mark will never set foot.

As we roll up our mats, I'm about to ask Shelly if she wants to head to O'Dell's again, but she beats me to it. She hugs her mat to her petite frame. "Do you want to grab a cup of coffee in the cafeteria?"

"Sure. Or maybe O'Dell's again?"

She shakes her head. A lock of sandy hair slips from her ponytail. "I better not. I'm trying to cut back, and if I go there, I'll drink too much."

Which is better for me, I think but don't say. Coffee's not a great truth serum. "Okay, that sounds good."

"Thanks. I want to run something by you."

"Your boyfriend troubling you again?" Since Shelly never did mention Dr. Donovan's name or occupation, I pretend I don't know who he is.

"No, that's not it, although he did text me to see if I want to meet up tonight. I'm sure it's for a booty call. Or maybe he wants me to water his stupid plants while he takes off to a fancy resort for a conference. Isn't that how it always goes?"

I shrug, having no idea how it always goes.

"But considering what an ass he was when he dumped me, he can probably forget about that." She picks at a loose thread on her yoga top. "That's not what I want to talk to you about though. I… well…I'd like to run something by you. Since you're a doctor and all."

"Sure. I'm happy to help." Curiosity makes me almost mean what I say.

With our rolled-up mats under our arms, we make our way to the cafeteria. It's on the same floor as the Sweat Lodge but closer to the inpatient units. At this late-afternoon hour on a weekend, the hospital corridors have less traffic. A glance out the window reveals a sparse visitors' parking lot too.

Inside the dining room, a spicy scent wafts from the taco bar. A few feet later, I'm hit with the smell of dough at the pizza counter, on which a food worker in a tight hair net has just placed a fresh pan of pepperoni. I might grab a slice later, but for now I follow Shelly to the self-serve coffee and tea bar. While she pours coffee for herself, I place a cardboard sleeve on a cup and fill it with hot water.

Shelly pulls her hospital ID badge out of a small pocket in the front of her yoga pants. Not only do the cards give us access to secure places, they allow us to charge our meals.

"This one's on me," she says. "For your time." When I reach for a Berry Blend tea bag, the tone of her voice shifts. "Oh no. I can't face him right now."

Expecting to see Dr. Donovan, I look up, my muscles already tensing. Instead, I see Trey over by the sandwich bar. Given his scrubs and the fact it's Saturday, I assume he's on call. He picks up a plate but lowers it when he sees us. His expression seems confused, like the one my mom makes when she's trying to remember who she is.

Shelly puts her coffee down on the counter. "I'm sorry, Liza. I think I'm just going to head home."

Before I can protest, she hustles out of the cafeteria.

I turn back to Trey, but he checks the screen of his pager and darts off as well.

With my tea in hand, I stand there, wondering what just happened. It appears I suffered Mark's spinal touches and peace-seeking mantras for nothing. I leave the hospital with no more dirt on Dr. Donovan than what I came in with.

20

I slide into an apple-red booth at Delilah's Diner on Main Street and place my usual order of blueberry pancakes. When I first started coming here, I thought the waitress's beehive hairstyle was just for fun, a gimmick to match the restaurant's old-fashioned decor, but I've since seen her around downtown Morganville sporting the very same look. Maybe, like me, she's her own island. I always tip her well.

Normally, when I'm not fretting about how to stop a killer, Sunday is a peaceful day for me. After a leisurely run or some time at the gym, I grab breakfast at Delilah's, study or work on any projects coming due, and then relax at home reading nonfiction, playing video games, or creating graphic designs. The latter stems from the freelance work I did as a student for some extra cash (in addition to my part-time job), and sometimes I still like to mess around with it.

But today I'm restless, not only from craving revenge against Sam for killing my father, but from knowing he'll kill again if I don't find a way to stop him, a way that doesn't land me in prison or make me roommates with my mom at Home and Hearth Healing. Breaking into Dr. Donovan's home is surely one of those ways.

But Shelly might still have his keys.

Trying desperately to heed my father's often-repeated advice, I mute the thought. "Always think of the potential consequences," he'd say, usually in response to some impulsive choice I'd made. But I feel like my hands are tied, and with each day my patience grows thin.

My only solace is believing that Sam won't take another life so soon after killing the heroin addict. That was a month ago, and based on what I found in my personal research study, he kills once, or at most twice, per year. I pray that's the case, because having the death of the waitress or car mechanic on my conscience is not something that'll easily roll off me, no matter how impassive my brother thinks I am.

The pancakes form an inviting clump of carbs in my mouth, and I take a moment to savor them. They're not as good as the ones my mom used to make, but they're close. Around me, silverware clinks, busboys clear checkered tabletops, and competing conversations make it impossible to decipher just one.

As I observe my surroundings, I again think of the irony that I'm the only one who sees Dr. Donovan for the monster he is. Everyone else gets sucked into his magical orbit, including Megan, who of all people should spot his duplicity.

She was right about Waseem. With closer scrutiny, I see that now. His easy smiles for our studious colleague John. The way he brings him DVDs to watch or graphic novels to read. The long glances when he thinks no one's watching. Without Megan's input, I wouldn't have looked for these nuances. According to her, Waseem's longing is unrequited, and I see that now too. John seems far more interested in a second-year pathology resident named Claire.

Although the personal lives of my colleagues don't interest me, Waseem's situation bums me out, especially since his homeland outlaws such feelings. I know all about having to pretend to be someone you're not in this complex world of human interaction.

After scraping the last bits of syrup-drenched pancakes from my plate, I wash it all down with the remains of my orange juice. When

I reach for the bill, my phone buzzes in the front pocket of my shorts.

It's Megan. Why is she calling me? Is she finally going to drag me to the mall for a purse? Is there some get-together today I forgot about? Between Dr. Silverstein's dinner party and Jen's barbecue, I've paid my social dues until Christmas.

I debate letting it go to voicemail, but since that will just prolong the inevitable, I take the call. The beehived waitress collects my plate, and I nod at her.

My colleague sounds breathless. "Liza, you'll never guess where I am."

"You're right, I won't."

"I'm at a crime scene not far from the hospital. A body's been found. Discovered by a jogger's dog. Just off Danford Road, back in the woods."

I cross my legs, and my knee strikes the support bar beneath the table. Wincing, I rub the spot. "How did you manage that?"

"I've already spent time with the forensic pathologists, getting to know them. It's never too early to get planning on a fellowship."

Of course you have.

"They know I want to go into forensics, so Dr. Munson agreed to let me visit a crime scene and help with the autopsy should one come up. I never thought it would happen so soon though." Her excitement is palpable, and I find myself getting drawn in. "They've got the area roped off, and it's pretty deep in the woods, but there are still onlookers trying to get a peek. The emergency vehicles must've tipped them off that something big was going on."

"Who's the victim?"

"It's a woman. Looks like a head injury at this point. Maybe killed somewhere else and dumped here. We're just finishing up."

I'm not sure what she wants me to say. Is she calling to rub my nose in it? Is she calling because as a fellow first-year she knows I'll be interested? Is she calling because she still has the idea that she and I will become best friends?

"I took some photos," she says. "I'll show you guys."

This surprises me. "They let you take pictures?" I wipe a fallen bit of pancake off my shirt. I'm tempted to eat it but refrain.

"Well...I kind of did it covertly. I'll delete them after you guys see them, but I wanted us all to learn from the case. It's confidential, of course."

So my second guess is correct. She wants to share in the education, which I have to admit is decent of her. But maybe guess numbers one and three factor in there too.

Her voice drops to a whisper. "Again, this is confidential, but given that the news vans are already here, it'll get out soon anyway. The victim works at the hospital."

"How do you know? Was her purse still with her?" That seems implausible to me.

"No. Her purse is gone—they think it might be a robbery—but she had a hospital ID badge tucked inside a small pocket of her leggings."

At those last words my throat globs up, as if the pancakes are still in it. "Who is she?" I ask thickly.

When Megan confirms what I feared she might, my knee bangs the table a second time.

Shelly Parsons is dead.

Back in my apartment, I pace the small area between my bed and desk and try to make sense of what Megan told me.

Shelly Parsons, the woman I did yoga with and watched drink whiskey sours at O'Dell's, the woman who dated Dr. Donovan, the woman who used to be married to the new orderly at my mother's mental health facility, is dead. Murdered.

But who's her killer?

Is it Dr. Donovan? In some ways that makes sense. One, he's a killer, and two, Shelly mentioned he wanted to hook up with her last night. Hitting her on the head though? Leaving her in the woods? That's not his M.O. That's not how an arrogant, plotting, take-his-time murderer behaves. And as far as I know, he never performed surgery on her. Then again, she told me she wanted my advice as a doctor. Maybe she had a health issue I don't know about.

Or is the killer Pete? According to Shelly, he's a "sadistic bastard," and from what I've seen at Home and Hearth Healing, I agree. He has more motive for killing her than Sam does. Jealousy. Revenge. Maybe even money since their divorce isn't final yet. I may not be a forensic pathologist, but the head injury Megan described seems more in line with a murder committed in a fit of rage than anything Sam has done.

Pacing to my kitchenette counter, I grab one of the chocolate chip cookies April brought over yesterday. Mindlessly, I munch. Maybe the killer is someone else entirely. I'm no cop. What do I know? The only thing I *do* know is that I want Dr. Donovan stopped. I want him locked away so he'll never hurt anyone again.

I reach for another cookie. Mid-bite, I pause. I toss an idea around in my mind.

Stuffing the rest of the cookie into my mouth, I hustle to my desk and seize my cell phone. I fumble with the passcode and open up my voice recording app. The audio file I labeled SD a month ago is still there.

I play it now, the argument between Dr. Donovan and Shelly springing to life. When I finish, I back up and replay something the surgeon said, his voice cruel and cold. "Stop calling me, stop bugging me, stop chasing after me. Or you'll wish you had."

Excitement prickles inside me. With jittery fingers I email the recording to myself so that the attachment will be easier to forward. Whether Dr. Donovan killed Shelly or not, I don't know, but I imagine the police would be eager to get their hands on this conversation.

I grab my satchel. Time to visit Tam again.

21

On Tam and Shawna's front porch, I ring the doorbell a third time. The day is cloudy, and a muggy dew sticks to my skin. Inside the house, Betts's barking grows to a feverish pitch. I try to reassure the border collie through the door, but her yapping only intensifies.

After a round of knocking, I have to assume no one is home. Shawna often takes Seth to her sister's in Boston on Sundays. Tam usually spends the day working on her small boat in the backyard. The thing was barely functional when she bought it last fall, but her toil and touch have transformed it into a cool-looking skiff that she'll soon take out on the water.

I peer into the backyard where she tinkers with it, but no one's there. Maybe she's been called into work. The discovery of another dead body in Morganville—this time a woman who's been dead less than twenty-four hours—likely requires all police hands on deck, unlike my attacker who'd been there a while and whose death was determined to be from a drug overdose.

Back in my car I type out an email to Tam on my phone. I tell her I know about Shelly's death through my colleague, who's working with the medical examiner. I explain the story behind my recording of Dr. Donovan and Shelly's argument in the hospital pavilion. Hopefully she'll believe it was an innocent capture because it was. After yesterday's disastrous conversation, she might think I purposely recorded him, which is why I didn't mention it at her house. The fact the tape starts with my own voice making reminder notes to myself should help convince her.

In my email, I type that I forgot all about the recording. It wasn't until I heard the news about Shelly's death that I remembered I had it. This is a partial lie. Although I haven't thought about the recording for a couple weeks, I knew it was there.

It dawns on me Tam will be curious how I know Shelly. After debating the best way to approach this, I simply type that I know the respiratory therapist from the hospital yoga class. No need to add that I purposely sought her out.

As a final note, I tell Tam that Shelly's husband works at Home and Hearth Healing. Pete will likely be a suspect, and Tam might get suspicious if I omit this tidbit. If she isn't already.

After proofing what I typed, my thumbs not always the best spellers, I send the email with the voice recording of Dr. Donovan and Shelly's argument attached. Although his threat doesn't make him guilty of murdering her, it might make him a person of interest.

When I pull out of my friends' driveway, Betts no doubt barking again at the sound of tires on gravel, I head down Waverly Boulevard toward Sherlock Road and Home and Hearth Healing. If Pete really is a killer, I need to make sure my mother is safe.

After stopping for doughnuts, I enter the facility and hand the pastries to the receptionist, an older woman who works part-time. She greets me warmly, and although I acknowledge her, I don't spend time chatting. I used up all my social chips on Tiana's placenta talk on Friday.

Given the light drizzle that started outside, the rec room is busier than it would be on a nicer day. I pause in the doorframe. Some residents and their visitors play board games at tables. Others battle each other at ping pong or the bean bag toss. A few, like my mother and Maisy, sit on couches and chairs scattered around the room.

This time, instead of my mother teaching guitar to Maisy, the gangly woman is teaching crochet to my mom. Neither seems bothered by their weather-induced confinement. Nor do they seem bothered by their endless monotony, for surely that's what living here must be.

My chest squeezes in a way that hurts. I lean against the doorframe and try to breathe it away. Dr. Lightfoot's reassurances run through my mind: The center is a wonderful place. She's better off here. You couldn't take care of her alone. She needs around-the-clock supervision. Yada, yada, yada. I know each and every one of these things is true. I also know my father would tell me the same thing, but no matter how much I rationalize this truth, I can't reconcile the taciturn Emily over there on the couch with the woman who made me blueberry pancakes on Sundays, took me to Body World exhibits instead of theater shows that bored me, and never forced me to wear dresses or makeup or smile nicely or do any of those things that girls are expected to do.

"The fact you feel this sorrow at all," Dr. Lightfoot once told me, "means you're not quite as soulless as you think you are."

I close my eyes. I breathe in and out. Finally, I move on and make my way to join them.

"Hi, Mom," I say, taking a seat beside her.

She looks up and offers a faint smile. Her hair smells like the raspberry-scented shampoo I bought her. Her eyebrows are beautifully arched. Her nails boast a fresh coat of pink polish. These things reassure me. They mean she's stable. Maybe even better than stable. In psychosis, grooming takes a backseat to delusions and hallucinations.

I greet Maisy as well. The awkward, curly-haired woman smiles and starts softly singing a song I can't identify. I wonder who she is to Dr. Silverstein. A family friend maybe? I never did ask. My crappy social skills once again at work.

To my mom, I say, "How are you feeling?"

"I'm okay. A little tired."

We talk about trivial things like what meals she's had, movies she's watched, music lessons she's taught the other residents. Although her affect is flat, dulled by the medications, her communicativeness buoys me. I don't see any side effects of abnormal facial or body movements from the drugs either, which is a relief. Maybe just a fine tremor. All the while Maisy hums, sings, and crochets.

Once assured of my mother's coherence, I choose my words delicately and ask if anyone's bothering her here. When she says no, I take it a step further. "It's been okay outside too? When you're playing your guitar on the rock?"

She lowers her eyes. "I don't go out there anymore."

"Why not?"

She looks around the room and whispers, "He watches me."

My stomach sinks to my knees. No bizarre statements follow, nothing delusional about the king, or Hitler, or dungeons, or gas chambers. Her non-dramatical statement scares me more than her paranoid rants.

At that moment Pete Parsons enters the room, wearing his white shirt and pants, below which yellow socks with purple stripes peek out. He's guiding an elderly resident and chuckling about something. A hundred thoughts collide in my mind. Does he know Shelly's dead? Does Home and Hearth Healing have a killer on their staff? Is he tormenting my mother?

I point to him. "Mom, is that man bothering you? Is he the one watching you outside?"

Confusion creases her brows. "That's Pete."

"Yes, Pete Parsons."

"It's not hiiiimmmm," Maisy sings out.

I study the bony woman. "What do you mean?" When I look back toward Pete, he's staring at me. From his position behind the old man, whom he's just seated at a table in front of a chess set, his upper lip snarls and his eyes narrow.

My mother is shaking her head. "No, not Pete. Not Pete Parsons."

Maisy puts down her knitting. "I'll shoooow you." She stands and holds out her hand to me.

Not wanting to but doing so anyway, I grab her hand and stand. "You know who's watching my mom?"

Maisy giggles and nods. "Come, I'll shoooow you."

I don't know what to think. Does Maisy really know who's been spying on my mother, or has she merely joined in the paranoid delusion? Without knowing the woman's underlying diagnosis, it's not a leap to think psychosis might be part of it.

"Come, come, come, come, come," she sings.

I reach out for my mom's hand, and she rises to join us. Like three girls going to play, we leave the rec room.

As soon as we do, Pete Parsons is at my side. Getting right up in my face, so close that the dark shadows below his eyes look blue, he says, "What's your problem?"

I release my mother's and Maisy's hands and usher them behind me. I inch even closer to Pete. "I'm sorry?" Though taller than my landlord, the orderly doesn't intimidate me anymore than Sinclair does.

"I don't know what you said to Dr. Dhar, but they're watching every move I make," he says. "Can barely take a piss without another staff member breathing down my neck. Quit telling lies about me."

I hold his gaze. My own lip starts to curl. "Nothing I've said about you is a lie. In fact, Shelly told me all sorts of interesting things about you."

At the mention of his ex-wife's name, his face shifts, but I can't tell if his expression is one of surprise or worry. I'm tempted to ask if he killed her, but I don't want to scare my mother or Maisy.

He sniffs a few times and then backs away. "Just stay out of my business."

"Come, come, come, come, come," Maisy sings again.

She grabs my hand and tugs me down the hallway. One turn later we reach my mother's room. Maisy opens the sweater drawer. I look at my mom to see if this is okay, but she just stands there, her arms hugging herself, her gaze on the rivulets of rain slipping down the window.

To my surprise, Maisy plucks out the photo book I made. She flips through it and points. "Heeeere he is. Heeeere's the waaaatcher."

Maisy's gaunt finger taps on the picture from my father's

funeral. A red circle has been drawn around the head of the person she's pointing to.

The room shrinks around me. It's Dr. Donovan. It's Sam.

I grab the book and thrust it toward my mom. "Is that true? Is this the man you've seen behind the trees? Behind the fence?" She stares at the image and hugs herself harder. When she doesn't answer, I ask Maisy, "Have you seen him too?"

She nods up and down and sings, "Yes indeeeedy, I have indeeeedy."

I'm not sure what to believe. "Mom? Is this the man who's been watching you?" I repeat.

Finally she speaks, but her voice is so low I barely hear her. "I…I think so, but…oh Liza, it doesn't make sense."

My mother trembles, and I fear she'll fall. I guide her to the bed and sit down with her, placing the photo book to the side. She's more lucid than I can remember of late—Dr. Dhar has done well with her meds—and yet I still can't be sure she's really seen Sam here. Or at least outside the vicinity. It's possible, I suppose. Her favorite rock is not far from the fence, and although the trees and bushes are dense there, bits of the road can be seen behind them.

Has the surgeon really hid there undetected, other than the few times my mother or Maisy might have spotted him? But why? He's already killed my father. What interest is she to him now?

Clearly, if it is him, he's doing it as a warning to me. That means I've endangered my mother's life. Remembering the beige Taurus that followed me, I'm even more convinced it was him. Maybe after seeing me in the surgical waiting room, back when I started this whole thing, he decided to buy himself a little insurance by tormenting my mom.

Wait, I tell myself. My mother fell apart when I showed her this book back in February. Though I had enough worries about who the mysterious man was to flip-flop my top residency choice, I assumed the most likely reason for her meltdown was the photo album itself, too many memories for her to handle. Was Sam spying on her even then? Or maybe not her, but had she recognized he was spying on my father and in her delusional state couldn't get anyone to believe her? Was talk of the king and Hitler and their punishing ways really about Dr. Donovan in disguise? If her psychiatrist—or my father when he was alive, or me, or whoever—would have listened to her, would my father still be here today?

I steel my jaw. Acid burns its way up my throat. This revelation confirms I did the right thing by switching to Titus McCall, to hell what anyone else thinks. I circle back to what my mother said, wanting her to clarify it. "What doesn't make sense, Mom?"

"He's... I don't understand... I think he was your father's surgeon. Maybe I'm confused—"

Her words are cut off by a commotion down the hall. A woman is shrieking, and a man is shouting. It sounds like Pete. "I don't have to go anywhere with you," he yells. "What's going on?"

I bolt off my mother's bed and skid into the hallway. When I see nothing, I jog a few feet to the corridor that leads to the rec room. In front of it stand two police officers. Next to them is Pete Parsons. I step closer.

"We need you to come with us, Mr. Parsons," the taller of two male cops says.

"But I didn't do anything. What the hell's going on?" In his agitation, the orderly's shoulder knocks over a painting of a puppy sleeping in a basket. It looks to be the work of one of the residents.

A few patients and staff members watch the exchange. Some of the patients cower and cling to the employees. Others lean against the wall with smirks or raised eyebrows. One, probably the woman who was shrieking, is now sobbing into a staff member's chest, perhaps unable to handle the excitement.

Pete's face is the color of cinnamon. When he glares down the hallway and spots me, his eyes narrow to slits. "Did you do this? Are you behind this?"

The police officers haul him away. I know I should feel safer with him gone, especially if he killed Shelly, but if what Maisy and my mother say is true, that it's Dr. Donovan who's been the "watcher," then I was wrong about Parsons. He might be a sadistic bastard, but he's not the one terrorizing my mother.

I wish I could take her home with me. Wish I could keep her

with me every second to keep her safe, but that's not possible. I couldn't care for her alone back in her big house; how am I supposed to do so in my studio apartment? With a full-time job to boot?

Home and Hearth Healing is the safest place for her. I know this. Everyone knows this. Still, my instinct is to protect her. I have to hope Tam will take the recording I sent her seriously enough that the police will question Dr. Donovan. Maybe that'll give him pause about further antagonizing my mother.

On the other hand, what if it fuels him even more?

22

M onday begins with a visceral unrest I can't seem to tame. Not with my neighborhood run at dawn and not with the steaming Earl Grey tea I sip in my cubicle as I wait for morning teaching rounds to begin.

Part of my unrest stems from Shelly's death. Part of it is worry for my mother. Another part of it comes from Tam's short email response to the audio recording I sent her yesterday. Her email simply said, Okay. Nothing to suggest she was happy to get it. Nothing to suggest she'd look into it. Not even questions about how I obtained it. What I ended up reading into that one-word response was, *Shawna and I are worried you're becoming your mother.*

The tea burns my throat, but I drink it anyway. My stomach won't stop churning. Is that what Shawna and Tam now think of me? That I'm a paranoid, delusional mental case? How did my orderly and solitary life get to this point? How did I become so entwined with other people?

It's perhaps this human enmeshment that causes most of my angst. I want things to go back to normal. I want to go to work, exercise, tinker on my computer. But normalcy is impossible until

Sam is stopped. I can't pretend none of this ever happened. If I do, more people will die.

By eight twenty, all of my colleagues except Megan have arrived in the residents' room. When she comes in a few minutes later, she summons us to her cubicle. "I want to show you guys my crime scene photos from yesterday." We form a huddle around her. "The victim was Shelly Parsons, a respiratory therapist here at Titus McCall." Her professional tone matches her pencil skirt, collared blouse, and flawless ponytail. "I need to delete these pictures after you've seen them, but I thought you'd all like a chance to learn from them. After all, murder is rare in Morganville. Thankfully."

Not so rare as you might think. Just ask your new boyfriend.

Jen is closest to Megan's phone. "This is so cool of you. It'll be a while before any of us get to see an actual crime scene."

"Well, we're a team, right?" Megan points to a spot on her phone. "You see here?" We all crane our necks behind Jen to look. "There's no blood pooled around the body. That implies she was killed somewhere else and then dumped in the woods."

She zooms in on the photo, and Waseem draws a sharp breath. Jen averts her eyes and shakes her head before looking back at the picture. A very dead Shelly Parsons lies supine on the wooded ground, a halo of dirt, twigs, and fallen leaves surrounding her body. Her blond hair fans out in all directions, except where it's matted to her temple in a bloody clump at the site of the head injury. Were it not for her wide-open eyes and gaping mouth, she'd appear every bit the sleeping princess on a forest bed awaiting her prince's kiss. On the other side of me, John's breathing grows shallow.

I glance up at Megan. She's watching me. Just because I don't react like my colleagues doesn't mean I'm not bothered by Shelly's death. But my focus now centers more on making sure whoever did this to her pays.

"Was the head wound her only injury?" Waseem asks.

"It appears to be. She has a compound fracture of her temporal bone. Probably ruptured the temporal artery. Autopsy is later today."

"Do the police know who did it?" John asks.

"I'm not sure where their investigation is at this point," Megan answers. "I only know she has an ex-husband who's a suspect."

"Aren't they always?" Jen muses.

I listen as my colleagues discuss the case, Megan scrolling through a string of pictures from the scene. Then she passes it to each one of us in turn. While they wonder about the timing between head injury and death, the weapon used, and the motive, I wonder about her killer. Was it Pete Parsons or was it Sam Donovan?

The phone makes its way to me last. As I'm examining the images, Martin comes in, rubs his hands together like a mad scientist, and asks if we're ready to get our butts kicked in the Death Chamber. "I've got some doozies for you this morning, and they're not all path-related questions."

While Megan asks Martin about a biopsy she read on Friday, the rest of my colleagues head to the microscope room. I decide to take the opportunity to message myself some of the photos Megan took. I'd like to examine them more closely later, and I can't do that if she deletes them.

Her iPhone is a newer model than mine but nothing I can't navigate, and as I imagined it would be, my number is in her contact list. In between furtive glances to make sure she's not looking, her attention still on Martin, I choose five photos and send them to my number. Then I open her messages. I manage to delete the string of photos I sent to myself just as she finishes her conversation and reaches back for her phone.

Phew. It would've been difficult having to explain why I stole them.

After we finish teaching rounds, I return to my cubicle and spend two hours in front of my microscope reading blood smears from the weekend's lab orders. The work serves as a peaceful escape, and for a short time Shelly Parsons, Dr. Donovan, and even my mother's safety fade from my mind.

I'm just packing up the slides and cleaning up my area when Dr. Silverstein, dressed in a loose summer dress and her usual Birkenstocks, enters the room. Residents greet her from their cubicles. She nods and gives a little wave, but when she steps up to my area near the window, her discomfort is obvious.

"Liza," she says, twisting the fitness tracker on her wrist, "can you come to my office for a minute?"

"Uh, sure. Did we have a meeting I forgot about?"

A long strand of silver hair escapes her loose bun, and she tucks it behind her ear. "No. There's just…something we need to talk about."

My fog of unrest returns, and as I trail behind my advisor, I wonder what I might have done. Did I violate my research parameters without realizing it? Did I mishandle biohazardous waste in the gross lab? Was my impassive nature deemed rude by an ordering physician?

Oh God. My step falters. Did something happen to my mother?

By the time we reach Dr. Silverstein's office, I'm convinced this is the case. "What's wrong? Is it my mom? Did Home and Hearth Healing call you? Is she——"

When I see who's sitting in her office, my words cut off. There, in front of her cherry wood desk, with its jar of lemon drops and plastic models of brains and spinal cords, is Dr. Donovan. This can't be good.

My advisor invites me to take a seat next to him. Barely has my bottom touched the chair's fabric when the surgeon bursts up from his own. Dressed in scrubs with his hair ruffled, he appears to have just come from the OR. A manila envelope is tucked under his arm.

"Enjoy our proximity, Dr. Larkin," he says, "because it's the last time you'll get this close to me." His fury makes his eyes squint, and the mole beneath his eyelashes disappears into the crinkled flesh. He pulls something from the envelope and slams it on my advisor's desk. "She'll get her own copy soon."

"Samuel, surely there's a…" Dr. Silverstein's voice tapers off as she skims the papers he's just given her. She looks up and blinks. "You can't be serious."

"Oh, I'm dead serious."

Before I can ask what the document says, Dr. Donovan rushes on.

"Your new resident here has been asking about me, following me, telling lies about me to the police." His torrent of speech is so loud I look over my shoulder to make sure Dr. Silverstein closed the door when we entered. She did, but it's probably a poor barrier. The others in the department will still hear his tirade.

I have no idea what he's up to. Dozens of thoughts race through my mind, and for a moment I can't grasp just one. Then a hopeful idea breaks through. This must mean Tam took my email with the attached recording seriously. Why else would the police question Dr. Donovan?

My advisor stares at me, lips parted, brow creased. She starts to speak, stops, starts again, stops again. Maybe she needs one of her lemon drops to make her tongue work. Finally, she sputters, "Tell me this is a misunderstanding, Liza."

Technically, everything Dr. Donovan has said is true. I *have* been asking about him. I *have* followed him. I *have* been speaking to the police. What I'm unsure about is how he knows these things. Until I do, I decide to play it safe and deny. "I have no clue what he's talking about."

"That's bullshit and you know it," he says to me. He turns to my advisor, his nostrils flaring and his hands fisting. "Because of her, I had the pleasure of the police visiting my home last night. They questioned me about a hospital employee who died. As if I had anything to do with it. I told them I didn't even know she was dead."

The cops would never reveal their source, so Dr. Donovan obviously assumed it was me behind their visit. Wise man. But this isn't him. He's too cool and poised for this type of embarrassing display. His fury is an act, I'm sure of it. Just like me, he's pretending. Only instead of feigning innocence, he's feigning outrage.

"Please, sit down, Samuel," my advisor says. "Let's all be civil here." When he does, the chair creaks in protest at his exaggerated drop onto it. Dr. Silverstein continues. "I heard about that woman—a respiratory therapist—but why would the police question you and why would Liza instigate it?" She again implores me. "Liza, help me out here."

"Because she has some bizarre vendetta against me," Dr. Donovan shouts. "God knows why, but she seems determined to destroy my reputation." The more he puts on a show, the more I understand what he's doing. He wants people to hear him, wants the whole department behind him so that when his house of murder starts stinking, they'll be on his side.

Dr. Silverstein massages her forehead. "Let's try to figure this out."

"There's nothing to figure out." The surgeon crosses his legs dramatically. "It's obvious what's happening. I know her family. I operated on her father several years ago. A very difficult surgery that he survived, I might add."

At the mention of my father, the furnace in my belly heats up. My face feels on fire too.

"You'd think she'd be grateful, not out to get me. And, well, I hate to say it, but it looks like she's slipping down the same road as her mother who has—"

"Now, Samuel, that's uncalled for."

It's a good thing Dr. Silverstein stepped in. If she hadn't, I might have jumped up and thrown Dr. Donovan to the ground. Ripped that mole from his arrogant face and shoved it down his throat. I inhale and exhale loudly, willing my anger to dissolve.

"Well, it's in your hands now. You figure her out. All I know is this has to stop." He points to the form on my advisor's desk, which I still can't read from my distance. He turns to me and says, "That's a request form for a restraining order. I'll call my lawyer and have him file it if your behavior doesn't stop." To Dr. Silverstein, he says, "And I expect you to make her do so."

Ah. That's what the paper is. Figures a man like Sam would have a lawyer at his beck and call. Good thing too. When I get my revenge, he'll need one.

"What do you mean?" Dr. Silverstein asks, sinking back in her chair. I imagine she wants to be anywhere but here, and for that I feel bad. With her husband gone and his early stage of dementia, she has enough to deal with.

Dr. Donovan leans forward and scoffs. "Do I need to spell it out? I want her suspended. She needs to go. Today."

I stiffen. *Well played, Sam, well played.* A lump takes root in my throat. "You have no right to demand that," I say.

His face reddens, and he squeezes the armrests of his chair so tightly they creak. He's a good actor. A great one, even.

We lock eyes. I stare deeply into his until I find what I'm looking for. Yep. There it is. Satisfaction. Pride. Smugness. I recognize the look because I've worn it myself many times. He knows he's won Round 5.

Only when Dr. Silverstein sighs and dismisses me, telling me to go home for the day while she and Dr. Thomas "sort this mess out," do I realize how big of a round it was.

23

I feel like I should applaud. Dr. Donovan has landed a haymaker to my gut. By involving Dr. Silverstein and putting my residency at risk, he's deepened my stress, so much so that while I'm eating lunch in the hospital cafeteria, I have to abandon my soup and salad and rush to the bathroom to relieve myself. These stomach cramps, this anxiety—it's all new to me. I can almost hear Ned rejoicing in my mind. *Hey sis, you might just be human after all.*

But I'm not out of the match yet. I still have some punches to throw. Before I pounce though, I need to confirm these patient deaths of Dr. Donovan's are not a coincidence.

After returning to the cafeteria to clear my lunch tray, the mish-mash of culinary odors heightening my queasiness, I head to the hospital library. Dr. Silverstein is unlikely to see me there. She believes me gone for the day, and I will be once I complete my research. By showing that the other surgeons' bedposts aren't full of murderous notches like Sam's is, I'll look less delusional to Tam. And Shawna. And now Dr. Silverstein too, who's probably still speechless over the fact that her favorite surgeon threatened to slap a restraining order on her new mentee. Soon the whole department will know. Word always gets around. Being the subject of gossip and whispers isn't what makes my stomach flip. It's losing my residency that does.

Something still puzzles me. Why hasn't Megan said anything about my battle with her new beau? I assumed his cozying up to her was to glean information about me—not that I've shared any—but maybe I'm wrong. Maybe their relationship is just one more *gotcha!* gift from him to me. Or maybe it's even simpler. Maybe he's just a libidinous male who enjoys spending time with smart blondes and then dumping them when he gets bored or they get too close.

Inside the hospital library, I sit behind the same computer monitor as last week and log in to HealthEMR. Though the room is once again vacant, it's noisier today than it was when I was here in the evening. Five stories below from a nearby window, a truck backs up and beeps annoyingly, and muffled voices from offices down the hallway make their way through the walls.

For the next two hours, using the same search criteria as before, I research five other surgeons over the last three years. This should give me a decent enough sample to confirm my suspicions.

In that time frame with these surgeons, I find four patients who underwent emergent surgery but died from other causes a relatively short time later. One was the result of a shooting in a bar fight. Two were clear-cut heart attacks confirmed on autopsy (unlike my father whose coronary artery disease was iffy). The fourth patient died from a ruptured cerebral aneurysm, again confirmed on autopsy and leaving little doubt as to the cause of death. None of the patients shared the same surgeon. No doubt there are other deaths I didn't find, but if the patients weren't autopsied, they wouldn't show up in my search.

My findings suggest these four deaths were random and legiti-mate and not the result of murder like Dr. Donovan's patients. When I finish recording them in my notebook, I sit back and massage my neck. A med student in a short white coat rummages through a shelf of radiology textbooks. I didn't even notice him come in.

Satisfied I now have more proof to support Dr. Donovan is a killer—though the how and why remain unclear—I weave my way down two hallways and four flights of stairs until I exit into the parking lot that holds my Civic. Pulling my sunglasses from my satchel, I raise my face to the hot glare and let the summer rays warm away the library's chill.

I don't allow myself to get cocky though. This new proof is flimsy, I know that. Although it won't come without risk, I need something physical. I need to find something tangible that ties Dr. Donovan to these deaths. Though I've been trying to avoid it, knowing how much committing a crime would break my father's heart, not to mention possibly land me in jail, I need to get inside the surgeon's house.

Since nothing suspicious showed up on the victims' autopsies, potassium chloride seems a likely and logical weapon. It's so efficient that it's used in lethal injections for those on death row. Both components are normal body electrolytes, and yet an overdose would effectively stop the heart. This means the drug would elude the pathologist, especially if the injection site didn't get close scrutiny. Then again, it demands a good-sized vein for delivery. How easy would that be to do?

Finding a vial of it in Dr. Donovan's home—or any other dubious drug—would not only strengthen my case, it would get me one step closer to keeping him from killing anyone else. Not that I could tell the police where I found it, of course, but it would at least objectively confirm my suspicions. The big hitch to my theory is that on occasion he's given Shelly access to his house to water his plants. A man with incriminating evidence in his home would be unlikely to pass out keys.

Still, I have to try.

Crossing the remaining distance to my car, I retrieve my phone from my satchel. Inside my Civic, I pull up my notebook app. There it is. 9536. The security code for Dr. Donovan's fancy-pants house in Cheshire Hill Estates.

Next I open my contacts. I find the number I typed into my phone when it was offered to me at Jen's barbecue. Before I press *Call*, my dad's voice materializes in my head. *Liza, are you sure you want to do this? Is this what a reasonably thinking person would do?*

The imaginary question makes me hesitate, my fingertip a hair above the phone tab. I think about the waitress and mechanic who could be Sam's next victims. I think about my mother at Home and Hearth Healing and her and Maisy's belief that Sam has been watching her through the trees and bushes, a belief I still don't know is grounded in fact or delusion. I think about my residency and how hard I've worked to become a pathologist.

I think about getting the police to believe me and getting Sam locked up once and for all.

I think about getting revenge for my father's death.

I press *Call* and phone Trey.

Asking Shelly for the keys is no longer an option.

24

W ithin three minutes of my call, Trey meets me by my car in the parking lot.

"That was quick," I say.

"I was about to grab a coffee in the atrium when you called." The way his gaze darts between the cars and his hands fidget with the drawstring of his surgical scrubs suggests caffeine is the last thing he needs.

I open the passenger door of my Civic. "Get in."

As I'm about to do the same on my side, he says, "I don't have time to go anywhere. Dr. Donovan and I are on call tonight."

"Weren't you just on call a couple days ago?"

"I'm covering for someone."

"Whatever. We're not driving anywhere. I just need to talk to you. Urgently." My pointed stare across the car roof must convince him because he climbs in.

The air conditioning has been running for a while, so the temperature inside the car is comfortable. Next to me, Trey smells of latex, probably a remnant of the many surgical gloves he dons throughout the day. His face shows a hint of beard regrowth but nothing like Waseem's afternoon moss. Staring at him, I wonder how best to proceed with my request. It's not one a reasonably thinking person would propose.

My silence must unnerve him because he runs the back of his hand over his mouth and says, "Oh God, you know, don't you?" He closes his eyes and rests his head against the seat. "Of course you do. You two were friends."

Though I have no idea what he's talking about, my curiosity is piqued. Instinct tells me to let him elaborate, so, like my psychiatrist, I simply nod and allow Trey to fill the silence.

"Shelly must've told you what I did, and after she died you put two and two together." Trey bangs his skull against the headrest and groans. "Of course you did. You're too smart not to."

Normally veering off topic annoys me, especially when I'm on a one-track brainwave like now, but this feels worth my time. "You're right, so why don't you tell me exactly what happened?"

His complexion sallows to a sickly shade. "I don't even know where to start," he whispers.

"Start at the beginning."

The surgical resident exhales loudly and slowly. Chest hair peeks out from the V of his scrub top, and his phone pokes out of the left pocket. "It started last Monday night when I was on call. I...a patient..." He buries his head in his hands. "Oh man, I don't think I can do this."

"Tell me, Trey. Just spit it out. It'll be easier that way." I try my best to sound like Dr. Lightfoot.

He straightens. "It was crazy on the ward. Four patients came through the ER after a car crash. Three needed urgent surgery. The nurses were pulled all over the place—new patients, old patients, post-op patients. Every patient and their uncle seemed to need something that night.

"One guy, a post-op bowel repair with pancreatitis, had been hollering for pain meds all night. I wrote an order for a one-time dose of morphine, but the nurses couldn't get to it right away. Finally, after I kept pestering them, Sarah, a new RN on the floor, unlocked the med-dispensing cabinet to do it. She grabbed a syringe and was about to pull up the drug when one of her patients stumbled up to us. His IV was ripped out, and blood was dripping down his arm and all over the floor. She cursed and promised she'd be right back, but she wasn't.

"Meanwhile, the poor guy with pancreatitis—that hurts like a son of a bitch, you know—kept crying for more pain meds. I could hear him all the way over from the drug cabinet." Trey's eyes plead with me. "I had to do something, Liza. He was hurting."

"What did you do?"

"I drew up the morphine myself, or at least I thought I did, and gave it to him."

"What's wrong with that?"

"I…" Trey's voice shakes. He swallows and tries again. "I grabbed the wrong vial and drew up one cc of hydromorphone instead of morphine. That's ten times…"

"More potent," I finish for him.

"Yes. So instead of ten milligrams of morphine, he got ten milligrams of hydromorphone."

"Couldn't you reverse it with Naloxone?"

"Yeah, if I would've realized my mistake in time." His voice rises in pitch, and his hands start to tremble. "Things were so crazy on the unit, insane. By the time I realized what I'd done he was already breathless and his heart was thready and his—"

"Slow down," I tell him. "It's okay."

Trey exhales and steadies his voice. "We tried to resuscitate him. As you already know, Shelly was the respiratory therapist working that night. But it was too late."

"What happened then?"

He snorts. "You already know. Why make me repeat it?"

Clearly he's convinced Shelly told me what happened, but I'm still completely in the dark. "I want to hear your version."

"It's awful, Liza." His eyes pin mine. "I feel like a piece of shit."

When nothing follows, I have to guess what comes next. "You didn't tell anyone you dosed the wrong drug, did you?"

His face flashes anger. "You know I didn't. I didn't admit to giving anything. Everyone figured the guy just died because he was an old man who had a tough surgery and severe pancreatitis. No one expected him to survive anyway."

"But Shelly figured it out." I try to hide my dismay.

"Yep. Said she walked past the room and saw me injecting a drug into the guy's IV line. She didn't think anything of it at the time, but once things settled down, she made the connection. Was going to report me right then and there."

"Why didn't she?"

"I begged her not to. Begged her to give me some time to come forward on my own. I told her the patient was old and really sick, and that it might not have been the overdose that killed him. I just hope they don't discover that small amount of drug missing." Trey squeezes his thighs, the tendons in his hands jutting like rip cords. "She agreed to give me a week."

This surprises me, but I stay silent. At least it explains what Shelly probably wanted to talk to me about in the cafeteria. *Since you're a doctor and all*, she had said.

He shifts in his seat toward me. "Remember when we went to O'Dell's?"

I nod.

"Remember I said Dr. Donovan did a solid for me when I was a second-year resident? I effed up big time. Could've been kicked out of the program, but he covered for me. A patient didn't die or anything like that," he adds quickly. "But it was still a serious mistake."

I don't enjoy hearing anything benevolent about Dr. Donovan, but I nod again.

"If this gets out about the morphine mix-up, I'll be a goner. No third strike allowed. Four years of med school and three-plus years of surgery residency down the toilet just like that. I'll be lucky to get a job draining boils."

"And then you saw Shelly in the cafeteria with me and…" When he doesn't respond to my fishing comment, only buries his face in his hands again, I think I know where this is headed. And it isn't to a good place. "You followed her out when she left."

With his face still buried, he nods. A sob escapes him.

"And when she threatened to tell her supervisor—or maybe even your supervisor—about the overdose, you..." I stop here, hoping he'll pick up where I left off.

"Her death wasn't my fault, I swear. It was an accident and—" Another sob swallows his words. He roughly wipes his eyes and cheeks with his palms and implores me. "You have to believe me. It was an accident." He exhales slowly, and his torso deflates. "God, it actually feels good to finally get it off my chest. I was going crazy holding it in."

"And yet you haven't said much of anything." My voice hardens. "What happened?"

"We were talking in the hospital garden, just walking around. Somehow we ended up near that stairwell that leads down to the fountain. You know the one I'm talking about?"

"I do. My advisor warned me about it."

"Exactly." He slaps his thighs as if I just proved his point. "I was begging Shelly not to say anything about the morphine mix-up."

Though I'm trying hard to hide my judgment, my face must sour because he adds, "The guy was old, Liza, and he was really sick. He probably wouldn't have survived anyway. What good would it do to ruin my career over something that was inevitable?"

I grind my teeth. My opinion of Trey nosedives. Cowards are only one step above bullies in my book. I swallow my disgust and hope it doesn't show. "Of course. What happened then? How did she die?"

"Well, I didn't kill her if that's what you're implying." His quickness to defend himself fuels my ire.

"I'm not implying anything."

"I just...well...when she started to leave, saying she'd waited long enough for me to come clean about the hydromorphone, I grabbed her. She tried to jerk away, and I moved forward and... well...maybe I pushed just a bit to try and keep hold of her, and then she slipped and...and...oh God, Liza." His chest heaves. "She fell down those steps—Jesus, they're concrete, you know?—and conked her head on the ledge at the bottom. Had she hit anywhere else, she probably would've survived, but she hit right on her temple. Probably ruptured her—"

"I don't need an anatomy lesson, Trey." The car suddenly feels like an inferno. I crank the air and try to shake the disdain from my voice. "Her body's in the morgue. The autopsy's today. Megan's observing it."

His eyes widen. "You won't tell anyone, will you? The place was empty and nobody saw." He reaches over the gear shift and grips my hands. "Please, Liza, please. What good would it do to say anything now? It won't change anything. It won't bring that man back."

My initial instinct is to report him. To rat him out and make him take responsibility for both deaths, a move of which I'm sure my father would applaud. *Now you're making rational choices, tiger.* Then I realize how much Trey's situation benefits me. How useful it is to have something to lord over him. I'm not proud of this decision. In fact, I might need a shower for just thinking it. But desperate times and all...

I file my father's advice away. "Listen up, Trey. I'll keep this to myself, but I need you to do something for me, something that's going to make you uncomfortable, but I need you to not question me on it."

He slowly releases my hands. "Are you blackmailing me?"

"Yes."

He blinks. "Seriously? You're not joking?"

"Oh please." I swat the air at him. "Don't get up on your high horse now. Besides, maybe blackmail is the wrong word, especially since what I need you to do will ultimately help you. It'll make this whole thing go away."

His eyes narrow. "What are you talking about?" Wariness in his tone. "What do you need me to do?"

"I need you to get me Dr. Donovan's keys. Early tomorrow morning while he's in surgery, so I can copy them before teaching rounds."

Trey straightens to full posture. It's easy to read the shocked disapproval on his face. In fact, in his present state, his expressions are so discernable he could model for those emotion cards Dr. Lightfoot used to show me.

"What are you talking about? I can't do that."

His sudden sanctity makes me want to slap him. "You just confessed to killing two people. Sainthood doesn't suit you."

He shakes his head. "I didn't kill them. They were accidents. Both of them."

"Yeah." My voice drips with sarcasm. "I'm sure the police will be totally cool with that explanation."

He sags back down.

"Look," I say. "Dr. Donovan isn't who you think he is. He's a killer. A *real* killer, not just an idiot like you."

Trey seems so baffled by what I just said he doesn't appear to notice my insult. "That's the most ridiculous thing I've ever heard."

I don't want to give him details. I worry he can't keep his yap shut. "You're going to have to trust me, but once this is over, I'll tell you everything."

"You're insane."

"And you're a killer who could go to prison for a very long time."

That shuts him up.

"He's been stalking my family," I say. "He killed my father. Did he tell you he threatened me with a restraining order today?"

Trey looks even more dazed. "No, why?"

"Because he knows I'm on to him. Also because I got the cops to question him about Shelly's death. I have him on tape threatening her."

Trey's mouth hangs open for a good five seconds. "Good God, I don't understand any of this."

"You don't have to understand it. Not now. You just have to get me his keys. Grab them while he's scrubbing in for his first case. Tell him you've got to see a patient urgently. Whatever. Just make up an excuse and meet me here in the lot with his keys at seven fifteen tomorrow morning. If you do this, I promise no one will suspect you in Shelly's death."

He swallows but says nothing, his eyes glazed.

I snap my fingers in front of his face. "Can you do that for me? Can you get his keys from his locker while he's scrubbing in?"

Trey nods. "It wouldn't be the first time I've had to fetch something for him. I know the combination. Right-hand man, you know?" he says weakly.

"Good. So you'll do it?"

"Sounds like I don't have a choice. I'll try, anyway."

"Don't try. Do. And," I grab his wrist and push my fingertips into it. "If I need your help again, you'll say, 'Whatever you need, Liza,' right?" When he says nothing, I push deeper into the nerve space and repeat, "Right?"

Finally, he nods, his Adam's apple bobbing up, then down.

"Good. Trust me, Trey. I'm going to find proof that'll put Dr. Donovan away. Then all of this will be behind us and we can get on with our residencies and our lives."

Early the next morning, Trey gives me Dr. Donovan's keys. His hands shake so badly I have to steady them in my own.

"It's okay," I tell him. "I'll get them back to you as soon as I can. No one will ever know."

Unfortunately, the drugstore with the key duplicator doesn't open until eight. I was stupid not to have checked. I bounce my thighs on the seat of my car and drum the steering wheel in impatience. As soon as the business's doors unlock, I rush inside and have four big keys and two small ones copied. If only I could duplicate the emergency key inside the key fob, but that's beyond the drug store's capability, and even a hardware store probably couldn't—or wouldn't—do it for me. For now, the regular keys will have to do.

By the time I get back to the hospital and return the keys to Trey, it's eight forty. I'm ten minutes late for teaching rounds. When I whip open the door to the Death Chamber, I apologize to Dr. Thomas for my tardiness. As usual, he's at the head of the table in front of the master microscope. Martin is to his left. The other first-years are in their usual spots, their gazes glued to their viewing heads. None of them look up at me, which I find strange.

Dr. Thomas stands and asks Martin to take over teaching rounds. To me, he says, "Let's go to my office, Liza." Despite the kindness in his tone, it doesn't put me at ease.

I trudge behind him, and when we reach his dark-hued office, I'm not surprised to find Dr. Silverstein already there. Dr. Thomas indicates I take the seat to the right of her, and then he sits in a large leather chair behind the desk. After a long pause he nods to Dr. Silverstein, indicating that she start. I already know what's coming. Maybe he thinks it'll be gentler coming from her.

"Liza," she begins, her hands folded on her lap, her loose pants skimming the carpet. Her hair is back in a braid, and her face makes a half smile, half frown. "I'll be honest. This whole thing with Dr. Donovan has us confused. The possibility of a restraining order, his accusations you're stalking him, his claims you sent the police his way. None of it makes any sense."

I start to protest, but she raises a hand.

"Truthfully, I don't know what to believe. We need to sort some things out, but in the meantime, Dr. Thomas and I feel…"

When Dr. Silverstein's words fade off, my program director steps in. "We feel it might be good for you to take some time off. Just until we resolve this issue."

"You're suspending me?"

Dr. Thomas shifts forward in his squeaky chair. "Suspend is a harsh word. It's more like a leave of absence."

I look back and forth between my two supervisors and bite the inside of my lower lip until I taste blood. My stomach swirls, and I worry I'll need to race to the bathroom again. Ever since my mother's brain reached the point of no return, neuropathology is the only thing I've wanted to do. A suspension will tarnish me forever.

My chest rises and falls, each breath heavier than the one before it. "You don't understand," I say. "Dr. Donovan isn't who you think he is. He's a—"

"Dr. Donovan is a skilled surgeon who's served this institution since 2012." My program director's tone suggests nothing else but this could be true about the man.

"No, he's a killer."

Dr. Thomas shakes his head. "Now why would you make such an absurd statement?"

"Because it's true!"

The two pathologists exchange glances. I realize I'm blowing it. This is not how I wanted things to go, especially when I see my advisor's shoulders sag and her eyes fill with pity. Given my mother's illness, my father's early death, and my own messed-up personality, pity is a look I recognize well.

"Liza, dear, I wonder if there's someone…you know…maybe someone you could talk to?"

I breathe in deeply and conjure whatever calm I can find. "A psychiatrist isn't going to help anything. What I need is Dr. Donovan's arrest. He killed my father." When Dr. Thomas opens his mouth to interject, I quickly add, "And he's killed at least six other patients. I can prove it with my research." My words speed up. "The first one was in 2014. Since then, he's killed at least one patient a year, and now he's stalking—"

"That's enough." Instead of sounding angry, my program director sounds sad, like when my dad told me he didn't think my mom would ever get better.

I close my eyes tightly and then open them. More deep breathing. "You both think I'm delusional, don't you? You think I've made this all up. That I'm crazy. That I've become my mother."

Dr. Silverstein scoots her chair over to mine. She takes my hands. "We don't think you're crazy, Liza. That's an awful word."

Her voice is so soothing I want to crawl up inside of it and surrender. Why keep up with this hopeless task anyway? No one believes me. Not Tam, not Shawna, not my attending physicians.

She continues. "We think maybe you stumbled upon something that's confusing you, that's all. With the stress of your residency, the difficulties with your mother, your father's death, well maybe you're…"

"Maybe you're imagining things that aren't there," Dr. Thomas finishes for her.

I laugh. It's harsher than I would like. "That's the very definition of delusional." I retrieve my satchel from the floor. Escape from this stifling room is paramount. "I won't fight you on this suspension for now," I say, my hand on the doorknob. "But I will show you. I'll prove to you I'm not making this up. Dr. Donovan is a killer, and if we don't do something, more people will die."

With that I leave the room and storm out of the department. While I stomp toward the hospital exit, I slam every door that will allow itself to be slammed. Frustration and fear sting my eyes. My entire body shakes. Blood rushes behind my eardrums. Not since I broke the girl's arms in Shawna's defense have I felt so out of control. In fact, were I not so convinced of my findings, I too might think I've slipped off the deep end.

"But I'm not delusional," I say out loud in my car. "I'm not. What I've found is real. I know it is. Doesn't matter if I'm skipping my psych appointments or not."

As I squeal out of the parking lot, a sudden, horrible, awful thought hits me. One that makes me almost slam into a truck at a stop sign: Every time my mother rants about the king burning her at the stake or Hitler sending her to the gas chamber, she probably says the very same thing.

25

From a distance, I stare up at Dr. Donovan's house on its coveted lot in Cheshire Hill Estates. There's no movement behind the main floor windows, nor those of the rounded turret, at least not what I can see from my car. The French doors of the second-floor balcony are quiet too.

Then again, why wouldn't they be? It's only been forty minutes since I flew out of Dr. Thomas's office. The rest of the world is still at work. It's only us suspended, delusional lunatics who are free to do as we please this morning.

As far as I'm concerned, Dr. Donovan can take his restraining order application and shove it down his narcissistic piehole. We both know it's more for show. Still, he bested me. He managed to get me suspended.

Bravo, Sam, bravo.

A cardinal flits onto the surgeon's mailbox and starts pecking at the fancy bricks. A few minutes later the motor of a lawn mower down the street scares it off. I saw the landscaper exit his truck a short time ago. I'll have to wait for him to clear out, or at least move on to the backyard. Within seconds, the smell of freshly cut grass fills my car.

What a fool I was to think anyone would believe me. In my naiveté, I actually thought the police would have nabbed Sam by now. I gave Tam my pictures. I gave her my research findings. I gave her my recording. Was I wrong to trust someone so close to me? Maybe my mother's history is clouding Tam's judgment. Maybe I should have gone to a different cop, like the one who took my statement the night of my attack in the gym parking lot. Ben, wasn't it?

Too late now. In Tam's and Shawna's opinion, I'm cuckoo. Dr. Thomas and Dr. Silverstein think so too.

A sharp pain shoots through my jaw, and I realize I'm grinding my teeth. I try to relax my facial muscles. In Tam's defense, she did instigate Dr. Donovan's questioning by the Morganville PD. That's something. And even though I now know Trey killed Shelly—at least accidentally—and not Sam, I feel no remorse for sending the cops sniffing Sam's way. After all, he's killed seven people. What does it matter if he's accused of one more?

It occurs to me I didn't ask Trey how he moved Shelly's body from the bottom of the steps to the woods. Leaving her in the hospital gardens would've been risky, so I can see why he didn't, especially if someone saw them walk out there together, but I wonder how he managed to move her. For one thing, he must've been in an area free of security cameras. The sitting area is tucked down inside the garden maze, and with all those trees he'd be well hidden.

My mind visualizes him concealing her body in the trees by the steps, bringing his car around to a closer parking lot, plopping her in a wheelchair to make her look like a patient, and wheeling her up the nearby ramp and out the maze. It was late afternoon on a Saturday and probably deserted, so I suppose this is feasible, especially if there wasn't much blood on the concrete. Maybe the less I know the better.

I stare at the surgeon's house, finding my courage. I may not always make the best choices, but I'm smart enough to understand the consequences of breaking into someone's home should I get caught. But what's my alternative? Let things remain as is? Let Sam go on killing patients just so I can get back into my residency program? That would sink me to his level. Make me his accomplice, even.

No, I have to do this. I have to see if there's something inside his house that links him to the murders. Even if I can't show it to the police without letting them know how I found it, I'll be one step closer to bringing Sam down.

The lawn mower stops. The landscaper adjusts his bandanna over his bald head, wipes sweat from his face and neck, and starts toward the backyard.

Aside from the cardinal who's just returned to his mailbox perch, I'm now alone. I step out of my car and stroll up to Dr. Donovan's driveway. From there I take a stone pathway that winds around the house toward the back door, inside of which I assume another security panel awaits. I try not to look around. Acting like I belong there will make me less noticeable, or so I reason. Nothing about me stands out. I'm still dressed in my work pants, blouse, and loafers. I could just be a friend stopping by or someone watering the plants.

Once I'm out of sight at the back door, I slip on a pair of hospital gloves and ready the keys, wondering again about the sensibility of my actions. Dr. Donovan could be watching me from a security phone app this very moment. I scan the area thoroughly but see no camera.

Still, my actions seem justified. An incident from fourth grade springs to mind. Shawna had gotten a new pen in her Easter basket, one with a thick cap and a bunny eating a sparkly carrot on its shaft. One day it disappeared. In order to prove Carla, a brute of a girl with broad shoulders and a perpetual frown, stole it, I had to dig around in her backpack during recess when all the other kids were outside. Sure enough, there it was, nestled against a half-eaten candy bar and a yoyo, both of which were probably stolen as well. Although I got reprimanded by Miss Simpson for snooping inside Carla's bag, I was at least able to return the pen to Shawna. Her joy at getting it back made the violation of Carla's property worth it.

Isn't this the same thing, only on a more grown-up level?

One by one I start inserting the larger keys. The third one's the charm. I open the door and step inside. As I suspected, a security panel sits nearby on the wall, its warning alarm beeping. Praying the code's still the same, I type in 9536. The alarm silences, and I exhale, unaware I was holding my breath. I lock the door behind me.

A state-of-the-art kitchen greets me: stainless steel appliances, a six-burner gas stove, and ecru cabinets that blend perfectly with the speckled granite counter tops and central island. To the left is a glass breakfast table with a chrome base, and as I wander across the dark-wood flooring into the living and dining rooms, it's easy to see Dr. Donovan's taste leans toward modern and minimalist. The furnishings are sparse, and stark stretches of wall sit between the occasional bold print or painting. Arched doorways with exquisite wood trim separate one room from the next so that a continuous flow is maintained.

Shelly wasn't kidding about his obsession with plants. Greenery adds a burst of life everywhere—ironic given his trail of death—and some plants sprout such exotic-looking leaves and flowers I wonder if they originate from other countries. Maybe he got his green thumb from his mother. Shelly mentioned the woman was a renowned gardener. Wonder what she'd think of her son now.

It seems unlikely anything incriminating would be found within these open spaces, so I take a look in a half-bath off the laundry room. A pedestal sink void of cabinets allows no place for hidden objects. Next to the bathroom is a door with another security panel, and I assume this leads to the garage. A quick peek confirms it. No beige Taurus inside though. I wonder where he keeps it, assuming it was indeed him who followed me.

Next I wander into the primary bedroom. The king-sized headboard matches the pale-wood furniture, its surface so smooth it feels like butter. How my mother would love its design. I move on to the en suite bathroom, where I encounter a space so large and so appealingly tiled with black and gray flooring that were I to live here I'm not sure I would ever leave. I poke around a bit, opening vanity drawers and cabinets more out of curiosity than of an expectation of finding evidence.

I return to the bedroom and sit on the bed. With a gloved hand, I rub the immaculate down duvet, its fabric clean and white like clouds. Lying back on it, I inhale the lingering sandalwood scent of Dr. Donovan.

"Look at me, Sam," I whisper, making angel wings on his bed. "Who's got the advantage now?" It's intoxicating to get this intimate glimpse into his personal world.

After a few more minutes of cottony repose, I rise from the bed. I need to get moving. My father's voice in my head is nudging me on. It's barely after ten a.m., so there's no worry Dr. Donovan will come home, but I shouldn't linger longer than necessary. Though the other houses on the street are mostly silent, I can't be sure my car won't raise suspicions. I smooth out the duvet and readjust any pillows my respite has nudged out of place.

Moving onto the massive dresser, I find a lot of precisely folded socks, underwear, and gym clothes. Same for the impressive walk-in closet, where I sift through every drawer, feel inside every polished shoe, and rummage through boxes and bags. I go through suit and pants pockets too. Though most of the clothes look expensive and tailored, a section in the back of the closet holds bland chinos, boring polos, and leather loafers not unlike my own, along with some other nondescript clothing. His blend-in garb, no doubt. I pull my phone from my pocket to take a few pictures. Then I head to the upper level.

Upstairs I find two bedrooms connected by a Jack-and-Jill bathroom. One bedroom contains typical furniture with a bed, an armoire, and a small sitting area. The other serves as a gym with a nice collection of weights, tubing, and cardio machines, all positioned on top of generous mats that protect the flooring. Leave it to a narcissist like Dr. Donovan to make movers carry his gym equipment up a flight of stairs. Though I haven't been to the basement yet, I assume this means it's unfinished.

I wander into the last room on the upper level. From the outside of the house, I initially assumed it was the primary bedroom given the small walkout balcony beyond the French doors, but it's actually a large den. An incredible den, one that might be the size of my entire studio apartment. Dark-wood shelves make up two of the walls, a fireplace occupies the third, and the fourth wall contains the glass French doors that open onto the balcony. On the right, inside the turret which makes up that corner of the room, sits a massive desk.

I cross over to it and look out the turret windows. From here I can see my car, as well as a good portion of the neighborhood. Both the cardinal and the landscaper's truck are gone, and no other life presents itself. Still, a squeeze of urgency tightens my chest. This is a big house to search. If I don't find anything in the den, I'll quickly snoop around in the basement.

I run my gloved hands along the glossy surface of the surgeon's mahogany desk. It's obvious he spared no expense in renovating this house. Extravagant. Opulent. Showy yet sophisticated. It's Dr. Donovan to a T. Except when he's out stalking.

Rifling through the top two drawers on the left, I find nothing concerning. Simply pens, legal pads, printing paper, and other office supplies. The bottom drawer, which is the largest, is locked. From my front pocket, I pull out the keys I copied and separate out the two smaller ones. The gods are smiling upon me because the first one I try opens the desk drawer. Inside are thin metal bars with files suspended from them. Flipping through the folders, I find the usual: tax information, home-related papers, personal documents. For now, none of them interest me. None of them are capable of killing someone.

I start to close the desk drawer. *Wait, what's that?* I get down on my knees for a closer look.

Shoved far back behind the suspended files lies a small lock box. It's about the length and width of a standard envelope but measures at least four inches deep. A small keyhole sits in the center.

As I remove the metal box and place it on the desk, something rolls inside it. With tremulous fingers, I try the second small key.

The box unlocks.

I'm aware of my increased breathing, the uptick in my heart rate, the moisture in my palms beneath my gloves. This could be it.

This could be the proof I need to take the next step in outing the killer surgeon.

Slowly, I lift the top of the metal box. Despite what I see inside it, my muscles relax and my lungs exhale with relief.

Because I was right.

I close my eyes, and when I open them again, the vial of potassium chloride is still there, along with three unused syringes. There's no reason in the world to keep this drug in your home, especially locked inside a box, hidden away from where any girlfriend or plant-waterer would look.

Unless you're a murderer.

And I've just proved Dr. Donovan is.

Knowing I can't take the vial with me (who would believe I found it there?) and knowing a picture won't do much good either (someone could say I planted it), I take a few photos with my phone anyway. My hands have never been so unsteady. Maybe I can't use my find as proof for the police, but at least it's proof of something else: I'm not delusional. I'm not imagining things that aren't there. Dr. Donovan is a murderer.

After replacing the box where I found it, I push the chair back from the desk and stand. Just as I'm wondering whether to search anything else in the house, the alarm system chirps.

My heart jumps to my throat. I recognize those chirps. They're the same chirps my parents' alarm system made whenever the door was opened or closed. "That way I know if you guys are sneaking in or out," my father would joke to Ned and me.

In this case, someone is coming in.

Dr. Donovan is home.

26

I stand frozen in Dr. Donovan's den, my heart galloping in my throat. The triplet of chirps repeats as the downstairs door shuts. This is followed by a few footsteps. After that there is absolute silence. I imagine Dr. Donovan standing in the foyer, or by the garage, or by whatever door he entered, head askance, wondering if he forgot to set the alarm.

Stupid. I should have remembered to reset it. At least then I wouldn't have made him suspicious. My gaze darts from the den door to the turret windows behind the desk and then back again. *Stupid. Stupid. Stupid.* This time it's my dad screaming it in my head.

Or maybe it's even worse. Maybe Dr. Donovan has an app on his phone that tells him his alarm system is disarmed. Otherwise why would he be home so early?

Then I remember. He's post-call. Trey told me they were both on duty last night. Maybe Titus McCall's surgeons leave early after a busy call shift. Either way, I was stupid. *Stupid, stupid, stupid.*

I could be arrested. Worse, if Dr. Donovan convinces the police I'm delusional, I could be committed.

My pulse shoots higher. I'm unused to this type of panic. Every muscle in my body quavers with uncertainty, and my mind races to find the best course of action. I could hide in a closet. I could wait until he's asleep. He's post-call. Maybe he'll rest. I could try to run past him, his surprise at seeing me slowing him down.

Still no sounds from below. Has he already slipped into the primary bedroom to sleep?

When his voice breaks the silence, I jump. "Well, well, well, I seem to have a visitor." Although he's down below, his words carry upstairs over the banister. His tone is frightening in its playfulness. "Why don't you come down and chat with me, Liza?"

I take a slow step back from the desk, hoping the floor doesn't creak. How is he so certain it's me? Did he see my Civic down the street? If he's been following me, he'll recognize that Dyno Blue Pearl color. Or maybe he has a security camera app after all.

Stupid, stupid, stupid.

I squeeze my stubby nails into my palms and edge closer to one of the five turret windows. *Oh, my little tiger*, my father's voice groans in my head, *what have you done?*

From downstairs I hear, "I underestimated you, that's for sure. With your plain-Jane clothes and penny loafers, I assumed you were simply a microscope nerd, but you're far more determined than I realized. You're quite the worthy opponent."

His voice sounds closer than before, and I imagine him wandering through the rooms, searching for me.

"The police mentioned you've been snooping through the medical records of my former patients. They even asked me about some of them." He continues in a devilish tone. "And I have the sneakiest suspicion it was you who gave them that recording of Shelly and me, may she rest in peace. And in return she gave you my house key. I had asked for it back, but I guess she decided to punish me. Didn't the two of you become quite cozy." He chuckles, and the fact he does so at a time like this chills me.

But I'm relieved he doesn't suspect Trey of stealing the keys. I'm also relieved Tam passed my research findings on. She doesn't completely think I'm nuts.

I keep inching toward the windows, adrenaline surging through my body.

"Of course, once I told them about you, told them about your mentally ill mother and your dead father, well, they now see it for what it is. You're simply a sick young woman who has a weird obsession with me." His voice fades and then grows louder again, and I wonder if he's just searched the laundry room and bathroom. "Poor thing, you've gone off the deep end. Bonkers. Loco. The craziest of the crazy train." His laugh makes my skin crawl.

No longer caring about making noise, I close the last of the distance to the windows. The roof from which the turret extends is only a few feet down. Though it's slanted, I could jump onto it and hopefully grab hold of the rust-colored shingles to avoid sliding off too quickly. From there to the ground is only one story. I can hang down by my arms and make the jump.

"Don't you get it?" His voice grows louder. Shoes thump hardwood. He must be climbing the stairs. "No one believes you. They think you're a paranoid schizophrenic like your looney-tunes mother."

My fists clench at his cruel words about my mom, but I resist the urge to confront him. My father would sag in relief at that decision. I unlatch a window and raise it. There should be just enough room for me to fit. Barely.

"In a weird way, this is actually your saving grace," Dr. Donovan says, very close now. "By making sure no one believes you, by making myself the victim and you the deranged stalker, I won't have to hurt you again."

I kick out the screen. So he did send the junkie to get rid of me. Did he kill the guy after the failed mission? A leave-no-witnesses-behind kind of thing? After the police identified the body, I learned through HealthEMR that he had indeed been a patient of Dr. Donovan's in the past, but for a relatively minor procedure.

I start squeezing my body out the window, trying to find the best angle to escape without falling headfirst onto the shingles below.

"How fun to see another Larkin curl up and die, at least metaphorically this time around." His voice sounds like it's coming from the hallway. It takes all my energy not to crawl back inside and kick the crap out of him for talking so callously about killing my father.

I escape from the window and lower myself to the shingles below. When he speaks again, his voice is so close he must be in the den. "But I'm warning you, let this go." No playfulness in his tone now. Just a cold, cutting evilness. "I've taken your career and your reputation. I won't hesitate to take something else—or maybe even some*one* else—from your life too."

With my arms out for balance, I totter my way to the end of the slanted roof, its shingles rasping under my weight. When I reach the ledge, I squat down, take a deep breath, and go over the side, nothing but my gloved hands clinging to the gutters. My muscles strain from the load, but my arms are strong enough to hold me. Sam is looking out the window now. I hear and feel him rather than see him, but I know he's there.

I jump to the ground, which is only four feet below me, and roll a few times before righting myself. With grass staining my slate-gray pants and mulch sticking to my loafers, I hobble and then run away down the yard, my ankle the only thing hurting. While I'm fleeing, Sam calls out the window, "And really, Liza, with your personal circle so small, can you afford to lose anyone else?"

Panting and sweating, I race to my car. I have to get to Home and Hearth Healing.

27

Inside my mother's center, I sit at one of the dining room tables with her and Maisy while they finish lunch. The crust from a piece of quiche remains on my mom's plate, along with three cucumber slices she's picked out of her salad. She's never been a fan of the vegetable, and I take comfort in knowing some things remain the same.

Today is a fair day for her, which means she's not Emily like on her good days, but neither is she Joan of Arc like on her bad days, nor Anna the Holocaust prisoner like on her worst ones. On fair days she becomes Meryl Streep, and currently she's pontificating for me in great detail the toils of working on a movie set. Instead of a coherent narration, her speech is disorganized and difficult to follow, and for reasons I don't understand, she's calling me Betty. I don't think I could look less like a Betty if I tried.

But at least she's safe. For now.

I've informed the staff I'm going to stay with her tonight and possibly longer. Though such a thing is not encouraged, it's also not forbidden. It's an upscale private facility that wouldn't exist if not for the pocketbooks of the patients' families. Occasionally, a son or daughter or other loved one visits from a distance and is welcome to stay for a short time (emphasis on the *short*). They sleep in their family member's room on the chair that folds down into a bed. As such, only one family member or friend is allowed at a time. There have to be some rules, I suppose.

Dr. Dhar heard of my plans to stay while he was making his rounds and asked why, especially since I live nearby. I wanted to tell him my mother might be in danger and I've received threats against her, but that didn't seem the smartest move. Instead, I simply said I had some time off and wanted to reconnect with her (no need to involve the word *suspension*). When he looked at me with concern, I assured him I wasn't losing it, or, to quote Sam, I wasn't becoming "the craziest of the crazy train." Like so many other people in my life now, Dr. Dhar didn't seem convinced.

While my mother talks about lighting and sound and the hours spent in the makeup chair, Maisy laughs and claps beside her. I scan the dining room, the food smells making me queasy. Like everywhere else in the building, decorative iron bars cover all the windows. Though the bird-on-branches design is elegant, the bars mean only one thing: no one can get out. For me, the assurance lies in the fact that no one can get in either. At least not without checking into reception first.

Still, despite the facility's security measures, my mother's safety isn't guaranteed. How can it be? I simply can't take the risk, no matter how small, of Sam gaining access, not when he's made threats against her. But I can't stay here indefinitely. I need to keep an eye on him. So I may have no recourse but to call my brother for help.

I wipe at the grass stains on my knees, the pants probably ruined for good. There was no time to go home and change. I sped directly from Dr. Donovan's house to here. My mother has what I need for an overnight stay. A shower, deodorant, and a spare toothbrush from the supply closet will do. Though she's not as tall as me and is sparrow thin, I should be able to fit into a pair of her looser shorts and a T-shirt, maybe the one from my father that says *Music Teachers Never Look Bach*. She's always loved it, but it's too big for her now.

My heart rate has returned to baseline, and my muscles are no longer tight. Even my twinged ankle from the jump feels better. But I still feel a low-grade unease. I expect the police to charge in at any minute, just as they did for Pete Parsons after Shelly died. My DNA is all over Dr. Donovan's bed from my ill-thought-out antics. I was so smug invading his space, as if I had the upper hand. *You should have listened to me*, my father says in my mind, his face sad. It would be easy to prove I was there. I guess this means Round 6 goes to Sam. Then again, I found the potassium chloride, so maybe it's a draw.

But as an hour passes and then another, I realize he must not have reported me after all. The only conclusions I can draw from this are: One, he doesn't want the cops to find incriminating evidence in his house that he doesn't think he can hide or get rid of. Two, he wants to let things simmer and avoid any more attention on himself now that he's convinced the police of my mental instability. Or three, he's enjoying our fight too much to stop.

When I got to Home and Hearth Healing, I texted Tam and asked where things stood with Dr. Donovan, hoping she could find out what he's been spewing about me. She hasn't responded. Maybe she's worried she'll encourage my crusade further. I'd also like to know what's going on with Shelly's investigation. Now that Dr. Donovan is no longer a suspect (if his words are to be believed), they must be leaning toward Pete Parsons again. And why wouldn't they? He's an angry and emotionally abusive ex-husband who plays tricks on institutionalized patients. If I hadn't heard Trey's confession about Shelly slipping down the concrete steps in the hospital garden, I'd put my money on Pete too.

I check my phone for the hundredth time. Still nothing from Tam. I texted Shawna a while ago too, but she said she was out jogging and couldn't talk. With each passing second, my angst grows and my sense of control diminishes. I feel like there's something I'm missing, something I haven't thought of, and that uncertainty fills me with dread.

My mother and Maisy leave the dining room and stroll to the rec room as if I'm not even there. I follow, and for the next fifteen minutes, I watch my mom direct a group of residents (some active participants, others passive) in an incoherent play over by the ping-pong table. Then my phone finally buzzes. Tam is calling.

"Thank God," I mutter. I retreat to a quieter spot near a couch where a sleeping man wears mittens and a winter hat in a room that's already too warm. I start talking the moment I accept the call. "Tam, I need to know—"

She cuts me off. Her voice is high-pitched and strained and far more emotional than I've ever heard it. When she tells me what's wrong, I can hardly breathe. I now realize what I was missing.

I messed up. Horribly. I thought only of my mother, the need to keep her safe. Meanwhile, I forgot about the other people who make up my inner circle.

Sam didn't forget though.

And now one of them is in the hospital.

28

As I race to Titus McCall, I understand one thing. Although I wasn't delusional about Dr. Donovan's extracurricular activities, I *was* delusional to think he and I were an equal match. In reality, I'm nothing but a lightweight boxer in his heavyweight world. While I'm licking my wounds, he's out hurting people. While I'm worrying about my mother, he's going after someone else. He's outmaneuvered me every step of the way.

And now Shawna's the one paying for it.

"Relax," I tell myself at a red light on Sherlock Road. "You can't know it was him." My self-assurances do nothing, and it takes all my willpower not to blast through the intersection on squealing tires.

As I drive the winding, wooded course of Waverly Boulevard to the hospital, I replay my phone conversation with Tam.

"What happened?" I asked her.

Tam gulped. "I don't know for sure. All I know is I was home with Seth when Shawna went jogging and got hit by a car. The car took off and she—"

"It was a hit and run?"

"I think so, but by the time I got to the hospital the ambulance was gone. All I know is what the nurse told me. She said a Good Samaritan happened by and called for help, and now my wife is in surgery, and Liza I need you here. I don't know this world like you do."

As soon as Tam said the word *surgery*, I knew Dr. Donovan was behind the accident. His next move in the ring. I don't know how, but somehow he made it happen. Made me think my mother was the one at risk, knowing all along I'd watch over her, leaving him free to hurt someone else. I should've realized he knew about Shawna. Not only was she at my college graduation and my dad's funeral, Sam the stalker probably followed me to her house. He's a much better spy than me. Stupid of me to think otherwise. And he might be operating on my friend this very minute.

In case I'm wrong though, I told the Home and Hearth Healing staff to watch my mother like a royal guard. If I could be in two places at once, I'd gladly cut myself in half.

When I get to Titus McCall, I park in the lot closest to the surgical unit and fly out of my vehicle, catching my satchel on the side mirror. I'm still dressed in my grass-stained work slacks, compliments of the jump off Dr. Donovan's roof, and my no-frills blouse now bears pit stains from my high-adrenaline state. Not only do I see them, I smell them as I whip open the hospital door and sprint to the second-floor surgical wing.

When I reach the waiting room, panting and breathless (*Oh, Ned, if you could see your Teflon sister now*), I stop so short I almost fall.

Someone gasps. Although a few people are scattered about, it's probably me who made the vocalization because my suspicions were right. My nightmare continues to unfold.

There, talking to Tam, in the same tailored scrubs and monogrammed surgical cap he wore the day I first observed him in this very waiting room over six weeks ago, is Dr. Donovan. Only this time he's not updating a mother and teenage son on their loved one's surgery. This time he's updating Tam on Shawna's.

I hear the words "suffered a compound femur fracture, hairline fracture of the pelvis, bleeding liver laceration, and a splenic hematoma" come from his thin lips, and I see Tam sigh in relief when he adds, "but she'll be okay. I got her through the worst of it. The orthopedic surgeon is finishing up now with the leg fracture."

"Oh thank God," Tam says, her hands cupped over her mouth. She lowers them. "Thank God you passed by when you did."

"That's a dangerous road to jog on." As he says the words, his eyes find mine. There's a joy in them that matches the wickedness of his smile, which Tam no doubt believes comes from his happiness to give her good news. But I know that look is meant for me. It's a look to remind me I was knocked down in this match long ago.

Tam glances over her shoulder to see who Dr. Donovan is looking at. When she spots me, she turns around and hugs me, something she's never done before.

"Thanks for coming." She does a quick swipe over her red eyes. "When I called you, I didn't know what was going on. Dropped Seth off with our neighbor and hurried over here. I was so worried Shawna would—"

Dr. Donovan squeezes Tam's shoulder. "No need for your mind to go there. She'll be okay. Healing will take a while, but she's young and healthy and will do great." He smiles at me a beat too long before returning to Tam.

Her body visibly relaxes. Whether she even realizes this man is Dr. Donovan or not, I don't know. In her state, she might not have processed his name.

The question is quickly put to rest. "Liza," she says. "If Dr. Donovan hadn't driven down Waverly Boulevard when he did, Shawna might not have...she might not have made it."

The surgeon shrugs in false modesty, a shrug I've seen him make several times before. How am I the only one to spot his duplicity? I can read him as well as I can read myself.

"I have the day off and was running some errands," he says. "Luckily I saw her in time."

"He rode along in the ambulance with her," Tam says to me. "Took her right to the OR."

Bullshit, I want to scream. He's the one who did this. I don't know the details, but I know he's behind it. How can Tam swallow his fiction? From the absolute reverence she's bestowing upon him, I see she has.

Once again I have the sudden urge to clap. Sam has performed splendidly. How brilliant to save the wife of the cop I've been talking to. Round 7 goes to him without dispute. Tam's gratitude for the surgeon will only make her disbelief of me grow. Whatever I say against him now will make me look more delusional. If he were a killer, why would he hit Shawna with his car only to save her in surgery? Even my father would question my logic. "Liza," he'd say, his lips flattened in that pensive manner of his, "if Dr. Donovan wanted to hurt your friend, why not leave her at the side of the road or let her die in surgery? He could've nicked a major vessel and blamed it on an injury from the trauma itself."

"Will I be able to see her soon?" Tam asks.

"The nurses will let you know when she's stable in recovery, then you can pop in. Why don't you make sure the receptionist has your cell number." When Tam nods and heads to the desk where a male staff member is helping two other people, Dr. Donovan turns to me and says, "Let's have a chat."

He grabs my elbow and starts leading me toward the door. When I try to jerk away, his squeeze deepens on my arm until his fingers pinch my nerve and send a bolt of pain down my forearm. All the while he smiles, nodding to the family members as we pass. I'm torn between my desire to bolt and my greed to hear what he has to tell me. No, my *need* to hear what he has to tell me.

Once we're in the hallway with a steady stream of hospital employees and visitors passing by, he leads us to a quiet corner off the main corridor. "You see what happens when you mess with me?" he asks quietly.

When I open my mouth to speak, he presses a finger that smells of soap and latex to my lips. His body shields me from the few passersby, and his other hand still grips my elbow, but more loosely than before. The pain is now down to a tingle. I maneuver my body to reach into my satchel and pull out my phone, but he seizes the mobile from my hand before I can stop him.

"Oh no, Liza dear," he says, his tone threatening. "There'll be no more recording." He slips my phone into his back scrubs pocket. "Be good, and you might get it back."

I remain mute.

"This is the point where your little investigation of me stops. Hopefully, you've learned your lesson." He pauses as a staff member in scrubs greets him. He waves to her and smiles as if all is well on this beautiful day. When she's gone, he says, "I have proof of you in my home. Your DNA is all around it, I imagine." He leans in and sniffs me. "Your scent too." When he pulls back, he adds, "Stupid of you to break in, of course, but I'm glad you did. Should be enough to guarantee you a bed next to Mommy Dearest at the nut house should I choose to disclose it. Tell me. Does she still enjoy playing guitar on her rock?"

Fury ignites in my gut. I welcome it. Anger is much easier for me to navigate than pain and grief. "Why do you do it?" I ask, the muscles in my jawline stiffening.

To his credit, he doesn't feign ignorance. All traces of levity leave his face. "Life shouldn't be squandered. Not everyone gets a second chance, you know. My mother sure didn't. Cancer took her like that." He snaps his fingers. "For the lucky few who do get a second chance, it should be treated like the gift it is."

I shake my head in disbelief.

"Don't you get it?" He releases my arm, raises his palms, and lifts his face to the ceiling as if he's a deity. Indeed, the fluorescent lighting in the hospital corridor casts an almost ethereal glow to his refined features, the dark mole beneath his lashes the only visible flaw. I imagine his pastor father looking the very same way from the pulpit.

He lowers his head and stares at me, his cheeks flushed. "Every day I repair them, heal them. I even bring some back from the dead. That's the most precious gift they'll ever receive, and yet so many of them squander it. They return to drugs. They soak in their alcohol, their livers hardening to stone. They grow into obese sloths who wallow in their gluttony."

My mind races through the people he's killed. I recognize these habits in some of them but not all. "My father," I spit out. "What about my father? He squandered nothing."

"Nothing?" Sam barks a laugh. "He gave up the law where he made a name for himself. He withdrew from public office. Just think of the good he could've done. And for what?" He stares at me, his jaw rigid, and I can tell he's trying not to raise his voice. "To grill meat in a food truck? To make pennies a day? What a waste of a life." He taps his chest. "A life I gave him. He might have been the worst offender of all. He might as well have just died on my table."

"How...what...? Who are you to make such a call?"

A vein on his forehead swells. "I'm the man who gave them back their lives! No other surgeon could have pulled off what I did." Blinking rapidly, he steps back and glances over his shoulder, probably to see if anyone heard him. He sniffs, adjusts his scrub top, and pins his focus back on me. "You act like I'm no better than a junkie on the street who murders for drug money."

"Like the guy you sent to kill me? You polished him off, didn't you? Couldn't leave him as a loose end. Not after he failed the job."

Dr. Donovan taps my forehead. "You're not hearing me, Liza."

I take his silence on what I just said as confirmation of its truth, though technically he hasn't admitted to anything, not even killing those patients. But I know he did, and I know he hurt Shawna.

He scratches vigorously at his scalp. It doesn't take a shrink to see I've touched a sore spot. "I'm looking after my patients. Like a parent, I take pride in their accomplishments, and like a parent, I'm hurt by their failures. Children should strive to make their parents proud." He exhales. "You can't stop this, you know." When I say nothing, he adds, "You're tenacious, that's for sure. You're not a quitter like your father. Well done on breaking into my house." He claps his hands softly. "But you can't stop me. You have no real proof."

"I saw the potassium chloride in your desk."

He shoos my statement away. In his riled state, it's clear he's not questioning my access to the locked box. Shelly wouldn't have had that key. "I'll say you put it there. Given everything you've done so far, no one will have trouble believing it. Even your program director and hippy advisor think you're psychotic."

He cowers, and his voice takes on a mock innocence. "Help me, officer. This woman won't leave me alone. I'm scared she'll hurt me." His normal timbre returns. "But you're going to stop your games now, right? Because I just performed surgery on your friend, and you know what that means…" His lips curl up. "That means I gave her life." He jerks his fist through the air as if yanking something away. "And I can just as easily take it back."

For a long beat, neither of us says anything. Then he leans forward and kisses my cheek. The gesture is so shocking, I jump.

He winks at me, dumps my phone in a pocket of my satchel, and whistles his way down the corridor and back into the waiting room, where the reverent Tam waits.

I press against the wall near a window. I have to stop him. Doing nothing is not an option. I have to stop him now. But how? He's immobilized me. I'm trapped against the ropes. He's painted me as psychotic and delusional when in reality it's *him* who's most like my mother. Plus, his delusions of godlike superiority are textbook psychopathy.

I stare out the window, the late afternoon sun a blinding orange sphere. I know Tam needs me, but I have to corral my scattered thoughts first.

Slowly, as I gaze past the parking lot toward the distant edge of the gardens in whose fragrant greenery Shelly died, an idea floats into my mind.

Yes. It's perfect. So perfect that I allow myself a small smile.

I pull away from the window and return to the surgical waiting room.

29

I wait until after eight p.m. to proceed with my plan. Luckily, the morgue is two floors away from the pathology department. I can't risk having someone see me. I enter the hospital complex and take the stairwell down to it now.

Shawna was moved from recovery to the post-op surgical ward a short time ago. Tam is by her side. Their infant son and their dog are staying with a neighbor. They know better than to ask me to watch either one of them.

After helping Tam navigate the medical lingo and hospital world and promising I'd be by tomorrow, I drove home to change into clean clothes, ones that weren't stained with grass and soaked in adrenaline. Now, dressed once again in work-suitable attire, including my never-worn white doctor's coat with tools I'll need for tonight's task inside its pockets, I act like I have every right to be in the morgue, which prior to my suspension I did.

Though call duties started for us this month (we serve alongside a more senior resident while we learn the ropes), I've not yet covered a night. My first was supposed to be Wednesday, August seventh, which is tomorrow. Now that I'm suspended, it won't be happening.

Both Waseem and Jen have taken a shift, and after teaching

rounds Monday morning when I still had a job, Waseem mentioned how quiet and creepy the morgue is at night, especially when the pathologists' assistant (or PA as he's called) takes his dinner break at eight. "It's as quiet as a ghost city," Waseem said.

As I tiptoe down the bland tiles of the dark, vacant corridor, my own curiosity of the place is piqued. Even the rubber soles of my shoes echo in the stillness of the basement. Being down here alone is an unusual feeling, like entering a haunted house after closing. Your brain says nothing can hurt you, but your nerves wonder otherwise.

Still, my dry mouth and goosebumps aren't from fear of being alone in a place full of corpses. That doesn't bother me. It's knowing there's a security camera in the hallway watching my every movement that does.

As I use my ID badge to unlock the heavy door to the cold room, I avoid looking around, even though I'm tempted to. It's basic human instinct to scour an area for other people when you're not supposed to be there, but security has no reason to suspect I'm up to anything. I'm a pathology resident who belongs in the department, and that includes the morgue. At least I was as of this morning, and since my badge is still active, security likely has no knowledge of my suspension. My status will probably remain active for at least a few days while Dr. Silverstein and Dr. Thomas "sort things out."

Once inside the cold room, I close the door and lean against it. The lights are already on. A chemical smell prickles my sinuses, and the sudden buzz of a whirring fan gives me a start.

The place is otherwise—quite literally—a tomb, one with a stainless-steel table, sink, and drain hole, all of which are remnants from an earlier time since Titus McCall's autopsies are now done in different rooms. What I seek is across from me. Two large-door refrigerators where the bodies are stored. At least there are no cameras in here. One quick look around confirms this.

Not wanting to dawdle, I hurry to the first cold-room storage area and shove all thoughts of what I'm about to do from my mind. That includes thoughts about potential consequences and repercussions, even though a part of me knows I might not be making the best choice here. Somewhere in the cosmos my father frowns.

From our orientation tour, we learned this storage area is the one used most often, its inhabitants being moved quickly through the postmortem process. The other one, its temperature deeper, holds bodies that remain in the morgue longer than usual.

Once more resisting the urge to peer around me to make sure no one's watching, I open the thick metal door and step inside. The cold is immediate, my white coat not much of a buffer. An occupancy sensor turns on an overhead light, and I'm able to get my bearings. On each side of me, stacked, stainless-steel trays hold corpses. Only four bodies are inside.

Shivering, either from the cold or from what I'm about to do, I quickly identify the one I need. The autopsy was done late yesterday, and I assume the body will be moved soon. Thank God it hasn't been already.

I reach into my lab coat pocket and pull out the gloves I placed there. After putting them on, I grab the scissors and resealable plastic bag from the other pocket. Wiping my mind free of judgmental voices, including those of my father, my shrink, and even myself, I focus only on the task at hand.

Narrowing my nostrils against the unpleasant scent, I unzip Shelly Parson's body bag and cut off a snippet of her hair. Then I scrape skin from the back of her neck with the blade of the scissors, just beneath her hairline where it's less likely to be noticed. Finally, I widen the body bag, and with the scissors I cut a section of tissue from beneath the crudely closed Y-incision. It's not ideal and wouldn't be the best fragment for testing, but I only need it for trace evidence. I'm no expert in forensics, and I have no idea if Luminol will detect the blood within the sample I've taken, especially after she's been dead for three days, but I figure it's worth a shot.

Once I seal up my macabre goodies in the plastic bag, I stuff it in my lab coat pocket and start zipping up Shelly's body bag. When I get to her face, I pause. Though I wouldn't say she looks peaceful, she at least no longer looks in pain. I find it difficult to swallow. Images of us downward dogging together in the hospital wellness center flash in my mind, followed by drinks at O'Dell's. As I did with my father before his coffin was closed, I press my hand to her cheek, her gray flesh cool against my glove.

"You didn't deserve this," I whisper. Then I zip the bag all the way up, step out of the cooler, and exit the morgue.

Outside the hospital beneath the darkening sky, I stride back to my car. Am I happy about what I've just done? Of course not. Desecrating Shelly's body leaves me no joy.

Nevertheless, a determined satisfaction washes over me, and like Dr. Donovan did earlier, I whistle while I walk. The identity of Shelly's true killer may never be revealed, but I guarantee *someone* will pay for it.

30

A t seven thirty the next morning, I again meet Trey in the hospital parking lot closest to the atrium. The sky is overcast, and dew glistens on the shrubs lining the sidewalk. Though it's already warm, I wear a sweater hoodie over my blouse. Despite my suspension, I also wear work-appropriate pants and shoes. For what I'm about to do, I'll need to blend in.

"This isn't right, you know. You making me take this." Trey slams the key fob for Dr. Donovan's Highlander into my hand.

"But moving a woman's body after watching her die is?"

He stares up at the sky, his chin trembling. "I effed up. I wasn't thinking."

I know a little something about that. "Is Dr. Donovan suspicious of your absence?"

Trey shakes his head. "I told him I had to meet with my research advisor. There are plenty of other residents to help him."

"Good." I tuck the surgeon's key fob into my pocket.

"Do you know they arrested Shelly's ex-husband for the murder?" Trey asks.

I do. When I called to check on Shawna after my trip to the morgue last night, I asked Tam about Shelly's case. I tried for subtle and hopefully reached it. Though as a patrol officer, Tam doesn't work homicide, she knows the details. "All I'm allowed to tell you is that Parsons was a pretty rotten dude," she said. "Ex-girlfriend who claims he choked her. Another one who says he liked to mess with her head. Of course, as so often happens, neither of them reported it. He's locked up for now."

Trey starts to mumble something, and I tune back in. He says he's not sure he can live with letting an innocent man rot in prison for a crime he didn't commit and that maybe he should come clean. I remind him that he's let four days go by without reporting his role in Shelly's death, which will make the police question the whole "accident" part.

"So you might be the one to rot in prison," I say, "especially since you killed a patient with a narcotic overdose and stayed mum about it."

This is cruel, I know, and I have no idea whether the police will believe Trey or not, but it's too late to play by the rules.

He moans and leans against my car. Thankfully, he doesn't cry. I don't have time for that.

"Listen," I say. "Someone *will* pay for Shelly's murder, but it will be someone who deserves it, someone who's not innocent at all."

He stares at the key fob in my hand. He opens his mouth but then closes it without saying a word. Instead, he scratches the flesh near the neckline of his scrubs, first with one hand, then both, as if he wants to climb out of his skin.

I try to reassure him. "The less you know the better, but I promise you'll come out smelling as clean as fresh laundry. In fact, if my idea goes south, I'll confess my role in this whole thing. I'll tell the police you were going to come forward about Shelly's death from the start, but I wouldn't let you. I'll take the fall."

He stops scratching. "I can hold you to that?"

"You can." I mean it, too, because if my plan doesn't work, all hope of catching Dr. Donovan will be lost, and I'll be the one locked up.

Trey exhales, and his body seems to relax, making me question his sincerity about confessing in the first place. His nonverbal cues suggest he's greatly relieved to have a way out.

I open my car door. "Twenty minutes," I say. "Back here."

I start my Civic, pull out of the lot, and drive a short distance to the employee lot closest to the surgical wing. I already located Dr. Donovan's Highlander there earlier this morning. I confirmed the license plate number from the picture I took of it back when I staked out his house.

After grabbing the first parking spot I find, which is three rows down from his, I pull my hoodie up and put on the medical gloves I placed under the seat earlier. I get out and tuck my hands in my pockets. A quick scan of the area tells me I'm alone. I purposely chose this time of the morning because the seven-to-three workers are already in the hospital, and the overnight eleven-to-seven shifters have already left. Most residents and med students are here by now too. The last few stragglers would be late-arriving surgical attendings, but I doubt there are many of those.

Whether or not Dr. Donovan's vehicle is in the eye of a security camera, I don't know. I'll have to risk it and hope that my plan works and that there'll be no reason to check it in retrospect. In the meantime, I keep my face as hidden inside the sweater hoodie as I can.

I reach the black Highlander. With deliberate but casual moves, as if I'm simply opening the back of my own vehicle, I press the unlock button on the key fob. When the hatch raises, I retrieve the small plastic bag in my pocket. From it, I pull a few strands of Shelly's blond hair and scatter them inside the trunk. Flecks of her scraped skin follow. Next I rub the chunk of tissue I cut from her Y-incision over the carpeted trunk floor, removing any particulates of tissue that cling there. The deposited clues should be inconspicuous on first glance, which is how I want it.

Even I'm enough of a sensibly minded thinker to know my actions cross a line, a low blow of the crudest kind. I mentally apologize to Shelly for this callous desecration of her remains. *But at least this way you won't die in vain*, I tell her. *This way, you'll help stop a murdering psychopath.*

The whole thing takes only a few seconds. I close the hatch, relock the car, and stroll back to my own vehicle as if I don't have a care in the world.

A short time later, I stop at my apartment to change into shorts, a T-shirt, and sandals. I also pack a bag for another night's stay at Home and Hearth Healing. Even though Dr. Donovan is at the hospital and should be there all day, I don't like leaving my mother alone, not even for this brief amount of time. But I have things I need to do, including visit Shawna in the hospital, and since I don't have a clone, I'm going to have to call my brother for backup.

I sit at my desk and unlock my phone. After three rings, Ned answers. "Hey, sis, this isn't a good time." A guitar strums in the background.

"Are you at the music store?" I ask.

"I am."

"Can you get a few days off?"

"What's wrong?" His pitch rises. "Is Mom okay? I called a couple weeks ago, and that doctor said she was messed up and needed her poisons upped."

I doubt very much the eloquent Dr. Dhar used any of those words. "She had a medication adjustment, yes."

"Why didn't you call me? What's wrong with her?" When I don't respond, he says, "You gotta keep me informed."

"I'm keeping you informed right now."

"I'm keeping you informed right now," he repeats in a robotic voice, which I assume is meant to be me. "Always so stingy with the emotions."

I stop swiveling in my chair and slam my fist on the desk. "You want emotion? How's this for freaking emotion? I need you to get your skinny ass over to Morganville and stay in Mom's room for a couple days. Can you do that? Huh? Can you?"

Silence from the other end. I can almost see his narrow face blinking in shock. Then, "Wow, Liza, I'm sorry. Didn't mean anything by it. I've got the dark fiend in me today, you know? I told you it wasn't a good time."

I soften. I shouldn't have overreacted. As a doctor I understand depression, even though I might not always recognize it as a sister. My voice returns to its normal tone. "It's all right. Sorry I snapped. Look. Mom's okay. I just need you to spend some time with her." I hesitate, wondering how to phrase it. "We've…had some threats. Nothing to worry about, but—"

"Threats? What kind of threats?"

"Mom should be safe at the center, safer than she'd be at my place, but I can't guarantee it, and someone should stay with her for now, that's all. I need to fix a few things to make the threat go away, and I can't do that if I'm with her."

"What kind of things?" he asks warily. His fear makes me remember my father's advice. *Watch out for your brother, tiger. He may be older than you, but he doesn't have your fortitude.*

"Nothing I can't handle. Really. I'd just feel better having you here."

With Ned, the less detail the better. He'd rather be oblivious, his guitar pick in one hand and the strings in the other.

"Come on," I say, hoping to lighten my voice into something he won't construe as robotic. "It'll be fun. We'll play board games like we used to. Home and Hearth Healing has a lot. Remember how much Mom liked playing *Pictionary*? And *Boggle*? She might be well enough now to play both."

He sniffs. "Yeah, okay. I guess I can get away. Give me thirty minutes to pack a bag, and another couple hours to drive there."

"Thanks, Ned." Once again, he's risen to the challenge when it counts.

"It'll be good to see you, Liza Lou."

When we disconnect, I return to my desktop computer. As it powers up, I reach for the plate of peanut butter cookies April delivered a short time ago. I was just putting my key in the door when she caught me. Jasmine was with her, giggling and pointing at the cookies. "I put the little peanut butter cups on top," she said.

I told her they were the best part and shoved one into my

mouth. After I swallowed, I said, "You and your mom should go into business together. You can call it April and Jasmine's Delicious Delights. I'll be a lifelong customer."

They both laughed, and after I thanked them for the cookies and made sure Sinclair was leaving April alone, Jasmine asked me to solve the Rubik's Cube again for her.

"Can't right now. Too busy." When her smile faded, I added, "Hold on a sec." I went to my closet, retrieved the cube, and gave it to her. "Here, practice it in the meantime. Then *you* can do it for me."

She giggled again, and we went our separate ways.

When my computer is fully booted, I open the folder containing Megan's photos, the ones she took at Shelly Parson's crime scene and subsequently deleted, but not before I sent some to myself. To be safe, I saved them on my hard drive and deleted them from my phone. I study the five I have. I go through them a second time. On the third run-through I find something. It's in the photo Megan took of the small crowd gathering around the perimeter tape.

I lick my lips. Peanut butter cookie crumbs litter my keyboard. An excited tremor runs through me.

This is it. Jesus, this is it.

How did I not see it before? With a little help from me, this is exactly the catalyst the police will need to search Dr. Donovan's property. A search warrant is only a call away. They'll find nothing in his home, of course. He'll have ditched the potassium chloride by now. But they'll find something in the trunk of his car, that's for sure. I get to work on the picture.

Ding ding ding. There's the bell.

Round 8 to Liza.

31

C onvincing Tam that the surgeon who saved her wife's life yesterday is actually the one behind her accident will not be easy. The idea of even trying to ties me in knots. Tam could end up hating me. Though I wouldn't like that outcome, I could live with it, but losing her as a resource to put Dr. Donovan away is unthinkable.

Hopefully, with what I carry in my satchel, she'll have no choice but to pass the idea on to the detective in charge of Shelly's case. That should get me one step closer to stopping Sam permanently.

At least Shawna is having a stable hospital course. That gives me some comfort as I exit the second-floor stairwell and press open the automatic doors that lead to the busy surgical unit.

The blipping monitors and pungent antiseptic smells take me back to my clinical rotations in med school, which, aside from the satisfaction of solving diagnostic puzzles, were my least favorite rotations. My poor bedside manner should surprise no one. It certainly didn't surprise my psychiatrist. I remember Dr. Lightfoot's expression when, as a seventeen-year-old, I told him I was pursuing medical school. If a look could be translated into words, his would have said, "Good God, please tell me you're joking." When I mentioned that pathology was my specialty of choice, he exhaled as if he'd been holding his breath for days. "Oh good. Yes, good. I think that could work. We might need some extra sessions during your clinical years though."

When I find Shawna's room, I pause outside. A wall-mounted defibrillator rests near my head, and a guard rail runs the length of the wall should I need help walking if Tam dropkicks me out of the room. Soft voices drift through the partially open door, along with a weird whirring noise.

It's now or never, Liza Lou. The stupid nickname from my brother gives me a weird urge to laugh. Finally, I knock and push the door open.

My face immediately heats. I'm not often embarrassed, but I am now. Not only is Shawna's right leg casted and suspended in traction, her upper torso is at a forty-five-degree angle and completely exposed save for the mechanical pump emptying both breasts and the surgical bandage covering her abdomen. That explains the whirring noise I heard through the door. Tam flips through a news magazine in a chair near the bed, her legs crossed and her shorts reaching her knees.

"I'm sorry," I mumble and start to leave.

"Don't be silly." Shawna's voice is hoarse and lacks her usual zing. "Come in. I was out of it when you were here yesterday. I still look a mess."

Tam greets me with a nod. I stand there in front of them, not sure where to look.

Shawna lowers her own gaze to her chest, one hand on each plastic collecting bottle, both of which are a third full. "I can't use any of this—too many drugs in my system—but I'm determined to keep up my milk supply."

Tam sets the magazine on the bedside table, next to a pink emesis basin and a matching pitcher of water. "Good thing Seth weaned himself. Otherwise, when Angie brings him in, he'd be royally pissed to not get the goods from the best containers ever."

While the wives smile at the joke, I stand there stupidly, hands at my side, satchel digging into my back. Lactation is not a world I care to know.

Shawna chuckles and then winces at the pain the motion causes. "Look at Liza's face. It's like she just ate roadkill."

Tam laughs too, and my face grows even hotter.

Luckily, I'm saved by a woman entering the room. "Knock knock," she says, seemingly oblivious to Shawna's milk-pumping.

Her hair is long and loose, and her limbs are those of a dancer. I assume she's their neighbor, Angie, because Seth is in her arms. He's dressed in crimson shorts and a Morganville Police Department onesie that must've been custom-made. His chubby legs kick the woman's side, and his teething ring takes a similar beating. Not only is his onesie soaked with saliva, so is the shoulder of Angie's linen tunic. There may be some snot there too, and I'm suddenly grateful that sex isn't a priority for me. In fact, I may never have it again.

"There's my sweet baby." Shawna's shadowed and sickly eyes brighten. "Can you take him, Tam? As soon as I'm done pumping, I'll see if I can hold him without too much pain."

"You probably shouldn't," I say, the doctor in me surfacing. "He's too active. He might kick your incisions. With a liver laceration and a splenic hematoma, that wouldn't be good." I'm recalling Dr. Donovan's listing of injuries in the waiting room yesterday, and the fact he caused them makes the organs inside my own belly burn.

Shawna looks disappointed. We've been friends long enough that she's pretty easy for me to read. "You're right." To Tam, who has just received the slobbering eleven-month-old, she says, "Just bring his head here so I can sniff it and kiss it."

Weird, I think to myself. Did my mom ever smell my head?

Angie asks how Shawna is doing.

"It's going to be a long road, but I'll be okay." Her eyes tear up.

I unstick my feet and step forward to awkwardly pat her left foot, which is tucked underneath the blanket. "You're healthy. You'll heal well." It's the best I can do.

"That's what the surgeon said too," Shawna tells Angie. "I'm so grateful he drove by when he did." I notice neither she nor Tam look my way as she tells Angie about the "lucky coincidence" of Dr. Donovan's arrival. "If he hadn't found me at the side of the road and got an ambulance there so quickly, I could have—"

"Don't even say it," Angie counters. "You've got people who need and love you. It's not your time yet. Have your parents come down from Maine?"

"They'll be here shortly."

As they talk more about Shawna's surgery, I approach Tam and ask if I can speak to her in the hallway. Her body seems to tense. Clearly, she's wary and has a pretty good idea of what our topic of conversation will be. With what seems like reluctance, she hands Seth back to Angie and tells them she'll be right back. Together we exit.

Given Shawna's room is not far from the nurses' station and has lots of foot traffic around it, I lead Tam to an empty waiting area I passed on the way in. It's a small room with a few chairs, a table holding magazines, and a countertop with a coffee and tea machine. We both take a seat.

The moment I reach into my satchel, Tam presses her lips together. "I know what you're going to say."

"What am I going to say?"

She falters for a moment and then brings an ankle up to rest on her other knee. "Okay, I don't know what you're going to say, but I know it's something about Dr. Donovan."

I glance around the windowless room, trying to find a way to phrase my words so she doesn't immediately dismiss me. "I stumbled on something that I think implicates Dr. Donovan in Shelly Parsons's death."

Tam leans her head against the wall and closes her eyes. When she opens them, she turns to me and says, "You need to let this go. We're worried about you." When I don't respond, she adds, "You're talking about the man who just saved my wife's life. You expect me to believe he's a killer?"

I shift to the edge of my seat and pivot my body toward her. "That's just it. That's what he wants you to think." My words sound delusional even to me, so I bite my tongue and shuffle things around in my head. "Look, don't you think it's a bit weird he happened to drive past after Shawna was hit?"

"If you're asking me if it's a coincidence, sure, but impossible?

No. Waverly Boulevard is a pretty well-traveled road."

"Then why didn't anyone else spot her and call for help?"

"She was running close to the woods' edge, as far from the cars as she could. The idiot who hit her must've swerved over." A muscle in Tam's jaw twitches. "Probably on his cell phone. Knocked Shawna clear into a thicket of trees. Even with her bright running clothes she might've been easy to miss."

"Then how did Dr. Donovan spot her?"

"I don't know, Liza, but thank God he did, don't you think?"

"It's just…hear me out…what if he was the one to hit her?"

Tam's laugh is more a snort. "Ah jeez, why would he do that? It makes no sense. If he wanted her dead, he'd have left her there." She makes like she's about to get up. "Listen, I've been patient with you. I know how much you did for Shawna when she was younger, and I'll always be grateful to you for that, but you've got to stop these accusations and—"

"But that's the whole point, don't you see?" My head is shaking so hard my cheeks wobble. *Must look rational*, I remind myself. "He wanted to save her with surgery first. That's his M.O. He gives a life, and then he and he alone decides if he takes it back. He told me so himself, right before he warned me that if I keep looking into him, he'll finish what he started with Shawna." When I see her expression, which might be a cross between exasperation and pity, I add, "I know it sounds crazy, but no one can explain why psychopaths do what they do. They don't think rationally, at least not when it comes to killing."

I pause. My throat tightens, and I don't want to admit the next part, but I do. "And it's my fault Shawna is hurt. She could've died because of me. She could still die because of me." I close my eyes and breathe.

Tam places a hand on my knee. Her voice finds its patience again. "Let's think this through logically, okay? If Dr. Donovan was the one to hit her, his car would be dented and covered with evidence."

I open my mouth, then close it. Clearly my forensic skills don't match Megan's.

"But it wasn't," she continues. "At least not as far as I know, because when he drove in the ambulance with Shawna to the ER, a cop at the scene drove Dr. Donovan's SUV to the hospital for him. I'm sure my colleague would've noticed evidence of a hit and run."

"What if Dr. Donovan didn't use that car? What if he used a different one, stashed it someplace, and then drove back with his Highlander to 'rescue' her." I make quote marks with my fingers. "You said yourself she was hidden away from sight."

She says nothing for a moment. Does that mean she's considering what I said? Or does it mean she's ready to commit me?

Finally, she sighs. "But how would he know Shawna jogs along that road? There are so many holes in your theory."

"No, there really aren't. Not if you'll just hear me out. I think he's maybe followed me, including to your house, and I've since confirmed he's been spying on my mother outside Home and Hearth Healing." Tam's rubbing of her temples keeps me from admitting that the witness who confirmed this for me is another patient at the center, a woman who sings most of her speech. I continue on before she can ask. "A beige Taurus followed me to Home and Hearth Healing once, I'm sure of it. It was beat up and dented on the back door. I'll text you a picture of the license plate. Maybe your department could look for it and—"

"If what you're saying is true,"—nothing in Tam's voice suggests she thinks it is—"what would the surgeon have done if someone else had found Shawna and not him? That would've ruined his whole plan."

I shrug and text her the photo of the Taurus's license plate that I took the day I spotted the car at Home and Hearth Healing. "Sure it would've, but he might've still driven to the hospital, offered to operate on her. He was post-call yesterday and had already gone home, but he could've come up with some excuse for being there. Maybe he'd claim he saw the ambulance and police cars and wanted to offer his help."

Tam tilts her chin and narrows her eyes. "How do you know he'd already gone home?"

Crap. I didn't mean to let that slip. Maybe Tam should be a detective.

What should I say? I can't tell her I broke into his house. Nothing would end this conversation more quickly than that. I haven't even told her and Shawna I've been suspended. Doing so certainly wouldn't help my case.

Deciding to ignore her question, I reach into my bag and pull out what I hope is the *pièce de résistance.* "Look at this. Maybe this will convince you he's not who he says he is."

She takes the photograph from me, a five-by-seven I printed out from the pictures I got from Megan's phone. Within seconds she shifts from friend to cop. "What am I looking at?"

"This is a picture from Shelly Parsons's crime scene. I have others in my bag too, but—"

Through gritted teeth, Tam says, "How did you get these?"

My brain flounders. Megan asked us to keep her pictures confidential. Just because I don't want to shop at Nordstrom with her or set up study sessions doesn't mean I want to get her in trouble. I have to offer Tam something though. "Remember I told you one of my colleagues is going into forensics and was at the scene? She called me when she was there, and I couldn't resist stopping by for a peek myself."

"Jeez, Liza, and they allowed it?"

"I kept myself well hidden. My colleague didn't even know I was there. Too much going on. But...I took a few pictures." When I see a flush in Tam's cheeks, I quickly add, "I deleted most of them, but then I remembered I uploaded a few to my computer for a closer look. I just wanted to learn, you know?"

I don't need Dr. Lightfoot to tell me that lying to the people in my life is the surest way to make them want to exit my life, but this is a lie I have to tell. If I admit I sent the photos to myself while Megan wasn't looking, it'll only make me appear more complicit. Plus, it'll bring Megan into my deceit, and I can't risk the police questioning her.

Before Tam can say anything, I continue. "I found them this morning and was about to delete them, but something caught my eye that hadn't before. Here. This is what you need to see." I point to an area in the left side of the photograph where Megan captured —inadvertently or not—a closely packed group of curious bystanders trying to get a look at the scene in the wooded park, beyond where it was cordoned off. My foot taps restlessly. "Look at that man in the crowd. He's partially hidden behind that big guy's shoulder, but look at his face. I think that's Dr. Donovan. I was paying attention to what the crime scene techs were doing, not the crowd, so I didn't even notice the surgeon at the time."

At first, Tam merely scans it at arm's length, her posture slouched. I imagine she's had just about enough of me and my theories today. Then her spine slowly straightens, and she raises the image to study it more closely. "I don't know. His eyes are shadowed by the baseball cap, and though the nose is narrow like his, you can only see half of his mouth and chin." She lowers the picture and sinks back down, as if deciding the photo is worthless.

I pull out another five-by-seven photograph I printed. My breathing is once again shallow. "Look. This is a blown-up shot of the same image. It's a little blurry, but do you see that under his right eye?"

Tam squints. "It looks like a speck."

I shake my head. My cheeks feel warm. "No, that's Dr. Donovan's mole."

Tam says nothing, and I worry I've lost her. Then her whole face shifts. "Why hasn't anyone else spotted this?" she asks, maybe more to herself than me.

"Remember, this was my photograph. It's not really of the crime scene itself. It's more of the perimeter. Plus, that big guy's easy to hide behind."

Tam rubs a hand over her mouth, her silver wedding band shifting with the motion. "Jeez, Liza. I can't believe...I mean...wow."

"Does that mean you realize I might be right?"

She gives me a stern look. "It doesn't mean anything yet, okay? It just means we might need to dig a little deeper into what you've told me. A detective questioned him about Shelly's death, and they found no evidence—beyond your recording of their argument—that implicates him. No one really thought he was guilty. Her ex-husband is a surer bet."

"But after seeing this picture?" I say. "After seeing that Dr. Donovan might've been at Shelly's crime scene? I mean, that's weird, isn't it?"

"Yeah, it's weird, I'll give you that, especially since he told the detectives he didn't know about her death until they came to question him." She looks up. "Crap. I shouldn't have told you that. Vance—the detective—passed it on to me in confidence. Shawna's accident has got my brain rattled."

"I won't say anything."

"Murderers sometimes like to show up at their victim's crime scene. Twisted minds, you know?" She flicks the photograph with her fingernail and says the words I was praying she would. "At the very least, the fact he appears to have lied about not knowing she was dead, combined with the recording you gave us, might be enough to get us a search warrant of his property." She holds up a finger. "*Might*, I said. I can't make any promises."

"And until then," I say, trying not to sound gleeful at such a somber moment, "I think either you, Angie, or Shawna's parents should stay with Shawna at all times. Make sure she's never alone."

Tam stares at me for a long moment, and then her face hardens into a mask I wouldn't want to encounter on a dark street. On any street, for that matter.

"Don't worry," she says. "If Dr. Donovan is behind Shawna's accident, he'll pay for it with the rest of his life."

32

My phone buzzes while I wait for my brother inside the lobby of Home and Hearth Healing. I snatch it off the plaid couch, where it's fallen out of my shorts pocket. Hopefully he's not canceling on me. It wouldn't be the first time he's had to bail last minute, but it *would* be the worst time. I need him here to stay with our mom.

Turns out the caller isn't Ned. It's Dr. Silverstein. Somehow, right now, this seems worse.

"Hello?" I say, a little tentatively.

"Oh good, thank you for answering, Liza. I'm just calling to see how you're doing."

My suspension was two days ago. My friend has been hit by a car. One of Titus McCall's best surgeons is a serial killer who murdered my father. How does she think I'm doing? But she knows nothing of Shawna's accident, doesn't believe me about my father, and is a very nice woman who cares, so I say, "I'm all right."

"I'm sure you're wondering what Dr. Thomas and I discussed regarding your leave of absence."

Ha. Leave of absence. "It's crossed my mind."

She laughs softly. "You're an excellent resident. We don't want to lose you, but, well, it's a tricky situation, you see. Dr. Donovan says his need to file a restraining order against you is because you've been stalking him."

"Not true." Well, not technically.

"Yes, so you've said. I don't want to rehash it over the phone, but with those accusations you raised about him, well, you can see how his actions might have some merit."

"Only if you believe him." There's no point in arguing. I'll only seem more delusional in my advisor's eyes. "So does this mean I'm done for good?"

A sigh from the neuropathologist. "Not necessarily. For now, Dr. Thomas and I would like you to get some therapy. Not just a counselor but a psychiatrist."

"I have one. I haven't seen him for a while, but I can make an appointment after—" I almost say *after I've taken care of Dr. Donovan*, but I catch myself in time. "After we finish this call."

"Very good."

"I can come back then?"

"Let's take it a day at a time. With regular appointments with your psychiatrist, and maybe with documentation of your...um...your improvement, we'll be able to get you back into the department. We haven't suspended your privileges, so it won't be difficult." She's quick to add, "Assuming you'll leave Dr. Donovan alone."

My impulse to scream is almost unstoppable, but I manage to hold it in. Once Sam is put away, they'll see I've been right all along, and this ridiculous belief I'm mentally unwell can end. "Okay," I say. "Thank you."

"You take care of yourself, Liza. Maybe I'll see you at Home and Hearth Healing. I should visit Maisy again soon. Her mother is a good friend of mine."

Shortly after we end our call, the center's security alert buzzes. Tiana, who knows my brother is coming, checks her screen and buzzes him in. A second later, Ned strolls through the center's door. I stand, and we greet each other like we always do, with a simple hello and a fist bump.

He's still as thin as ever, his frame small like our mother's. Like always, he arrives with a guitar case slung over his shoulder. In the other hand is a carryall. His T-shirt and jeans smell faintly of weed. Understandable, I suppose. My phone call and cryptic explanation of threats no doubt spooked him.

"Thanks for coming," I say.

Even though he's been here before, he says, "This place looks like Paula Deen barfed all over it."

I shrug. "The residents seem to like the country look. It's homey."

"I think you mean *homely*."

We both laugh, and I'm pleased it feels genuine. I lead him to my mother's room, greeting the staff members as we go and introducing Ned to the newer employees he hasn't yet met. His last visit was almost seven months ago. My mother's favorite nurse, Luis Vargas, is on duty tonight, and I relay to Ned how well our mom responds to him.

Even this small bit of socializing is taxing, especially in my hyper-vigilant state. Though it's not as if I expect Sam to pop out of a dark corner, I've been chewing the skin around my thumbnail all day, unable to relax until I hear from Tam that the police got a warrant to search his house and—more importantly—his car. That's where the good stuff hides. But no text from her comes. I wonder how long it takes to get a warrant. Every time I'm tempted to text her and ask, I refrain. Playing it cool from this point onward seems critical.

When we reach our mother's room, her shower is running, and the bathroom door is closed. "She wanted to look nice for you," I say to Ned, taking his bag and guitar case and placing them near the fold-down chair near the window. I've already replaced the sheets I used last night with fresh ones.

He examines the trinkets on the dresser, including the tiny blown-glass guitar he bought her for Mother's Day a few years ago. "She's with it then?"

I don't like when he phrases it that way, as if our mother is a feeble-minded imbecile rather than an intelligent woman who happens to have a serious medical condition. Just because her illness is psychiatric and therefore less tangible doesn't mean it's not worthy of the same respect as diabetes or cancer. But I know what he means. "She's been better lately. Well enough to shower on her own right now. Ever since Dr. Dhar adjusted her medications she's spending less time in psychosis. Still bouts of delusion, but her speech is more coherent. No major drug side effects yet either. She understands that you're staying here for a bit. She's excited to have you."

"Three nights. That's all I can spare. I got a gig back in Providence on Saturday."

I nod. Hopefully that will be long enough.

He saunters across the room to our mom's bed and sinks down on it. I take a seat on the makeshift one he'll be using. The heels of his sneakers are worn down, and the original white coloring is now a dirty gray. Even the laces appear to be on their last tie. I get up and grab my satchel from my mom's small desk. After fishing out the three hundred dollars I withdrew from the ATM this afternoon, I hand it to him.

"Aw, you don't have to do that, Liza Lou."

"Please, take it. I make a decent salary now."

He pockets it, and I can see the gratitude in his eyes. "So, you were pretty mysterious when you called me. Said you've had some threats. Do I need to be worried about mom and me here?" He's trying for casual, and though I might miss it in a stranger, I can easily read the nervousness in my brother's face.

"No," I lie. "I'm just tied up with something and might not be able to be here as much. Don't worry though. I'll get it sorted out."

This lame explanation would satisfy few people. For my cautious brother, who never enjoyed trick-or-treating and who rarely watches horror movies, it's enough. Though his the-less-I-know-the-better attitude has frustrated me in the past, it suits me perfectly now.

The shower shuts off. I plop back down on his chair-bed. "You still with Mary?"

His face melts into a hangdog expression. "She left me."

"I'm sorry."

"Gave some bullshit story about needing her space. Says I'm too morose and needy."

I say nothing.

He rubs his face with both hands and then lets them flop to his thighs. He sags down on my mom's bed and leans against the wall. "Women say they want a sensitive guy, someone who listens to them and is always there, but guess what? They don't." He runs his fingers over my mom's soft alpaca blanket. "Shit, what're you gonna do. Just write more music, I guess. Until the next one comes along."

Although my brother is not a womanizer, he's had enough girl-friends to more than make up for my lack of boyfriends. He's good-looking, and women initially flock to him. Later into the relation-ship, however, he's usually the one to get dumped. I doubt it's because he's too sensitive.

I'm about to console him about Mary, wondering how to make it sound real, when I'm saved by my mother coming out of the bathroom, her raspberry-scented shampoo freshening the air around us. Her joy at seeing her son matches my relief at seeing the mother from my youth. At least one part of me feels at peace now.

My phone buzzes as they greet each other. I whip it out of my pocket, but my body deflates when I see it's Megan and not Tam. I let it go to voicemail, and it's a long while before I feel the buzz that the message is complete, during which my brother has already pulled out his guitar and handed my mother hers. The two of them sit on her bed, my mother's legs pulled up and crossed at the ankles, my brother's dangling over the lavender comforter.

My phone buzzes a second time and again it's Megan. Like before, I let it go to voicemail, but when the second message is equally long, my curiosity is roused. As my mother and brother tune their instruments, I listen to my voicemail. Megan's friendly tone fills my ear. She tells me she and the other first-years are having a late-afternoon coffee in the cafeteria. They miss me and want to talk to me. I find that difficult to believe.

"But before I go back to the table and put you on speaker-phone," she says in the message, "I wanted to say something in private to you first. I'd rather not do it in a voice message, but I doubt you'll call me back, so I guess I'll have to." She chuckles, and I can't fault her reasoning. I brace myself for what's about to come. What I hear surprises me.

"Look, I don't know what went on between you and Samuel." Her ongoing use of Dr. Donovan's first name doesn't surprise me. Though I don't know the extent of their relationship, the fact he accompanied her to Jen's barbecue tells me they're well beyond formal titles.

"And yes," Megan continues, "it did leak in the department that he might seek a restraining order against you. I can't imagine why he'd do such a thing, but I'm going to give you the benefit of the doubt." She pauses, and I hear passing voices in the recording. Maybe she's in the hallway outside the cafeteria. When it's quiet again, she says, "He never mentioned anything to me about a restraining order. It came as a complete surprise. But he *has* said negative things about you, things that, quite frankly, made me uncomfortable. Things I didn't see from you in our day-to-day inter-actions. You might keep to yourself, Liza, but I get a good feeling from you. I'm a good people-reader."

I think about the things she so quickly picked up on, including Waseem's unrequited feelings for John. "That you are," I say, as if she can hear me through a voice message.

"I'm not sure why it took me so long to get the weird vibes I'm getting from Samuel now. Maybe his good looks and status blurred my sensors. Believe me, I'm embarrassed to admit that, but listen, Liza, I'm picking up on them now. Something seems off with him." She pauses again, and in that brief interlude her thoughtful words shower me with guilt for every time I turned down her offer of tea at the kiosk or lunch in the cafeteria or even—dammit—taking me to Nordstrom to shop for a new purse.

Her voice message picks up again. "I don't know what it is. Maybe it's just his arrogance, or the way he seems to pay me atten-tion one minute and his eyes glass over the next. Or maybe it's because he's always so busy when he's not at the hospital. Every time he makes an excuse for why we can't go out, I imagine he's with someone else. No big deal—we're not that close—but at least own up to it, you know?"

Oh, he's with someone else all right, I want to say. He's stalking his next victims.

Now that the tuning is done, my mother and brother's duo guitars grow louder. I step out into the hallway to listen to the rest of Megan's message.

"I guess I'm babbling now, but I just called to, you know, tell you I'm on your side. We all are. In one way or another, you've helped each of us, whether you realize it or not, and we want to offer our support. Okay, enough sap. I'm heading back to the others now, but I'll have to hang up and call back. This message is long, and I'll get cut off soon."

My chest fills with an unfamiliar warmth that's almost painful. Massive relief, too, because at least someone else has seen through Dr. Donovan. Maybe not to the extent I have, but still, it helps. Someone out there doesn't think I'm crazy.

On the new message, I hear Waseem's voice, followed by Jen's and John's, their greetings overlapping and competing for time on the speakerphone. In their own way, each one says they miss me and that although they don't know the whole story behind my suspension, they're sure it will work out. To this, Waseem adds, "You got a bum shuffle" and "those powers-that-be wouldn't know a rat from a bat if it bit them in the ass." This makes me smile. I'm sure he's punking us all with his botched idioms. His English is better than mine.

The second voice message ends, but my newfound calm doesn't. After a few minutes of listening to my mother and brother play, I leave them until tomorrow. Though Sam is never far from my mind and a low-grade unease persists, the peace at knowing my mother and brother are safe, combined with my colleagues' kindness, soothes my agitation like a topical anesthetic. And with Tam at Shawna's side, she remains safe too.

Everyone in my circle is accounted for.

33

After a long morning run followed by core work and push-ups in my studio apartment, I shower and head to the hospital to visit Shawna. It felt good to sleep in my own bed after the previous night at Home and Hearth Healing, and I'm relieved to have Ned's help.

At eleven thirty I enter Shawna's room on the surgical floor. Tam isn't there, but Shawna's parents are. (Yay me.) An uncomfortable fifteen minutes ensue while I respond to questions about Shawna's recovery, which, considering I haven't seen her medical records nor am I a surgeon, isn't particularly easy. I then endure irrelevant banter about what I'm doing with my life, whether or not I'm married yet, and where I hope to see myself when I've finished my residency. What's not raised is the question of whether the very surgeon treating their daughter is the same man who rammed her with his car and left her with life-threatening injuries. I'm betting Tam didn't pass that tidbit on. Why would she? No need to worry Shawna or her parents unnecessarily, especially since Tam probably still leans heavily toward thinking I'm bonkers.

I'm itching to talk to her. Not wanting to seem unhinged or pushy (probably too late on both counts), I haven't dared call or text her, not since I gave her that picture yesterday. At the same time, my mind is driving itself mad wondering if she followed up with it yet.

Unable to stomach another question about my personal life, I interrupt Shawna's dad and ask, "Tam's not working today, is she? I thought she was taking the rest of the week off to be with you."

"Oh she is," Shawna assures me. Her hair is brushed out today, probably by her mother, but her normally made-up face remains bare, shadowed with the pain of broken bones and a postsurgical abdomen. She taps the cast on her leg, which is still in traction, and adds, "I think my accident hurts her more than it does me. She'll be here soon. Said she had to do a couple things first. Took Seth with her so my parents could have a break."

I nod and withstand ten more minutes of small talk about Seth's upcoming first birthday party, his inability to eat peaches without a stool blowout, and the winter predictions for Maine this year. When Mr. Vasquez rolls his rotator cuff around and says his shoulder won't survive "another winter of shoveling, picked the wrong state to retire in," I pretend I have an incoming phone call. Awkwardly, I pat Shawna's arm and tell her I'll see her later. As I exit, I hear Mrs. Vasquez say in a hushed tone, "She's always been a weird little duck, hasn't she?"

It doesn't bother me. Her words roll off me like liquid mercury. I've heard them many times before from many mouths, and I don't doubt their veracity.

On the drive home, Trey texts me. He wants to know if I have any news to share yet. At a red light, I text him back, Not yet. Soon. Promise. At the next red light I add, Everything is going to work out fine. Trust me.

When I drop my phone back on the passenger seat, I hope I'm right.

Back at my apartment, I know I must be seriously out of sorts because after I drop my satchel on my desk, I willingly knock on April's door. An enticing scent of baking bread seeps from the crack beneath it. Thursday is usually her day off.

She answers, and Jasmine stands behind her. When they see it's me, their mouths fall open. I ask Jasmine if she's been practicing the

Rubik's Cube I gave her. She nods and says, "Watch, I'll show you." She runs off into the single bedroom, presumably to get my puzzle cube.

April remains near the doorframe, an apron over her tank top and jean shorts. The apron's fabric is so colorfully patterned her arm tattoos seem part of it. She invites me in, and I go as far as the kitchen counter, across from which is a small living room. Mother and daughter share the single bedroom from which Jasmine now bolts. The only other room is a bathroom, yet the apartment is still twice the size of mine.

Jasmine climbs onto a bar stool. With her tongue out, she starts twisting the cube. Meanwhile, April cuts a loaf of banana bread, grabs a tub of butter and a knife, and pushes the whole lot toward me. While I watch Jasmine twist the colorful panels, I butter myself a piece of bread. It's so fresh and warm the butter instantly melts into it. By the time Jasmine manages to get all the red panels on one side, I've polished off two pieces.

She looks at the clock on the microwave and sighs. Her shoulders slump. "Five minutes and I only got one side done. I suck."

I wipe my hands free of breadcrumbs. When my mouth is empty, I say, "Are you kidding? That's really good. It took my brother an hour just to get one side matched up."

"Really?"

"Really." Honestly, I have no idea if that's true. I only remember Ned could never solve the one he got for Christmas. When he saw that I could, on only the second day of it being in our house, he never touched it again. But my words seem to reassure Jasmine. "Keep practicing," I tell her. "You'll get it. You're way ahead of the average person."

"I can keep it still?" She looks up at me.

"Of course. You can keep it until you master it."

April has said little this whole time, but she smiles at me now. The visible brown spot high on her incisor says it's a genuine one. Even I recognize my chattiness is out of place, but a thousand jolts of electricity are surging through me, and I can't seem to calm them, not until I hear back from Tam. Each thought of Dr.

Donovan and what I left in his car cranks the voltage higher. I'm halfway through my third piece of banana bread when my phone finally buzzes.

It's Tam.

"It's work," I lie to April. "Sorry, I have to take it." I answer Tam's call and ask her to hold on a second. Then I thank April for the banana bread, salute Jasmine, and leave.

Back inside my own apartment, I lock the door and hurry to my bed. "Thanks for waiting," I tell Tam, trying to sound casual. "What's up?"

"I tell ya, Liza, when you came to me yesterday with that messed-up story about Dr. Donovan running down Shawna with his car, well, I'm not gonna lie. I thought maybe you needed some mental help."

"And now?" With a tremulous hand, I put the call on speakerphone and lower it to the bed.

"Now? Well, after thinking about it last night, I called Vance, the detective on Shelly's case. We also called Malia, the detective working Shawna's hit-and-run, and had a three-way conference call. Told them about your theory about a beige Taurus that could've been used to hit Shawna and then later ditched. Gave Malia the license plate number from the picture you took of it. I'll be honest, Liza, I felt like an idiot passing it on to them. How could I know if it was true or just a...just a..."

"Just a delusion on my part?"

"Yeah, that. Sorry. But between that and the picture you gave me from the crime scene, I couldn't get it out of my head. Then I started thinking about that audio recording of him threatening Shelly and those seven patients you researched, and I thought, 'What if she's right? What if instead of assuming she's, um, delusional, why don't I start from the standpoint of thinking she's on to something?'"

"And?" My bare thighs bob up and down on my duvet.

"And after sharing it all with Vance, he got back to me this afternoon."

"And?" I can barely breathe.

"You'll never believe this."

Try me.

"Malia sent a patrol car to look around the junk yards and salvage lots around the area. You know that one out on Mansfield Road? The one that's got row upon row of twisted and abandoned cars?"

"I do."

"Well, Malia's guys found a beige Taurus. Beat up. Dented back door on the driver's side, just like you said. Plate matches the picture you gave me."

"Did Malia run it?"

"Of course, but the license traces back to an old guy who lives downstate. Or I should say 'lived.' He passed away a while back. Wife said he kept his old Plymouth out back near the alley. She hasn't driven it since he died."

My thighs stop bouncing. "I don't understand."

"After Malia called the wife, the woman went out to check the Plymouth and discovered the license plates were gone."

"So someone stole the plates."

"Yep. And put them on a beat-up beige Taurus. So with that being a dead end, Malia checked the VIN. Traced it back to a gal— a sketchy gal at that—who says she sold the car to some guy for cash a year or so ago. Doesn't remember the guy's name, but says he was 'skinny with eyes so wide they looked like they'd pop.' Which doesn't sound like Dr. Donovan."

"Probably had his druggy gopher-boy buy it. The guy who attacked me."

"Basically it means we don't know who was driving the Taurus. It's still registered to the previous owner."

I scoff. "I do. It's Dr. Donovan's stalkermobile, stored far from his precious Cheshire Hill Estates." I admit to myself I don't know this for sure. After all, he didn't use it while spying on the mechanic and waitress. Then again, he stopped at the hospital first. Maybe he figured it would be riskier being seen driving the Taurus.

Tam ignores me again. "Here's the kicker. The dented bumper has been wiped down, but there were still traces of..." Her voice catches before she speaks again. "Traces of blood and skin on the headlight."

I inhale and close my eyes. I can't believe it. Well, I can believe it because I know who Sam really is, but I'm amazed I called it so spot-on.

Tam is still talking. I tune back in.

"Of course, we've got no digital experts here in Morganville—we'll need to send it to Boston."

I'm not sure what she's talking about. I must have missed something. I temper my excitement and listen more closely.

"But Liza, finding that car, combined with your crime scene picture that shows Dr. Donovan was lying about not knowing Shelly was dead and the threat he made to her on that recording? Makes a search warrant only a call away. At least that's what Vance says, but hey, this is between you and me."

I sit up even straighter on my bed, which, considering how taut my spine is, doesn't seem possible. "A search warrant for what?" *Please include his car.*

"For his house, his car, his office, you name it."

I press my hand to my chest. "Today?"

"Maybe not that quick, but hopefully by tomorrow. We'll want it before the weekend for sure. Vance is pretty keyed up about this. They had to release Shelly's ex-husband. Not enough evidence to hold him, so this put Vance in good spirits. In the meantime they'll check the car for prints, though I imagine anyone who did this would've wiped them all away. Unless they're stupid, which, if this really is Dr. Donovan, I doubt he is."

Though she can't see me, I shake my head. No, he's definitely not stupid. He's been one, if not two, punches ahead of me this whole time. Until now, that is.

Because while I may have been knocked down, I'm far from being knocked out.

34

E arly Friday morning my phone shrills its loud ringtone and awakens me from a deep sleep. When I see the caller is Tam, I jolt awake. I don't even bother with hello.

"What is it?" I say, half croak, half sputter.

"It's good news, that's what it is," she says. "Guess whose home is getting searched as we speak?"

I grip my phone and close my eyes.

Thank God. Round 9 to Liza.

"Vance got the search warrant late yesterday afternoon," Tam says. "They headed over to Donovan's house at six this morning, hoping to catch him before he went to work. They wanted to give him the courtesy of being home for it, not that he deserves it."

From her words, not to mention the bite in her tone, it's clear her opinion of the surgeon has done a one-eighty. I'm not sure what it was that ultimately convinced her. Maybe Shawna told her I've never been anything but level-headed before. Maybe the Taurus with the stolen license plate revealed some fingerprints. Maybe Dr. Donovan's presumed presence at the crime scene with the other onlookers was one oddity too many. It really doesn't matter what it was. The relief over finally being believed is so great I can barely speak. "And was he home?" I manage.

"He seemed to be, at least at first. An upstairs light was on, and Vance heard noises from inside, but after he knocked and announced himself, saying he had a warrant to search the property, no one came to unlock the door. When the cops finally forced it open, the security alarm was off and the place was empty."

I squeeze a handful of blanket in my fist. "Did he take his car?" This whole thing will be a bust if the police don't search Sam's car and find the presents I've deposited there. There's no way he'd leave the vial of potassium chloride in his desk.

"No, the SUV was still in his garage. Vance got a warrant for that too but couldn't snare one for Donovan's office. Not yet, anyway."

I exhale in relief and sink back down against my pillow. "So where did he go? How'd he get away?"

"Who knows? Maybe he got spooked. Grabbed a bike from the garage and took off out the back with it. Our guys were out front, at least at first. Vance said there were plenty of trees in the yard to hide an escape, and one of the guys spotted a thin tire impression in the grass beyond Donovan's deck. So maybe that's exactly what he did." Tam pauses, and her voice grows steely. "But Liza?"

"Yes?"

"The fact the prick fled makes him look guilty as hell. He didn't go to the hospital for work either. Vance checked on that. From what you've told me about Donovan, he'd normally put up a hissy fit if someone searched his place."

My mind ignites as I race through the possibilities of why he'd take off like that. He doesn't know I planted evidence in his car, does he? For a moment, I panic, but then I dismiss the thought. I was very careful. But if he assumed the cops would find nothing in his house, why wouldn't he stay and defend himself?

The answer that comes to me is simple. It's something I understand. Dr. Donovan is a psychopath. He's a psychopath who thinks he's smarter than everyone else. And while the police are busy in what he assumes will be a fruitless search of his property, he's busy setting up his next move, a move that will be aimed at me because he'll assume—correctly—that I'm the one who kick-started the search warrant. The only question that remains is what that move will be.

Oh shit.

I bolt upright, kicking the tangled sheets from my legs. "Tam!"

My urgency cuts off what she's saying about the search process. "What?"

"Please tell me you're with Shawna. Are you with her? You can't leave her. He'll—"

"Hey, hey, slow down. Yes, I'm here at the hospital with her. My in-laws are at our house with Seth. You think I'd leave her not knowing where that guy is?"

Though her confirmation should reassure me, I pace my small studio, my nerves as twisted as my bedsheets. I know Dr. Donovan is not simply going for an early morning bike ride through the scenic streets of Morganville. No, he's planning to get back at me. He must be seething over my latest punch to his throat. A search warrant is a heavyweight move. So first and foremost, he's going to make me pay. He's going to hit below the belt. Then, after he's gotten his revenge, his absolute confidence of victory back in place, he'll return to the police and tell them how absurd it is they're allowing a delusional resident to destroy his life.

Tam's voice interrupts my thoughts. "I have to go," she says. "The doctor just came in to talk to us. The orthopedic surgeon, that is, not the criminal one."

After hanging up, I resume my pacing. Normally, seeing my unmade bed would make me twitch with discomfort. With a space as small as mine, tidiness is key, but right now I don't care. I need to figure out what Sam's next move will be and I need to figure it out quickly.

He threatened to hurt Shawna again—this time permanently—if I didn't let things go, but he can't do it with Tam there, a cop no less. He's an arrogant killer who thinks he can get away with anything, but he's not dumb. No, he'll go after someone else in my circle.

I race to the bathroom, which is literally only six feet away. While I brush my teeth with a speed that would make dentists weep, I pull up Home and Hearth Healing on my phone and call the number for my mom's room. A sleepy Ned answers. I spit toothpaste out into the sink and put the phone on speaker. "Ned—"

"What the heck, Liza? It's barely six thirty."

"Are you guys all right?" I rinse quickly and spit again. Then I return to my closet with its clunky door and pull out a pair of shorts and a clean T-shirt from one of the two shelves.

"We're fine, what the fu—" Fear now enters his voice. "What's wrong? Are we in danger?"

I throw the phone on the bed and start getting dressed. I need to be honest with him. "I don't know. Maybe." I speak loudly to make sure the phone catches my words from the short distance. "Probably not with the security measures there, but please, just stay by Mom's side. All day." Before he can protest or question me further, I hang up and phone the center's front desk. From eleven p.m. to eight a.m. the calls are directed to the nurse on duty. I identify myself and insist that neither she nor anyone else should allow outside visitors near my mother today, especially a man with a mole under his right eye. "If someone does try to get in to see her, call the police." Again, I disconnect my call before she can protest.

Now, dressed and as groomed as I need to be, my hair so short nothing but my hands are required for styling, I resume my pacing. Shawna's safe. My mother and Ned are safe. Sam will know these are the people closest to me, but he'll also be aware of his limited access to them.

He *will* pay me back though, of that I'm sure. More sure than I've ever been of anything in my life. An egomaniac like Dr. Donovan will never tolerate me getting the upper hand. The question is, who else could he hurt?

I stop short near my desk and look toward the door. I can almost taste her banana bread in my mouth.

I tear out of my apartment and pound on April's door. I keep pounding until she opens it, a dazed and sleepy look on her face. Poorly removed mascara clumps and blackens her eyelashes, and her oversized pajama tee shows a picture of a blond woman with an electric guitar.

"Do you have to work today?" I ask her.

"What?…Liza, what are you doing here so early?"

"Do you?"

"I…" April rubs her eyes and looks like she's trying to orient herself to date and time. "No. It's Friday, right? Then no. I'm spending the day with Jasmine."

"Good. Don't go anywhere. Don't leave the apartment until I get back to you. And don't let anyone in. No one. Understand?"

"No, I *don't* understand. What's wrong?" Her eyes widen, and her features, aged beyond her years thanks to prison and a tough life, settle into an expression of fear. "Did you have a break-in?" She seems to think through possibilities. "Is it Sinclair? Is he going to evict me?" Now obvious terror is on her face. "Oh God, no."

I shake my head with impatience. "No. It's not him. Just promise me you'll stay put and call the police if anyone tries to get in, okay?" When she just keeps staring at me, I grow sterner and holler. "Okay?"

"Sheesh, yes, okay, but—"

"Good. Thanks." I start back toward my studio.

"Wait. Aren't you going to tell me why?"

"I promise I'll fill you in later. As long as you keep the door locked and stay put, you'll be okay. Trust me."

Before she can say anything else, I hurry back inside my place. I grab my satchel, drop my phone into it, and snatch my car keys from my kitchenette counter. Then, like a tiger with no prey in sight, I stand there. Frozen.

Where should I go? Who should I go to? Everyone seems to be protected. Who else could be Sam's target?

My brain shifts to my colleagues. *Shit.* My circle has grown. It's larger than I thought. But other than Jen Lopez, I don't know where any of them live. It's almost seven. They'll either be getting ready for work or on their way to the hospital.

The cyclone in my gut swirls faster. I can't get to them all. I don't know how to. Who would Sam pick? Whose demise besides

Shawna's and my mother's would he feel would hurt me the most? Wallop me with the most grief and guilt? Because that's what this is about. I didn't stop when Sam told me to, and now someone will pay. It can't be me. Not only would that take the fun out of the fight for him, it would look too suspicious to the police if I suddenly turned up dead or disappeared.

But who have I grown closest to?

Think, Liza, think.

So far he's only killed people he's operated on, including the junkie he bribed with drugs or drug money to silence me early in our match, but that doesn't mean he won't change his M.O., especially with things spiraling out of control for him. He might very well deviate from his structured and restrained murder routine. He might act rashly.

Still, police protection or no police protection, Shawna seems the most vulnerable.

My decision is made. I'll go to the hospital. Make sure he can't finish what he started.

I hurry out to my car, and although I start the engine, I don't pull out yet. I ask myself again if there's anyone else who could be Sam's next target.

Like a giant boulder rolling down his precious Cheshire Hill Estates, it hits me. Slams me so powerfully I can't believe I didn't think of it sooner.

Sam's not going after Shawna. He's going after someone else. Someone else in my circle he's performed surgery on. And now I've put her life in danger.

The Civic's digital clock reads 6:52.

I grope my portable GPS, almost knocking it off its weighted base on the dashboard. My fingers stumble over the small screen.

Please oh please oh please don't let me be too late.

35

Tearing out of the parking lot of my apartment building, I wonder how I didn't see it sooner. Dr. Silverstein. My advisor, not to mention the department chair. The woman who's done nothing but try to help me may now be the next pawn in Sam's game.

In my urgency to get to her house, I almost run a red light. At the last second, my wheels screech to a stop. The man in the car next to me glares in my direction.

Another awful thought surfaces. Sam will make her murder look like I was the one who committed it. I'll get blamed for her death, of course I will. Who'd have more of a motive to kill her than the psychotic resident she's just suspended? And by choosing my advisor, Sam won't have to break his M.O. Her gallbladder was on the receiving end of his scalpel a couple years ago. He even paid her a house call afterward, so he knows where she lives. The cherry on top? Her husband, a man with early signs of dementia, is currently in Italy on sabbatical.

Her home is on the other side of town, and even though Morganville is easier to navigate this early in the morning, a good number of cars still clutter its roundabouts and streets, the drivers probably getting a head start on their work commutes. In its quaint downtown, gift shops, candy stores, and restaurants pass by at an agonizingly slow pace. I could detour around to the side streets, but with their illogical one-ways and circuitous routes, they tend to be a maze of frustration. Though I dreaded Dr. Silverstein's dinner party at the time, I'm now grateful she had it. If not, her address wouldn't be in my GPS.

When I finally escape the mousetrap of the historic town center, I feel like an anchor's been lifted off my chest. If I recall correctly, all that remains of the drive are a couple long stretches of residential roads.

I want so badly to call the police, or at least to text Tam who can then summon them. I even go so far as to unlock my phone, eyes on the road as best I can, but I decide against it. If I'm wrong about Dr. Silverstein being a target, I'll be the girl crying wolf. Not only will I look even more delusional, I'll lose all chance of returning to my residency program. Whether I'm armed with glowing progress notes from my psychiatrist or not, no program director is going to reinstate me if I raise a false alarm about my advisor's imminent murder.

So I drive on, making a deal with myself that if I see anything suspicious at Dr. Silverstein's house, I'll text Tam straightaway.

Fifteen minutes after leaving my apartment, I arrive at her home, a stately yellow Victorian with a long front porch, dark roof shingles, and white shutters. Its unattached garage is closed, and no cars are parked in the driveway. At seven fifteen she wouldn't have yet left for work, so I imagine her car is inside. Other than a minivan on the street two houses down, I see no means of transportation for Dr. Donovan. The neighborhood's garage doors are closed, and the driveways are empty. I don't even see a bike.

But that doesn't mean he's not here.

The police started searching his place at six a.m. If he bolted right away as Tam suggested he did, he'd have a little over an hour to make it here. Though a brisk walk couldn't pull that off, a dedicated run could. Then again, I don't care if he hitched a ride with an eagle. I only care whether he's inside the house and about to kill my advisor. Or if I'm already too late.

Parking across the street so as not to alert him of my engine, I exit my car. I leave my satchel inside but take my keys and phone. A block away, a woman has just exited her house with a German Shepherd, but they head out in the opposite direction.

As I approach the yellow Victorian, I look for signs of life. I see none, but with the sunshine it's difficult to tell if any lights are on inside. Halfway up the driveway, I wonder whether I should ring the doorbell or peek through the windows first. If Sam is in there, he won't answer the door. If he isn't there (but has been), my advisor might already be dead.

Just as I'm about to cross over the grass, I stop short. A bike is leaning against the back of the garage, its front wheel jutting out.

My mouth goes dry. I tell myself it might mean nothing. Dr. Silverstein's energy-conscious and active. Maybe she bikes a lot.

But it could be Sam's.

For a moment, I'm torn. Call the police that he's here or confirm it first?

Screw it.

If it means saving my advisor's life and finally putting Sam away for his crimes, I'll take the risk. With one foot on the lawn and the other on the driveway's concrete, I type out a message to Tam, telling her to call 911 and send the police to Dr. Silverstein's address, which I give her. Then I add, DR. DONOVAN IS HERE! As soon as I press send, I pray I've done the right thing. It's times like these I feel the absence of my father's guidance most acutely. He provided that extra instinct I lack.

Except when it comes to Sam. For him, my instinct shouts loud and clear. One aberrant mind to another.

I cross over the lawn and step through a flowerbed to look through the front windows. Who cares if someone sees me? They'll call the police, which is exactly what I need anyway.

Pressing my face to the glass, I see no one. Not in the bay window of the dining room, not in the windows adjacent to the front door, and not in the two big windows on the far end of the house, which appear to showcase the living room.

I backstep and hurry around to the side of the house nearest the garage. A dandelion gets stuck in my sandal. When I kick it away, it flaps around but doesn't dislodge. I let it be and peer into the only window on this side of the home. Its blind is pulled. Judging by the small size, it might be a bathroom window. I move quickly to the backyard, where a small vegetable garden takes up a quarter of the trimmed lawn and a stone patio with wrought-iron furniture abuts the house. I step onto it and peer into the first set of windows.

My heart leaps to my throat. Facing me, inside what appears to be a home office with hunter green walls and oak bookshelves, is my advisor, Dr. Rina Silverstein, dressed in a terry-cloth robe and restrained with duct tape to a chair by her forearms and ankles. Behind her is a man wearing sweatpants and a T-shirt. Whether they're his pajamas or he took time to change out of his fancy work clothes when the police arrived to search his home, I don't know. I only know he's Sam, and he doesn't appear to have seen me yet.

I seize my phone from my pocket. Why hasn't Tam responded? I'll have to call 911. When I unlock my phone screen, I see in horror that my message to Tam didn't send. I press *Try Again*, and this time it goes through.

Within seconds my phone buzzes. Tam responds, **I'm on it. Don't do anything stupid before they get there.**

Her response to me now is day-and-night different from her response back when I first told her of my suspicions. It's that knowledge that gives me the confidence to keep going. I may very well be about to do something that meets her definition of stupid, but I can't just stand here and wait.

I peer through the glass once again. Behind my advisor, Sam wears surgical gloves and fills a syringe.

36

Having no idea how long it will take the police to reach Dr. Silverstein's house on the west side of Morganville, especially with the morning commute picking up, I have no choice but to act.

Beyond the window, Sam pockets the vial of what I assume is potassium chloride and lowers the just-filled syringe with his gloved right hand while grabbing Dr. Silverstein's chin with his left. The neuropathologist, her eyes wide and her mouth sealed with duct tape, shakes her head vigorously and bucks her chair with impressive strength for a sixtyish-year-old woman. In the quiet morning, her muffled protests reach me through the window.

I slam the glass with my palm, hoping to shatter it. The window cracks but doesn't break. Sam's head jerks up at the thump, but I don't take time to find out if he sees me. Instead, I rip off my sandal, grip it in my hand sole first, and punch it into the bottom windowpane, putting all my years of heavy-bag boxing to use. The glass smashes. With my sandal, I bash away the shards around the edges.

As I push the screen inside and heft the front of my torso onto the ledge, Sam calls out, "You're too late, Larkin."

The remaining pieces of glass in the window frame slice my

belly through my T-shirt as I dump myself into the house. In my adrenaline rush, I barely register the pain. My only focus is on knocking that syringe out of Sam's hand before he injects the contents.

I get to my feet. It's obvious my presence has surprised him. Dr. Silverstein, too, has stilled in her chair prison.

Sam stares at me, eyes wild, hair stuck up and ruffled from his bike ride, mouth twisted in a jagged scowl. He looks nothing like the refined Dr. Donovan who commands the OR. He looks every bit the psychopathic Sam who murders people.

Seeing him like this, so barbaric and evil, shocks me. In my mind I knew he was a killer, but it's a very different thing to see him in action.

From her confinement, my advisor resumes her chair-bucking and moaning, her eyes pleading at me. Not wanting to act rashly, I inch my feet—one wearing a sandal, the other bare—over the plush area rug, hoping to close the six-foot distance that separates Sam and me. I must get that syringe.

"Let her go," I say, knowing it's a futile demand.

"You've forced me to change my routine, Liza." Despite his feral appearance, his voice is eerily calm.

"Oh yeah? How's that?" I take another step forward.

"Normally, I don't use restraints. They leave marks. Besides, I'm their friendly surgeon. They trust me."

"Then how do you do it?" Not only am I stalling, I'm genuinely curious.

He stares at me, the syringe rolling between his fingers. Just when I think he won't answer, he behaves like the psychopath he is and brags about his brilliance. "Simply slip up to them in a quick embrace and inject them under the tongue. Such a rich blood supply there. Absorbs the drug quickly but no doubt burns like a bastard going in. Of course, some put up a struggle, but I manage. Easy for a pathologist to miss that injection mark." He leans down and speaks softly into my advisor's ear. "Right, Rina dear?"

Only once in my life have I been truly, utterly terrified. Back when that neighborhood bully locked me in the old steamer trunk his father kept in the garage. I wasn't in there long. The garage door was open, and a neighbor across the street witnessed the commotion. But those few minutes when I was locked inside? I couldn't see, couldn't think, couldn't breathe. I could only claw and scream.

I feel the same way now. What started as an intriguing puzzle for me has turned into a real-life, horrifying nightmare. What a hotshot fool I was to think Sam and I were in an equal weight-class.

When he raises the syringe and starts removing the duct tape from my advisor's mouth, I know it's now or never. I charge toward him, rounding Dr. Silverstein's chair. I slam into him. We both stumble, but neither of us goes down. I draw back to punch him, but he ducks and I punch a bookshelf instead. Paperbacks go flying.

When he sidesteps me to return to his prey, I kick out a leg and trip him. The syringe sails out of his hand. Then I'm on top of him, throwing punches, the two of us rolling on the soft rug like animals. I imagine his torso and head are just another one of Brian's heavy bags, and I pound and pound and pound.

But Sam isn't an inert bag. He fights back and deflects my punches. He's strong. Stronger than me. A fist in my face, my side, and my kidney as we tussle on the rug first and then the hardwood floor when we exceed the tapestry's limits. I have no idea where the syringe is, but I'm acutely aware of how deadly its contents are.

A blow to my nose brings a gush of blood. His panting and grunts match my own. Some of the sputtering might be coming from Dr. Silverstein, whose bucking has just toppled her chair over, but I'm too frenzied to tell.

"You can't win," Sam yells, breathless. "You have to know that." More punches and deflections. "You'll go down just like your father."

With those words, fury powers my next punch, and I land it hard over his jaw. Then I knee his groin. This buys me enough time to get up on my haunches and shake myself into coherence. My flank burns, my jaw screams, and my nose—likely broken—pulses a throbbing beat. While I try to rise to full height, my gaze darts frantically around the room to locate the syringe. There's only one person who should be on the receiving end of it, and I'm determined to make that happen.

But I overestimated my attack on Sam. While I'm searching for the syringe, he jumps up from the fetal position my groin blow folded him into and punches me hard in the solar plexus. My breath whooshes out with a force that could extinguish a torch. I fly back into the bookshelf, and before I can stop gasping and sputtering, Sam is in front of me, the syringe in his hand. He pushes me down and sits behind me.

He grips me in a headlock with his left arm and then pins my arms at my side with his thighs. At the same time, his feet criss-cross over my legs and force them down. This isn't one of Waseem's movies where a woman easily overpowers a bigger man. This is reality. Sam outweighs me and outpowers me. I can barely breathe, let alone move.

"I should've killed you when the junkie failed to do the job for me," he says, his voice nearly as breathless as my own.

"Bullshit," I sputter, trying to wriggle out of his grasp but unable to. "You kill me...more attention...on you." I gulp air, his arm tight around my neck. "What you're doing...so...insane..." I can't manage any more words.

"Don't you understand?" he hisses. "Are you that stupid? It's not about the killing. It's about eliminating those who have no appreciation for the life they've been given. The life *I* gave them. Who are you to stop me? And now look what you're making me do to poor Rina." Across the room my toppled advisor stares wide-eyed at the scene taking place in her den. "I warned you, and now her death is on you. Do you, with your stupid, mentally botched brain, get that? Huh, do you?"

I try to swallow. *I do get it. Painfully so.*

"And by the time I'm done, it'll look like it was done by your hand."

My earlier suspicion was right. He plans to frame me for Dr. Silverstein's murder. How he'll do that now that I'm here and about to die, I don't know, but I have no doubt he'll try.

His arm tightens around my neck and steals the last of my

oxygen. My thoughts start to slip. With woozy vision I see the syringe in his hand. In my confused and blurry world, I think I hear thumping. I can even feel the vibrations in the floor. Must be the footsteps of death coming to claim me.

"Oh, dear, sweet, crazy Liza," Sam coos behind me. The pound of his heart matches the thud of my own. "It's almost a shame to end this. You've been so much fun."

I know I'm dying. I can feel my life slipping away. Maybe I'm already dead.

In my growing weakness, he extends my right arm and traps it down with his shin. This holds my limb in place. His left arm still squeezes my neck and cuts off my windpipe. His right hand raises, and I see a blur of syringes and needles. It could be one. It could be a thousand.

He places the needle on top of the vein at the flexure of my elbow. My overheated body from our fight has plumped it up nicely for him. I feel it more than I see it and realize it's an easier target for him than getting through my clamped-down jaw.

He sticks the needle into my flesh.

He compresses the plunger. My vein immediately feels on fire.

The last thing I hear is Sam's whisper in my ear. "At least I still have Mommy Larkin to play with. And sweet Shawna too."

As I fade away, my chest gripping in excruciating pain, I imagine I see Tam appear in front of me. Dozens of Tams. Other people too. Is that Shawna? Dad, is that you? *I'm sorry, I'm sorry to all of you*, I try to say. *I couldn't stop him.*

But I'm long past speech now.

37

My chest howls in torment. Thousands of knives stab my lungs. My whole body sears, and my nose throbs like a human heart. Every time I take a breath, I want to disappear back into the void I've just awoken from.

Something squeezes my hand, but in the blackness I can't see who or what it is. Someone keeps calling my name. So loud. Please stop.

"Liza, Liza, can you hear me?" My hand is released. A shuffling sound follows, and I hear the same voice, more distant now. "Hey, she's waking up again. Hurry, help, she looks like she's in a lot of pain."

It's the hint of panic in the voice that helps me recognize it as my brother's. Ned is here. Once more my hand is gripped, and I assume it's him again, but everything is still so dark.

"Open your eyes, Liza Lou, please open your eyes." My brother's tone is softer now, still scared, but softer.

I try to oblige, but my eyelids are so heavy they flutter open only for a moment. In that flash, everything is blurry.

"Yes, that's it," Ned says. "Do it again."

I do, and this time, after blinking away the brightness, which may not be all that bright but compared to my sweet void it is, I keep my eyes open. Slowly, the figure of my brother materializes. Behind him a nurse in a coral scrub top and white pants comes through the door. I guess that means I'm in a hospital. Only now do I register all the tubes and cords extruding from my body.

"Well hello, miracle woman," the nurse says. Her accent sounds Caribbean.

"Does this mean she'll be able to stay off the ventilator?" my brother asks.

"I think so, but we'll see." The nurse places her stethoscope over my gown and listens to my heart and lungs. To me, she says, "You woke up this morning, but you couldn't stay awake. We were able to extubate you though, so keep up with that breathing on your own. Otherwise we'll have to tube you again, and we don't want that."

No we don't, I think, understanding now why my airway feels like gremlins are inside it, scraping at my vocal cords.

I try to speak. *Where is Sam*, I want to ask, but the pain is so intense, both from my chest and from my throat, I close my mouth.

"Don't worry, that morphine bolus will kick in soon." The nurse taps buttons on a square machine secured to a pole near the bed. "I've just upped your basal PCA rate. Should cover your pain better now that you're awake. Remember, push the button if you need a bolus."

PCA. Patient-controlled analgesia. Knowing the acronym calms me. My mind is still intact. And somehow, I'm still alive.

My gaze follows the nurse as she exits the room. Through the open door I see a round counter, behind which sit several staff members. I'm in the ICU. I recognize the unit from my orientation tour, which seems both a million years ago and only yesterday. Behind the circular desk, doctors and nurses type at computers and make phone calls. Others sit quietly for a moment's respite.

"Is that better?"

I return my attention to Ned. I assume he's referring to the pain relief, and I nod.

His dark hair is flattened on one side, as if he slept on the chair he's sitting on. Stubble dots his face, and his eyes are red and shadowed. My hand is back in his, or maybe it's never left it.

"You scared me, Liza Lou. You really scared me." I squeeze his hand. He smiles grimly, releases our contact, and sinks back in the chair. "That nurse is right, you know. You really are a miracle woman. Such a fighter."

"What day is it?" I manage to croak.

He must not hear me because he says, "You can't leave us, you know. You're the rock of the family, especially now that Dad's gone. You're the bravest person I've ever known."

I say nothing, partly because speaking is difficult, and partly because, although his words lift me, I simply want to know what day it is. And I want to know—no, I *need* to know—what's happened with Sam.

"Remember when that chick Twila left me? How she stole my amps and guitar and emptied what little money I had saved in that tin can in my drawer?"

I nod.

"I'll never forget how you tracked her down, and somehow—I don't know how—got her to write me a check for everything she owed me. She'd already sold my stuff." He shakes his head. "And that's just a little thing. There are so many more examples. If it wasn't for you, our mom would be one of those raving lunatics you see on the street."

"Inheritance," I mumble, not to mention that Morganville has very few "raving lunatics" on the street. "Nothing to do with me."

His head darts up. "Oh no, that's where you're wrong. It has a lot to do with you. You keep her grounded. You keep her playing her guitar. You treat her like the person she always was, whereas all I see is who she used to be, and it just makes me so sad."

"She adores you." It's true. The two of them are more alike than my mother and I will ever be and have always had a closer bond. That doesn't bother me. It is what it is.

He leans forward again. "I can be a moody brother, I know that. Mean too, and I'm sorry for that, but I used to hate that Dad spent so much time with you. Way more than he spent with me."

"He had to. I wasn't normal. He tried to help me."

"Yeah, I see that now," Ned says. "It still stings, but it doesn't bother me like it used to because I finally realized something."

I wait and let him say his piece. He probably doesn't know much about what happened with Sam anyway. For that I need Tam. It's not that I don't appreciate his unburdening—I do—but I just really, really need to know how I ended up in the ICU when the last thing I remember is dying.

Ned continues. "I realized that all those times I gave you grief about being a robot or not caring about my life, I was wrong. You *do* care. You just care in a different way. It's not through affection or compliments or coming to hear my band play. It's through making sure we're all okay. You do what you do based on what feels right, consequences be damned. You don't let anything hold you back."

Is he high? I wonder. Were it not for the oxygen prongs in my swollen nose, I might smell something other than plastic and starched bedding. I appreciate his words though, and altered state or not, he's speaking with more clarity than I've heard him do in a long time.

My eyes close, too heavy to keep open any longer. As Ned talks about the abandoned cat we nursed back to health when we were in grade school, about how I spent so much time cleaning its "gross" wounds, I drift away, back to my void. Only this time I'm in much less pain. This time I'm content.

The next time I wake up, I see a woman with long silver hair talking to a guy in scrubs outside the door. From the lack of windows in my room and the mess of tubes still coiling from my body and connecting to blipping machines, I understand I'm still in the ICU. It could be night. It could be day. The pain in my chest has returned and is probably what triggered me awake. I push the button on my PCA pump and wait for the narcotic to numb me.

Dr. Silverstein steps into the room, having finished her conversation with the doctor. Though I'm enormously relieved she's alive, it's

Tam I need to see. Tam will have the answers to the questions that keep circling in my head.

"Oh, Liza, I'm so happy you're okay." My advisor leans over and gives me the loosest of hugs. "I want to squeeze you tightly and never let you go, but I don't want to hurt you." She smiles, and when she takes the seat Ned occupied earlier (*where is he?* I wonder), I'm surprised to see moisture in her eyes.

"What day is it?"

Her eyebrows lift, maybe at my brusqueness, which I didn't mean to be. I'm feeling more alert now. I even find I can shift a bit on the bed. I'm desperate to know about Sam.

"It's Sunday. Sunday evening."

"So it's been two days since…"

"Since you saved my life, yes." She presses her hands against her face. "What would I have done if you hadn't showed up? I can't even imagine. And to think I let him into my house. I should have known something was up when he came over so early." She fidgets in the chair. "I should have listened to you. I should have believed you."

"It's okay," I say. "I probably wouldn't have believed me either. I'm sorry he came after you." It feels good to hear my voice stronger. I want out of this bed. I want this catheter out of my bladder so I can piss on my own. I want these nasal prongs—I reach up to my nose and am relieved to find them gone. I no longer need supplemental oxygen.

"You don't have to apologize for anything," my advisor says. "It's you who is owed one. We should have—"

Tam enters the room. She promises the nurse behind her, who's insisting on only one visitor at a time, that she won't be long. My relief at seeing my cop friend is so great I try to prop myself up on my elbow. This proves a mistake, and I cry out at the bolt of pain.

"That would be your broken ribs," Tam says, approaching my bed. "But I'm sure as hell happy you're awake to feel them. The nurse just told me they'll get you out of the ICU within the next couple hours."

"What happened?" I say once the pain subsides.

"Dr. Silverstein gave you CPR until the ambulance came. Your ribs were a casualty, as they often are when it's been done right."

That's not what I meant, but this only prompts more questions. "But she was tied up. How…were you there too?"

Tam nods and places a hand on the guardrail. "I was just a short time behind the patrol car that came out. While we took care of Dr. Donovan, she took care of you. Saved your life."

My advisor flicks her hand. "It's nothing any of you three officers couldn't do." Her gaze falls on me. "Your friend here had the smarts to call an ambulance on her way over. Between the compressions and the meds the paramedics gave you, you managed to survive. They had to bag and mask you, of course, even shock you. You got intubated in the ER. Not many people survive a potassium chloride overdose, I can tell you that."

This humbles me, of course it does, and I'm grateful to be alive. I'm grateful for their quick thinking and quick acting. But it's not what I meant when I asked Tam what happened.

She seems to understand. "I bet what you're most interested in is what happened with Dr. Donovan."

I nod so briskly that another stab of pain ignites me.

She turns her head toward Dr. Silverstein. They must share some silent communication because my advisor stands and says, "I'll give you two some time alone. I'll check in with you later, Liza." She smiles at me and leaves.

Once the door is closed, Tam says, "Things aren't looking too good for Donovan."

"Where is he?" Alarm props me back up on my elbow. "My mom. Is she——"

"She's fine, she's just fine. Ned's with her. As for Donovan, he's enjoying some quality time with some other lowlifes in jail." Tam steps back and leans against the wall. "Listen, you've gotta keep everything I tell you confidential, got it? I shouldn't be sharing the details I got from Vance's interview with Donovan, and I can't tell you everything, but, well, after what you've been through, seems cruel not to give you something. 'Course, it'll be in the news quick enough."

She seems to be waiting for my assurance of secrecy, so I give it to her.

"Donovan denies everything, of course," she begins. "Tried to accuse you of being the one to bring the potassium chloride to Dr. Silverstein's house. Said he was only trying to save her from you."

"That's ridiculous. Does he forget there's a witness? Meaning *her*?" I grunt. "I should've taken time to snap a picture of him before I broke the window."

"If you had, your advisor might be dead." Tam bends a leg and rests the sole of her shoe against the wall. "Still, he's clinging to it being a smear job. Even after Vance told him they found hair and traces of blood in his trunk. Donovan's blaming you for that too, of course. I hear he's a good actor. Acted like he knew nothing about it."

That's because he didn't. Despite my aching body and throbbing nose, I can't help but smile a little when I imagine Sam's shock at hearing the news of Shelly's tissue traces in his car.

"Between Shelly's murder and his attack on Dr. Silverstein and you, we've got enough to put him away for a long time."

"And the seven other people he murdered?" Technically, since he didn't kill Shelly, I should have omitted the word *other*. "He needs to pay for them."

"We'll look into them, don't worry. They'll be harder to prove though, much harder. Still, even if we can't, we've got him on Shelly."

Which is exactly why I did what I did. Consequences be damned. *Sorry, Dad.*

"If it wasn't for that picture you took—which Donovan of course denies and swears his lawyers will bring us down over, even though he has no alibi for his whereabouts during the time of the crime-scene analysis—we might not have gotten our warrant. Then he might not have gone after Dr. Silverstein, and he'd still be a free man."

I look away, finding it difficult to maintain eye contact. That picture started it all.

"I know you don't like praise, but you gotta take it for this," Tam says. "Dr. Donovan getting put away? That's all on you." Her phone chirps, and she smiles. "Here. Someone wants to talk to you."

Tam lifts her phone to me. Shawna is on FaceTime. From the stark whiteness around her and the trio of pillows propping her up, I see she's still in the hospital too.

"Hey, look at us," she says, her dark hair billowing around her. Looking perkier and less tired than when I last saw her, she pinches a bit of her hospital gown from her upper chest and lifts it. "We're fashion twinsies." She lets the fabric drop. "God, aren't they awful? I look so washed out."

Her words remind me of Megan, and I smile. "My colleague would send an orderly to Nordstrom for a silk robe."

"She's a smart woman." Shawna's expression shifts into something more sober. "You scared us, Liza. We thought we were going to lose you."

Tam very lightly punches my shoulder. "Nah, Liza's as tough as they come."

At her words, my violent exchange with Sam comes back to me in detail, and I understand why it isn't only my ribs that hurt. My nose must be the size of my PCA pump, and bruises must cover my entire body.

"We both better heal up quickly," Shawna says, still staring at me from Tam's phone screen. "Seth's one-year birthday party will be here before we know it and don't think you're getting out of it."

Not conscious for even twenty-four hours yet and someone's already talking about parties.

Tam snorts. "Look at Liza's face. I think you scared her, hon."

They laugh, and though I don't join in, I don't mind that it's at my expense. In fact, it's kind of soothing.

I lay my head back against my pillow and close my eyes. Another press of my PCA button bathes me in a comfortable warmth. In my sublime drug haze, I wonder if widening my inner circle might not be so bad after all. It grew awfully small when my dad died.

38

By noon on Tuesday, I've had so many hospital visitors, including every one of my fellow first-years and my program director, that not only am I thrilled to be going home today, I'm rethinking my earlier, drug-hazed acceptance of an ever-widening social circle. At least I have a single room.

Even April and Jasmine stopped by yesterday. It wasn't until I saw them that I remembered my command three days earlier to not leave their apartment until I called to announce it was safe to do so. Fortunately, they didn't sequester themselves the entire time. When I didn't come home that night, April called the police. Though they didn't give her specifics, they let her know I was in the hospital. Once I was moved to the general ward, she stopped by. I admire her courage. I'm even touched by it, at least as much as I can be touched by anything. As a former inmate, calling the police must've been the last thing she wanted to do.

I haven't been released yet, but I'm dressed and ready to go. Just waiting on the cardiologist to clear me. She wants to see me again this afternoon first. Since the shorts and T-shirt I came in with were ripped, bloodied, and confiscated by the police, Megan brought me clean scrubs to wear home. No bra, but with broken ribs, I don't care to wear one.

Since I lost a sandal back at Dr. Silverstein's house after breaking the window, I'm shoeless. She said she would've brought it in to me, but the police took it as evidence. *Have fun with the smell*, I think. Hospital slippers make do in the meantime. My hair is too short to worry about its appearance, but I wouldn't mind tweezers to reshape my eyebrows. *Eyebrows can make or break you, right Mom?* I'm itching to check in on her. Ned returned to Providence yesterday, which means he missed his Saturday night gig.

My ribs still scream every time I move the wrong way—three of them broke during CPR—but I'd rather have ten-out-of-ten pain than be dead. I refused any more narcotics though. I don't need opioids in my cupboard. I've seen the devastation they can cause, both for the addicts and for the loved ones they leave behind. Ibuprofen will have to do.

My other bruises will heal fine. Nothing I haven't sustained from Brian's Gym, beating the heavy bag too much. My abdomen and flank still twinge when I move, but Sam's blows caused no serious damage. Though my broken nose is less swollen, I have shiners that would shame an eggplant. The internist following my care referred me to a plastic surgeon to have it repaired later, but honestly, I don't mind the boxer's nose. It suits me better than any tattoo or piercing could.

While I wait for my meal tray, hoping it comes with a brownie or a cookie, I read pathology articles on the iPad Ned dropped off for me. Given I was right about Dr. Donovan, I assume I still have a job. The alternative would sting far more than any of the injuries Sam gave me. While it would be a leap to say I miss my colleagues, I do miss my routine, and they're certainly a part of it. Waseem has already asked if he can write up my near-death experience as a case study. "Do you know how few people survive a potassium chloride overdose?" he asked at my bedside, his eyes wide with academic interest.

Jen chastised him, and the others agreed it was inappropriate, but I told him to have at it. What do I care? There are no patient identifiers in case studies, and he's spot on that it'll make for a great publication. As for me, I've already moved on from it. Sam, however, lingers in my mind. Is he enjoying his cell? With what he tried to do to Dr. Silverstein and then *did* do to me, Tam says he shouldn't make bail. I eagerly await any new updates from her because a niggle of uncertainty over that picture keeps nudging me.

My stomach growls, but before my lunch arrives, I have yet another visitor, one I didn't expect to see.

Trey.

Given his scrubs, I assume he came from the OR and is either finished with the day's surgeries or is in between cases. His usual strut is less buoyant, and his head hangs lower, which suggests guilt still plagues him. Though I'm still not sure how I feel about the guy, this gives him a check in the plus column.

The head of my bed is elevated, but I still feel too much like a patient in my reclined position, so with a grimace, being careful not to anger my chest wall more than necessary, I slowly swing my legs to the side of the bed and assume a sitting position.

Trey stands awkwardly for a few seconds and then sits in the lone chair. "Nice shiners," he says.

"You can't get these just anywhere."

He shuffles his feet and shifts his legs a few times, as if he can't find a comfortable position. Finally, he leans back and puffs air out of his mouth. "This is some effed-up shit, isn't it?"

"It is."

He pins me in his stare. "It's all over the news, all over the hospital, all over everywhere. Jesus, you were right, Liza. People thought you were crazy, but you were right."

I don't think Trey knows about my mother, so I let the term *crazy* go.

"I can't believe I worked with a killer." He chokes out a laugh. "It blows my mind that those words just came out of my mouth."

"They still need to prove he killed those seven patients. Maybe there are others too, I don't know." I take solace in knowing the waitress and car mechanic, who Tam has informed me were indeed former patients of Dr. Donovan's, are still alive. Whether or not they were squandering their lives in Sam's godlike mind, I have no idea, nor do I care. I'm just glad they'll see tomorrow.

"But what he did to you? What he tried to do to that pathologist lady? Well, that's messed-up."

"It is."

When I don't say anything else, he reminds me I promised to tell him the details when it was over. True enough, and fair is fair, so I ask him to close the door. After he does, I fill him in on everything. Finding Sam in my pictures, following him to Titus McCall to see what he was up to, researching patient records for former patients he might have killed, discovering he murdered my father, breaking into his house, getting tissue samples from Shelly in the morgue and planting them in his car, his confession to me about taking the lives of people he deemed unworthy, and finally to deducing he would go after Dr. Silverstein and finding him at her place.

When I finish, Trey stares at me, mouth agape. He swallows and says, "Wow. That's quite…" He scratches the back of his neck. "But you stopped it. That's incredible. If it wasn't for you, more people would be dead."

"You helped me." Then I think to add the words Dr. Lightfoot —who I'm booked to see this Friday—would encourage me to say. "Thank you for trusting me."

This seems to please Trey, which confirms I've said the right thing. He plants his hands on his thighs, his posture firmer. "But look, there's another reason I came to see you."

"Okay."

"I came to say…" He looks around, as if to confirm no one else is in the closed room with us. "I came to tell you that I'm going to confess to my program director about my role in the narcotic over-dose of my patient. It's hard enough letting someone else take the blame for Shelly's death when—even though it was an accident—it was my fault. But I can do it because Donovan's a psychopath who murders people. Even then I wonder if it's the right—"

"There's nothing to gain by you coming clean about Shelly's death," I say quickly. "You'll only draw suspicion to yourself."

Although I'd like to claim altruism as my motive for saying this, it's more self-protection than anything. I don't want to get caught for planting evidence. I'm not proud of what I did, but if it kept Sam from killing anyone else, then I'd do it again in a heartbeat. But what if someday Trey changes his mind and confesses?

I glower at him. "You can't tell anyone. Ever. We'd both end up in prison." I don't know if this is true or not, but I'm pretty sure he won't call my bluff. Just in case, I harden my voice and add, "I'll stop you if you try."

An expression of alarm—one that doesn't require social training to read—etches his face. He clears his throat. "I won't. Donovan can rot in hell for all I care, but not owning up to what I did to that old guy? I'm not sure I can live with that. It doesn't matter that he wasn't likely to survive anyway. I need to come clean."

"Good," I simply say. Another check in the plus column for the fourth-year surgical resident. A big check.

"Still a woman of few words, I see." He snorts. "Who knows if I'll still have a position here. I sure hope I do. The best way to deal with medical mistakes is to talk about them, right? So the same thing doesn't happen again?"

I nod. When he looks at me but says nothing, I deduce he needs more. Unfortunately, I don't know what to tell him. It wouldn't be the first time a doctor—or nurse, or whoever—caused a patient death with a medication error, but what the consequences will be, I'm not sure.

I settle on, "Your courage in coming forward is what's important, so that others can learn from the mistake." My shrink would give me an A+ for that response. "But Risk Management will get involved, and there could be legal action. You'll probably be put under more direct supervision too."

"I can live with that," he says.

For the next few minutes, he rambles on about things that don't interest me, like how his car is due for a tune-up, how he needs a new mountain bike, and how he's having a problem with a junior resident. What's notably absent, however, is any suggestion the two of us go out again. I'm pretty sure I've scared Trey off the Liza love train forever.

Which is fine because all I want is my lunch.

39

Inside a brown-accented room with furniture so comfortable that personal disclosure is inevitable, my shrink sits across from me, one ankle casually crossed over a knee and his hands clasped in his lap. His jeans are dressy, his russet sport coat matches his wingback chair, and his full head of wavy hair would make other fifty-year-old men pat wistfully at their own. A coffee table with two empty mugs of tea separates us. As with many professional providers in New England, Dr. Lightfoot's office is inside his house, an older home in a quiet Boston neighborhood.

Presently, his face wears that patient expression I can easily read because he's shown it to me so many times. It comes with a complimentary long stretch of silence that won't break until I say something. I shift my gaze to the wide window. The horizontal blinds are raised, and a cloudy, Massachusetts day lies beyond. A light drizzle patters the glass.

Finally, I buckle. "I'm going back to work on Monday."

"That's great, but that's not what I asked you."

"If Dr. Silverstein apologizes to me one more time, I'm going to transfer into psychiatry to escape her gratitude. Then the whole world will be at risk."

This gets a chuckle from my psychiatrist. "Funny, but still not what I asked you."

"I'm eager to get back to work, but I'm not looking forward to the onslaught I'll face. Everyone will want me to rehash things. I just want to leave it all behind. Not sure I can handle the attention."

"Of course you can. We've spent enough years together for me to know you're prepared for anything. You have a whole arsenal of cognitive and behavioral techniques to use."

"Doesn't mean I want to."

"It'll die down, but allow yourself to bask in the glory a bit. You've earned it. Especially with those shiners and that broken nose." He points to my healing facial injury, which is the only injury he can see. My unflattering oversized T-shirt (Megan would run from it screaming), hides the fact I'm not yet wearing a bra. My ribs are still too sore for that kind of confinement.

"I don't bask," I say.

"Maybe not, but you stopped a..." Dr. Lightfoot flounders for a moment. "I don't even know what to call the guy. He wasn't really a mercy killer."

"He thought he was."

"How so?"

"He thought he was helping us. By getting rid of people he thought were wasting their lives and polluting the world with useless pursuits and addictions, he was helping humankind. In his mind, anyway."

"But you stopped him. Which brings me back to my question." Dr. Lightfoot switches his legs, the other ankle now crossed over the opposite knee. "Which you still haven't answered."

"Tam told me they definitely linked the beat-up beige Taurus to Shawna's hit-and-run. Though most fingerprints were wiped away, they found a decent partial one under the seat. Matches Dr. Donovan's. Probably left there from when he first adjusted the seat."

"It's tragic what happened to your friend. How's she doing?"

"She took a hard hit, but she'll be okay. Probably won't run on Waverly Boulevard anymore though."

Dr. Lightfoot responds with another expectant silence. I'm not in the mood to give him what he wants, so I continue relaying what I've learned from Tam.

"They're looking at those seven patient deaths, including my father's." I swallow and gaze out the window. "In five of the cases, family members or coworkers remember Dr. Donovan coming around, either for a home visit or to their place of employment. Detectives found two more patients who fit the pattern too. Guess I missed them in my search. They think his first victim was in 2014, two years after he came to Titus McCall. They found nothing suspicious before then."

"But how do you feel about his—"

"You know what I think?" I lean forward on the chair, its comfortable grip reluctant to release me, especially when the pain in my ribs makes me wince. "I think at first, the power of saving a life was enough for him. Fed his god complex and made him feel omnipotent. Like he was above the rest of us."

Dr. Lightfoot hesitates and then says, "Many psychopaths feel that way. Of course, the vast majority of them don't kill people. Many live normal lives." He softens his voice. "You should know—"

"But I think after a while, saving lives wasn't enough for him, especially after his mom died, a woman who apparently could do no wrong. See, the first man he killed, Ted Overton, was an alcoholic. Impaled himself on a spiked fence while trying to climb it in a drunken binge. The surgery took hours. From what I read in the medical record, it initially seemed impossible, and it's probably what put Dr. Donovan on the map as one of the finest trauma surgeons in the area. I'm sure he devoured the Christlike accolades that followed, just like his father did behind the pulpit." I flutter my lips in disdain and shake my head.

"But then," I continue before Dr. Lightfoot can interrupt, "when he saw that same man, the man he spent hours painstakingly operating on, the man he gave a second chance at life, squander it by going on to drink himself to oblivion? Well, I think that was too much for him. His mother didn't get a second chance, so who was

Ted Overton to waste his? So once his mom died, Dr. Donovan lost it. Decided if he could give people life, he could take it back just as easily. He believed it was his right to do so, and once he tasted that power, he couldn't give it up."

My shrink dips his head my way. "You make a good case, Freud. You'll get no argument from me there." He studies a piece of metal artwork hanging on the wall near the door and rubs his chin. "Strange that his M.O. was so different with the respiratory therapist though. Makes me wonder——"

"Did I tell you my mom's doing pretty well? She's back to playing her guitar outside."

His gaze returns to me, and his chest rises and falls in a long breath that's probably rife with controlled exasperation. "I'm glad to hear it."

"I've stopped in every day. She slipped into Joan of Arc yesterday, but instead of fretting that the king would burn her at the stake, she was rejoicing his downfall." I didn't add that the king in this instance was Dr. Donovan, and that my mother was parading me around the facility as the victorious warrior who brought him down, Maisy clapping behind us. Apparently, Ned relayed the details before he returned to Providence.

I could've done without that spotlight, but my mother's enthusiasm and good mood were a welcome change. They also made up for the fact that she didn't use my name and probably didn't even realize I was her daughter. Something heavy presses on my heart, but Dr. Lightfoot cuts the feeling short.

"Don't you have a neighbor who spent time in prison?" he asks. "You mentioned her the last time we met. Months ago."

His abrupt topic shift surprises me. I also didn't miss the way he stretched out the word *months*. "Sorry I took so long to make an appointment, but yeah, April is my neighbor. The drugs were her boyfriend's though."

"Is he still her boyfriend? Do they keep in touch? Is he still in prison?"

I open and close my mouth, not sure how to answer his flurry of questions. I settle on, "No, he's no longer her boyfriend."

"But she can reach him if she wanted, right? He must have all sorts of connections on the inside—prison or jail."

My satchel is next to me. It's a new one, a soft leather carryall with plenty of compartments to organize my stuff. I finally went to Nordstrom with Megan. Well, technically, anyway. She traveled to the department store while I, with my healing rib fractures, stayed home and watched her through FaceTime. She marched from purse to purse, holding each one up to her phone's camera. Although I refused them all, we finally agreed on my new satchel. I wish she'd let me reimburse her for it, but she refused. She said all my colleagues chipped in for it. "Believe me, Liza," she said over the phone. "A weird man-bag is the least we can do for you."

I pull a bottled water from my weird man-bag and drink. When I recap the beverage, I finally respond to Dr. Lightfoot's last comment. "I don't know what April does in her spare time. It's not like we hang out much. She makes me baked goods. I pitched in with her rent. Watched her kid overnight once."

"I'm sure she's very grateful to you. Might even feel like she owes you."

"What are you trying to imply, Dr. Lightfoot?"

"I'm not trying to imply anything."

I check my watch. Our time is almost up. I want to get out of Boston before afternoon traffic hits. Although I'm still in no shape to punch the heavy bags at Brian's Gym, I could probably manage a light spin on one of the cycles.

"Do you want to answer my question now?"

I sink slowly back into the chair. "Still a nag, I see."

He laughs. "That's my job." A sigh follows. "But Liza, can we finally address the elephant in the room?"

"Which is?"

"How do you feel about Dr. Donovan's death?"

I take another long drink of water and shrug. The movement makes me wince. "If you're asking me if I care that someone shanked him behind bars, the answer is no. Karma at its finest, in my opinion."

"Some people…" Dr. Lightfoot pauses, seemingly measuring his words. "Even though the man was a murderer, some people might have an emotional response to his death, especially if they were the one who set it in motion."

"He set it in motion," I retort. "Not me."

"Well, yes, that's true," my shrink says, "but had you not switched your residency rank list last minute and put Titus McCall first—your own admission to me earlier—he never would have been caught." When I don't respond he adds, "Had you been seeing me regularly, we could have discussed this whole thing from the start. Worked through some options about how to best approach finding a strange man in your pictures and each step thereafter. As I've told you in the past, with your dad gone, I think you'd benefit from weekly sessions with me again. Someone to help you navigate life's more difficult choices."

I shrug. "Maybe."

He leans forward. "Most people wouldn't switch residency programs on a whim, and most people wouldn't personally investigate a man to such extremes. Do you understand that, Liza?"

My belly sparks that familiar flash of fury. "So I was just supposed to let it go? Some guy stalking my family? Stalking others? Just let him go on killing?"

"Of course not. That's not what I'm saying at all. Though you didn't know he was a killer at first, you had every right to explore why he was in your photographs. But who knows how it could have turned out? You're lucky his attempt to kill you failed."

"Maybe so, but I still got him."

"I'm just asking you to acknowledge that there were other avenues to take. More rational avenues." He scoots to the edge of his chair and rests his elbows on his thighs. "Look, I'm not saying what you did was right or wrong. I just want you to think about the other ways you might have approached it, that's all. Just as we've been doing for years."

The heat in my belly starts to dissipate. "I get that, but in this case, I think my way worked out just fine."

Dr. Lightfoot lets it go at that, but only after adding, "Let's readdress this next week, okay? We'll walk through the last couple months step by step and discuss other ways each action on your part might have been handled differently."

That sounds about as much fun as shopping with Megan. "Okay, but I can't make it here until five thirty at the earliest."

"That's no problem. I can extend my workday for one of my most, shall we say, interesting clients." He smiles, stands up, and fist-bumps me. "Until next week, Liza Larkin."

As often happens when I leave Dr. Lightfoot's office, I mull over what we talked about. It's this reflection that has kept me in therapy for so long, at least until I let things lapse last fall, because if I spend time thinking about our exchanges, they must be helping, right?

Whether I need to return to weekly sessions long-term, I don't know, but I won't ever go so long without seeing him again. He's right. Without my dad around anymore, a shrink is my best voice of reason, and these past several weeks suggest I probably still need one. Despite what others might think, I do want to fit in as well as I can. I love my job and want nothing more than to study the brain inside out. Doing so requires functioning as close to normal as possible.

You are not a list of symptoms, Liza.

But what's done is done. I can't—nor do I want to—go back now.

An hour of traffic and a doughnut stop later, I return to my apartment. With my pastries and a bottle of Belgian beer in hand, I plop down in front of my desk. While my computer powers up and loads its programs, I circle back to Dr. Lightfoot's question.

Do I care that Dr. Donovan is dead?

No.

Do I care that I'm the one who started the trajectory that led to it?

No.

I pull up the one remaining photograph I kept of Shelly's crime scene. I deleted all the others, just as I promised Megan I would, but this is the defining one, the one that set the Rube Goldberg machine into motion, the one without which the police would never have gotten a search warrant. Without a warrant, they would never have found the evidence I planted in Dr. Donovan's car. And without the evidence found in his car, the seven patient murders would never have been investigated. My father's death would never have been avenged.

Therefore, Dr. Lightfoot, whether or not the steps I took are the same ones other people would take matters nothing to me. What matters is I took them, and by doing so, justice was served. Dr. Donovan was a murderer. He admitted it to my face. Admitted to killing my father and others. He killed people to feed his own godlike ego, and from one psychopath to another, he got what he deserved.

Oh yes, let's not mince words. Dr. Lightfoot might not write the terms "psychopath" or "sociopath" in my file. He might not even write the medical name, antisocial personality disorder, since schizoid personality disorder is a better fit for me. But I'm sure it's crossed his mind. History of aggressiveness? Check. Deceitfulness? Check. Societal nonconformity? Check. Anyone who looked at his case files on me, which surely are copious by now, could probably read between the lines. After all, it's not my schizoid personality that made me prone to violence in the past. Those acts had psychopath written all over them.

I don't care. Though in many ways Dr. Donovan and I are alike (minus the charming demeanor he had in surplus but I lack), my father was right. I am not a list of symptoms. I am me. I don't purposely hurt people. I don't want to see them in pain. I will always stand up for those who are victimized. As Ned said in my hospital room, consequences be damned.

So I'll make no apologies for wanting Dr. Donovan dead. Were he still alive, his fancy lawyers would tie up his case for years. They'd call everything that has to do with the seven former patients circumstantial. They'd explain away the partial fingerprint in the Taurus as insufficient. They'd argue the photograph that led to the search warrant was doctored and that he'd never set foot at Shelly's crime scene, even though he had no alibi for that timeframe.

He'd be charged with his attack on Dr. Silverstein, of course, as well as his hit-and-run on Shawna if they could prove it. Both would send him to prison and ruin his career, but they might not put him away for life.

Plus, according to the information Tam gleaned from the detectives, Dr. Donovan was insisting I was the one who intended to harm Dr. Silverstein with potassium chloride, even with her testimony otherwise. He claims either my advisor was drugged and therefore confused about what really happened inside her home or she was siding with me. He asserts that in my delusional state, I cooked the whole thing up, and if he hadn't followed me to Dr. Silverstein's house, she'd likely be dead. He only injected me with the potassium chloride in self-defense, right when the police came in.

These ridiculous claims seem a fool's errand for sure, but when one sees himself an omnipotent god as Sam did, he probably thinks anything is possible. And with a team full of high-billing lawyers, maybe it is because, according to Tam, after Dr. Donovan met with his lawyers in jail, they presented all of these statements as truth.

"He's clammed up like a mute," Tam said to me when she paid me a visit the day after my hospital discharge. "Everything's going through his lawyers. Who knows? He might be out on bail before the week's over."

Had I seen more confidence in her body language, I would've been convinced such a thing could never happen, but even she worried he could possibly get off.

Then she gave me a start by locking eyes with me and asking, "That crime scene photo you gave us was real, right? No one else the cops questioned remembered seeing him there, and he wasn't in any of the photographer's pictures. You gotta promise me it was real, Liza, because if he gets off, after what he did to my wife?" Her face flushed crimson, and her jaw became hinged stone. "I swear, I'll kill him myself."

Fortunately, she didn't have to. Another cellmate took care of that for her yesterday. For the rest of the world too.

I realize how lucky I am the detective didn't question Megan, given she was at the crime scene as well. Otherwise, her deleted photos might have resurfaced and been compared to mine. Or maybe she *was* questioned but had my back and denied taking any pictures, not wanting an evil man like Dr. Donovan to get off. If that's the case, I owe her big time.

So no, I don't care that he's dead. The thought of that evil, murdering, arrogant monster getting off for his crimes, especially after all I went through to ensure he was caught, would have been too much for me to bear.

Guess he learned he's not the only one who can give or take a life.

I stare at the huddle of curious bystanders in Shelly's crime scene photo on my monitor. Within the wooded area, Dr. Donovan's face is partially hidden by both the baseball cap and the man in front of him.

Running my finger over his image on the screen, I feel nothing but relief. Because a digital forensic expert from Boston would have indeed studied the photograph once the Morganville PD sent it on. At the defense lawyers' insistence, an expert would have tried to determine whether that was really Dr. Donovan at the scene or not. But now with him dead and with the other evidence the police have, including his attack on Dr. Silverstein and me, they'll have no reason to analyze it further. At least I hope not.

It *is* him in the picture though, of that I have absolutely no doubt.

Because I'm the one who put him there.

It was that night I called Ned to come stay with our mom. Fueled by April's peanut butter cookies and empowered by my Photoshop prowess, I got to work. I cut his face from the picture I took of him while I cased his house, the one I snapped when he returned from his jog in all his shirtless jackassery. Then I pasted it right over that of another bystander.

The job is so well done and the area so small that I doubt even if digital experts were to examine the picture, they'd find anything to prove it's been doctored.

I delete the photo and bite into my vanilla-cream doughnut.
Match goes to Liza.
The opponent has been knocked out.

THE END

AUTHOR'S NOTE

Fatal Rounds is a work of fiction, and as always, liberties were taken to create it. The town of Morganville, Massachusetts and the businesses named within it stem purely from my imagination, including Titus McCall Medical Center.

ACKNOWLEDGMENTS

A big thank you to my editor, Kevin Brennan, for his insights as well as for coming up with the book's title. It was the perfect "punch" for the novel's theme. Another huge thank you to story coach Kate Johnston for her invaluable beta read, to Officer Johnsen for reviewing the police details, to Dr. Baccon for the pathology insights, and to Dr. Miller for the psychiatry input. Any mistakes I made with these professional fields are entirely on me. Thanks also to Lance Buckley of Lance Buckley Design for the cover art. Furthermore, I wish to thank my wonderful and supportive online community. Our social interactions prove the internet can be a sweet and wonderful place.

Another shoutout goes to my sister, Jo'Rinda Johnsen, for allowing me to use a portion of her original song, "House of Misery," in the *Fatal Rounds* book trailer. Music fans can check out her album on Spotify, Amazon, or other music retailers.

Finally, as always, I want to thank you, the reader, for giving me your time in this busy world. Without you, writing wouldn't be nearly as much fun.

ABOUT THE AUTHOR

Carrie Rubin is a physician turned novelist who writes medical-themed thrillers. She also has a cozy mystery, *The Cruise Ship Lost My Daughter*, published under the pen name Morgan Mayer. She is a member of the International Thriller Writers association and lives in Northeast Ohio.

For more information, visit:

www.carrierubin.com

ALSO BY CARRIE RUBIN

The Benjamin Oris Series:

The Bone Elixir

The Bone Hunger

The Bone Curse

Other Medical Thrillers:

Eating Bull

The Seneca Scourge

Pen Name Morgan Mayer:

The Cruise Ship Lost My Daughter

CPSIA information can be obtained
at www.ICGtesting.com
Printed in the USA
LVHW100550050123
736465LV00017B/350/J